PATH OF
THE SEER

THE STRIKING SCORPIONS and Dire Avengers scattered for cover as fire erupted from one of the windows, bullets and splinters from a wooden planter punching through the armour of one of Kenainath's warriors.

Thirianna returned fire without thought, her weapon sending a hail of shurikens through the window, slashing across the chest of the human within while volleys from the others tore apart his throat and face.

Without hesitation, Nimreith leapt across the breach and the One Hundred Bloody Tears followed her through. Thirianna was the fourth through the window and broke to the right as they had trained, her eyes scanning the shadowy interior for foes. She spied a door opening beneath an arching staircase and brought up her shuriken catapult. Another fusillade of monomolecular discs filled the air as a human guard clumsily burst into the hallway, his padded armour ripped and bloody in a heartbeat.

A WARHAMMER 40,000 NOVEL

PATH OF THE ELDAR SERIES
BOOK TWO

PATH OF THE SEER

GAV THORPE

BLACK LIBRARY

For Marc. If you wish to experience this tale as the
Farseer does, turn to the end, read backwards and plan
all life accordingly.

A BLACK LIBRARY PUBLICATION

First published in Great Britain in 2011 by
The Black Library,
Games Workshop Ltd.,
Willow Road, Nottingham,
NG7 2WS, UK.

10 9 8 7 6 5 4 3 2 1

Cover illustration by Neil Roberts.

A CIP record for this book is available from the British Library.

UK ISBN: 978 1 84970 080 1

US ISBN: 978 1 84970 081 8

See the Black Library on the internet at

www.blacklibrary.com

Find out more about Games Workshop
and the world of Warhammer 40,000 at

www.games-workshop.com

Printed and bound in the UK by CPI Mackays, Chatham ME5 8TD

IT IS THE 41st millennium. For more than a hundred centuries the Emperor has sat immobile on the Golden Throne of Earth. He is the master of mankind by the will of the gods, and master of a million worlds by the might of his inexhaustible armies. He is a rotting carcass writhing invisibly with power from the Dark Age of Technology. He is the Carrion Lord of the Imperium for whom a thousand souls are sacrificed every day, so that he may never truly die.

YET EVEN IN his deathless state, the Emperor continues his eternal vigilance. Mighty battlefleets cross the daemon-infested miasma of the warp, the only route between distant stars, their way lit by the Astronomican, the psychic manifestation of the Emperor's will. Vast armies give battle in His name on uncounted worlds. Greatest amongst his soldiers are the Adeptus Astartes, the Space Marines, bio-engineered super-warriors. Their comrades in arms are legion: the Imperial Guard and countless Planetary Defence Forces, the ever-vigilant Inquisition and the tech-priests of the Adeptus Mechanicus to name only a few. But for all their multitudes, they are barely enough to hold off the ever-present threat from aliens, heretics, mutants - and worse.

TO BE A man in such times is to be one amongst untold billions. It is to live in the cruellest and most bloody regime imaginable. These are the tales of those times. Forget the power of technology and science, for so much has been forgotten, never to be re-learned. Forget the promise of progress and understanding, for in the grim dark future there is only war. There is no peace amongst the stars, only an eternity of carnage and slaughter, and the laughter of thirsting gods.

jutting from the wall beneath each one.

Armed figures stood guard at the high doorways and patrolled walkways running along the red-tiled roofs. The men were dressed in loose black trousers tucked into knee-high boots, with bulky red jackets buttoned and braided with gold. Their heads were covered by black hoods, with tinted goggles to protect their eyes from the strange light of the local star. They walked their rounds and chatted with each other, thinking nothing was amiss.

Behind the line of trees that bordered the grounds of the manor, the air shimmered with colour. A swirl of energy broke reality and from the breach emerged a thin line of warriors. Clad in blue and gold armour, the Dire Avengers of Alaitoc stepped foot upon the humans' world, their shuriken catapults held at the ready.

They moved quietly between the trees as more Aspect Warriors appeared: the black-armoured Dark Reapers, the bone-coloured Howling Banshees. At the centre of the ten-strong squad from the Shrine of One Hundred Bloody Tears, Thirianna looked impassively at the imposing but severe structure of the mansion, assessing the lines of fire from its rooftops and windows.

There were fewer defenders than had been expected, but the farseers and autarchs had taken no chances with the size of the force that had been despatched. Several dozen Aspect Warriors converged across the grounds, more than enough to cope with the stiffest defence yet small enough to attack and withdraw without alerting the wider defences of the

PROLOGUE

A BLUE SUN reflected from the still waters of the lake, its yellow companion peeking just above the red-leaved trees that surrounded the edge of the water. Red-and-black birds skimmed above the lake with wings buzzing, their long beaks snapping at insects, their chattering calls the only sound to break the quiet.

A white stone building bordered the water, its long colonnaded veranda stretching over the lake on thick piles. Beyond the portico, it reared up amongst the trees, square in shape, turreted towers at each corner. Thin smoke seeped lazily from vents in the wall, the breeze carrying it away across the forests. Narrow windows shuttered with red-painted wood broke the upper storeys, small balconies

6

Life is to us as the maze of Limlian was to Ulthanesh, its mysterious corridors leading to wondrous vistas and nightmarish encounters in equal measure. Each of us must walk the maze alone, treading in the footsteps of those that came before but also forging new routes through the labyrinth of existence.

In times past we were drawn to the darkest secrets and ran wild about the maze, seeking to experience all that it had to offer. As individuals and as a civilisation we lost our way and in doing so created the means for our doom, our unfettered exploration leading to the darkness of the fall.

In the emptiness that followed, a new way was revealed to us: the Path. Through the wisdom of the Path we spend our lives exploring the meaning of existence, moving from one part of the maze to another with discipline and guidance so that we never become lost again. On the Path we experience the full potential of love and hate, joy and woe, lust and purity, filling our lives with experience and fulfilment but never succumbing to the shadows that lurk within our thoughts.

But like all journeys, the Path is different for each of us. Some wander for a long while in one place; some spread their travels wide and visit many places for a short time while others remain for a long time to explore every nook and turn; some of us lose our way and leave the Path for a time or forever; and some of us find dead ends and become trapped.'

— Kysaduras the Anchorite,
foreword to *Introspections upon Perfection*

world. It was imperative, so said the farseers, that this seemingly idyllic place was wiped from the skein of fate, lest some disaster spawned here befall the craftworld in the future.

Thirianna felt the touch of Farseer Kelamith upon her mind, as did the others around her.

The heavy blade pauses while the shadows deepen.

She knew exactly what was meant; the main force was to halt out of view while the rangers and Striking Scorpions infiltrated the humans' defences. She settled to her haunches in the shade of a tree and waited, mind fixed on the task ahead.

THERE WAS A flash of light through the sky and a massive explosion rocked the front of the manor house, shards of stone and cracked tiles thrown high into the air by the impact. A moment later, another blast seared down through the clouds and detonated, destroying one of the turrets in a cloud of dust, spilling mangled bodies to the close-cut lawn beside the mansion.

To Thirianna's right, the Dark Reapers had opened fire with their missile launchers. A rippling burst sent a volley of projectiles towards the roof of the house while the Dire Avengers and Howling Banshees dashed across flower-filled beds, vaulted over stone benches and skipped across bubbling fountains trailing splashes of water.

Nimreith, Thirianna's exarch, led the squad towards a long porch alongside the waterfront. Thirianna could see the heavily armoured forms of Kenainath's Striking Scorpions emerging from the lake, pistols and chainswords ready.

The Deadly Shadow launched their attack as Thirianna's squad reached the end of the portico, the Striking Scorpions' pistols spitting hails of molecule-thin discs, their chainswords purring. Caught by surprise, the soldiers stood no chance and were cut down in moments, dismembered, disembowelled or beheaded by the blades of the Striking Scorpions.

The warriors of the One Hundred Bloody Tears leapt over the balcony rail and joined the Deadly Shadow. Together they headed towards the back doors.

The Striking Scorpions and Dire Avengers scattered for cover as fire erupted from one of the windows, bullets and splinters from a wooden planter punching through the armour of one of Kenainath's warriors.

Thirianna returned fire without thought, her weapon sending a hail of shurikens through the window, slashing across the chest of the human within while volleys from the others tore apart his throat and face.

Without hesitation, Nimreith leapt across the breach and the One Hundred Bloody Tears followed her through. Thirianna was the fourth through the window and broke to the right as they had trained, her eyes scanning the shadowy interior for foes. She spied a door opening beneath an arching staircase and brought up her shuriken catapult. Another fusillade of monomolecular discs filled the air as a human guard clumsily burst into the hallway, his padded armour ripped and bloody in a heartbeat.

'To the ascent, we walk in blood, Dire Avengers,' said Nimreith, heading towards the stairs.

Thirianna fell into her place in the line, stepping effortlessly up the stairway as she trained her shuriken catapult on the landing above. There was movement and she opened fire instantly. The body of a human tumbled properly into view, throat slashed open.

Reaching the landing, the squad was directed to the right by Nimreith, towards a set of wooden double doors. Thirianna felt the wild presence of the Howling Banshees approaching from behind and then diminishing as they turned left along the landing. A dull aura of fear had settled on the manse, the dread of the human occupants polluting her thoughts.

She kept her eyes and weapon fixed on the doorway at the end of the landing, while subconsciously registering the explosions of more Dark Reaper missiles and the shouts of dying humans from below.

Luadrenin and Minareith opened the double doors while the rest of the squad stood ready. The chamber within was empty, the rough furnishings of wood suggesting some kind of recreational area. There was a wood-burning fireplace and a low table surrounded by couches. The carpet underfoot was threadbare from the passage of many feet. A painting of a human with heavy jowls hung above the fire.

Thirianna took it all in at a glance, her focus drawn towards another door on the opposite side of the room. The squad moved quickly, securing the door and a window that led to the balcony.

Thirianna was first into the next room.

It was some kind of eating area. A long table flanked by high-backed seats stretched the length of the room, set with plates and candlesticks as if ready for a meal. Thirianna heard a whimpering noise and leapt onto the table. She ran along its length, picking her way between the dishes and candlesticks without effort.

At the far end of the room was another seating area, with overstuffed chairs and a round table. In the corner cowered a female human. With her were three children: one male, two female. Their faces were red and wet, their eyes glistening.

The taint of Chaos permeates this place, said Kelamith. *All must be purged.*

The humans made whimpering, animal noises as Thirianna brought up her shuriken catapult.

THE AMBIENT LIGHT in Thirianna's bedchamber was dimmed. She lay on the soft floor and looked at the shadows on the ceiling, watching the slowly-changing patches of dim light and dark shifting. Her slight body, narrow waisted and slender shouldered, was immobile. Her thin face was half hidden by the long sweep of white hair that lay across it, obscuring the tattoo of Alaitoc's rune on her right cheek. Thirianna's deep blue eyes roved from side to side as her gaze hunted the darker shadows, which constantly slipped to the edges of vision, refusing to give up their secrets.

She smelled something strange: blood. A moment later she felt a pain in her hands. Lifting them up, she saw that she had dug her nails into her palms. She watched a droplet of her life fluid slide down to her wrist and drip onto her bare stomach.

Something was wrong.

A presence squirmed in the recess of her mind. The smell and the sight of the blood stirred it. The touch of Khaine, the anger of the Bloody-Handed God awakened. Thirianna closed her eyes, seeking peace in the darkness. Her vision was filled with the blood red of her war-mask.

With a gasp she opened her eyes again. She whispered the mantras she had been taught, seeking to put aside that part of her that was Thirianna the Dire Avenger. Her brow itched, feeling upon it the rune of her shrine that had been painted there in blood.

She lifted her finger to her forehead but felt nothing. There was no blood there. She had removed the rune and chanted the verses and still a remnant, a dagger shard, remained in her mind.

Trying to relax, Thirianna took a deep breath and laid her hands on her chest. She felt the beat of her heart through her fingertips, swift and strong. The nagging sliver of Khaine would not go.

She wondered if perhaps she should go to the shrine, to seek the guidance of Nimreith. She dismissed the idea. Thirianna felt that if something was amiss, she would be able to deal with it.

Closing her eyes again, she probed at the wound in her psyche, feeling around the raw edges, hesitant to look deeper. Veiled with mental curtains, the memories within were part of her war-mask, detached from the rest of her thoughts. She felt them throbbing behind the locked synapses of her brain, insistent for attention.

What could be so important that it demanded to be seen?

Slowly, Thirianna folded back the curtains of her thought for a glimpse, the tiniest flicker of acceptance.

She screamed, mind awash with a vision of crying children and the dying shrieks of their mother.

Part One

Poet

FRIENDSHIP

Tower of Torments – Vaul's Gaol. This is a rune of opposition, appearing in conjunction and used alongside the runes of two individuals. It represents the prison of Vaul, in which the Smith God was bound to his anvil by Khaine the Bloody-Handed One. When used deliberately, the Tower of Torments can guide one along the skein to a breaking of bonds, as Vaul broke free from his chains; when appearing unheralded upon the skein the Tower of Torments signifies abrupt departure, though whether the breaking is for good or ill requires further divination.

THE STYLUS NIB hovered over the shard of crystal set in its stand before Thirianna. She sat on a brightly embroidered rug in front of the writing stand, her legs crossed, free hand held to the small of her back. She focussed her thoughts, composing herself to commit her sentiment for eternity. Three runes intertwined in her mind, forming the concept, embellished with a unique flourish Thirianna had been devising for several cycles.

Picturing the edges and curves of the rune overlaying the facets and contours of the crystal, Thirianna started to move her hand. Light flowed between stylus and shard. Molecules rearranged, forming a design of shifting colours in the heart of the crystal. Her hand moved back and forth, left and right, shaping the poem-design in glimmering rainbow.

When she was finished, she returned the stylus to its holder on the writing tray. She regarded her work with critical eyes but was pleased with the result. Warm reds flowed into cold blues and jade green, separating the three runes yet linking them with the oranges and purples between. Thirianna plucked the crystal from the claw-like holder and turned it around in her fingertips. The colours shifted and the runes interleaved in different ways, each perspective creating a subtle new verse of shape and hue.

The poem-form came full circle in her hand, flowing without hindrance back to the beginning.

Thirianna smiled at the accomplishment. She read the poem again, satisfaction replaced with longing. Standing, she left the small composing area of her habitat and went into the main living chamber. Crossing the rug-scattered space Thirianna stopped before a blister-like protrusion on the wall. It peeled open at a wave of her hand, revealing rows of shelves, each holding a dozen poem-crystals. Thirianna placed her latest composition in its place on the lowest row.

She took a while to review them all, picking up each, reading and re-reading them, feeling the story of her life, of her love, unfolding once more. From the first few crude slashes to the elegant lines of her latest works, the poems told a story not only of her feelings but of her growing proficiency.

The poet delved deeper, examining the meaning as well as the form. The crudeness of the first poems mirrored their raw content, the pain and suffering she had felt. As she had moved away from that hard time, pushed her war-mask deeper and deeper into the past, the movements had come more fluently, the language more assured as her thoughts and emotions had settled. She smiled again at the recurring themes, her playful delves into possible futures of happiness.

Thirianna snapped out of her contemplation, suddenly aware that she was running late. She stepped into her robing area and swiftly chose an outfit suitable for the coming occasion. She pulled on a white ankle-length dress pleated below the knee, delicately embroidered with thread just the slightest shade greyer than the cloth, like the shadows of a cloud; sleeveless to reveal pale arms painted with waving patterns of henna. She wrapped a diaphanous scarf of red and white about her shoulders and summoned up a mirrorplate to appear in the wall of the chamber. Something wasn't quite right.

She opened a drawer and pulled out the pigment-comb. Its teeth were a haze of blue, which shifted to glittering silver. Thirianna's lustrous black hair changed to white as she ran the pigment-comb through her long locks. With deft movements, she picked out two stripes of blue to frame her face. She completed the transformation with a swift touch of an iris-petal to her eyes, turning them from bright green to dark blue.

Satisfied if not entirely happy with these hasty preparations, Thirianna left her apartment and headed to the docks. She had hoped to enjoy a leisurely journey to the Tower of Eternal Welcomes, but instead hailed a star-runner. The small tri-winged craft spun up to the docking lock of the dome in which Thirianna lived, gravitic vanes trembling in the fluctuating field of Alaitoc's artificial gravity as she boarded. The exterior portal cycled open, allowing the craft into the airlock, which gleamed with golden light. The ambient hue turned a deeper orange in warning as the outer gate detached. The star-runner was propelled out into the vacuum with a puff of air and freezing water droplets.

Thirianna relaxed and looked down at Alaitoc below as the star-runner skimmed towards the starward rim. That star, Mirianathir, bathed the craftworld with its ruddy glow. To Thirianna's right the glimmering webway portal rippled against a field of stars.

With a fluctuation of golden light, the webway portal dilated for a moment and where there had been vacuum drifted *Lacontiran*, a bird-like trading schooner just returned from her long voyage to the stars of the Endless Valley. Trimming her solar sails, she turned easily along the starside rim of the craftworld and followed a course that led her to the Tower of Eternal Welcomes.

Thirianna sighed with relief. Aradryan was aboard *Lacontiran*, and would not arrive before the star-runner made it to the Tower of Eternal Welcomes. She activated the filterglass and the stars were replaced with an opaque sheen so that it seemed as if Thirianna sat inside a pearl.

She hummed quietly, testing out timing and cadence for her next poem, trying to capture her mood of excitement and expectation.

WENDING HER WAY easily through the assembled eldar thronging the walkways of the Tower of Eternal Welcomes, Thirianna sensed the ebb and flow of emotion around her. It was not just from the snatches of conversation or the poise and expressions of the other eldar that she drew this information; as a poet she had taught herself to attune her feelings to the emotions of others, sensing their mood on an instinctual level.

She passed couples in love, groups of friends, siblings both loving and jealous, friends and rivals. She felt the heady swirl of these overlapping, colliding feelings washing over her from the crowd, enjoying every moment of expectation, every thrill of excitement; even the worry and dread felt by some was a sensation to be savoured. Without sadness happiness could not appreciated; without darkness light had no meaning.

In the midst of this kaleidoscope of craftworld life, Thirianna spied Korlandril. His slender frame was draped in an open-fronted robe of shining silk-like gold, his neck and wrists adorned with hundreds of molecule-thin chains in every colour of the spectrum so that it seemed his hands and face were wound with miniature rainbows. His long black hair was bound into a complicated braid that hung across his left shoulder, kept in place with holo-bands that constantly changed from sapphires to diamonds to emeralds and every other beautiful stone known to the eldar.

Thirianna saw something of the work of the ancient artist Arestheina in her companion's attire, though displayed somewhat too brashly for her liking. All the same, she felt a buzz of familiarity as she laid her hand upon Korlandril's in greeting, feeling the warmth of his affection.

They swapped intricate pleasantries while *Lacontiran* glided effortlessly towards the docking pier. Thirianna complimented Korlandril on his outfit and he replied in kind, a little too enthusiastically for Thirianna's comfort. She could see the longing in the sculptor's eyes, took considerable pleasure from it being directed towards her, but there was something else lingering beneath the surface. There was a hunger hidden away, and it gave Thirianna pause, frightening her with its intensity.

She dismissed it as part of Korlandril's assumed artistic temperament. Though the Poet and the Artist were close Paths, they were not trodden for the same reason. The Artist sought inspiration, to be utterly open to all influence from outside in order to render the universe into his work. The Poet was about reflecting the universe, using it as a mirror to examine oneself and one's feelings. The first was extrovert, the second introvert, and though they complemented each other well, Thirianna and Korlandril's chosen paths meant they viewed Alaitoc and its eldar with very different eyes.

Thirianna turned towards the approaching starship, alive with the excitement of Aradryan's return. Korlandril was good company, a very loyal friend, but she had missed Aradryan greatly. His humour, his laugh, had been taken away when he had chosen to tread the Path of the Steersman, and she longed to see his face again and listen to his soft voice. She trembled at the prospect and felt Korlandril stir with unease beside her. She glanced at him out of the corner of her eye and saw a frown briefly crease his brow as he looked at her, before he too turned his gaze towards *Lacontiran* sliding smoothly against the dockside.

A dozen gateways along the hull of *Lacontiran* opened, releasing a wave of iridescent light and a honey-scented breeze along the curving length of the dock. From the high archways passengers and crew disembarked in winding lines. Thirianna stretched to her full height, poised effortlessly on the tips of her boots, to look over the heads of the eldar in front, one hand slightly to one side to maintain her balance.

'There he is, our wanderer returned to us like Anthemion with the Golden Harp,' said Korlandril, pointing to a walkway to their left, letting his fingers rest upon Thirianna's bare arm for the slightest of moments to attract her attention.

Thirianna's gaze followed her friend's pointing finger. At first she did not recognise Aradryan amongst the dozens of eldar streaming down to the dockside. Only by his sharp cheeks and thin lips did Thirianna finally pick him from the crowd. His hair was cut short on the left side, almost to the scalp, and hung in unkempt waves to the right, neither bound nor styled. It struck Thirianna as roguish and she smiled. He had dark make-up upon his eyelids, giving him a skull-like, sunken glare, and he was dressed in deep blues and black, wrapped in long ribbons of twilight. His bright yellow waystone was worn as a brooch, mostly hidden by the folds of his robe. Aradryan's forbidding eyes fell upon Korlandril and then Thirianna, their sinister edge disappearing with a glint of happiness. Aradryan waved a hand in greeting and made his way effortlessly through the crowd to stand in front of the pair.

'A felicitous return!' declared Korlandril, opening his arms in welcome, palms angled towards Aradryan's face. 'And a happy reunion.'

Thirianna dispensed with words altogether, brushing the back of her hand across Aradryan's cheek for a moment, savouring the touch of his flesh, assuring herself he was real. She laid her slender fingers upon his shoulder, an exceptionally familiar gesture of welcome usually reserved for close family. Thirianna did not know why she had been so intimate, but enjoyed the touch of Aradryan's fingers on her shoulder as the steersman returned the gesture. Thirianna felt a hint of coldness from Korlandril and realised that she was being rude to monopolise their friend's attention.

The moment passed and Aradryan stepped away from Thirianna, laying his hands onto those of Korlandril, a wry smile on his lips.

'Well met, and many thanks for the welcome,' said Aradryan.

Thirianna noticed Korlandril holding Aradryan's hands for a moment longer than might seem necessary, and saw her friends scrutinising each other carefully but subtly. With the same slight smile, Aradryan withdrew his grasp and clasped his hands behind his back, raising his eyebrows inquisitively.

'Tell me, dearest and most happily met of my friends, what have I missed?'

THE THREE REUNITED friends spent some time catching up with each other's news, each noticing the differences in the other since Aradryan's departure. The steersman wanted to feel Alaitoc again beneath his feet and so they walked along the Avenue of Dreams, through a silver passageway that passed beneath a thousand crystal archways into the heart of Alaitoc. The dim light of Mirianathir was caught in the vaulted roof, captured and radiated by the intricately faceted crystal to shine down upon the pedestrians below, glowing with delicate oranges and pinks.

Korlandril was being garrulous, speaking at length about his works and his accomplishments. He could not help it; the mind of the artist had no place for circumspection or self-awareness, only sensation and expression. Thirianna exchanged the occasional patient glance with Aradryan as they walked, while Korlandril extolled the virtues of his sculptures.

Now and then Aradryan would intervene, sometimes when Korlandril was in mid-flow, to ask Thirianna about the changes in her life. Korlandril would take these interruptions with forced grace and was always eager to steer the conversation back to himself, as though he competed with Thirianna for Aradryan's attention.

'I sense that you no longer walk in the shadow of Khaine,' said Aradryan, nodding in approval as he looked at Thirianna.

'It is true that the Path of the Warrior has ended for me,' she replied, her eyes never straying from Aradryan. In a hidden part of her mind a memory stirred. Though she could not recall what was locked away there, she sensed the pain within and forcefully quelled the urge to examine it. 'The aspect of the Dire Avenger has sated my anger, enough for a hundred lifetimes. I write poetry, influenced by the Uriathillin school of verse. I find it has complexities that stimulate both the intellectual and the emotional in equal measure.'

'I would like to know Thirianna the Poet, and perhaps your verse will introduce me,' said Aradryan. 'I would very much like to see a performance, as you see fit.'

'As would I,' said Korlandril. 'Thirianna refuses to share her work with me, though many times I have suggested that we collaborate on a piece that combines her words with my sculpture.'

'My verse is for myself, and no other. It is not for performance, nor for eyes that are not mine,' Thirianna said quietly. Korlandril's attention-seeking was beginning to test her patience and she cast a glance of annoyance at the sculptor. 'While some create their art to express themselves to the world, my poems are inner secrets, for me to understand their meaning, to divine my own fears and wishes.'

Admonished, Korlandril fell silent for a moment. Thirianna felt a stab of guilt immediately and the brief silence that followed gnawed at her conscience. Korlandril recovered quickly enough and asked Aradryan whether he intended to stay. The steersman jested with him, showing some of his old wit, while Thirianna merely enjoyed seeing the two of them together again.

'Your return is most timely, Aradryan,' Korlandril said after another silent interlude. 'My latest piece is nearing completion. In a few cycles' time I am hosting an unveiling. It would be a pleasure and an honour if both of you could attend.'

'I would have come even if you had not invited me!' laughed Thirianna. For all of his patience-sapping self-aggrandising, Korlandril was exceptionally gifted and his sculptures allowed her to better see the spirit hidden behind the gregarious facade of the artist. 'I hear your name mentioned quite often, and with much praise attached, and there are high expectations for this new work. It would not be seemly at all to miss such an event if one is to be considered as a person possessing any degree of taste.'

Aradryan did not reply for a moment and Thirianna cast a concerned look at her friend. He seemed almost expressionless, as if a blank mask had been placed upon his face.

'Yes, I too would be delighted to attend,' Aradryan said eventually, animation returning. 'I am afraid that my tastes may have been left behind compared to yours, but I look forward to seeing what Korlandril the Sculptor has created in my absence.'

THIRIANNA SPENT THE next few cycles alone as Aradryan reacquainted himself with his family and other friends, and Korlandril continued the labours on his latest sculpture. She began the composition of a new poem, inspired by the return of Aradryan. His reappearance had stirred up old emotions; some pleasant, others not so.

She passed much of the time in the Dome of Wandering Memories, where archives of Alaitoc's greatest writers and poets were kept. She sought out her favourites – Liareshin, Manderithian, Noiren Alath and others – and spent whole cycles losing herself in their verses. She sought the runes that would blend the two facets of her feelings, not merging to grey but speaking in clear tones of black and white, light and dark.

In her research, Thirianna spoke with some of the other poets that she met there, never revealing her intent but seeking recommendations that would further her understanding. She enjoyed this phase of composition immensely, excited by possibility, unfettered by the reality of committing her words to eternity.

The evening before Korlandril's great unveiling she received a message across the infinity circuit from Aradryan, inviting her to join him at the dawn of the next cycle. She agreed and left arrangements for them to meet on the Bridge of Glimmering Sighs, one of her favourite haunts when away from the Dome of Wandering Memories.

She slept fitfully that night, alternately excited and oppressed by the thought of spending some time alone with Aradryan. He had lost much of his gaiety since becoming a steersman, not only in look but demeanour. She wondered what experiences had wrought such changes, and wondered also if she really wanted to learn of them.

It was the nature of the Path that friends and family changed, becoming new people, relationships waxing and waning as individuals made their own way through their long lives. Yet Aradryan, and Korlandril more so in his absence, had left a lasting impression upon her that she could not shake. He seemed more like a brother than a friend – Thirianna had no real siblings to compare – and it was hard for her to reconcile her warmth for him with the stranger who had returned upon *Lacontiran*.

Aradryan was already waiting for her when she arrived at the Bridge of Glimmering Sighs. The silver arc crossed over a ribbon of white-foamed water that cascaded through the Dome of Silence Lost, its span curving as it rose to the crest high above the river. Green-and-blue snapwings and red-crested meregulls trilled and squawked as they dived beneath the bridge and swept along the fern-filled banks.

She smiled as she approached Aradryan, who stood alone at the edge of the bridge looking down into the rushing waters. There was no rail, and he stood with the toes of his high boots poking over the edge, his balance poised at the delicate edge between stability and falling. With an impish grin, he looked over his shoulder as Thirianna called his name, and waved her to join him. The expression flooded her with happiness, reminding her of the Aradryan that she had waved goodbye to long ago.

'A very pleasant location,' he said, stepping back from the edge of the bridge to face Thirianna. 'I do not recall coming here before.'

'We never came here,' Thirianna replied. 'It is a well-kept secret amongst the poets of Alaitoc, and I trust that you will keep it so.'

'Of course,' said Aradryan. He looked out over the edge again. 'It reminds me a little of the gulfs of space, an endless depth to fall into.'

'I would prefer that you did not fall,' she said, reaching out a hand to Aradryan's arm to gently tug him back as he looked to take another step. 'You have only just come back, and we have much to talk about.'

'We do?' he said, delighted by the thought. 'Perhaps you have a verse or two you would like to share with me, now that Korlandril does not intrude upon us.'

'As you were told before, I do not perform my poems.' Thirianna took her hand away from Aradryan's arm and cast her gaze into the distance, seeing the haze of the dome's edge beyond a maze of winding rivers and gushing streams that cut through golden lawns.

'I thought perhaps they were written for a very select audience,' said Aradryan. 'It must be such a gift, to compose one's disparate thoughts; to embrace them and order them in such a way.'

'They have an audience of one,' said Thirianna, still not meeting Aradryan's gaze. 'That one is me, no other.'

'You know that we used to share everything,' said Aradryan. 'You can still trust me.'

'It is myself that I do not trust. I cannot allow any fear that my compositions might be seen by another to restrict my feelings and words. I would be mortified if my innermost thoughts were put on display to all-comers.'

'Is that what I am?' said Aradryan. He took Thirianna by the arm and turned her towards him. 'One of many?'

'It is no slight against you, nor against Korlandril or any other,' explained Thirianna. 'I choose to share what I share. The rest is mine alone, for no other to know. Please appreciate that.'

'Such an attitude does not sit well aboard a starship,' said Aradryan. 'One is part of the many, and in confinement with others most of the time. It takes several to pilot such a vessel, and we must each trust the others implicitly. I have learned that friendship is not the only thing that must be shared. Co-operation, the overlapping of lives in ways beneficial to all, is the key to understanding our place in the universe.'

'A grandiose conclusion,' laughed Thirianna. 'Perhaps there is something of the poet in you!'

Aradryan did not seem to share her amusement. He let go of her arm and glanced away. When he looked at her again, the expressionless mask had returned to his face, sincere but otherwise featureless.

'Korlandril will not be entertaining us until the dusk of the cycle begins,' he said. 'If you will not grace me with your poems, perhaps you could suggest other entertainments that will divert us until the unveiling.'

Thirianna did not like the change, the abrupt closing off of emotion. She supposed that she had deserved it, but could not bring herself to apologise for any unintended offence she might have caused Aradryan. It was his error to press her on her poetry and he would have to learn that she was not willing to talk about it.

With an effort, Thirianna brightened her mood and laid a palm upon the back of Aradryan's hand.

'The Weathering of the Nine takes place later today,' she said. 'I have not been for many passes.'

'Nostalgia?' said Aradryan, a smile breaking through his demeanour, eyebrow lifting in surprise.

'A return,' Thirianna replied. 'A return to a place we both know well.'

Aradryan considered the invitation for a moment,

the conflict showing in his shifting expressions. The internal argument ended with a look of happy resignation and he nodded.

'Yes, let us go back a while and revisit our youth,' Aradryan said. 'A return to happier times.'

'It is a truth that as we progress, our grief increases and our joys diminish,' said Thirianna.

The two of them started down the slope of the bridge towards the coreward bank.

'It does not have to be so,' said Aradryan. 'The universe may have grief in plenty to heap upon us, but it is in our power to make our own joy.'

Thirianna was about to argue that the greatest grief came from one's own making, but stopped herself. Such thoughts led to a place she was not willing to visit. Not yet. Not ever again, perhaps.

They walked on a little further and she considered what Aradryan had said and her reaction to it. Had she become morose, she wondered? Aradryan's return was a cause for celebration, a positive event. It was up to her to make the most of it.

'Yes, you are right,' said Thirianna, cheered by his words. 'Let us recapture the past and create some new happiness.'

'SHE IS SO serene,' Thirianna said. 'Such calm and beauty.'

Korlandril's creation was remarkable, stirring dormant thoughts within Thirianna's mind. *The Gifts of Loving Isha* it was called. She was struck by the simplicity of the sculpture, which hid a very complex web of themes.

The statue was bathed in a golden glow and tinged with sunset reds and purples from the dying star above. It depicted an impressionistic Isha in abstract, her body and limbs flowing from the trunk of a lianderin tree, her wave-like tresses entwined within yellow leaves in its upreaching branches. Her faced was bowed, hidden in the shadow cast by tree and hair. From the darkness a slow trickle of silver liquid spilled from her eyes into a golden cup held aloft by an ancient eldar warrior kneeling at her feet: Eldanesh. Light glittered from the chalice on his alabaster face, his armour a stylised arrangement of organic geometry, his face blank except for a slender nose and the merest depression of eye sockets. From beneath him, a black-petalled rose coiled up Isha's legs and connected the two together in its thorny embrace.

It was a monument to love, and the grief that it brought; a motif with which Thirianna was all too familiar of late.

Aradryan did not seem to share her opinion, flicking his fingers slightly in a sign of disagreement.

'It is self-referential,' Aradryan explained, his gaze moving from the statue to Thirianna. 'It is a work of remarkable skill and delicacy, certainly. Yet I find it somewhat... staid. It adds nothing to my experience of the myth, merely represents physically something that is felt. It is a metaphor in its most direct form. Beautiful, but merely reflecting back upon its maker rather than a wider truth.'

Though the criticism was evenly spoken, Thirianna sensed tension in her companion, as though his critique was directed at something more elemental than a sculpture. Intimidated by what Aradryan might have made of her verses had she shared them, Thirianna sought to defend Korlandril's work.

'But is not that the point of art, to create representations for those thoughts, memories and emotions that cannot be conveyed directly?'

'Perhaps I am being unfair,' said Aradryan. 'Out in the stars, I have seen such wondrous creations of nature that the artifices of mortals seem petty, even those that explore such momentous themes such as this.'

Thirianna felt a surge of anger close at hand and turned in time to see Korlandril, his face twisted with a sneer.

'Staid?' snapped Korlandril, stepping forwards. 'Self-referential?'

Her stomach lurched with sudden shared guilt at Aradryan's words, which the sculptor must have overheard. Aradryan seemed unperturbed, his posture calm, expression radiating sincerity.

'My words were not intended to cause offence, Korlandril,' he said, offering a placating palm. 'They are but my opinion, and an ill-educated one at that. Perhaps you find my sentimentality gauche.'

Korlandril hesitated, blinking and glancing away in a moment of awkwardness. The pause lasted only the briefest heartbeat before Korlandril's scowl returned.

'You are right to think your opinion ill-informed,' said the artist. 'While you gazed naively at glittering stars and swirling nebulae, I studied the works of Aethyril and Ildrintharir, learnt the disciplines of ghost stone weaving and inorganic symbiosis. If you have not the wit to extract the meaning from that which I have presented to you, perhaps you should consider your words more carefully.'

Thirianna stepped away from the pair as Aradryan folded his arms.

'And if you have not the skill to convey your meaning from your work, perhaps you need to continue studying,' Aradryan snarled back. 'It is not from the past masters that you should learn your art, but from the heavens and your heart. Your technique is flawless, but your message is parochial. How many statues of Isha might I see if I travelled across the craftworld? A dozen? More? How many more statues of Isha exist on other craftworlds? You have taken nothing from the Path save the ability to indulge yourself in this spectacle. You have learnt nothing of yourself, of the darkness and the light that battles within you. There is intellect alone in your work, and nothing of yourself. It might be that you should expand your terms of reference.'

Horrified, Thirianna wanted to intervene, but found herself helpless. She looked from Korlandril to Aradryan and back again, torn between her two friends. She detected animosity deeper than was being revealed, and wondered at its cause.

'What do you mean by that?' said Korlandril.

'Get away from this place, from Alaitoc,' Aradryan said patiently, his anger dissipated by his outburst. Now he was the picture of sincerity, his hand half-reaching towards Korlandril. 'Why stifle your art by seeking inspiration only from the halls and domes you have seen since childhood? Rather than trying to look upon old sights with fresh eyes, why not turn your old eyes upon fresh sights?'

Korlandril parted his lips for a moment, but then shut his mouth firmly. He directed a fierce glare at Aradryan, before stalking away through the blue grass, scattering guests in his flight.

As if realising for the first time that Thirianna had been witness to the confrontation, Aradryan turned towards her, hands raised in apology.

'I am sorry, I d–'

'It is not I that deserves your apology,' she said curtly, her feelings hurt more by Aradryan's treatment of Korlandril than his disregard for her. 'Perhaps such behaviour is tolerated on a starship, but you are back on Alaitoc. You are right, you have become gauche.'

With that parting remark, she left Aradryan, ignoring his call after her. She fought to retain her composure as she made her way through the dispersing audience, smiling at those who met her gaze though inside she felt like screaming.

She had been content with her life. Aradryan's return had thrown that into turmoil and she worried what that would bring. She had sought serenity and calm through her poetry, but it seemed that matters beyond her control were about to make her life far more turbulent.

AFTER LITTLE SLEEP, Thirianna woke before the next cycle had begun. She lay in the twilight of her apartment and thought about what she should do. It was unlikely that Korlandril and Aradryan would reconcile of their own accord. The prospect of choosing one of her friends over the other or, worse still, losing both of them, stirred her to action. Neither would be happy for her to interfere, but Thirianna was sure that if she was subtle she could bridge the sudden divide that had come between them.

It was not something she could attempt alone. She knew well the peril of unintended consequences when trying to steer the course of others' lives. Yet it was not an insurmountable obstacle. There were older, wiser minds that could be brought to bear on the problem.

As the darkness lightened into the glow of a new cycle, Thirianna ate a swift breakfast, cleansed herself and dressed in simple attire. She left the tower in which she lived and, along with a handful of other early wakers, crossed Alaitoc on a grav shuttle. The few eldar with whom she shared the carriage sat quietly, keeping to themselves. Thirianna was glad for their recognition of her desire for solitude and spent the time considering the changing nature of her relationships with Aradryan and Korlandril.

So wrapped up did she become in these thoughts that she almost did not notice her arrival at the Dome of Golden Sanctuary. There were no other eldar alighting from the shuttle as she stepped down to the curving platform, but she could feel the presence of many others close at hand: the infinity circuit.

Close to the heart of Alaitoc, the Dome of Golden Sanctuary was a maze of chambers and corridors, its walls gleaming with the energy of the craftworld's psychic energy conduits. Flickers of colour flashed past along the crystal matrix, each bringing a brief buzz of life to the empty rooms and tunnels.

It was in this place that the farseers conducted much of their esoteric work. All of the eldar aboard Alaitoc knew of it, though few ventured here. It was the first time Thirianna had visited, and she wondered if it was true that the layout of the dome's winding streets and soaring towers did indeed change over time, reflecting the will and whim of the infinity circuit and the farseers that used its power.

She came upon a broad space that at first glance appeared like any of a thousand other parklands that could be found across Alaitoc's many domes. In many ways it was quite mundane; the grass was green, as were the leaves on the trees, and the water that glittered in a pool at its centre was clear and filled with fish. There were certainly more exotic plants and habitats elsewhere on the craftworld; where gravity was inverted and waterfalls poured upwards; where species of birds extinct off-world continued to fly the skies; where pools of liquid silver reflected clouds of coloured gases.

Yet first impressions were deceptive. Walking along the narrow path of white stones, Thirianna could sense more than could be seen with the naked eye. Here the power of the infinity circuit was being used to weave a landscape across more than the usual number of dimensions, and the results could be felt rather than touched or heard. She passed across a bridge and was filled with a gentle melancholy; stopping beneath the wide boughs of a tree Thirianna felt a moment of adoration for the beauty and complexity of life.

Distracted, she wandered the park for a while, enjoying the changes of mood and emotion that the different areas brought. Thirianna found a bench that looked out at a tumble of rocks and boulders at the bottom of a grassy slope. There was a blue-robed eldar sitting on the bench, a number of rune pendants hanging on golden chains across his chest, his wrists laden with gem-clad bracelets and intricately crafted charms. His hands were sheathed in soft velvet-like gloves of pure black.

'You are late,' said the eldar, turning purple eyes to Thirianna. His expression was one of pleasant surprise rather than admonition, which further confused her.

'I did not know I was expected,' she replied. The eldar gestured for her to sit next to him and she did so.

'I am Alaiteir,' said the eldar. 'I have been waiting for you a little while.'

'You are a farseer,' Thirianna said, laughing at herself for foolishly asking if she had been expected.

'You are right,' said Alaiteir. 'Your coming here has been known to me for several cycles.'

'And do you know what I wish to ask?' Thirianna said, her smile fading.

'No,' admitted Alaiteir. 'Physical things, the interactions of beings, can be foreseen with practice, but their purposes and desires are far harder to discern. The will of an individual is a fleeting, capricious thing that is hard to locate.'

Thirianna accepted this explanation with a shallow nod. She looked at Alaiteir for a moment, wondering if she was doing the right thing.

'All that you say shall be kept in confidence,' Alaiteir assured her. 'You may ask without regret or shame. It is the burden of the farseer that we see and hear many things, but only few can we even discuss.'

Taking a deep breath, Thirianna steadied her thoughts and launched into her tale. She explained to Alaiteir how she had come to know Korlandril and Aradryan, and her changing feelings for both of them. She talked about her own life, the Paths she had walked that had brought her to this place. She finished with the story of Aradryan's return and the disruption it had caused. All the while Alaiteir said nothing, but listened patiently with the occasional nod of understanding or a brief smile to Thirianna to persuade her to continue.

When she was done, Thirianna asked the question that had been on her mind since Aradryan had stepped off *Lacontiran*.

'What is going to happen to my friends?'

Alaiteir laughed, earning himself a shallow scowl of annoyance from Thirianna. The farseer held up a hand in apology and he seemed genuinely contrite.

'A question that is so simple to ask, yet so difficult to answer,' he said. He moved closer to Thirianna and laid a hand on her leg: a bold intrusion of her space but well meant and a gesture of assurance.

'What you ask cannot be answered. Not by me and not in the way you have asked it. Could I see what will happen to them tomorrow? Possibly. The cycle after? Very likely. A pass from now? To the ends of their lives?'

Thirianna sighed, realising the enormity of what she had hoped and the futility of hoping for it. She moved to stand up but a gentle pressure from Alaiteir stopped her.

'Did Anatheineir give up so easily on the quest for the Silver Star?' said the farseer. 'I cannot see these things for you, but there is another way. It is this that truly brought you here.'

'You have seen something?' Thirianna asked, her excitement growing. 'Something about Korlandril or Aradryan?'

'No,' said the farseer, deflating Thirianna's mood. 'I know nothing more of these individuals than that which you have just told me.'

'Why can you not simply tell me what you have seen?' said Thirianna, annoyance replacing her anticipation. 'Why not give a straightforward answer?'

'You have not yet asked the right question.' Alaiteir held up a hand to quell Thirianna's next outburst. 'I do not speak riddles out of choice, but necessity. We each ask ourselves and others a myriad of questions in every cycle. Some are trivial, and some are not. Which are the trivial ones and which are important? We do not know until we hear the answers. I cannot give you a truthful answer to a question that has been unasked but I can tell that you have not yet divined your inner purpose in coming here.'

'Inner purpose?' Thirianna was sure she knew exactly what she wanted to know and said as much. 'I just want to know if things will be better between Korlandril and Aradryan.'

'And now we start to get to the heart of the matter,' said Alaiteir. He stood up, took Thirianna's hand and gently pulled her to her feet. The two of them looked down the slope towards the broken rocks. 'By what measure can "better" be defined? Better for Korlandril? Better for Aradryan?'

Thirianna knew the answer immediately but hesitated in saying it, suddenly ashamed of the realisation. She glanced at Alaiteir, who was studying the rocks below.

'Better for me?' Thirianna said quietly. Alaiteir nodded but did not look at her. Thirianna thought some more, working out what she meant by the statement. It was strange that her conclusion came as no shock to her. The farseer had been right, she had known all along what she really wanted to know. 'How will this division between Aradryan and Korlandril affect me?'

'That is good,' said Alaiteir. He looked at Thirianna, his expression stern. 'It is perhaps the first and last question we ask of any person or situation. Our selfishness is inherent and nothing that should bring you shame. Turmoil and change is upon you and you fear for what the future may hold. That is entirely natural.'

'And my wish is for Aradryan and Korlandril to mend this wound between them for my benefit,' said Thirianna. 'Surely it is to their benefit as well?'

'Who can say?' said the farseer, his necklaces sway-ing as he gave a shallow shrug.

'I thought perhaps a farseer could say,' said Thirianna, smiling again.

'You seek answers, but I cannot give them to you,' said Alaiteir. 'All I can do is steer you to the right questions. The answers you will have to find for yourself. The time is upon you to make a choice, Thirianna. It is this choice that I saw; this choice that persuaded me to come to you in this place at this time.'

'I must choose between Korlandril and Aradryan?' said Thirianna, dismayed by the prospect. 'How could I do such a thing?'

'Or perhaps choose neither,' said Alaiteir. 'Perhaps you must choose yourself over both of your friends. If you truly wish to know what the future holds, there is only one decision you have to make.'

Thirianna looked at Alaiteir for some time, trying to discern any extra meaning from his expression, seeking further guidance, but none was to be found. The farseer obviously intended that she must come to this decision entirely without direction from him.

It was only after much thought that the answer came to Thirianna.

'You think that I should move to the Path of the Seer?' she asked quietly.

'What I think is irrelevant,' replied Alaiteir. 'All I can tell you is that every cycle we each stand upon a branch in the threads of fate, every decision we make shaping the future we will live in. Some cycles the choices we face change little of what will happen.

This cycle, this moment, is not such a day. What you decide to do next, free of coercion or persuasion, guided by your own mind and heart, will set you on a new trail, whether you stay a poet or become a seer.'

'I cannot take such a decision now,' said Thirianna.

'I would not expect you to do so,' said the farseer. 'If I am to be honest, I must tell you that you have already made the decision. Now you must spend some time finding out what road you have chosen.'

Thirianna nodded and took a few steps along the path. She stopped and turned back to Alaiteir.

'Thank you,' she said. 'What should I do if I choose to follow you on the Path of the Seer?'

'If that is revealed to be your choice, I will know it and come to you.'

INTROSPECTION

Rod of Light – The Staff of Asuryan. This rune is one of conjunction, lacking any power or significance on its own, but of the highest potency when cast or seen alongside another. Its appearance colours the reading of any other rune, and characterises wisdom from within. When the Rod of Light comes unbidden to a seer, it signals great change, representing the flame of the Lord of the Heavens that consumes the old and brings rebirth.

ON RETURNING TO her quarters, Thirianna was greeted by a thrum of recognition from the infinity circuit interface in her main chamber. Placing a palm onto the smooth slate, she allowed her consciousness to touch upon the energies of Alaitoc. Thirianna's thoughts touched with an after-echo of Aradryan's presence; he had come to her apartment seeking her.

She detached herself from the infinity circuit while she considered what she should do. Part of her wished for solitude, so that she could think upon the choice presented to her by Alaiteir; the other part of her wanted to lose herself in mundane matters so that she could forget the dilemma for a while and return to it refreshed.

Thirianna decided on the latter course and meshed with the infinity circuit again, seeking the signature of Aradryan. She found him on the Boulevard of Split Moons, not far from the tower where she lived. Through the infinity circuit, she touched upon his thoughts, gently gaining his attention. In a moment they had exchanged feelings of greeting and conciliation and came to an understanding; Aradryan would wait for her amongst the storefronts and arcades and she would join him shortly.

Breaking the link, Thirianna changed her clothes, swapping her robe for a tight bodysuit of glittering purple and silver. She wrapped a light scarf about her neck and shoulders and a wide belt studded with sapphire-like gems about her waist. She pulled several torcs up her arm and finished with a long pair of white gloves and matching boots. She quickly coloured her hair and eyes green to finish the striking look and hung a small waistbag from her belt. Feeling ready to meet Aradryan, she set off for the Boulevard of Split Moons.

She found Aradryan waiting beside a jewellery

stall, picking through an assortment of plain gold earrings. He wore a wide-shouldered jacket of dark blue, flared at the hips, fastened by a line of tiny buckles from waist to neck and wrist to elbow. A heavy kilt of subtly blended greens and blacks covered his upper legs, above narrow boots studded with golden buttons. It was a style that had not been seen on Alaitoc for some time, and the sight of her friend caused a moment of nostalgia in Thirianna.

Aradryan looked up at her approach, smiling broadly, and held up a pair of earrings shaped vaguely like two leaping fish.

'Not really to my taste,' said Thirianna as they touched hands in greeting.

'Not for you, for me,' said Aradryan, nonplussed.

'I know,' said Thirianna, laughing softly. She took one of the earrings and held it up to the side of Aradryan's face. The curve of the jewellery matched well with his features and she nodded. 'Yes, they would look very good.'

'Then it is decided,' said Aradryan, recovering his composure. The steersman signalled his desire to take the jewellery to the stallholder, who nodded his head in appreciation of a choice well made and waved for the pair to continue on their way.

The two of them spoke little as they moved between the stalls and stores, examined gems and scarves, robes and headdresses. Thirianna was grateful for the opportunity to divert her attention away from herself and Aradryan. She enjoyed feeling the textures of cloth and seeing the rainbows of light in the gems, losing herself in every detail.

When Aradryan spoke, he raised trivial matters, commenting on the wares on display and those offering them. After a while, Thirianna realised that much of what he said was negative, and though never offensively phrased his words came across as a quiet but constant denigration of Alaitoc.

Eventually Aradryan's subtle complaints started intruding on Thirianna's appreciation of the objects on display and she turned to him, letting her irritation show.

'What is it about life here that chafes so badly that you must constantly gripe and find fault?' she snapped, taking Aradryan by the arm and guiding him to a small alleyway between two stores where they would not be overheard.

'I am sorry if I have broadened my view beyond the petty baubles on display here,' Aradryan replied. He was about to say something else but stopped himself and his expression changed to one of contrition. 'No, I am genuinely sorry. You say that life here chafes, and I can think of no better word to describe it. It rubs against my spirit, binding my thoughts like a cord around my limbs. Alaitoc is safe, and controlled, and suffocating. It offers comfort and dependability. I no longer desire these things.'

'So why did you return at all?' Thirianna asked, feeling guilty for judging her friend so harshly. 'There must have been a reason to come back.'

Aradryan gave Thirianna a look that she did not recognise; it seemed to be desire mixed with pleading, and a hint of desperation. The look passed quickly and Aradryan glanced away, pretending to flick away an imagined piece of thread from the shoulder of his jacket. When he looked at her again, he showed the studied, expressionless mask that he had worn almost constantly since his return.

'My memories of Alaitoc were fonder than the reality,' said Aradryan. 'Or perhaps the reality has changed to one of which I am less fond.'

'You speak of Korlandril,' said Thirianna. The mention of the artist's name caused a brief flicker of emotion to cross Aradryan's face; annoyance that turned to shame.

'And you,' said Aradryan. He sighed and leaned back against the wall of the alley, crossing his arms over his chest. 'I do not know my place here any longer.'

'It will take time, but you will adjust again, and learn anew to find the delight in each moment that passes, and meaning in the things you now find trivial,' Thirianna assured him. 'Alaitoc is your home, Aradryan.'

'Is it?' he replied. 'I have little bond to the family left here, and my friends are not those I left behind. Why should I choose to stay here when all of the galaxy is open to me?'

'Though it would sadden me to see you leave again, I cannot argue against your desires,' said Thirianna, feeling helpless against the force of Aradryan's disaffection.

'Is there some reason I should stay?' he asked. He directed a look at Thirianna similar to the one he had given her earlier; longing and hopeful. She could not hide her shock when she realised what he wanted to hear from her.

'I have only my friendship to offer,' Thirianna said. Aradryan's disappointment was instant, showing as a furrowed brow and parted lips for a moment before the emotionless mask descended again.

'Friendship was once enough, but not now,' said Aradryan, his tone even and quiet. He directed a quick bow of the head to Thirianna, in deference to her feelings, eyes closed out of respect. When he opened them, there was a glimmer of sorrow. 'It seems that even friendship is not possible with Korlandril. He has grown arrogant, I think, and he has no time for others. Thank you for your candour, Thirianna. I hope I have not caused you undue embarrassment or woe.'

Before Thirianna could reply, Aradryan had stepped out of the alley, quickly striding through the thickening crowd of eldar milling along the Boulevard of Split Moons. Thirianna considered whether to go after him and decided against it. She was certain that she could not offer what Aradryan desired and no other argument would convince him to stay.

It is probably for the best, she told herself. As much as it pained her to think of Aradryan leaving again, his return, and the feelings he had hinted at, had made her life a lot more complicated in a very short space of time. Thirianna was confident that whatever ennui or wanderlust plagued Aradryan, he would overcome it.

The question she had been ignoring returned to her, prompted by the thought that perhaps she could free herself from the uncertainty that surrounded her life. This brief episode had highlighted to her how little control of her situation she had, and that made her feel uneasy. To know something of what would come, to glimpse the possible consequences of these endlessly difficult decisions, was a huge temptation.

THE DOOR CHIME woke her in the early part of the following cycle. She sensed Alaiteir. Quickly slipping on a loose robe of white and silver, she thought open the door and welcomed her unexpected visitor.

'I apologise for the inconvenience, but I bear news that you will wish to hear,' said the farseer. 'I would not normally intervene in such a small matter, but considering the delicate balance of choice on which your life is currently poised I think it wise that you should know that your friend, Aradryan, has set himself aboard the crew of a new ship.'

'And why does this news bring you to my door at such an inopportune time?' said Thirianna. She could not remember the dream that had been interrupted but a hollowness lingered inside her, a vague after-memory that disturbed her.

'The starship is *Irdiris*,' said Alaiteir. 'It is due to slip its moorings before the dawn cycle begins.'

'So soon?' said Thirianna. 'Why such a swift departure?'

'Why not?' said the farseer. 'Your friend is in pain and seeks swift resolution to it. He is acting rashly, but we cannot blame him for that.'

'If he does not wish to share the courtesy of saying goodbye to me, then perhaps he is not the friend I thought he was,' said Thirianna, sitting cross-legged on the rug at the centre of the main chamber. She indicated an invitation to Alaiteir to seat himself on one of the low couches but he declined with a raised hand.

'The *Irdiris* is no normal vessel,' said the farseer. 'She is a void-runner bound for distant stars beyond the reach of the webway. It will be many passes until your friend returns, if he comes back at all.'

'A ranger ship?' said Thirianna, one hand moving to her mouth in shock. 'You think that he chooses to make himself outcast, leaving the Path behind him?'

Alaiteir simply nodded, his eyes never moving from Thirianna.

'I have to convince him to stay!' She jumped to her feet and made for the dressing room next door. She hastily dressed herself in the same outfit she had worn earlier in the cycle and hurried from the apartment. She stopped on the landing outside and waited for Alaiteir to join her. Realising that she did not know where the *Irdiris* was docked, she returned to her quarters and moved towards the infinity circuit terminal.

'The Bay of Departing Sorrows,' said Alaiteir from the doorway, just as Thirianna's hand was about to make contact with the smooth plate. He waved a hand towards the docking balcony behind him. 'You can take my cloudskiff if you wish to travel swiftly.'

'I do not understand why you have such an interest in this,' said Thirianna, hurrying past the farseer. The two-sailed anti-grav vessel hovered alongside the sky quay, its engines gently humming. 'You have my sincere thanks for passing on this news.'

'Wait!' Alaiteir called out as Thirianna nimbly leapt over the side of the cloudskiff. She turned, one hand on the tiller controls. 'Do you really want Aradryan to stay?'

Thirianna hesitated, and in turn that hesitation gave her a moment's pause for thought. Were her reasons selfish? She decided that it was in the interests of both herself and Aradryan that he stay, regardless of the difficulties that might cause.

'I cannot bear to think of him out there in the darkness, adrift from the Path and alone,' she said, thumbing the grav motors into life via the rune on the tiller handle.

She steered the cloudskiff away from the quayside and down towards the floor of the dome, the hum of its engines becoming a soft purring as she picked up speed. She brought the craft level with one of the many transit routes that stretched from dome to dome, and guided the cloudskiff towards the arched opening.

Glancing back she saw Alaiteir standing with arms crossed at the railing outside her apartment. As she passed into the shadow of the passageway she wondered if she was not being manipulated by the old seer. How could she tell if the decisions she was making were truly her own and not a meaningless dance to some design that favoured Alaiteir?

She dismissed her doubts, realising that such speculation could lead nowhere. She reassured herself that the life of one poet was far below the machinations of the Farseers of Alaitoc and forced herself to believe that Alaiteir was acting out of genuine regard for her, if not outright kindness.

SHE GUIDED THE cloudskiff from dome to dome, cutting across the disc of Alaitoc by the shortest route, passing over the central divide towards the darkward rim. Coming close to the edge of the craftworld, she saw the Bay of Departing Sorrows in the distance: a crescent of quays and docks attached to the darkside rim at a steep tangent. There were three ships moored there, but the *Irdiris* was easily recognised by its small size and single solar sail. It was little more than an armed yacht, built for speed, efficiency and range, crewed by only a handful of eldar. At the moment its hull was coloured a deep green mottled with black stripes, its sail glowing gold in the light of dying Mirianathir.

Steering the cloudskiff lower, she passed alongside the white hull of a short-range barque, dipping beneath its twin loading ramps along which a procession of egg-like package crates were floating into its hold. Coming around the prow of the barque, Thirianna saw two figures walking up the gantry beside the *Irdiris*. She recognised the tall, gaunt figure of Aradryan and slowed down, bringing the cloudskiff gently alongside the larger vessel. Stepping down to the quay, she saw Aradryan turning in her direction.

'Aradryan!' Her voice disappeared into the depths of the dimly lit hangar.

He stopped, hands on hips. Thirianna broke into a run and reached him as Aradryan's companion, a female eldar in a tight bodysuit of yellow and blue, shook her head and continued up towards the void-runner.

'This is madness,' Thirianna said as she reached her friend. She reached out a hand to his arm but he stepped away, avoiding the contact. Aradryan was dressed in the same severe outfit he had worn on his arrival and his expression was stern.

'It is freedom,' he replied, glancing over his shoulder towards the open iris-like door of the starship. He looked back at Thirianna and his expression softened. 'I did not wish to be parted like this. It is too painful to say goodbye.'

'It does not have to be this way,' said Thirianna. 'Do not leave.'

'You wish me to stay?' said Aradryan, one eyebrow raised. 'Would there be a purpose in remaining on Alaitoc?'

Thirianna had wrestled with the idea on the journey from her apartment, but had resolved no solid argument she could offer. It simply felt wrong that Aradryan should go in this manner, abandoning the structure and protection of the Path for a life as an outcast.

'There must be more to this than your desire to be with me,' she said. 'How can you hate Alaitoc, who has raised and nurtured you and given you so much?'

'I do not hate her,' said Aradryan. 'I am merely bored of her. Perhaps in time my thirst for new vistas and experiences will be sated and I will return. Would you come with me?'

Arguments sprang to Thirianna's mind, but they seemed trite against the yearning she felt in Aradryan's spirit. She stepped back, bowing her head.

'Be safe,' she said. 'See the stars and come back to us.'

'I will, Thirianna,' Aradryan replied. He strode close to her and laid a hand on each of her shoulders. 'Take care of Korlandril for me. I sense that he needs a good friend at the moment, if only to save him from himself.'

'And who is going to save you from yourself?' Thirianna asked, tears moistening her cheeks. She could not look at Aradryan and kept her gaze on the marble-like floor of the docking pier.

'Nobody,' Aradryan said.

Thirianna still did not look up as she felt Aradryan remove his hands and back away. She heard his faint footsteps on the gantry followed by the delicate whisper of the closing doorway.

Lights sprang into life along the length of the *Irdiris*, bathing the dock in a warm glow of oranges and reds. Thirianna turned away, not wanting to see the starship leave. With barely a sound, the breeze of its passing ruffling her hair, the void-runner lifted from the platform and tilted starwards. The force-field enclosing the dock shimmered into silvery life as the *Irdiris* passed through it.

Thirianna looked up at the last moment, catching a glimpse of the vessel's swallow tail before it disappeared through the energy barrier and was obscured from sight. She waited for the forcefield to settle, returning to its transparent state. By then, the *Irdiris* was accelerating swiftly towards the webway gate aft of Alaitoc. It became a shimmer against the stars as its holofield activated, and then it was gone from view.

THIRIANNA FOUND ALAITEIR sitting on the same bench as before. The aging farseer sat with his hands neatly clasped in his lap, watching yellow-feathered sawbeaks duelling over the tumble of rocks at the bottom of the hill.

'There is a final warning I must give you,' Alaiteir said as Thirianna sat beside him. She arranged her robe carefully and looked down the slope. 'Though you may step onto the Path of the Seer like any other part of the Path, and step off again when you feel the time is appropriate, it has the strongest lures of any we might tread.'

'I resisted the call of Khaine,' said Thirianna. 'That is perhaps the most treacherous trap of all.'

'It is not,' said Alaiteir. Thirianna detected a subtle note of annoyance in his tone and realised she had spoken out of place. She dipped her head in apology.

'The call of Khaine is strong but it is a harsh, unsubtle snare,' the farseer continued, mollified by Thirianna's contrition. 'The lure of the Seer is far more potent, for it promises unbounded power. Those of us who tread the Path of the Seer to the fullest extent know the doom to which we walk.'

He held up a hand, silencing another comment from Thirianna before she could make it.

'I do not mean the visions of our own deaths,'

Alaiteir continued. He chuckled. 'When you have seen the hundredth possible way you might die a gruesome death, the fear tends to have lost its edge.'

The farseer paused and Thirianna sensed that he was inviting her to speak.

'As a warrior I learnt to accept that all things die,' she said. 'I have faced real death many times; what is the phantasm of a possible future compared to that?'

'Yet none of us wish to truly die,' said Alaiteir. Without turning, he gestured towards the spirit stone fixed in an ornate brooch upon Thirianna's left breast. 'Our spirits pass on to the infinity matrix when our physical forms are spent.'

'This much I already know, as would any child of Alaitoc,' said Thirianna. 'I do not understand how that is so different for a seer.'

'For a seer one's spirit retains a greater sense of consciousness after death, but it is not of that which I speak,' said Alaiteir. He tugged at the fingers of his glove, removing it to reveal a hand that glittered like a diamond. The skin was transparent, slightly edged like a shaped gem, and within shining flashes of colour hinted at veins and capillaries and muscle. He held it up to the light of the dome, each fingertip sparkling like a star. He wiggled his fingers and laughed quietly. 'To tread the Path to its furthest end, to become a Farseer, is to resign oneself to a different fate. We do not join with the infinity circuit; we become it!'

Thirianna had heard of such a thing, indeed had walked in the Dome of Crystal Seers, but it was a different matter to see the effect first-hand whilst it was progressing. She stared at the jewel-like flesh of Alaiteir's hand, marvelling at the rainbows of light that danced from the surface.

'Does it hurt?' she asked.

'Not at all,' replied Alaiteir. 'It is quite pleasant in a way. It is not the changing of the flesh that I warn against, but the hardening of the spirit. When a farseer becomes part of the infinity circuit his mind is wholly intact. Not for us the half-limbo of the physically dead, dimly aware of the fate that has befallen us. Consciousness is retained, an eternity ahead to spend without form stretched across the reaches of the skein.'

'The skein?'

'If you choose to become a seer you will learn more,' the farseer said, pulling on his glove.

'If I choose?' said Thirianna. 'I have already chosen. You know this or you would not have been waiting for me.'

'You will reconsider your choice and the two eventualities of that decision still exist,' said Alaiteir. He stood up and extended a hand to Thirianna, graciously helping her to her feet, a sign of equality. 'If you choose the Path of the Seer, go to Farseer Kelamith and he will be your guide.'

'Not you?' Thirianna was saddened, having already become a little attached to the farseer's strange but charming ways.

'No, Kelamith's thread and yours will entwine if you choose as such. He has more of a gift with novices than I.'

'Even with your warning, I feel certain of my choice.' Thirianna asked. 'Why will I reconsider?'

'I do not know,' admitted the farseer. He glanced at Thirianna and smiled slyly. 'And If I did, do you think I would tell you?'

FATE

The Raven – Messenger of Morai-heg. One of the most powerful runes, the Raven can be used only by the most experienced seers, for it can be a wayward guide to the unwary. The eyes of Morai-heg see all, and the Raven leads the follower to a single point of fate, from which there is no escape. Such nodes of destiny are rare, for the future is eternally mutable, but where they exist, the Raven will find them.

THIRIANNA WAS AT Korlandril's statue, sitting at one end of a curving bench, gazing at the dim glow beyond the dome. She wondered what it would be that might cause her to change her mind. As far as she knew herself, her mind was set on taking the

Path of the Seer. The possibilities it offered were genuinely endless; the ability to gaze into the furthest reaches of the future and control her own fate.

She felt another approaching and turned to see Korlandril crossing the grass. He was a little late, but she did not mind; their appointment had not been precise. She smiled as he sat next to her, pleased that one of her friends seemed to be in good spirits.

The moment passed, as did her smile, when she turned her thoughts to the news she needed to pass on.

'Aradryan has left Alaitoc,' Thirianna said quietly.

Korlandril's face was a flurry of emotion. Assuming the mantle of artist he had rendered himself incapable of self-critical thought and restraint. Every feeling etched into his features; shock and then disappointment. There was another look, just at the end, and Thirianna detected a small measure of satisfaction. She was not wholly surprised at this. After all, Korlandril and Aradryan had parted on bad terms.

'I do not understand,' said the sculptor. 'I know that we had a disagreement, but I thought that he planned to remain on Alaitoc for some time yet.'

'He did not depart on your account,' said Thirianna, though doubtless the disagreement between the two had contributed. She realised that discussing Aradryan's declaration of feelings for her would not be prudent.

'Why would he not come to see me before he left?' Korlandril asked. 'It is obvious that some distance had grown between us, but I did not think his opinion of me had sunk so low.'

'It was not you,' Thirianna said, knowing she could have persuaded Aradryan to stay but had chosen not to.

'What happened?' asked Korlandril, a slight tone of accusation in his voice. 'When did Aradryan leave?'

'He took aboard *Irdiris* last cycle, after we spent some time together.'

Korlandril did not seem to recognise the name. That was no surprise; Thirianna had not heard of the starship a cycle ago.

'*Irdiris* is a far-runner, destined for the Exodites on Elan-Shemaresh and then to the Wintervoid of Meios,' she explained.

'Aradryan wishes to become a... *ranger*?' Incredulity and distaste vied with each other across Korlandril's face. He stroked his bottom lip with a slender finger, calming himself. 'I had no idea he was so dissatisfied with Alaitoc.'

'Neither did I, and perhaps that is why he left so soon,' confessed Thirianna. 'I believe I spoke hastily and with insensitivity and drove him to a swifter departure than he might otherwise have considered.'

'I am sure that you are no–' began Korlandril but Thirianna cut him off with an agitated twitch of her finger.

'I do not wish to speak of it,' she said. Her guilt gnawed at her and bringing out the sorry details into the open would do neither Thirianna nor Korlandril any good.

They sat in silence for a while longer, while lit-tlewings darted amongst the branches of the trees above them, trilling to one another. Deep within the woods a breezemaker stirred into life and the leaves began to rustle gently: a calming backdrop.

'There was something else about which I wish to speak to you,' said Korlandril, rousing Thirianna from thoughts of Aradryan. 'I have a proposal to make.'

There was something about Korlandril's look that excited Thirianna. The passion she could see in his eyes stirred the feelings she had kept secret between herself and her poems. She indicated with an incli-nation of her head that they should stand.

'We should discuss this in my chambers, with something to drink, perhaps?' she said.

'That would be most agreeable,' said Korlandril as the two of them made their way towards the dome entrance.

THEY WERE ABOUT to step onto the sliding walkway up to the towers where Thirianna lived when a large group appeared from the gloom ahead of them. Sensing something dark, Thirianna strayed closer to Korlandril, who put a protective hand upon her shoulder though she felt him tense and could sense his discomfort.

The group were Aspect Warriors and an aura of death hung about them as palpable as a stench. They were clad in plates of overlapping armour of purple and black, their heavy tread thunderous in the still twilight. Thirianna could feel their menace growing stronger as they approached, waystones glowing like eyes of blood. They had taken off their war-helms and carried them hooked upon their belts, leaving their hands free to carry slender missile launchers.

Dark Reapers: possessed of the war god in his aspect of Destroyer.

Something in the depths of Thirianna's thoughts stirred; a memory hidden away, an aftertouch of Khaine on her spirit. It both excited and appalled her, disgust warring with the thrill it brought.

Though their helmets were removed, the warriors still bore the rune of the Dark Reaper painted in blood upon their faces. Thirianna and Korlandril shrank closer to the edge of the passageway as the Aspect Warriors passed, seeking the faces of their friends. Thirianna took several deep breaths in an attempt to calm down, but she felt a quiver running through her as the Aspect Warriors approached. Korlandril's hand on her shoulder felt heavy and reassuring.

Thirianna pointed, directing Korlandril's attention to Maerthuin. Arthuis walked a little way behind. The brothers stopped and turned their eyes upon Thirianna and Korlandril. Their gazes were empty, devoid of anything but the remotest recognition. Thirianna could smell the blood of the runes on their faces and suppressed an urge to reach out towards it.

'You are well?' asked Thirianna, her voice quiet and respectful.

Arthuis nodded slowly.

'Victory was ours,' intoned Maerthuin.

'We will meet you at the Crescent of the Dawning Ages,' said Arthuis.

'At the start of the next cycle,' added Maerthuin.

Korlandril and Thirianna both nodded their agreement and the two warriors moved on. Thirianna relaxed and Korlandril gave a sigh of relief.

'It is inconceivable to me that one should indulge in such horror,' said Korlandril as the two of them stepped upon the moving walkway.

Thirianna said nothing. Horror was not the sensation she had felt, though she was sure it was there, hidden away behind the careful memeblocks erected by her war-mask.

They made a spiralling ascent, languidly turning upon itself as the sliding ramp rose around the Tower of Dormant Witnesses. Thirianna considered Korlandril's words and as they reached the top of the ramp realised the error in them.

'It is not an indulgence,' said Thirianna.

'What is not an indulgence?' replied Korlandril, who had been looking at the stars beyond the dome.

'The Path of the Warrior is not an indulgence,' she repeated. 'One cannot simply leave anger in the darkness, to fester and grow unseen. Sooner or later it might find vent.'

'What is there to be so angry about?' laughed Korlandril. 'Perhaps if we were Biel-Tan, with all their talk of reclaiming the old empire, then we might have a use for all of this sword-waving and gunfire. It is an uncivilised way to behave.'

'You ignore the passions that rule you,' snapped Thirianna.

'I meant no offence,' he said, obviously embarrassed.

'The intention is not important,' said Thirianna, still annoyed by Korlandril's flippancy. 'Perhaps you would care to ridicule the other Paths on which I have trodden?'

'I did not mean...' Korlandril trailed off. 'I am sorry.'

'The Path of Dreaming, the Path of Awakening, the Path of the Artist,' said Thirianna, shaking her head slightly. 'Always self-indulgent, always about your needs, no sense of duty or dedication to others.'

Korlandril shrugged, a fulsome gesture employing the full use of both arms.

'I simply do not understand this desire some of us feel to sate a bloodlust I do not feel,' he said.

'And that is what is dangerous about you,' said Thirianna. 'Where do you put that rage you feel when someone angers you? What do you do with the hatred that burns inside when you think upon all that we have lost? You have not learnt to control these feelings, merely ignore them. Becoming one with Khaine, assuming one of his Aspects is not about confronting an enemy, it is about confronting ourselves. We should all do it at some time in our lives.'

Korlandril shook his head.

'Only those that desire war, make it,' he said.

'Findrueir's *Prophecies of Interrogation*,' said Thirianna, knowing the quotation. It was a trite statement that she had once believed as well. 'Yes, I've read it too, do not look so surprised. However, I read it after treading the Path of the Warrior. An aesthete who wrote about matters she had never experienced. Hypocrisy at its worst.'

'And also one of Iyanden's foremost philosophers.' Amusement danced on Korlandril's lips.

'A radical windbag with no true cause and a gyrinx fetish,' countered Thirianna.

Korlandril laughed. His levity bordered on disrespect and Thirianna allowed her displeasure to show.

'Forgive me,' Korlandril said. 'I hope that is not an example of your poetry!'

Thirianna vacillated between annoyance and humour before breaking into a smile.

'Listen to us! Gallery philosophers, the pair! What do we know?'

'Little enough,' agreed Korlandril with a nod. 'And I suppose that can be a dangerous thing.'

THE TWO OF them reached Thirianna's chambers. She noticed Korlandril examining the interior in some detail and they made some small talk while she prepared drinks. They discussed Aradryan's leaving again, though Korlandril turned the conversation around to himself, and it was clear he was more concerned about Aradryan's low opinion of his sculpture than the fate of his friend, which irritated Thirianna.

'Your friendship has been important to me,' said Thirianna, wishing to change the subject.

'I have a new piece of sculpture in mind, something very different from my previous works,' Korlandril announced.

'That is good to hear,' said Thirianna. It was obvious it was this that Korlandril wanted to talk about. She was a little bit disappointed. 'I think that if you can find something to occupy your mind, you will dwell less on the situation with Aradryan.'

'Yes, that is very true! I'm going to delve into portraiture. A sculptural testament to devotion, in fact.'

'Sounds intriguing,' said Thirianna. 'Perhaps something a little more grounded in reality would be good for your development.'

'Let us not get too carried away,' said Korlandril with a smile. 'I think there may be some abstract elements incorporated into the design. After all, how does one truly replicate love and companionship in features alone?'

'I am surprised.' Korlandril's talk of love intrigued her. She watched him closely, trying to discern his mood, but he did not seem to notice her scrutiny. Thirianna thought of her poems, and the love they expressed. 'I understand if you do not wish to tell me, but what inspires such a piece of work?'

The artist looked perplexed, and Thirianna realised there was more to what he had said than she had seen. Before she could apologise for not responding to his gentle overtures, Korlandril spoke again.

'You are my inspiration,' he said quietly, eyes fixed on Thirianna. 'It is you that I wish to fashion as a likeness of dedication and ardour.'

Thirianna was shocked by Korlandril's openness, and a little dismayed that it perhaps had come too late. Her infatuation with him, hidden away within her verses, had always been her secret, and in writing her poems she had lessened its power over her.

'I... You...' She looked away, not sure what to say. For a moment she wondered if Korlandril knew what she had written about him. Suddenly she was scared by the whole issue and affected an air of distance. 'I do not think that is warranted.'

'Warranted?' Korlandril leaned towards her, his face intent on Thirianna. 'It is an expression of my feelings; there is nothing that needs warranting other than to visualise my desires and dreams. You are my desire and a dream.'

Thirianna did not reply. She stood and took a couple of paces away before turning to face Korlandril, her face serious.

'This is not a good idea, my friend,' she said gently. She wondered why he had said nothing before, when perhaps she would have been in a position to reciprocate. She realised that this was the dilemma that would make her reconsider becoming a seer. There was no doubt in her mind, and it was best to disappoint Korlandril as gently as possible. 'I do appreciate the sentiment, and perhaps some time ago I would not only be flattered but I would be delighted.'

'But not now?' he asked, hesitant, scared of the answer.

She shook her head.

'Aradryan's arrival and departure have made me realise something that has been amiss with my life for several passes now,' she said. Korlandril reached out a hand in a half-hearted gesture, beckoning her to come closer. Thirianna sat next to him and took his hand in hers. 'I am changing again. The Path of the Poet is spent for me. I have grieved and I have rejoiced through my verse, and I feel expunged of the burdens I felt. I feel another calling is growing inside me.'

Korlandril snatched his hand away.

'You are going to join Aradryan!' he snapped. 'I knew the two of you were keeping something from me.'

'Don't be ridiculous,' Thirianna rasped in return, trying to hide her guilt that Aradryan had offered to stay for her. 'It is because I told him what I am telling you that he left.'

'So, he did make advances on you!' Korlandril stood and angrily wiped a hand across his brow and pointed accusingly at Thirianna. 'It is true! Deny it if you dare!'

She slapped away his hand.

'What right do you have to make any claim on me?' she snapped. 'If you must know, I have never entertained any thoughts of being with Aradryan, even before he left, and certainly not since his return. I am simply not ready for a life-companion. In fact, that is why I cannot be your inspiration.'

Korlandril's trembling lip was a cliché of sadness and it melted through Thirianna's anger. She took a step closer, hands open in friendship.

'It is to save you from a future heartache that I decline your attentions now,' she continued. 'I have spoken to Farseer Alaiteir and he agrees that I am ready to begin the Path of the Seer.'

'A seer?' scoffed Korlandril. 'You completely fail to

divine my romantic intents and yet think you might become a seer?'

'I divined your intent and ignored it,' lied Thirianna, laying a hand on his arm. 'I did not wish to encourage you; to admit your feelings for me would be to bring them to the light and that was something I wished to avoid, for the sake of both of us.'

Korlandril waved away her arguments, pulling his arm from her grasp.

'If you have not the same feelings for me, then simply say so. Do not spare my pride for your comfort. Do not hide behind this excuse of changing Paths.'

'It is true, it is not an excuse! You love Thirianna the poet. We are alike enough at the moment, our Paths different yet moving in the same general direction. When I become a seer, I while not be Thirianna the poet. You will not love that person.'

'Why deny me the right to find out?' Korlandril's fists were balled at his side and anger flashed in his eyes, scaring Thirianna. 'Who are you to judge what will or will not be? You are not even on the Path and now you think you can claim the powers of the seer?'

'If it is true that you feel the same when I have become a seer, and I feel the same too, then whatever will happen will come to pass.'

Korlandril caught an angry reply before he said it. His expression changed to one of hope.

'If you feel the same?' he said. 'You admit that you have feelings for me.'

'Thirianna the Poet has feelings for you, she always has,' Thirianna admitted.

'Then why do we not embrace this shared feeling?' Korlandril asked, stepping forwards and taking Thirianna's hands in his. Now it was her turn to pull away. She could not bring herself to look at him when she spoke.

'If I indulge this passion with you, it would hold me back, perhaps trap me here as the poet, forever writing my verses of love in secret.'

'Then we stay together, poet and artist! What is so wrong with that?'

'It is not healthy!' Having seen what obsession had done to Aradryan, Thirianna was in no mind to suffer it herself. 'You know that it is unwise to become trapped in ourselves. Our lives must be in constant motion, moving from one Path to the next, developing our senses of self and the universe. To over-indulge leads to the darkness that came before. It attracts the attention of... Her. She Who Thirsts.'

Thirianna waited while Korlandril flexed his fingers. She could hear the quick beating of his heart and feel his pain rising to the surface. Yet for all that she felt for him, he would have to be the second friend in a cycle that she would turn away.

'What we feel is not *wrong*!' said the artist. 'Since the founding of the craftworlds our people have loved and survived. Why should we be any different?'

'You use the same arguments as Aradryan,' Thirianna admitted softly, turning on Korlandril. 'He asked me to forget the Path and join him. Even if I had loved him I could not do that. I *cannot* do that with you. Though I have deep feelings for you, I would no more risk my eternal spirit for you than I would step out into the void of space and hope to breathe.'

Seeing the agonised expression on Korlandril's face was too much for Thirianna. To part with Aradryan had been a heartache; to spurn Korlandril for whom she had once felt so deeply was too much. Tears welled up in Thirianna's eyes.

'Please leave,' she said.

Korlandril's anguish was all-consuming and it frightened Thirianna. His eyes narrowed to slits and he bared his teeth as he stalked back and forth across the room.

'I cannot help you,' Thirianna said, staring with misery at the anguish being played out in Korlandril's actions. 'I know you are in pain, but it will pass.'

'Pain?' spat Korlandril. 'What do you know of my pain?'

Korlandril half-raised his hand, fist clenched. Stepping back, fearing he would strike her, Thirianna raised a hand to her mouth in horror.

Korlandril fled, crying and trembling. Thirianna took a step after him, full of concern. She stopped herself, fearful more of what he might do to her than himself. She had seen something in his eyes that she had only before witnessed in the sanctuary of the Aspect shrines: hate and anger.

This did not bode well for either of her friends and more than ever she wanted to know what would happen.

* * *

WALKING AMONGST THE forest of seers past, Thirianna allowed her mind to open to their thoughts. She passed between them, near the heart of the Dome of Crystal Seers, intrigued by their diamond-like bodies, still clothed in the robes they had worn when they had finally passed into the otherworld of the infinity circuit.

Their thoughts were like a background noise in her mind. It pulsed around her, under her, over her, threading along the microscopic veins of psychic crystal that enmeshed the dome. She could feel their sentience around her, each coming to the fore as she walked past his or her immobile form.

She caught glimpses of life in the infinity circuit; a world of colour and sound and light. She saw also beyond the veil, peering at snippets of the realm of the purely psychic. Since she was a child she had been taught to raise barriers against that world, to protect herself and others against the creatures that lingered within.

It was a hard habit to break and she could not open anything more than a chink in her psychic defences to let in the vibrant minds of the crystal seers. Just as she glimpsed something interesting, instinct would snap her away, moving her thoughts elsewhere, throwing up defences against the psychic intrusion.

'It will be the fate of Kelamith to end here,' said a voice behind her. 'Perhaps it will be the fate of Thirianna. That is not yet known.'

Thirianna turned to see a farseer standing beside one of the statue-like eldar, one hand on its shoulder. He was clad in a robe of thick black velvet, embroidered with runes and sigils in golden and silver thread. About his neck and wrists were many charms.

He was a little shorter than Thirianna, and broad of shoulder for an eldar. His eyes were mismatched; one a vibrant purple, the other a luminous yellow. They glittered with psychic energy.

The farseer had his other hand outstretched and above it a single rune gently spun in the air, turning end over end. Thirianna recognised it immediately. It was her name, her rune.

'Are you Kelamith?' she asked. 'You were expecting me?'

'Kelamith will expect you, yes,' replied the seer. His voice carried more gravitas than any other Thirianna had heard. His intonation, his choice of words, seemed archaic yet spoke of the future. It was difficult to understand what he was saying. 'He will know that you would come. He will be here.'

'When will he be here?' she asked. 'If you are not Kelamith, who are you?'

'He will be here now,' said the seer. His hand closed around the rune and his eyes dimmed. They focussed on Thirianna. 'Apologies, child. I am Kelamith. I will guide you on the Path of the Seer.'

VISION

The Seeking Shaft – Arrow of Kurnous. A guiding rune, the Seeking Shaft will always find its mark, no matter where or when it is released. In the most complex journeys across the skein, cause-and-effect cannot be easily attributed to a single personality. In these circumstances, a wise seer will turn to the Seeking Shaft to identify a particular individual not yet known to the seer.

A SENSE OF relief filled Thirianna as she watched the crystal-verses of her poems melt away in the reblender. As she fed each into the warm interior of the device, their words lifted away from her, seeping deeper into her memory, becoming a thing of the past rather than the present.

She had saved this task until last, unsure what the destruction of her work would do to her. She was glad: a final closing of the chapter of Thirianna the Poet, as Thirianna the Seer would concern herself only with the future.

As the last of the crystals dissolved in the orange glow of the reblender, Thirianna felt the last ties to her previous life slipping away. For many poets what she had done bordered on vandalism, but in her mind Thirianna knew that nothing good could ever come from her poems being known by another, least of all Korlandril.

She had not heard from him since their argument; she had missed the appointment with their friends while she had been in the Dome of Crystal Seers. She had spent the last cycle tidying up her apartment for whoever next chose to live there, and her few belongings were gathered in a shoulderbag waiting for her by the door. There was little she wanted to take with her on the next part of her life, and even less that she wanted to keep to remind her of the past.

Content that she was ready, Thirianna stood up, slung the bag over her shoulder and left the rooms. From now on she would dwell in the Chambers of the Seers.

ARRIVING IN THE heart of Alaitoc, close to the gardens where she had met Alaiteir, Thirianna secured herself new quarters. Having received no guidance or instruction from Kelamith on how to proceed, Thirianna located a suite of unoccupied rooms – the trace on the infinity circuit showed that the seer who had lived there had moved on to walk the Path of Service, which Thirianna considered a good omen.

It took hardly any time at all to unpack the few books and crystals she had brought with her. She inspected the view from the apartment's balcony and found that it overlooked the rock-strewn slope where she had spoken to Alaiteir. Never one to trust coincidence when farseers and the infinity circuit were involved, Thirianna smiled to herself.

'Thirianna will be late.'

Kelamith had arrived without announcement by the infinity circuit. Surprised, Thirianna blushed as the farseer stepped onto the balcony. He had the same strange, distant look in his eyes as when they had first met.

'I did not remember receiving an invitation,' she confessed.

'Kelamith will not send the invitation as he sees that Thirianna will be late, so instead he will come here for Thirianna himself.'

'Do you always speak like that?' Thirianna asked, annoyed at the farseer's presumption.

Kelamith slowly closed his eyes. When he opened them again the witchlight had disappeared. He bowed his head slightly in apology.

'A risk attached to the work I undertake,' he explained. 'I delve deeper along the skein than my companions. I examine with the narrow eye that which attracts the attention of their broad gazes.'

'Where will I be late?' Thirianna said.

'I do not remember,' said Kelamith. 'The thread has gone. My presence here has assured that.'

'You do not remember?' Thirianna said. 'Only a moment ago you spoke about it.'

'And a moment ago it ceased to be a possibility and thus never existed,' said Kelamith. 'One cannot remember a thing that has not existed. Really, child, you need to grasp these fundamental realities quickly if we are to make any sort of progress.'

Taken aback, Thirianna had no answer to that. She thought it better to keep to a specific topic.

'Where are we going?' she asked.

'Into the mind of Alaitoc,' Kelamith announced with a broad smile. 'I hope you are ready.'

THE CHAMBER WAS one of many, egg-shaped and arranged alongside the others like a maze of bubbles in a foam, joined by narrow archways. The walls were glowing with the conduits of the infinity circuit, thousands of crystalline capillaries interwoven with each other and the fabric of the rooms.

As they had walked through an arterial tunnel into the depths of Alaitoc, Thirianna had glimpsed other eldar in the adjoining chambers, some alone and others in groups. Each was surrounded by a small constellation of runes, turning in the air, bobbing up and down, spiralling and climbing, curving and dipping in their eccentric orbits. Kelamith paid them no attention and offered no explanation as to what they were looking for.

Kelamith stood in the centre of the room and held out his hands, palms down, thumbs splayed and touching. Thirianna felt a surge of psychic energy and a node of the infinity circuit extruded from the interlaced conduits on the floor, pulsing with green and blue light.

'Our minds are a fragile thing, child,' said Kelamith. 'From the moment we are born to the moment we pass on, our thoughts are open for all of the universe to see. There are creatures that desire them, powers that hunger after them, and for that reason even as you learnt to speak and walk, to master your joy and woe, you were taught how to suppress the energies of your mind.'

The farseer took a step back and waved to Thirianna to stand beside the node. She did as he instructed, wanting to reach out and touch the glimmering crystal stalagmite but afraid to do so.

'We all possess the ability to unleash the power of our minds in amazing ways, child,' said Kelamith. 'Whether it is in the shaping of a thought or the mastery of the deadly Aspect arts, our mind is our most powerful tool. We suppress that power to ward away the dangers such ability will bring, but as a seer you must embrace it.'

'What do you wish me to do?' asked Thirianna, full of trepidation.

'You must let go of your thoughts,' said the farseer. 'You must allow them to be free and boundless. You must give up a lifetime of worry and cast away all of the protection, unlearning that which you had to learn.'

'Does that not attract the attention of the Great Enemy?' The slightest thought of She Who Thirsts sent a shudder through Thirianna, of fear and loathing.

'In time you will use the runes as your shield, focussing the psychic energy you will channel,' explained Kelamith. 'The defences will always be there, yours to call upon should you need them. Do not be cautious though, for such interruptions may set back your development and retard your ultimate power. At first you will conduct this unlearning within the safety of the infinity circuit. And do not be afraid, for I am also here with you, child.'

Kelamith gestured for Thirianna to place her hands on the infinity circuit node. It was cool to the touch, though veined with warmth on her palms.

'Speak after me, and let your thoughts flow with the words,' said Kelamith. Thirianna closed her eyes, concentrating on the feel of the node in her hands and the voice of Kelamith, which came slowly, rhythmically on the edge of hearing.

'In the skein there is nothing. There are no names and there are no beings. This is where the mind originates. There is the mind but nothing is physical. Forms obtain the mind and thoughts are created. This is called Passing. In the not-yet-formed the skein divides and splits but there is no time passing. This is called Being. There is an energy that gives life to all things, allowing form to obtain mind and create thought. Forms that create thought share in this energy. This is called Life. Let slip Life, and become Being. Let slip Being and become Passing. Let slip Passing and become Mind. Become Mind and be one with the skein.'

Thirianna chanted the words, matching the pitch and cadence of the farseer. She dimly recognised them from her childhood, though they seemed in a different order. As she spoke each syllable, she felt herself relaxing, in body and thought.

She could no longer feel the node between her fingers. She continued chanting, repeating the words, feeling them entering her subconscious, triggering reactions in her thoughts that she could not feel but sensed in other ways.

Her body dissolved away, as the crystals had melted in the reblender. Her limbs, her torso, her fingers, her face, all had gone, leaving Thirianna as a floating core of thought.

'Open your eyes, child.'

Thirianna did so, though she had no eyes to open.

She found herself in a realm of light and movement. She could see the flicker of other eldar around her, like candles in twilight. A tracery of white, the infinity circuit, linked every other light together, stretching on without horizon into the impossible distance.

Energy flowed along the maze, back and forth, surging and ebbing, binding everything together with its movement, linking the eldar with one another.

And beyond.

Beyond was something even more spectacular, defying rationalisation. Beyond were the constantly shattering panes of existence; the overlapping planes of destiny; the interwoven threads of fate. The present surrounded Thirianna, but just out of reach was the future, and in the darkness behind was the past. Every life, every thought, every movement, every motive, every emotion, weaving together in a dazzling tapestry of cause and effect. It branched out, splitting and dividing like cells, spawning entire new universes and possibilities with every passing moment.

This was the skein, and it was beautiful.

And too much. Too much to see, to comprehend, to understand.

Thirianna passed out.

IT TOOK THREE cycles until Thirianna had recovered sufficiently from her first experience of the skein to contact Kelamith. The farseer had been notably absent as Thirianna had rested in her new rooms, and had offered no explanation of what had happened to her. Thirianna considered the possibility that Kelamith had known what would happen, and had foreseen that she would regain her mental harmony in time, and chosen not to intervene.

Just that briefest glimpse of the skein had opened Thirianna's mind to the wondrous possibilities that lay before her. Rather than being fearful of approaching the infinity circuit again she was excited by the prospect. Yet it had taken three days of meditation and contemplation before she had been able to think of the skein without being dizzied by its power.

Midway through the fourth cycle after the episode, she received an invitation from Kelamith to join him in the gardens next to her chambers. He made it clear that the two of them would be venturing into the infinity circuit again, which set

Thirianna's mind racing in all directions.

As she made her way down towards the parkland, her first thought was one of concern. What if she were incapable of interacting with the skein? What if she lacked the psychic power to deal with its infinite possibilities? She dismissed the idea as she reached the edge of the gardens. Kelamith had hinted that her mind's defences would be more of a hindrance than a help at this early stage; if he had any further worries over her suitability he would have voiced them or refused to become her mentor altogether. His lack of concern for her wellbeing led Thirianna to believe that what she had encountered, and her reaction, was commonplace.

Following the path up to the top of the rock hill, she wondered how many attempts it would take before she could interact with the infinity circuit. She was impatient, more than at any time in her life. She had a lifetime to perfect any art or skill she turned her mind to, but her desire to see what the future held for her propelled her forwards more swiftly than on any previous Path. It was possible, she concluded, that in her haste to comprehend the skein she was unwittingly stalling her development.

Kelamith stood beneath the branches of a tree near to the bench atop the hill. His eyes were free of witchlight and his expression was one of almost paternal pride, which confused Thirianna.

'Greetings, child,' said the farseer. Thirianna nodded her head in return and sat on the bench. 'I trust you feel restored and recuperated? You have not been unduly perturbed by your recent experience?'

'I am rested,' said Thirianna. She smiled at the far-seer as he walked over to her and stopped in front of the bench. 'And I am eager to try again. I hope that with your guidance I will not fail this time.'

'Fail?' Confusion knotted Kelamith's brow. 'There was no failure. Not on your part, at least. I failed to divine the extent of your instinct and natural ability, and did not take suitable precautions for your safe-keeping.'

'I do not understand.'

The farseer sat beside Thirianna, closer than would normally be acceptable between recent acquaint-ances. Thirianna tried to ignore the intrusion into her personal space.

'You went further into the infinity circuit than I considered possible,' explained Kelamith. 'For most of us, our first steps upon the Path are tentative and short-lived. We see no more than a fraction of the infinity circuit, and nothing of the great realm of which it is part. You, on your first attempt, looked upon the skein itself. The skein is a thing of wonder, but it cannot be seen without training and prepara-tion.'

Thirianna tried not to look smug at the thought that she had done so well, but evidently failed. Kelamith's frown of confusion turned to one of annoyance.

'You have natural power but no control, child,' he said. 'Once the shackles have been loosed from our thoughts it is easy to look at the skein. The skill comes in understanding it; in seeing only a part and choosing a singular thread to follow. Any fool can look at the mass of the future, but a seer must separate the detail from the noise, the important from the unimportant.'

Kelamith stood up and waved for Thirianna to follow him.

'We will return to the infinity circuit and we will try again,' said the farseer. 'This time I want you to only peek at what can be seen.'

'And how do I do that?' Thirianna asked as they started down the hill.

'As a child we blinded you, and now that you have opened your eyes again the light burns them,' said Kelamith. 'I will teach you the means to open them only slightly and protect yourself from the harsh glare of the unbounded skein.'

As before, they made their way into the heart of Alaitoc, walking through the interlinked Chambers of the Seers until they came to the same room as before. The infinity circuit node rose from the floor at Kelamith's command and he indicated for Thirianna to approach it.

'Do you still remember the words?' he asked.

'I do,' replied Thirianna. The verses were etched into her thoughts as deeply as her poems had once been. Oddly, she realised, she could barely remember her compositions when once they had come to mind at the slightest thought. The destruction of the crystals had been mirrored by her memory.

'Concentrate on the sense of form,' said Kelamith. 'Retain a foundation within your form rather than letting your spirit free. Chain your mind with the reality of your being and the restrictions of form.'

Thirianna did not quite understand what the farseer meant, but she was eager to link with the infinity circuit again. This time when she placed her hand on the node, she tried to picture the way she had interacted with the infinity circuit countless times before, skimming across its surface without delving into it.

'That will not do,' said Kelamith, sensing her intent. 'You cannot simply look upon the infinity circuit, you must still become part of it, while keeping yourself detached.'

'That is a contradiction, surely?' said Thirianna.

'Remember: Mind, Being and Form,' said the farseer. 'Three intertwined parts of you, each separate and the same. If such concepts prove difficult, there is nothing I can do to help you.'

Nodding her submission to this logic, Thirianna took a breath and allowed herself to slip into the infinity circuit.

At first she did as she had planned, touching only lightly upon the huge matrix of psychic energy that ran through every part of Alaitoc. She allowed her thoughts to dance towards the distant rim, where ship manifests and passenger lists inhabited the frameworks of the docks; to the Pinnacle of Mornings, where a group of poets were reciting the *Epic of Eldanesh*; to the Dome of Crystal Seers; to the Arc of the Turning Suns.

She felt a presence beside her: Kelamith, not physically, but within the structure of the infinity circuit.

'Thirianna will delve a little deeper,' he said.

She felt warmth from his presence, like the glow of

safety that wrapped her as a child when her mother had held her. It was sanctuary and it bolstered Thirianna's confidence. She started to recite the words taught to her by Kelamith and felt her consciousness slipping further into the infinity circuit.

'Thirianna will stay where she is, deep enough to see,' said the farseer.

The sensation was different this time. Thirianna understood what Kelamith meant about being part of the infinity circuit while remaining separate. Her form had become the infinity circuit but her being remained as it was and her mind lingered between the two.

Her world had become a glittering web of power, but rather than try to see it all, she concentrated on what was close at hand. She was inside the Arc of the Turning Suns. She could feel the flutter of the engineers touching upon the infinity circuit as they tended to the star-sails gathering energy from the dying sun. With another part of her mind she could witness them at their stations, making gentle adjustments to the massive solar collectors to maximise their efficiency.

She became aware of Kelamith beside her, watching without comment. He appeared as a golden spark in the infinity circuit, his psychic energy diffusing along dozens of conduits but concentrated close at hand.

Something else flickered into her consciousness. At first they were too fast to comprehend; flashing pinpricks that had raced past by the time her mind had become aware of them. Thirianna narrowed her focus, picking a handful of crystalline threads to interact with. The speed of everything seemed to slow as her thoughts coalesced, making the workings of the infinity circuit plainer to see.

The constant thrum of psychic energy became a slower pulse, moving outwards along the conduits of the infinity circuit in rhythm to Alaitoc's ponderous heartbeat. It rippled from the core to the rim, near-instantaneous in reality, but to her mind's eye becoming subtle, entrancing waves.

More of the bright sparks she had seen passed close by and Thirianna caught them with her thoughts, her scrutiny slowing their progress.

There were several dozen of them, clustered in groups each a handful strong. They appeared as tiny creatures, each group occupying the area of a fingernail. Yet there was immense power contained in their miniscule forms. Looking even more closely, she saw tiny clawed legs splaying across the threads of energy and she realised she looked upon the warp spiders from which the Aspect Warriors of the same name drew inspiration.

Each warp spider raced along the infinity circuit's threads, dozens of legs moving faster than thought. They rode upon the pulses of energy, then dashed back to the core before the next, heaved out on the tide of psychic power before returning to the hub.

They became aware of Thirianna and investigated. They circled around the mote of consciousness that was her mind, scurrying to and fro while they inspected her. Created to guard the infinity circuit from malign presences, the warp spiders quickly realised that Thirianna was no foe and relaxed their guard.

Rather than move on, they circled playfully around her, excited by this new presence. She could feel the tiny pinpricks of energy passing through her as the warp spiders danced across the infinity circuit, joyfully clambering around and through her thoughts.

The warp spiders were like a psychic tickle running through her mind, each a particle of purity and happiness that left a warm trail where it touched her, criss-crossing her memories and thoughts with tiny footsteps.

The experience was cleansing, the warp spiders feeding on tiny shreds of negative energy that leaked from Thirianna's deepest fears and worst emotions; fears and emotions kept locked away in the recesses of her mind but never wholly secured.

'It will be enough for the moment.' Kelamith washed through Thirianna, scattering the warp spiders. 'Thirianna will have her first true taste of the infinity circuit, but she must quell her curiosity and retain control.'

Kelamith's mind linked with Thirianna's and pulled her across the infinity circuit back to the Chambers of the Seers. For a strange moment Thirianna found herself looking at her own form. She realised that no matter how graceful and poised her body seemed, to the realm of the purely psychic it was crude as any other physical structure, with the same imperfections and compromises as any living being.

It was a humbling moment, right before she was

reunited with the shell of her body.

Thirianna felt a wave of claustrophobia as she was restricted to her normal, physical senses again. The weight of her form was a burden to her thoughts, which struggled across chemical synapses and along physical nerves.

The sensation of loss passed and Thirianna opened her eyes, looking at her hands upon the infinity circuit node. Kelamith stood to her right, eyes blazing with psychic energy. He turned that otherworldly stare upon Thirianna.

'Thirianna will do well, but she must be told that this is only the beginning,' said Kelamith. 'She will return here in the next cycle and we will continue.'

'Yes, she will,' Thirianna said, her mind still tingling with after-effects from the warp spiders.

FOR CYCLE AFTER cycle Thirianna returned to the Chambers of the Seers and explored the infinity circuit with Kelamith. Often he would guide her, leading Thirianna to strange places she had never seen before; places made of crystal cliffs and plains of sapphire, ruby seas and star-lit voids. Sometimes Thirianna was left to wander. Though never wholly alone – Kelamith's presence could always be felt in the distance – Thirianna started to learn how to navigate the infinity circuit more speedily.

Freeing herself from the constraints of form, she noticed junctions and pathways that were separate from the physical crystalline matrix, existing only in the psychic realm. At first these transitions jolted her consciousness, bringing the strangest sensation of disassociation, almost bereavement. In time the translocation of her spirit became less jarring, her consciousness slipping between the nodes of the infinity circuit with less effort.

Thirianna spent more time with the warp spiders, following them back to their roosts in the core and letting her mind free to be washed across the infinity circuit on the tides of psychic energy. Kelamith encouraged her, in his own odd fashion, and from the warp spiders she learnt more of the secret routes of the infinity circuit and the space in-between. Thirianna would chase the creatures, following them around the complex maze, never quite catching them. The warp spiders were more than happy with her company, staying just ahead of her flowing mind, teasing her with their presence.

When she was not delving into the secrets of the infinity circuit, Thirianna spent her time studying the runes of the seers. Kelamith furnished her with a learning crystal that contained thousands of the sigils, embedded with commentary from Alaitoc's greatest farseers.

At first, like the skein they represented, the volume of the runes was overwhelming: a near-incomprehensible labyrinth of meaning that overlaid and meshed in mysterious ways. Through the learning crystal, Thirianna was able to focus on one rune at a time, absorbing its meanings and uses, before following the branches and threads that led to other runes. Cycle by cycle her understanding expanded exponentially, her knowledge of the seers' codes and language spreading even as her comprehension of the infinity circuit broadened.

Thirianna admired the pattern and asymmetry of both; the organic flux of circuit and rune in conjunction with each other. Even as she was chasing warp spiders through the psychic maze of Alaitoc, Thirianna was associating the runes from the crystal with the experiences she underwent.

Yet not every cycle was a playful or joyous experience. The infinity circuit delved into every part of Alaitoc, from the restoration chambers to the weapons batteries. Through her deepening knowledge of the circuit's ways, Thirianna learnt to read the telltale signs of danger that appeared when she encroached upon areas she was not yet ready to look upon. Some of these she ventured into later with the aid of Kelamith; others remained a mystery to her.

Some of these regions were the places haunted by the spirits of the disquieted dead. While the energy of most eldar was subsumed into the greater consciousness of the infinity circuit, there were some that refused to relinquish their grip on the physical world. Many were warriors, killed in battle, trapped with their rage and their bloodlust. Some were great leaders, notable orators and philosophers, acclaimed artists; their personalities so strong that they existed after death to suffer eternity in the limbo of near-life.

Not all of the spirits that survived were dangerous. Many were simply mournful, filled with self-loathing and depressed at their fate. Some had strange mood swings, moving across the infinity circuit between joy and despair.

Kelamith advised Thirianna to be wary of such spirits, but not to shun them entirely. They were wise and many had noble intent, but their division from the world of the living gave them a twisted view of affairs. Thirianna had not yet developed the skill or focus to converse with these wandering ghosts, but communicated merely in sense and emotion, feeling happiness or woe, longing or regret when she came upon them.

Of particular distaste to Thirianna was the increasing habit of the warp spiders to seek refuge near the Aspect shrines during their games of psychic hide-and-seek. Thirianna could sense the brooding presence of the Aspect Warriors, their warlike minds corralled within the infinity circuit away from the thoughts of others. Like a shadow cast across the psychic maze, the temples of Khaine's followers touched on the infinity circuit with rage and hatred, tainting its energy.

The psychic landscapes of the infinity circuit were twisted as well. Gone were the rainbow bridges and waterfalls of silver, replaced by dank grottos, forbidding caverns of black ice and harsh red deserts. Fire glimmered across the infinity circuit, corrupted by iron and war, ash and blood.

It was not just a general abhorrence and fear that kept Thirianna from exploring these dark reaches further. The memory of her time as a Dire Avenger grew in strength when she came closer to the power of the Aspect shrines. It nagged harder and harder to be free from the bounds that kept it within Thirianna's unconscious, forcing her to withdraw, feeling polluted by its presence.

Part Two

Warlock

CONTROL

The Brother's Gaze – Eye of Ulthanesh. It is often tempting to follow a thread across the skein in a single direction, linking event to event, catalyst to outcome, to arrive at a final fate. While this allows one to see the progression of the future, it is to surrender the initiative to fate. The Brother's Gaze is a rune of contradiction, approaching a juncture from the opposite angle, providing the path from outcome to catalyst so that the course of destiny might be better steered.

SEVERAL DOZEN CYCLES had come and gone since Thirianna's first foray into the infinity circuit when Kelamith came to her early after the artificial dawn. She awoke, sensing his presence in her chambers, and found the farseer standing on the balcony of the apartment. Thirianna was instantly aware of something different; not about Kelamith but Alaitoc itself. The atmosphere was pregnant with energy, the infinity circuit buzzing with a growing presence, stronger here near the Chambers of the Seers than she had felt it before.

No, not stronger, just different. It had been stronger in the Shrine of One Hundred Bloody Tears.

The Avatar of Khaine was waking. The incarnation of the Bloody-Handed God was coming to life, stirring on its iron throne.

'War comes,' she said, pulling on her robe.

Kelamith turned towards her, eyes alight with psychic power. He said nothing for a moment and the light faded.

'Yes, child, war is coming,' he confirmed. 'You have the opportunity to witness something you have only experienced from afar.'

'No,' said Thirianna. 'I do not wish to see the Avatar awakening. I am a warrior no longer, and I will not suffer Khaine's touch upon me again.'

'You must,' said Kelamith. 'It is not the fate of the seers of our age to look upon joyous ends. War and death, blood and misery are the veils we must lift to see what the future holds for Alaitoc. We must confront our own destruction every cycle, in order that it can be avoided. If you cannot resist the lure of Khaine, if you cannot tread in his fiery trail, you are of little use as a seer.'

Shuddering at the thought, Thirianna finished dressing. She felt Kelamith's eyes on her, curious and invasive, but pushed away the self-consciousness his attention brought forth. She looked at the farseer but he said nothing, features set in a look of polite determination.

'There is no other way?' asked Thirianna. Kelamith shook his head, eliciting a sigh from her. 'Very well. I will come with you into the infinity circuit.'

'Our journey does not end in the infinity circuit, child,' Kelamith said, raising a finger in a gesture of correction. 'The nerves of Alaitoc are a cipher of the skein, an artificial construct that is only a representation of the realm into which you will eventually delve.'

'I understand,' said Thirianna. 'I remember seeing the skein itself.'

'And the coming battle will provide us with a great opportunity to return there,' said Kelamith.

'Battle?'

'Surely, child,' replied the farseer. 'In battle the skein is a stark, living thing. It will be an excellent introduction for you. Where else do fate and chance come into such vivid contrast? A battle narrows the score of the skein, revealing the myriad twisting ways of destiny in a confined space and time. You are fortunate.'

'Fortunate?' Thirianna laughed with bitterness. 'I have tasted battle, and though I do not remember it, a sense of fortune is not my recollection.'

'Your protests are tiresome, child,' said Kelamith. He shrugged dismissively. 'We both know that you will accompany me. I know this because I have seen it. You know this because in your heart you desire to become a seer and this is what you must do.'

'You think I should just accept what you decide?' snapped Thirianna. 'I am a slave to your instruction because you have seen the results?'

'Never succumb to fatalism, child,' said Kelamith, growing concerned. He approached Thirianna and laid a hand on her shoulder. 'There are rarely no choices. As a seer you will find that there are too many decisions to make, not too few. In time you will have a power that lesser creatures dream of possessing; you will be able to shape the future consciously and not be a powerless leaf on the river of time.'

The farseer's words conjured up vistas of possibilities in Thirianna. She was momentarily suspicious that Kelamith seemed to know the right thing to say when it mattered, but her doubt faded as she envisaged the power he described. It was the desire to have that power and control that had brought her to the Path of the Seer and it would be foolish to be fearful now of the obstacles she would have to overcome.

WITH GREAT TREPIDATION, Thirianna walked along the corridor that led to the Shrine of One Hundred Bloody Tears. It had not changed since she had quit the Path of the Warrior; had not changed in ten lifetimes of the eldar since it had been founded. The portal to the shrine was a pointed arch at the end of the corridor, of blue metal embossed with runes in gold, like etching on crossed sword blades. One hundred tear-shaped rubies decorated the edge of the metaphorical swords, symbolic droplets of blood, their tiny facets each reflecting ruddy images of Thirianna as she approached the shrine.

The gate opened as she stepped up to it, revealing a landscape of wooded hills. Over the trees soared the pinnacle of the temple tower, its summit lit with silver light, its walls a smooth ochre. The only light came from the tower, bathing the woodlands in an odd twilight that seemed to hang on the edges of narrow leaves and clung to the deep ridges in the bark.

Taking a step across the threshold, Thirianna felt a surge of different feelings. She remembered her fear when she had first come here, mind awash with rage at her father. Other recollections danced in her thoughts as she followed the strip of golden slabs that led to the tower: learning the mantras of the Dire Avengers; taking up her armour for the first time; the hiss of the shurikens the first time she fired her weapon.

Deeper memories, of acts committed while she wore her war-mask, edged into consciousness but were held back by the mental barriers she had put in place. Her war-mask writhed inside her subconscious, brought into life by the growing presence of Khaine's Avatar, awakened by her coming to the shrine.

Eventually she came to the base of the tower.

The doorway was open, golden light spilling from within. Thirianna walked into the light, feeling its warm touch envelop her like the arms of a lover, caressing the memories that were hidden away behind the locked doors of her mind.

Thirianna swiftly ascended a spiralling set of stairs to the armouring chamber in the upper reaches. She could hear the soft chants of the Aspect Warriors as they prepared themselves for battle, but blocked out the urge to speak them herself.

Coming to the main hall, Thirianna found eight Dire Avengers half-dressed in their armour. The rune of the shrine was already upon their foreheads, written in the blood of each warrior, and between the two lines of Dire Avengers walked Nimreith, her voice leading the chant. Thirianna recognised the glazed looked in the eyes of her former squad members, and another memory, a longing for acceptance and harmony, wriggled in her mind.

Nimreith paused in her ceremony, eyes falling upon Thirianna. The exarch said nothing, but waved a hand towards an archway to Thirianna's right. It had always been closed when she had been a Dire Avenger, but now the portal lay open, the room beyond dark.

Nimreith had taken up the chant again, turning her back on Thirianna. Realising that she would receive no further instruction, Thirianna stepped through the open doorway and into the room beyond.

There was no light save that which glowed from several objects hanging upon the far wall. A deliberate rumble and a hiss of air caused Thirianna to turn around. The door had closed behind her, leaving her alone in the antechamber.

Crossing the small room, Thirianna examined the glowing objects. There were three triangular breastplates, wrought from silver wraithbone, formed into rune-shapes and inscribed with tiny sigils from which the light was glowing. The psychic energy emanating from the rune armour was palpable, connecting with Thirianna as she held out her hand towards the closest piece. Above each set of armour was a helmet, studded with gems, the eyepieces seeming to glint with their own power as they reflected distorted images of Thirianna.

Between the armour and helmets were several swords. An aura of menace surrounded each one, leaking thoughts of death into Thirianna's mind. Her war-mask quivered in response, rising from the depths of her unconscious like a hunter scenting prey, eclipsing her other thoughts.

Thirianna moved to the armour on the far left, drawn to its organic form. She lightly drew her fingers along its lines, feeling the small indentations of the runes and a surge of psychic energy.

She realised she was chanting, whispering the mantra that would bring forth her war-mask. Part of her wanted to stop, knowing that pain and suffering was waiting for her beyond that bloody veil. Another part of her, a stronger part, wanted to embrace the oblivion of the death-dealer, to shred away conscience and remorse and become Khaine's Bloody Hand.

She lifted the armour from its hooks and turned it around so that she could slip it over her shoulders. Bands and belts writhed like tentacles, wrapping around Thirianna's body, drawing the armour tight to her chest. It felt reassuring to be in the armour's embrace and its protective energies flowed through and around Thirianna, surrounding her with a dim gleam of power. The armour melded around her waystone, drawing it from its brooch to move it over Thirianna's heart. The waystone was bright with power, throbbing in time to her racing pulse, hot to the touch.

The matching helmet came next, resplendent in the blue and gold of the shrine. Still chanting, Thirianna brought the helm over her head, taking a deep breath as the darkness consumed her. Flashes of memory were surfacing now; glimpses of battle and death. Looking through the eyepieces was like seeing with fresh eyes.

Lastly she took up the accompanying sword. As Thirianna's fingers curled around its hilt, the blade glimmered, every rune glowing blood red for a moment. It felt like taking the hand of a child, uplifting and comforting yet bringing a sense of responsibility. The witchblade's murmuring desires for blood trickled into Thirianna's consciousness, pushing back the last of the barriers holding her war-mask in check.

She felt complete.

She stood in the centre of the room and held the witchblade in front of her at the salute. From this pose she began a series of slow movements, the memory of her ritual fighting stances coming back to her. The sensation was strange. She had practised countless times with a shuriken catapult, but now every gesture and manoeuvre seemed to match perfectly with a blow or defence with the sword.

Something was subtly different. With a mixture of surprise and happiness, Thirianna realised that it was the witchblade that moved her, teaching her its unique style of fighting, directing her limbs and body in the way of war imbued within the weapon.

Faster and faster she practised, her muscles, her instinct, remembering everything. She whirled and chopped, spun and sliced, sidestepped and parried. An age ago the witchblade had been given its purpose and now it had another vessel through which it could act.

She allowed her mind to drift from its anchors as she had learnt with the infinity circuit. Mind detached from Being, Being detached from Form, leaving her as a single moving entity of pure thought. The sword was no less a part of her than an arm or a foot or even her heart. Its edge shone bright as Thirianna allowed herself to be drawn into the blade, her own essence powering its lethal energies.

Thirianna and witchblade became one.

'IT IS A simple enough task,' said Kelamith, betraying no sign of impatience.

The same could not be said for Thirianna. She glared at the witchblade lying on a purple rug spread out across the floor of her room, where it had been for the best part of the last cycle.

'Lift the sword, child,' said Kelamith.

Gritting her teeth, Thirianna held out her hand towards the hilt of the witchblade and tried to imagine it in her grasp. She pictured it floating gently upwards, blade downwards, and gliding across the room to her waiting hand.

The sword did not so much as twitch and sat on the rug with what Thirianna thought was a defiant expression, if such a thing could be said of a sword.

'It won't move,' she snapped, letting out an explosive breath and letting her hand drop to her side.

'Perhaps it is not the sword that needs to move, child,' said Kelamith.

'If I am allowed to move, then I would simply cross the room and pick it up!' said Thirianna, exasperated by Kelamith's tone and cryptic suggestions. She was sure the farseer spoke in improbable riddles simply to prove himself superior.

'I did not say to move your form,' Kelamith replied. 'You are a seer now, a mystic with limbs not made of flesh. The sword is not of your form but it is now part of your being, linked to you by the power of mind. You are bound together, sharing your travels along the skein.'

'I cannot do it,' said Thirianna. 'It will not come.'

'The paralysis is in your thoughts, just as paralysis in your arm would stop you from lifting your hand. Do that now. Lift your hand.'

With a sigh of reluctance, Thirianna did as she was asked, holding her right hand up to Kelamith.

'Was there any difficulty?' asked the farseer.

'Of course not,' said Thirianna. 'My hand is attached to me by my arm. I do not feel this link you speak of.'

'You ignore it,' said Kelamith. 'You allow your warrior-self to intrude upon the mind. The warrior is a creature of Form and Being and no thought. The warrior cannot lift the sword, only the seer can.'

Thirianna turned back towards the witchblade, sneering at its reluctance to be commanded. She was not going to lose a battle of wills with an inanimate object.

She extended her mind, focussing her thoughts again on the lifting of the blade. She visualised as Kelamith had instructed, imagining the witchblade to be as light as a feather, gently wafting across the room at her beck and call.

Nothing happened.

'How much longer are you going to force me to do this?' Thirianna snarled, folding her arms petulantly. 'I promise I will not drop my witchblade.'

'Perhaps you would rather I tied it to your wrist?' Kelamith replied, with no hint of mockery. 'It is not the blade that you require; it is the act that you need to perform.'

He delved a hand into one of the pouches at his belt and brought out three runes. With a flick of his fingers he cast them into the air. As they fell the runes slowed and veered, coming together in a group to spin around the farseer's pointing finger. Two of them continued to circle slowly and the third sped up, passing around twice for each rotation of the others. One of the others then began to move up and down, describing an undulating wave in its orbit.

'The mastery of our minds is an exercise in control, child,' said Kelamith. He moved his hand to his nose and the runes changed their route, circling around his head. As Kelamith lifted his hand away a rune took its place, gently turning end over end in front of his nose like a propeller. Thirianna laughed, the ridiculousness of the scene puncturing her annoyance.

In the next moment, the runes flashed across the room, darting past Thirianna's face. She ducked out of instinct and it was Kelamith who now laughed.

'Grab one,' said the farseer as the runes started to weave around Thirianna's body.

She swept her hand towards the closest, but it darted between her fingers as they closed, pinging gently from her forehead. She tried again, lunging after the next, but it swerved away from her hand and took up a fresh orbit around her leg. Thirianna kicked at the rune out of irritation and instinct, but missed once more, almost unbalancing herself.

'Mind is quicker than Form,' said Kelamith. 'In the time it takes your thought to move to your arm, to your fingers, to your knee and toes, I can have five thoughts.'

The runes spun faster and faster, circling around Thirianna's head. In quick succession they bobbed against her nose, her lips, her ear, like a group of especially irritating flies. Thirianna glared at Kelamith and saw a brief smile of amusement.

'Pick up the sword,' he said, bouncing a rune from the back of Thirianna's hand.

She reached out towards the witchblade. She did not will it into her grasp, did not visualise its movements. She simply desired it in her hand so that she could swat away the annoying runes.

With a screech, the witchblade flew from the rug and slapped into Thirianna's open fingers. She closed her hand quickly and turned on her heel, looking to knock the runes out of the air.

The runes were already back with Kelamith, dancing to and fro from outstretched fingertip to fingertip.

'When you move your arm, you do not think about it, you simply do it,' said the farseer. 'When you are hungry you feel it. When you fall asleep, it happens without consent. Form must conform, but Mind is free, bound together by Being. Try it again.'

Heartened, Thirianna returned the witchblade to its place on the rug. She walked back to her position and flung out her hand.

The sword did not move and Thirianna's exasperated sigh filled the chamber.

THE TIME TO depart was fast approaching. For six cycles Thirianna returned to the Shrine of One Hundred Bloody Tears. For six cycles she and her witchblade became accustomed to one another, learning a little bit more about the other with each encounter. For six cycles she practised the exercises taught to her by Kelamith, seeking to refine her psychic control so that it came as easily as breathing and walking.

In contrast to her worries before going to the One Hundred Bloody Tears shrine, Thirianna found no difficulty in letting her war-mask slip away when she had concluded each session. It was as if she had moved that part of her into the witchblade, allowing it to take possession of the anger and the hate, soaking up the merciless desire for death that came from the war-mask.

The next time she put on her rune armour and took up her sword, Thirianna would not be removing it again for some time. She and Kelamith would be amongst the Aspect Warriors of the strike force being assembled. She would be returning to battle.

THE RUNE PROJECTED from the crystal consisted of three glowing loops, bisected by two crossbars. The image turned slowly in front of Thirianna as a female voice spoke quietly.

'The Sign of Daitha was first configured by Nemreinthera of Iyanden and its use spread quickly to other craftworlds, coming to Alaitoc during the Fourth Pass of the Wintering in the Age of Hallowed Dusk. It was first adopted by Kordanrial Alaineth, who introd–'

The recording paused as it detected the door chime. Thirianna realised she had been so intent upon her studies that she had not noticed the approach of a visitor. She cast her mind into the infinity circuit – feeling a moment of pride that she could do so now without physical contact with a node or interface – and suddenly recoiled in surprise at the identity of her guest.

She thought open the door and plucked the crystal from the floor, stowing it in a pouch at her belt.

'Aradryan!' she said, turning towards her visitor. 'This is unexpected.'

He was dressed in a tight-fitting suit of greens and

blues that were constantly shifting, masking his form. It was a holo-suit, frequently used by rangers, though there was no sign of the heavier cloak or coat that such eldar usually wore. Thirianna noticed a long knife was sheathed at his hip, and he wore a belt laden with packs and pouches.

'Hello, Thirianna,' said Aradryan, stepping into the apartment. He smiled and offered a palm in greeting. Thirianna laid her hand on his for a heartbeat, still nonplussed at her friend's arrival. 'Sorry I could not warn you of my return.'

'I did not expect to see you again for much longer,' said Thirianna. She sat down and waved to a cushion for Aradryan to sit but he declined with a quick, single shake of the head.

'I cannot stay long,' he told her. 'It seems my attempt to get far away from Alaitoc was destined to be thwarted. The *Irdiris* intercepted a transmission from Eileniliesh. It's an Exodite world that has been attacked by orks. We thought it wise to return to Alaitoc with the news.'

'Preparations are already under way for an expedition,' said Thirianna. 'Farseer Latheirin witnessed the impending attack several cycles ago.'

'Such is the way of farseers,' Aradryan said with a shrug. He laughed. 'Of course, you are becoming a seer now. Perhaps I should choose my words more carefully?'

'I do not take any offence,' replied Thirianna. 'They are an enigmatic group, that is sure. I have been around them for some time and I do not yet understand their ways.'

She studied Aradryan and sensed restlessness. It was something more than the wanderlust that had taken him away from Alaitoc; an unsettling energy emanated from her friend.

'How have you fared?' she asked.

Aradryan shrugged again.

'There is not much yet to say,' he said. He gestured at his outfit. 'As you see, I have decided to join the rangers, but in truth I had not set foot off *Irdiris* before we had to return. On Eileniliesh we will fight the orks.'

'That would be unwise,' said Thirianna. 'You have never trodden the Path of the Warrior. You have no war-mask.'

'It is of no concern,' said Aradryan with a dismissive wave of the hand. 'My longrifle will keep me safe. It seems I have a natural talent for marksmanship.'

'It is not the physical danger that concerns me,' said Thirianna. She stood up and approached Aradryan. 'War corrupts us. The lure of Khaine can become irresistible.'

'There are many delights in the galaxy; bloodshed is not one that appeals to me,' said Aradryan. His brow creased deeply. 'I never realised how blinkered you could be. You see the Path as the start and the end of existence. It is not.'

'It is,' said Thirianna. 'What you are doing, allowing your mind to run free, endangers not just you but those around you. You must show restraint. Korlandril, he has been touched by Khaine. His anger became too much.'

'He is an Aspect Warrior now?' said Aradryan,

amused by the news. His smile was lopsided and there was something else, something fey in his eyes. 'I did not realise my critique of his work was so harsh.'

Aradryan's short laugh cut at Thirianna's spirit. There was a harshness there that had not existed before. Her friend had always possessed something of a delight in irony and sarcasm but his happiness at Korlandril's predicament was entirely misplaced.

'Why have you come here?' said Thirianna. 'What do you want from me?'

'Nothing,' said Aradryan. 'You made it very clear I should expect nothing from you. I came as a courtesy, nothing more. If I am not welcome, I shall leave.'

Thirianna was not sure how to respond. Having Aradryan here, in her apartment, was unsettling. She could feel the wildness hovering beneath the surface of his spirit. He appeared normal and polite, but every now and then that unfettered spirit showed itself. He was prey to every passing whim and fancy, every vague emotion and thought that came to him, and was unpredictable and dangerous because of it.

'Yes, I think you should leave,' said Thirianna. Aradryan's lip curled a fraction but he nodded his acquiescence. For a moment the look of hurt and betrayal he had worn before he left returned. Thirianna relented slightly. 'Please take care of yourself, Aradryan. I am pleased that you came to see me.'

The ranger seemed caught in two minds, taking a step towards the door but keeping his eyes fixed on Thirianna, perhaps hoping for her to change her mind. She hardened her spirit to his departure, knowing that he was a distraction she could not afford, especially this close to leaving for Eileniliesh.

'Goodbye,' he said, one hand on the edge of the open door. 'I do not expect us to meet again. Ever.'

It was difficult but Thirianna refused to respond to the overly dramatic statement. It was nothing more than a blatant attempt at emotional blackmail and she was determined not to succumb.

'Goodbye,' she replied. 'Travel well and find contentment.'

With a sigh, Aradryan turned away and moved out of view. The door swished across the opening, leaving Thirianna alone with her thoughts. She stayed there a moment and then dashed towards the door, which opened before her. She shouted Aradryan's name as she ran out onto the landing. He was just at the turn towards the stairwell and stopped to look over his shoulder.

'Please see Korlandril,' Thirianna called out to him. He nodded and raised a hand in acknowledgement, and then disappeared down the stairs.

As THE CYCLE entered the night period and the lights of her apartment dimmed, Thirianna sat in the main room with a small object in her lap. It was a simple thing: a small white box. Inside was a rune, shaped from silvery-grey wishstone. It was the mark of the Dire Avenger, a small souvenir she had kept from her time as an Aspect Warrior. She was not sure why she had taken it. It had once hung from the grip of her shuriken catapult and in a moment of foolishness or sentimentality she had brought it with her when she had quit the Path of the Warrior.

She did not know what to do with it, but the rune nagged at her. Returning to the shrine had awakened dormant passions and desires, and though they were faint now, the rune was responding in some way. She could not throw it away; that would be disrespectful to herself and the Shrine of One Hundred Bloody Tears. She could not keep it, its presence was becoming a distraction. She would feel embarrassed to return it.

Another option occurred to her.

Though she had concentrated of late on her own development, she had heard that Korlandril had been overpowered by his rage and succumbed to the lure of Khaine. In a move that Thirianna thought of with delicious irony, Korlandril had become an Aspect Warrior, a Striking Scorpion of the Deadly Shadow. The name of the shrine struck a chord in her thoughts when she had heard it, resonating with that memory she kept placated in a way she did not understand.

She was a seer now, and Korlandril a warrior.

Thirianna remembered their argument about the Path of Khaine before Korlandril's turn to anger. Knowing that, just as with Aradryan's abandonment of the Path, she was in part responsible for Korlandril's lapse into rage, Thirianna thought that she could show her former friend some measure of understanding and atonement. It was a message from one warrior to another, one that she was sure he would appreciate in the difficult time he was surely experiencing.

THIRIANNA WAITED IN front of the door to Korlandril's apartment. She knew he was not inside; she felt none of his presence and with her heightening psychic awareness needed no foray into the infinity circuit to discern his whereabouts.

She wondered if it would be better to wait for him, to place the gift in his hands and explain its meaning.

Thirianna decided against this course of action. It would be of no benefit to Korlandril or her to meet again under these circumstances. To whatever end, both of them had changed, moved on to new Paths, and they were still discovering their new selves.

She placed the box in front of the door where it could not be missed. Leaving her hand lingering on it for a moment, she allowed a little of herself to seep into the rune within: sadness and longing, regret at their parting, pride in his actions and, most of all, forgiveness and understanding.

BATTLE

The Suin Daellae – Spear of Khaine. As with all runes associated with the Bloody-Handed God, the Suin Daellae reacts only to bloodshed. Its purpose is the location of pivotal moments of war and is used to detect the violent death of a significant individual. It must be employed with care and strictly controlled; the Spear of Khaine has an inherent desire to show the seer myriad versions of his or her own bloody demise.

'KEEP YOUR MIND closed,' warned Kelamith. 'You are not yet ready to see the webway with your thoughts.'

Thirianna and her mentor sat on the padded bench of a light skiff, awaiting the arrival of the seers that would join them. The vehicle was a slender deltoid, its wings flaring sharply at the stern, the lights of the launch bay blocked by the golden, curving sail above, leaving the two seers in shadow. Seated in a small cockpit behind the passenger compartment, the driver adjusted the trim of the vehicle, the sound of the engines increasing briefly to a soft purr.

The farseer was garbed in his full regalia: flowing dark robes beneath the golden chestpiece of his armour, rune-furnished clasps and jewellery hanging from neck and wrists. His face was hidden behind the mask of an ornate helm with a high crest decorated with oval gems. A long witchblade was scabbarded across his back, and in his hand he carried a staff taller than Thirianna, topped with a sculpted detail of Vaul's anvil surrounded by lightning bolts.

Thirianna also wore her rune armour and helmet, her long witchblade hanging at her left hip, a shuriken pistol holstered on the right.

Another farseer and three warlocks hurried up the extended ramp into the main body of the skiff, murmuring apologies for their late arrival. They sat on the opposite bench as the crystalline canopy extended from the hull and encased the group, distorting the glow of the hangar lamps into a rainbow. With a momentary surge that pushed Thirianna into her seat, the skiff lifted off and turned towards the shimmering field that acted as the door to the flight deck.

Thirianna was apprehensive as the skiff detached itself from the dock of the starship. Through the canopy Thirianna looked out at the webway with only her eyes. She had travelled it many times as a Dire Avenger, but her thoughts had always been engaged on the upcoming battle. Now her war-mask was less intrusive, her anger held in check for the moment. The witchblade twitched in its sheath, sensing her thoughts.

The starship receded into the distance as the webrunner accelerated through the psychic tunnels of the eldar webway. Burrowing through the space between the real universe and the immaterial realm of the warp, the webway appeared as a shimmering tunnel of energy. The psychic field enclosing the corridor moved constantly, like a branch swaying in a breeze, undulating gently across the shifting warp tides. It appeared red through the lenses of Thirianna's helm, but in truth was of no real colour; the mind interpreted the swirling energies of the warp held at bay as a kaleidoscope of ever-changing rainbows and patterns.

Thirianna could feel the weight of psychic pressure surrounding her and was not in the least tempted to disobey Kelamith's instruction. She had no desire to let her mind free so close to the lair of daemons and other warp entities.

A pulsing gateway opened ahead, ringed with shimmering gold. Thirianna felt the wash of reality pouring into the webway like the draught from an opened door. It prickled her senses, bringing images of life and vitality after the cloying numbness of the webway's protective barriers.

The webrunner's driver steered towards the

opening. There were other craft too – grav-tanks with sleek hulls and transports carrying Aspect Warriors. Around the main webway tunnel other passageways were forming – temporary creations that delved through space directly to the surface of Eileniliesh. Thirianna could see rangers moving on foot through these ad-hoc tunnellings, followed by squads of Striking Scorpions.

She wondered if one of them was Korlandril.

'Breaching the gate,' the driver told them.

The portal loomed around the webrunner, large enough for several vehicles to pass through at a time. It hung across the webway like a gate to the heavens, twin pillars of white and gold topped by a sharply curving arch. The runes on its surface shimmered with the light of the webway, small flickers of psychic energy dappling its pale surface. From this perspective, it seemed as if the webway simply carried on past the archway, but even without opening herself to the skein, Thirianna could feel the strange interface of warp and reality contained within the faint haze that spanned the gateway.

A Wave Serpent transport swept past, its curved hull a mottled blue and white, marked with the symbols of Alaitoc. Glancing back, Thirianna saw a swarm of jetbikes closing fast, their riders wearing silver, blue and white, laser lances in their hands: Shining Spear Aspect Warriors.

As the skiff approached the opening, Thirianna sensed the titanic energies contained by the web gate's crystalline circuitry. Passing through the plane, she felt as if a strong wind blew through her mind, sweeping away the background noise of the webway, leaving only the calm and quiet of the natural world. Peace and clarity filled her thoughts.

One moment Thirianna was in the webway, the next she was on Eileniliesh, looking back at the towering gateway of the web portal set against a star-filled clear sky. It was situated in a forest-ringed dell, two curving stone-like upthrusts marked with runes, a crackling sheen of energy flaring between them. The Shining Spears burst from the portal, banking their jetbikes to skim towards a roadway leading towards the settlement of Hirith-Hreslain. At the direction of Kelamith, the skiff pilot brought the craft to a gentle stop, hovering just above the ground.

Immediately, Thirianna ventured a portion of her mind into the skein and felt a familiar-yet-different sensation. Eileniliesh, like all Exodite planets, possessed a world spirit that ran through large parts of its crust. It seemed to Thirianna to be a locked, barren place in comparison to the throng of the infinity circuit, barred to her entry. For the briefest moment she was aware of the entire world, her mind spanning continents, flowing along gushing rivers, soaring between mountain peaks and delving into deep caverns.

The sensation passed and Thirianna was brought back to herself by Kelamith's light touch on her arm.

The canopy slid back and Thirianna took a breath of air through the filters of her helm. She smelt the freshness of the night air, leaves mulching beneath their branches bringing an undercurrent of autumnal decay. She could hear the buzzing of insects and a moth the size of her hand fluttered past in the light of Eileniliesh's moons. Over the tips of the trees Thirianna could see a tall tower, its summit a blazing beacon of bluish light that threw harsh shadows through the forest canopy.

Kelamith and the other farseer, Donoriennin, dismounted from the webrunner as a similar craft pulled alongside. A heavily armoured figure wielding a long spear and sporting an impressive crest of white hair on his helm alighted from the vehicle and met the two farseers on the soft turf.

'Arhathain,' said one of the other warlocks, an eldar almost twice Thirianna's age, called Keldarion.

'The autarch,' replied Thirianna, recognising the name. Arhathain was one of Alaitoc's foremost military leaders, destined to be remembered for generations for his victories. Thirianna was filled with admiration and a little fear by the fabled warrior. Like all autarchs he had trodden the Path of the Warrior several times in different Aspects, and that spoke of a frightening bloodlust unfamiliar to Thirianna; yet he had emerged from each occasion without succumbing to the entrapment suffered by the exarchs, and that spoke of immense willpower, discipline and personality.

Autarch and farseers held a short discussion, during which it seemed that Kelamith did most of the talking. Arhathain nodded frequently, listening to the advice of his counsellors. He made a few quick replies and returned to his transport. Kelamith and Donoriennin took their seats in the webrunner and the driver turned the craft after the departing autarch's vehicle.

'The settlement straddles a river,' said Donoriennin. 'The orks still revel in their destruction and their stain has yet to spread. The Exodites have done well to destroy the crude landing craft and keep the aliens from expanding their conquest, though they lack the strength to drive the invaders from the lair they have built. We will contain the orks in Hirith-Hreslain and then destroy the foul horde. Our ship will deal with the ramshackle ork transport in orbit, ensuring there is no possibility of reinforcement or escape. The main attack will come from this side of the river, into Hirith. Fire Dragons and Striking Scorpions have been despatched to intercept ork reinforcements coming across the river from their camp in Hreslain, the other part of the town.'

'Thirianna will accompany me in the main attack,' said Kelamith. Even through the lenses of his helm Thirianna could see the psychic light in the farseer's eyes. 'Donoriennin and Keldarion will be with the vanguard, Lurithein and Simmanain will lend their support to the flanking force moving along the river bank to relieve the squads lying in ambush at the bridge.'

There could be no argument. Kelamith and the other farseers had spent much of the journey to Eileniliesh delving into the various future paths the battle might take, reviewing each for the best outcome for Alaitoc. Though no fate was ever assured, their foresight did not just provide an advantage for the eldar, it guaranteed it; they had seen the victory for Alaitoc and divined the means by which to bring about that outcome. If the eldar stuck to the plan as drawn up by Arhathain from the prophecies of Kelamith and the others, they could not fail. The only uncertainty remaining was the courage and discipline of the individual warriors taking part.

The skiff was zipping between the broad trunks of the trees, cutting away from the roadway towards a glittering curve of river ahead. Jetbikes swooped and swerved between the boles, flashes of brightness in the darkness, while the larger vehicles made their way along the road.

Turning to follow the river, the eldar army stopped a short while later when they came into sight of the first buildings. The woods did not end abruptly but diminished in density as Hirith-Hreslain took over, nature and settlement blending seamlessly into each other.

The bulk of the town formed a crescent, arcing away from a curving span that crossed the slow river, leaving a wide space at its centre. The air was thick with smoke from ork fires and the stench of their encampment hung in Thirianna's nostrils despite her helmet's filtration systems. She snorted with disgust as the army moved out slowly, breaking into two distinct parts: transports carrying Howling Banshees crept along the river bank accompanied by Shining Spears. Kelamith and Thirianna dismounted along with the main force, the skiff moving away quickly to take the other seers to their appointed positions. Dire Avengers loped through the trees, shuriken catapults at the ready. Dark Reapers made their way into the nearby buildings, their dark forms reappearing at windows and balconies in the high towers. A pair of Falcon grav-tanks glided across the grass, heading towards an archway that led to the main thoroughfare.

Ahead of the main force, vague flitters of movement in the shadows showed the progress of the rangers, Aradryan most likely amongst them. They carried with them psychic beacon-markers that would enable the squads still in the webway to create openings in the heart of the town and launch the first wave of attacks against the orks.

Coming closer to Hirith-Hreslain, Thirianna could see the evidence of the ork occupation. Several towers had broken roofs and the walls were pocked with shell holes. Soot from burning marked many buildings, windows had been smashed and doorways broken in.

Worryingly, Thirianna could see no bodies and she shuddered to think of what had become of the Exodites slain in the ork attack.

The raucous talk of the orks echoed along the white-paved streets, along with the crackle of fires and the snap of random gunshots. Engines could be heard from across the river, faint but discordant against the sighing of the wind and the calls of night birds in the forest surrounding the settlement.

'Join me,' said Kelamith, coming to a halt in an arched alleyway at the edge of the town.

It was a moment before Thirianna realised the farseer wished her to conjoin their minds. Thirianna whispered the mantras, letting her psychic defences slip away so that her spirit and Kelamith's could enter the skein together. She felt the farseer's thoughts overlapping hers, soft but insistent. Relaxing, Thirianna allowed herself to drift into a psychic trance, trusting the warriors around her to protect them in this vulnerable state. Her last sight was of a dozen runes dancing above Kelamith's outstretched palm, and then she was inside the skein.

AT FIRST EVERYTHING seemed to be anarchy.

Threads of fate wound about each other in impossible knots, tying together and splitting, writhing like a disturbed nest of serpents. Dozens of images flashed through Thirianna's thoughts: images of death and destruction, of dying orks and slain eldar. It was impossible to make any sense of the confusion, to discern meaning from the mass of seemingly random information. Her mind recoiled as it had done during her first foray into the infinity circuit, but now she knew how to respond.

Thirianna ignored the huge tides of fate washing over her and picked out a single thread, as she might locate a node or conduit of the infinity circuit. She concentrated all of her thoughts on that short stretch of time, pushing away everything else. Like leaves falling from the tree, the other fates being revealed to her fell away, allowing the thread on which she was focussed to expand and gain detail.

Before she could work out what she was looking at, Thirianna felt Kelamith's touch on her thoughts. Runes appeared across the skein, glowing with power, moving in strange patterns, interacting with the ever-shifting warp and weft of time.

'Follow me,' said Kelamith.

He seemed like a bolt of gold on the threads of fate. Latching on to Kelamith's psychic signature, Thirianna allowed herself to be dragged along in the wake of his divination, seeing flashes of the battle unfold. The runes acted as navigation beacons, and Kelamith steered towards one and then another, before veering wildly from the path for a short time to investigate a newly unfolding passage of events.

As they travelled, Thirianna was bombarded with sights and sensations. The crackle and bark of guns, the hiss of shurikens cutting the night air, the roars of the orks and the war shouts of the eldar. Warriors fought and died over and over, buildings crumbled and rebuilt, vehicles exploded and were miraculously restored as possible futures laid themselves upon Thirianna's mind.

The filth of the orks was everywhere, a cloying, overwhelming brutality that blotted out rational thought and compassion. Their bestial urges ran through every future, a mass of green-skinned violence and anger. Its power obliterated armies and engulfed planetary populations, fuelled by war and domination. It was in every ork and every ork was in the mass, a surging force of nature, elemental in its randomness, cataclysmic in its devastation. It could be beaten back, sometimes even tamed, but never destroyed.

And then came fire and blood.

'The Avatar!' said Thirianna.

It was like a vortex of fate, dragging in hundreds of

other threads to itself, the rune of Khaine lingering above it. The Avatar's presence was like flames on a woven cloth, burning along the weave, destroying everything nearby. Blood soaked the skein, drowning lives by the score, washing over Thirianna with a wave of hatred and base rage.

The sensation almost overwhelmed her as her war-mask surged from the depths of her psyche, threatening to obscure her witch-sight. She struggled to keep her bloodlust at bay, to concentrate on the unfolding patterns of destiny, and after some struggle she repressed the urge to kill, the desire for war and death.

In doing so, she looked upon the skein with greater clarity. Suppressing the bright glare of the Avatar, she could see the winding and unwinding of lives in the knots and coils that had formed around it; enemies slain and followers tainted.

Thirianna had come to a standstill, halted by the encroachment of the Avatar; Kelamith blazed across the skein, seeming to be everywhere at once. Through his mere observations the skein was changing, becoming simpler, as redundant fates were cast away, never coming to pass. To see and reject a future was to consign it to non-existence, paving the way for new threads to emerge, new fresh possibilities to weaken or grow in strength.

All of a sudden, the farseer was back with Thirianna, surrounding her in an aura of gold.

'Tell me what you see,' said Kelamith.

Thirianna concentrated again, not seeing the skein itself but delving into its contents. She noticed a rune she recognised from her teachings – the Cave of the Mon-keigh. She allowed her thoughts to be guided by it, plunging into one possible future. She saw a massive ork, blade in hand, cutting apart Striking Scorpions, only to fall to the blades and shimmering fists of their exarchs; the alien's death howl echoed in her thoughts.

As she was about to depart, Thirianna caught a sense of something else, flavoured with recognition. Retracing her steps, the scene seeming to rewind through her thoughts, Thirianna paid more attention to the ork warlord's victims.

She froze, gripped by sudden anguish.

Korlandril was one of those that would fall to the ork's attack. Panicked, Thirianna pulled back, seeking the life-cord of Korlandril. It continued for a little while and then frayed, becoming dozens of ragged threads before disappearing into a haze of uncertainty.

'Does he die?' she asked.

'I cannot see any more than you,' said Kelamith.

'I should warn him,' said Thirianna. 'He could die.'

'There are some that die tonight and he may be one of them,' said Kelamith. 'You cannot prevent them all, and it may not even be desirable to save them.'

'He is my friend,' said Thirianna. 'I cannot just ignore this.'

'You focus on the wrong detail, child,' replied Kelamith. 'It is not the injury of your friend that is important. The ork warlord will die if we follow that path, and in its death others will be saved.'

'How...' Thirianna gave up trying to argue.

A miniature battle raged inside her thoughts. Her instinct was to save her friend, but Kelamith's logic fought back and the two sides reached an impasse. Was Korlandril's life worth two other eldar? Ten? Twenty?

'I understand,' she said, guilt threatening to consume her.

'There is no time for self-pity, child,' said Kelamith. 'The battle begins and Arhathain must make a few changes to the plan.'

Blotting the image of wounded Korlandril from her memory, Thirianna allowed herself to be drawn back into her body. She opened her eyes and saw in the small time display of her helmet that everything she had seen had taken less than two heartbeats to pass in the physical world.

Even as she was making sense of this, feeling disjointed and split between the real and the psychic, another presence intruded on her thoughts. It was like the bow wave of a boat, pushing everything before it, sending ripples far out through the skein.

Blood and fire.

Thirianna turned, as did many of the eldar moving into the town. A patch of air was alive with psychic energy, like fire crawling along an ember. The scent of blood, of charring flesh and melting iron filled the air, and again Thirianna was forced to fight back against her rising war-mask.

In the skein it had only been the Avatar's potential that she had fought against. Here she struggled against its actuality, with her mind still open like a portal left unlocked.

Waves of anger and hatred poured into her. Her witchblade threw itself out of its sheath into her hand, crackling with psychic energy, its edge keening for blood. As the air split and a coruscating ring of fire appeared, Thirianna gritted her teeth and fought back the urge to slay and maim.

Feeling her will buckling as the Avatar approached, Thirianna became desperate. She ripped her mind free from the skein altogether, letting the barriers of her mind slam back into place, shutting her off from the deluge of rage. She fought to stay conscious, blood pounding through her veins, vision swimming.

The Avatar stepped from its portal, trailing smoke and sparks.

More than twice the height of Thirianna, the incarnation of the war god was a towering creature of metal and flame. The air around the Avatar recoiled from its heat, causing smoke and steam to writhe wildly. Psychic energy emanated from the creature, bringing a distant screaming and wailing to the edge of hearing. Its body was of ancient iron, a form of shifting plates barely holding in check the fiery being within.

A cloak of red cloth and flame trailed from its shoulders, held in place by a pin shaped like a long dagger. In its right hand, the Avatar held aloft a spear of immense proportion, its triangular head engraved with runes that burned with white flame. The weapon shrieked its bloodthirst – the Wailing Doom. The Avatar's left hand formed an enormous iron fist, blood dripping and steaming from its spiked knuckles.

Eyes of fire turned on Thirianna, who backed away from the apparition. The Avatar's gaze pierced her spirit for a moment, burning through her mental defences, bringing forth flashes of dying aliens and slain beasts – memories long repressed. The Avatar turned its head away and Thirianna let out a gasp of relief.

Leaving smoking footprints in its wake, the Avatar strode into the town, the eldar following close behind.

THE ELDAR ATTACK struck like lightning.

Guided by the web-beacons and signalled by Kelamith, the warriors that had remained in the webway opened temporary portals around the centre of Hirith-Hreslain. Tiny stars expanded into glowing gateways through which Dire Avengers, Howling Banshees and Fire Dragons stormed.

Power swords gleamed in the darkness of the night; the whisper of shurikens echoed from the white walls of the half-ruined town; the blaze of thermal guns and detonating plasma grenades lit up the plazas and streets. The orks, many of them still slumbering, died in their dozens to the sudden assault.

Roars and shouts, drums and horns sounded the alarm as the main force of the eldar closed in, sweeping around the ork camps to pin them against the river while the strike force tore into their centre.

The Avatar raced forwards, Wailing Doom in hand, charging directly for the greatest concentration of orks. More Aspect Warriors followed close behind, their exarchs leading their squads along rubble-choked streets and through the shells of destroyed buildings.

Kelamith and Thirianna followed a little distance behind. Every now and then the farseer paused to consult his runes; Thirianna joined with him during these moments to see the battle unfolding upon the skein.

As Kelamith had told her, the battle was a micro-cosm of the whole skein. Every bullet and shuriken, every sword blow and axe swing created uncertainty and possibility, the future branching out so quickly that it was impossible to follow every thread. Shadowing Kelamith, Thirianna observed how the farseer used his runes to seek out the pivotal moments, following the course of the Avatar, the ork warlord, the autarch, individual exarchs. Through these means, sense could be made of the senseless. The white noise of destruction gave way to specific detail and vivid scenes.

Thirianna moved back from Kelamith as his mind ventured towards the fighting on the bridge, fearing to look again at the fate of Korlandril. Instead she turned her attention to one of the other seers: Simmanain. He had progressed far further along the Path of the Seer than Thirianna, though his presence was a candle flame compared to the bonfires of the farseers. She watched Simmanain dancing along the narrow threads, moving from fate to fate, focussed on a handful of individuals.

As those threads were severed, she realised with

a shock that she was witnessing the deaths of those Simmanain was fighting. It was frightening and yet invigorating to see cruel fate in action, brought about by the warlock's witchblade.

'Come, child, our presence is needed,' said Kelamith a moment before he withdrew from the skein.

Thirianna detached her mind and followed the farseer as he broke into a run, stepping nimbly over fallen blocks of masonry that littered the street ahead. Kelamith brought them to a small square just a short distance from the main plaza. Fire and smoke erupted from a building on the opposite side, followed by the crash of large cannons. Shells screamed along a street towards the main eldar attack, detonating out of sight; Thirianna felt the sense of life lost as pinpricks of tragedy on her consciousness.

A squad of Dire Avengers appeared from the rubble to Thirianna's right, summoned by Kelamith. She recognised the rune on the back banner of their exarch: the Shrine of the Golden Storm. Together the Aspect Warriors and seers converged on the ork artillery.

'Ready your weapon,' warned Kelamith.

Thirianna felt the touch of his mind on hers, coaxing her into the skein for an instant. She glimpsed a wall of fanged, green faces and saw herself with witchblade raised, fending off the swing of a heavy maul.

Reacting without thought, Thirianna swung her witchblade up to the guard position as the eldar leapt through a broken wall into the artillery position. Deflected, an ork club swung harmlessly past her shoulder. The witchblade moved in her hands, taking off the beast's arm below the elbow as it pulled back for another swing.

Reality and possibility flashed together, creating a near-instantaneous flow of images in Thirianna's mind. With her eyes she saw more than a dozen orks pouring from an adjoining room; with her thoughts she saw the ork next to her blazing a hail of bullets into her chest.

She leapt to the right as the ork opened fire, its shots spewing wide of their mark. Taking her witchblade double-handed, Thirianna thrust the point into the ork's chest. The psychic sword thirsted for energy and she poured her power into it, plunging the blade through breastbone and heart and spine.

The growls and grunts of the orks filled the room along with the blare of pistols. Muzzle flashes illuminated leering, savage faces. In Thirianna's mind she saw an ork jumping down from the shattered floor above, its axe carving into the shoulder of a Dire Avenger.

With four swift steps she crossed behind Kelamith and shouted a warning, pointing her witchblade towards the hole in the ceiling. The Dire Avengers parted as an ork almost twice their size plunged into their midst. Shuriken catapults sang, shredding the greenskin from several directions.

A shockwave of psychic power burst from Thirianna and she stumbled forwards as something crashed into her back. Her rune armour crackled with energy as she spun around to face her attacker.

She had been too occupied by warning the others to foresee the blast of the ork's pistol into her back. Kelamith's sword parted its head from its neck with one sweep, blood spattering across the farseer's gem-encrusted helm. Kelamith said nothing as he turned away, directing the tip of his staff towards more orks lumbering through a doorway to his left.

Psychic lightning crackled.

The closest ork exploded into a mist of vaporising blood and bone dust. The one behind it was engulfed in flames as its padded jacket caught fire, fat bubbling away, muscle charring. A third juddered uncontrollably, finger tightening on the trigger of its gun, sending a hail of rounds into the back of another green-skinned brute.

As the glow of the attack faded, the Dire Avengers opened fire, sending a storm of shurikens into the survivors, slicing flesh and bone.

Behind their exarch, the Aspect Warriors dashed into the next room, shuriken catapults at the ready, Kelamith and Thirianna just two steps behind. They opened fire again, cutting down the small slave creatures manning three large-bore cannons.

'Disable them,' said Kelamith, nodding towards the artillery pieces.

Thirianna moved forwards, sword gripped in two hands. Copying the exarch, she brought the blade down into the breech of the crude gun, sending up a shower of sparks and droplets of molten metal as she poured psychic energy into the weapon. The witchblade sheared through the breech and lock, cracks running along the poor-quality metal of the barrel with loud crackles and shrieks.

Glancing out of the ragged hole in the wall through which the pieces had been firing, Thirianna could see the main plaza. The Avatar was surrounded by a swarm of greenskins, the war god's incarnation carving left and right with the Doom that Wails. The flare of Dark Reaper missiles fizzed across the dark sky, exploding inside the buildings where a large number of orks had taken refuge.

'We must join the battle,' said Kelamith.

Seers and Aspect Warriors sprinted along the road towards the rest of the Alaitocii. Feeling the presence of other eldar, Thirianna glanced up and saw the dim figures of rangers, their longrifles rested on the broken rails of balconies and the sills of shattered windows. Unseen in the distance, orks died to their silent fire.

Reaching the main space at the heart of Hirith-Hreslain, the picture of the unfolding battle was clear. The orks occupied the few buildings left standing near to the river, a horde of leering faces and muzzle flares at the windows. The wreckage of several vehicles burned on the bridge, and in the light of the flames a squad of Fire Dragons and two groups of Striking Scorpions battled against the ork reinforcements. Thirianna wondered if Korlandril had fallen yet, but could not bring herself to seek the answer in the skein, fearing to see his thread cut short like those of the orks.

Two Falcon grav-tanks pounded the tallest of the remaining towers with pulse laser and shuriken cannon fire while other eldar forces moved from building to building, avoiding the killing field of the open plaza. A wildly corkscrewing rocket erupted from one of the ork lairs, fizzing across the square with a trail of sparks to hit the curved prow of a Falcon grav-tank, ricocheting from the angled armour before exploding. The thud of heavier weapons drowned out the whispering of shurikens and zip of lasers.

A sizeable mob of orks appeared from the river banks, clad in heavier armour than the others. More rockets and heavy calibre shells flared from their weapons as Thirianna and Kelamith took shelter behind the ravaged remains of a pool and fountain. The warriors from the Shrine of the Golden Storm broke to the right, crossing the cracked flags of the plaza as gunfire erupted around them.

Thirianna saw two Dire Avengers fall to the fusillade before they reached the shelter of a wall. She glanced at Kelamith, wondering why he had not warned them, but the farseer was intent on the newly arrived orks pushing forwards from the river.

From a sidestreet emerged the Shining Spears, their laser lances crackling with energy. In two lines, the jetbike riders curved around a toppled statue of Kurnous the Hunter and arrowed into the heart of the ork reinforcements. Laser blasts exploded with white light, smashing open armour and disintegrating flesh. Axes and claws gleaming with power fields were swung back at the swift Aspect Warriors, unseating one and smashing the jetbike of another. The Shining Spears swept past out of range and turned sharply, the shuriken catapults of their

jetbikes spewing a hail into the orks that had survived the first charge. As the green-skinned brutes
returned fire another jetbike exploded, sending the
rider crashing into the burnt remnants of a tree. The
Shining Spears lowered their weapons and dashed
in again, sweeping away the last of the barbaric
aliens in a bright ripple of laser lance detonations.

Fuelled by battle-lust, or perhaps possessing just
enough foresight to realise they were trapped, the
orks poured out of the buildings they had occupied
in a haphazard counter-attack. Gunfire roared from
the ruined buildings and flashed across the plaza.
The orks charged in groups towards the eldar, their
bellows and roars turning to shouts and howls of
pain as las-fire and shurikens greeted them.

The Avatar strode towards the fray, spear keening
madly. The war god's incarnation hurled its rune-
etched blade into the approaching orks, the burning
tip of the Wailing Doom ripping through half a
dozen aliens in a bloody arc before returning to the
Avatar's hand. Howling Banshees sprinted into the
fray, their masks emitting piercing shrieks that
coursed along the nervous systems of the orks, stopping them mid-stride. Swords gleaming with blue
power fields sliced effortlessly through armour and
flesh, flashing and sweeping in sinuous arcs.

Following Kelamith as he advanced on the orks,
bolts of energy leaping from his fingertips, Thirianna
skimmed across the surface of the skein, glimpsing
the possible movements of her foes. A half-track
vehicle that had eluded the ambush on the bridge
appeared in her vision, its turret spewing flames.

She glanced towards the alley from which it would emerge and saw that a squad of Fire Dragons were already waiting, alerted to the attack by Kelamith or one of the other farseers.

No sooner did Thirianna glance in that direction than the crude ork vehicle burst out of the darkness, fire licking from the muzzle of its small turret. The Fire Dragons opened fire as one, their thermal guns melting through the fuel tank being towed behind the orkish contraption. The explosion filled the narrow street with flame and debris, coating the walls and roadway with patches of burning oil.

The orks were now desperately trying to break through the encircling eldar line, hurling themselves forwards despite their heavy casualties. At a mental nudge from Kelamith, Thirianna headed right, glimpsing a possible breakthrough amongst the many futures unfolding. Dire Avengers poured hails of shurikens into the orks.

Yet the aliens pressed on, heedless of the growing number of deaths. Detonations erupted amongst the attacking aliens, scores cut down by the missiles of the Dark Reapers now in position in the upper storeys of the surrounding buildings. Still it was not enough to halt the reckless ork assault and the Dire Avengers took the brunt of the charge, firing their weapons until the last possible moment.

Their exarch leapt to the fore, a glimmering shield of energy on one arm deflecting the first flurry of blows, power sword slashing at limbs and throats. Kelamith and Thirianna arrived a few heartbeats later, their psychic weapons shimmering with energy.

Thirianna slashed the tip of her witchblade across the neck of the closest ork, cutting through its spine. She side-stepped the clumsy lunge of an ork with a growling chainsword and chopped away its leg as it stumbled past, swiftly following with a thrust into its back, her sword erupting from its chest as it fell.

Thirianna's rune armour flared as bullets hammered into her from the left. She winced at the shock of their impact, unhurt but startled by the unexpected storm of fire. There was simply too much happening to pre-empt every enemy action. Kelamith came to her assistance, casting a serpent-shaped rune into the air above the orks. A whirling apparition appeared out of the night sky, a burning snake that enveloped a handful of orks in flaming coils.

Recovering quickly, Thirianna rejoined the fight, her witchblade moving with speed and precision, slicing and thrusting, despatching three orks in quick succession. Guided by her precognition, the warlock evaded their counter-blows, swerving away from danger, picking the right moment to strike at every instant.

Darkness fell upon the skein, blinding Thirianna's othersight. A torrent of brutish rage pummelled her thoughts, crushing her mind. A wave of cataclysmic energy engulfed her, accompanied by a psychic roaring that swamped all other sensation.

Mid-stride, Thirianna was hurled from her feet by an explosive blast. The detonation echoed in her mind as much as it had hurt her body, a wall of pure psychic power unlike anything she had experienced.

While patches of light danced across her vision, Thirianna righted herself and saw an energy-wreathed ork beyond the scattered bodies of the Dire Avengers. Green crackles of power crawled across its near-naked form and sparked from wildly wide eyes. It held a copper staff in one hand, trailing copper wires that jumped and fluttered with more psychic energy.

Thirianna delved into the skein, trying to find out why she had not detected the ork psyker earlier. She was swamped again by a deluge of orkish brutality, like a mental war shout that drowned out everything else. Like a volcano erupting, the psychic ork was a detonation of power, shredding the skein with its presence, blotting out everything else.

The ork shaman had a bodyguard of half a dozen warriors who laid down a curtain of fire from their automatic weapons, sending poorly-aimed volleys into the disorientated Dire Avengers. Kelamith threw out a blanket of darkness, shrouding the Dire Avengers from view as they leapt into the cover of a nearby ruin.

Ripples of green energy pulsed from the shamanistic ork, cracking the paving tiles underfoot. The waves hit the eldar, tossing them from their feet, a deep welt opening up in the ground beneath them.

Thirianna leapt nimbly over the widening crack, running into the darkness projected by Kelamith. The gleam of her witchblade was extinguished and she could see nothing for a moment. Keeping in a straight line, she sprinted on, sword ready for the attack. Bursting from the psychic cloud, Thirianna found herself just a few strides from the closest of the shaman's minders. A moment later and her witchblade had taken off its head, fiery sparks pouring from her sword.

As Thirianna ducked beneath the crackling power claw of the next ork, five figures appeared from the shadows behind the orks. Clad in heavy, segmented armour, their chainswords purring quietly, the Striking Scorpions fell upon the unsuspecting orks. Their exarch wielded a long, two-handed chainsword with which he cleaved down the spine of the shaman, splitting the alien's body to the waist.

The psyker's bodyguard were hacked down in moments, but there was little time to hesitate. The orks had been funnelled towards a single street by the rampaging Avatar and the missiles of the Dark Reapers. There were only a few dozen left, but their desperation made the orks dangerous.

Above the bark of guns and the whine of shurikens, ear-splitting screeches split the night air. Monstrous winged shapes dropped down from the clouds, silhouetted against the setting moons. Blasts of multicoloured lasers stabbed into the orks as the Exodite dragon riders plunged into the attack.

Thirianna felt a surge of awe when a chorus of ground-shaking bellows reverberated through the town as more of the Exodites' war-beasts entered the battle. Gigantic forces of nature harnessed by the Exodites, the immense reptiles thundered across the plaza towards the orks. With laser lances and fusion pikes, the Exodites closed, determined to exact revenge for the destruction of the town and the deaths of their kin. To them Arhathain had granted the final act of destruction, an opportunity to settle a bloody score with the green-skinned invaders.

Some of the Exodites were mounted on bipedal, predatory lizards with dagger fangs and slashing claws. Armed with pistols and blades, the Exodite knights slashed into the retreating orks, striking and withdrawing continuously. Other eldar crewed heavier weapons in howdahs upon the backs of gigantic reptiles. Pulses of white fire and burning lasers strobed through the orks, cutting down a score in one salvo. The dragons soared above, their riders raining down more las-fire and showers of plasma grenades.

Against the fury of the Exodites, the orks did not survive for long. They were cut down in short order, the wounded crushed beneath the feet of the advancing behemoths.

'The battle is won,' announced Kelamith.

Thirianna looked around the square and saw the hundreds of dead orks and several dozen wounded and slain eldar. She knew she should be sickened by the sight, that the memory would be enough to drive any eldar mad, but her war-mask shielded her from these dark thoughts, leaving them only as an abstract, intellectual consideration.

The warlock felt composed, recognising the scene from many like it witnessed on the skein. Thirianna was relieved; some of the glimpsed vision had showed far more eldar dead. She detached her thoughts from the skein, left with lingering images of the Alaitocii and Exodites scouring the ruins for hidden ork survivors.

The battle was indeed won, but the killing was not yet over.

LOST

The White Guardians – The Warp Spiders. The skein is not a benign realm, to be wandered without heeding its dangers; perils of a very fatal kind await the unwary. Not only this, the skein is open to manipulation, and there is no power more mutable than that of the Great Powers of the warp. In dealing with matters associated with such entities, the employment of the White Guardians is essential to keep the seer safe from both physical harm and psychical misdirection, as their namesakes guard the infinity circuit for similar dangers.

A CLOUD HAD settled upon Thirianna's spirit. Following the battle with the orks, she had returned labouring beneath a feeling of guilt and shame; guilt of foreseeing Korlandril's injury and shame for allowing it to happen. She cried for a cycle and half, swallowed by frustration and the burden of what she had seen. The limitation of her power was very evident. Without Kelamith to guide her, Thirianna could not find out what lay in wait for her friend, and she did not know whether he would live or die.

Something more tenebrous also nagged at her subconscious. It was not the misery of death or the bloodlust of battle; these things she had experienced before and her war-mask protected her from them. She could dimly recall being overwhelmed by the shamanic power of the orks, swept away by its elemental force. Like a rock caught in an avalanche, she had been tumbled across the skein, unable to find purchase, while Kelamith had remained unaffected.

She had seen nothing of the farseer in the five cycles since they had arrived back on Alaitoc, and knew better than to seek out Kelamith. If he was not to be encountered it was of his choosing.

Left to her thoughts and worries, Thirianna felt a stirring of jealousy for the farseer. His powers were prodigious, in reality as well as upon the skein. There were few places he would not venture – places he had forbidden his apprentice to enter – and Thirianna was sure that there were secrets out on the skein that she could uncover. Glimpsing the short, obvious intent of an attacking ork was one matter; discerning the interweaving web of motion and action of a group was something beyond her. Thirianna needed to know how to look further and deeper into destiny, and chafed at having to wait for Kelamith to lead her back into the infinity circuit.

At dawn-light on the sixth cycle since coming back to the craftworld, Thirianna decided to take matters into her own hands. She rose early from her bed, ate a light breakfast and headed to the Chambers of the Seers by herself. She easily found the node employed by Kelamith and started her preparations to immerse herself into the infinity circuit.

Before completing the mantra, Thirianna paused, her hand hovering above the warm, inviting curve of the node. Kelamith had explained nothing of the mores and taboos about the skein and Thirianna felt a pang of guilt, wondering if she was about to commit a transgression of seer tradition. Was it disrespectful to proceed without the authority of Kelamith? Would she be bringing disorder to the work of the other seers by her solo intrusion?

Thirianna dismissed her concerns; Kelamith had made no edict or ban on her using the infinity circuit by herself, and even for one whose communication was as esoteric as Kelamith she concluded that he would have made any such prohibition plain.

She placed her hand onto the node and started the mantra anew, peeling off the layers of physical form, ego and consciousness, allowing her unfettered mind to slip into the realm of dreams and futures.

TO ACCLIMATISE HERSELF, Thirianna headed first to some of her familiar haunts, allowing herself to be borne along by the pulsing energies of the infinity circuit. She loitered around the Eye of Aetheniar, dancing on the starlight that poured into the observatory, becoming one with the waves and particles that fell upon the banks of sensors and lenses.

Her mood lightened and she moved her presence across Alaitoc, spanning a distance in an instant that would take the best part of a cycle to travel by conventional means. She swam through the crystalline threads beneath the Dome of Haunting Whispers, catching snatches of poetry and lectures from the early cycle orators performing before crowds only they imagined. Thirianna bored quickly though, having spent too often in this place in her body, and skimmed along the craftworld's conduits towards the docking spires.

Even now she could still feel the after-presence of Aradryan, a light echo of his parting etched on the fabric of the infinity circuit. She delved into the transmissions and archives, seeking any news of where her friend's ship had gone after the battle with the orks. There was nothing, an emptiness left by the desire of the rangers to travel unheralded.

Saddened by this, Thirianna was about to head to the Dome of Crystal Seers when she felt a ripple through the infinity circuit. It was the gate astern of Alaitoc dilating, sending a shivering pulse of energy through the craftworld as a ship emerged from the near-warp of the webway.

Thirianna bobbed on the ripple for a moment, enjoying the sensation of distant stars seen and far-flung planets visited that was borne to Alaitoc in the starship's wake. As the webway closed again, Thirianna noticed something she had not seen before.

Kelamith had warned her not to stray too close to the portal, for reasons he had not disclosed, but Thirianna now felt herself drawn in that direction. Curiosity, helped along by no small measure of petty defiance, urged her to have a closer look.

She was taken aback by what she discovered, though when she had thought about it for a moment she realised it should not have been a surprise.

The infinity circuit did not stop at the webway portal, but continued along insubstantial threads woven into the energy of the webway itself. Freed from crystal conduit and psychic lattice, the infinity circuit became a hazy fluctuation of energy that dispersed into the fabric of the webway tunnels.

It made sense, Thirianna decided. Though in many ways the webway was a physical thing, a tunnel that delved between the warp and the material universe, it was just as much a psychic construct. It was fixed in places, but for the most part was a shifting, ephemeral thing, its gates linking the distant, moving craftworlds together.

She had not considered such a thing before, or the implication of it. The webway was more than just a means of travel, it was the interstellar link between the surviving craftworlds, powered by and powering them in equal measure.

Edging closer, a little fearful of the power sustaining the webway, Thirianna saw that there were smaller portals, extending from other parts of the craftworld. In theory she had known about such things; to be part of them was a different experience entirely. Many of the older Aspect temples had small webway doors; there were likewise others that led to the Chamber of the Autarchs; the private residences of Alaitoc's oldest families had openings erected in the times before the Fall. Many were little more than vestigial passages, cut off and defunct, their purpose now forgotten or unnecessary. Some were still active but locked, barred by psychic shields and rune-forged barriers. She veered away from these, knowing that they had been closed for good reason. Like the Mirror of Nandriellein, they were tainted forever, doomed to betray any that used them.

Thirianna hesitantly moved into that part of the infinity circuit that was not physically encompassed within Alaitoc. The transition was seamless, from the partly physical to the purely psychic. As she neared the webway portal, the vagueness of the threads ahead resolved into more distinct pathways. Emboldened by this discovery, Thirianna ventured further.

There was a brief moment of dispersion as she moved into the fabric of the webway itself. She stopped, suddenly aware of how far she was from her body. The thought of her physical self interfered with her clarity of thought and for an instant she struggled to retain her collective presence, fighting against a pull that threatened to drag her back to her mortal shell.

Repeating the last verse of the mantra she had learnt, she stabilised her presence, reassuring herself that in the world of the skein, distance was as meaningless as time. Should she get lost or in trouble, Thirianna was confident that she could detach herself from the infinity circuit and would be brought back to her body without effort.

For a while she lingered close to the webway portal. There was a coldness here that seeped through her spirit. She realised that she was alone, though the presence of other seers flickered past occasionally as they made their own forays across the interstellar distances between craftworlds.

She felt a tremor of life as the portal opened and a ship passed into the webway, bringing its own miniature version of the infinity circuit. Spirit stones at the heart of the starship sent out psychic tendrils, their feathery touch on the webway moving through Thirianna as the ship accelerated away from Alaitoc towards its unknown destination. The crystalline matrix within the ship drew energy and information from the structure of the webway, becoming part of its psychic construction whilst its physical form remained distinct.

Thirianna suppressed an urge to take hold of one of the psychic tendrils and slide aboard the departing vessel. That would be too much of a risk, and she was content to wander by herself, glorying in the ever-widening branches of the infinity circuit as it traversed the galaxy.

There was no sense of time in this place, but Thirianna knew that she had been inside the infinity circuit for quite a while. In comparison to her earlier travels, this journey was by far the longest. Undeterred, she allowed herself to drift away from Alaitoc, following the after-echoes of the ship that had left, buffeted gently by its psychic wake.

The webway split not far from the Alaitoc portal, becoming several large shafts and many more smaller ones. With a metaphorical last glance back at the portal, Thirianna chose one at random and swooped along it, breaking free from her worries as she broke free from the psychic well of her home.

Here it was truly lifeless.

The coldness of the void between stars permeated the webway's walls, dissipating its energies. As Thirianna moved on, she encountered patches of resistance, areas of thinness in the fabric of the webway where the physical universe was trying to encroach upon the framed space created between realities.

There were signs of damage, or perhaps poor maintenance. She did not see them, she had no eyes to speak of, but became aware of the frailty of the infinity circuit along certain stretches.

Everything had been silent and blissful after the relative metropolis of the dead that was Alaitoc's circuitry. Now came a distant whispering.

Fear gripped Thirianna as she realised how far she had come and how foolish she had been to venture here without protection or escort. She felt alone and tiny, a mote of existence suspended between life and death by a fragile thread of ancient engineering.

As the whispering grew louder, coming closer, Thirianna moved away from it, frightened by its presence. It was not just the material world that could break into the webway; the warp also exerted its own pressures on the structure, and where it was breached, the denizens of that immaterial realm could enter.

Thirianna stopped her retreat, aware that she could not discern whether she was moving back towards Alaitoc or further from it.

She had ventured far enough and it was time to return, Thirianna decided. The seer let her grip on the psychic matrix loosen, expecting to be drawn back to her body.

Nothing happened.

She tried again, thinking of her body, of the physical Alaitoc, of the singularity of Mind and Being and Form. Still she was bound within the twining energies of the webway and the haunting whispers were now almost upon her, chilling her spirit with their presence.

Thinking that perhaps she could broaden the vista of her interaction and find the way back, Thirianna allowed her presence to dissolve, spreading along the skein in every direction. She thought she saw a glimmer of heat, of life, of energy that could be Alaitoc. Yet at the same time, her spirit touched upon something utterly alien and utterly repellent.

Disembodied, Thirianna could not scream. Her flare of despair and dread caused a ripple across the skein as she drew herself back to a single point of consciousness. The wave of fear seemed to echo forever, betraying her presence to every sentience in the vicinity. Thirianna was aware of being discovered, of being exposed to any passing predatory thing. She tried to make herself invisible, to blend with the fabric of the webway, but her fear caused convolutions to pulse across the infinity circuit, spasming its structure as sobs might wrack her physical form or a twitching fly might alert a waiting spider.

Like a noose tightening around her, the things that hunted Thirianna closed in. If she stayed where she was, she would be trapped and helpless. Mustering all of her courage, Thirianna summoned up as much willpower as she could find. She became a sparkling mote of energy in the webway and in a moment she had fled, flashing across the infinity circuit, turning left and right, heading up and down, turning around and about, heedless of the direction as long as it was away from the things that had stalked her.

Stopping, Thirianna knew that she was truly lost now. There was not the faintest glimmer of Alaitoc's warm presence.

There was something else though, bending the skein with its weight, distorting the webway. Thirianna could not sense it directly; whatever it was had a masking field around it, shielding it from detection. It was only by its effect on the nearby strands of the webway that it could be located, like a glass lens that can only be seen because of the light passing through it.

Thirianna had a suspicion that she knew what it was: a reality pocket. A piece of the material universe had been wrapped up in the fabric of the webway, hidden from both the mortal and immortal realms. There were many reasons for such pockets to exist, and most of these webway sanctuaries pre-dated the Fall. Given her recent experiences, Thirianna was reluctant to investigate further, but necessity outweighed caution; she had to find some means of getting back to Alaitoc and the bubble world might contain someone that could help.

Thirianna moved towards the reality pocket, probing gently at its borders. It did strange things to her sense of self, like a convex or concave mirror bending her image; she felt herself simultaneously stretched thin and yet terribly heavy.

Pushing past the discomfort, Thirianna slid into the pocket world. A moment later she saw that she had made a terrible mistake.

A spire of dark material speared up from a rocky foundation, extruded from the inner surface of the webway duct. At first Thirianna had no comprehension of scale; she was a fragment of consciousness with no form to judge her surroundings. As she observed the black tower, she realised that it was enormous, and that the flecks of darkness spiralling around its summit were in fact eldar with winged flight packs.

Everything moved with such slowness here, compared to the thought-quick interactions of the unfettered infinity circuit. Dragging herself around the edge of the reality pocket, catching a glimpse of a miniature dark blue star above the tower, Thirianna saw three long walkways extending from one side of the tower. The pair of starships docked at two of them revealed their function as quays, but the ships were like nothing Thirianna had seen coming or going from Alaitoc.

They were undoubtedly warships: weapons blisters extended the length of their hulls. Their lateen-like solar sails were raked heavily back, two large and one small, and the prow of each vessel had a ram-like extension that glittered with an energy field.

The webway encompassed the world of the tower but did not penetrate it. The threads of the infinity circuit surrounded the bubble but made no inroads towards the tower itself. Thirianna could see small figures of eldar walking along gantries and the docks, but she had no means of approaching closer.

When she realised what the eldar on the dockside were doing, she decided that it was for the best that she could not come any closer.

The eldar, garbed in highly stylised, barbaric clothing, bearing whips and scourges, were leading a seething mass of aliens from their ship to a yawning gate in the side of the tower. As the portal opened, the sound of shrieks and moans filled the air. Thirianna felt wave after wave of torment roiling around the reality bubble; agony unending poured like a flood from the gate of the tower.

Turning her attention to the newest arrivals, Thirianna recognised humans, several dozen of them, amongst the miserable throng. The other creatures, some hairy, some scaled, some squat and misshapen, others upright with two arms and legs like eldar, were not known to her. They were all bound in energy cuffs, glowing bands of red around their ankles and necks. She could not see any more detail, and for that she was grateful.

Thirianna felt herself being ripped apart as a portal appeared in the fabric of the pocket, tearing from the webway into the compressed region of reality. Another ship appeared through the gate, an armed sloop smaller than the two other vessels.

Its black and red hull glistened like the scales of a fish as it banked towards the highest of the docks.

The pirate lair could not provide the information Thirianna required and to be here was dangerous in the extreme. She extricated herself from the reality pocket with another mind-churning sensation, leaving the raiders to their despicable lives.

Now that her panic had subsided, Thirianna was able to take better stock of her situation. She was lost in the webway, some distance from Alaitoc. The best way to locate the craftworld would be aboard a ship, and her best chance of finding a ship would be to locate one of the larger arterial routes. She could sense that the webway around her was a tangled mess of smaller passages and tunnels, caused in no small part by the distortion of the pirates' sanctuary. She would be lost in here forever if she tried to get past the lair, so she turned back, her nervousness returning as she considered the fact that she was moving back towards the place where whispering creatures had come for her.

A MOMENT OR an eternity passed, it was impossible to tell which. Thirianna was sure that she was heading in the right direction. The webway seemed to be widening, but Thirianna could not shake the nagging feeling that the further she moved, the greater the distance was growing between her and Alaitoc.

Her mood flitted through various phases: frustration, fear, hope, anxiety, and back to frustration. The infinity circuit responded to her presence, her state of mind, echoing back her inner thoughts, reflecting her sudden moments of excitement and dread.

After some time Thirianna realised again that she was not alone. This time she tried her hardest to master her fear, balling it up deep inside her, not allowing it to disturb the skein of the webway. Things, formless things of dead eyes and dagger fangs and eternal hunger, flitted past her.

Their touch was freezing, but Thirianna did not respond. She was a patch of energy in the webway, an aberration not prey, nothing of interest to the mindless hunters.

The predators circled slowly, nudging at the fabric of the webway from without, trying to push their way in. Thirianna moved slowly away, so slowly it was almost imperceptible in comparison to the lightning-fast speeds she had travelled before.

Now and then she stopped, sensing the hunters coming closer again, their interest piqued by this fuzzy patch of warmth and life. Thirianna tried not to panic, tried hard to dim her thoughts, to suppress memories of home and friends, giving nothing for the predators to seize upon. She was a mote of existence, a part of the universe, and nothing more.

Heat suffused the infinity circuit. It grew gradually, like dawn breaking. From its warmth the hunters turned tail and fled.

Relief flooded through Thirianna. She was sure the warmth was something good. As it crept across the skein, it filled her with hope. It was like the caress of a lover, gentle and relaxing, coaxing her into sleep. It was the embrace of a mother, swaddled in soft cloth, gently rocking into somnolence.

Violet surf lapped at the pale blue sand, the warm water touching Thirianna's toes. Above, a bright orb of silver illuminated the scene, casting soft shadows across the rippled beach. A figure approached from Thirianna's right still some distance away. She smiled, recognising the gait of Aradryan. He was dressed in a loose-fitting robe of white and grey, and held a hand to his brow to shield his eyes, which glittered in the silvery light.

Thirianna stood up, reaching out a hand in welcome. As her friend came closer she realised she had made a mistake. It was not Aradryan that approached, but Korlandril. The sculptor's face was masked by his hair, tousled across his features by the gentle breeze. He was smiling, eyes alight with amusement.

'This is a nice place,' said Korlandril, stopping beside Thirianna. He looked out across the glittering water. 'It was nice of you to invite me.'

'I thought we should spend a little time together,' said Thirianna, though in truth she could not recall any agreement to meet her friend. 'We have to talk.'

'We can spend more than a little time,' Korlandril said, smiling lopsidedly. He reached out a hand and stroked Thirianna's arm. His touch set her nerves alight, sending a shiver of pleasure through her body. 'We can stay here as long as we want.'

'I'm not sure,' said Thirianna. She wanted to pull away her arm, but Korlandril gently gripped her wrist and tugged her closer. His dark eyes bored into hers, full of passion.

'I made something for you,' he said, producing a fine golden bracelet from his robe. He held it out for Thirianna to slip her hand into.

She hesitated.

'When did you start making jewellery?' she asked. 'I thought portraiture was your speciality.'

'Let us see what it looks like on your arm,' said Korlandril, ignoring the question. He pulled her hand closer. 'Just put it on and we can see.'

'You have never given me a gift before,' said Thirianna, disturbed by Korlandril's insistent manner.

'You have never declared your love for me before,' replied her friend. He moved the bracelet towards Thirianna's fingers but she snatched away her hand.

'This is not right,' she said. Thirianna looked around, not recognising where she was. There were few parts of Alaitoc she had not visited, in person or in spirit, and her surroundings felt unfamiliar. The thought spurred a memory.

'You stopped being a sculptor,' said Thirianna, taking a step back from Korlandril. 'You became a warrior.'

'I could not bear to be away from you,' said Korlandril, pacing forwards to stay beside her. 'Your love has conquered my hate. Why not just accept my gift for what it is? Put it on and we will sit here and talk. We have as much time as we want, nobody will disturb us.'

'No,' said Thirianna, shaking her head. She tried desperately to recall how she had come back to Alaitoc. She could not. The last thing she remembered…

'This is not real,' Thirianna said, backing away from Korlandril. 'I was stuck in the webway. I still am, aren't I? What are you?'

'I am your friend,' said Korlandril. 'You know who I am. Put on the bracelet and together we will go home. I know the way.'

'You are not Korlandril.' Thirianna felt panic rising in her breast. She did not know what the apparition was, but it was certainly not her friend.

Korlandril looked genuinely hurt, his brow furrowing with disappointment. Clouds gathered quickly overhead, obscuring the silver sun, swathing the beach in gloom. The figure of Korlandril pursed his lips and gently shook his head.

'Why did you have to spoil this beautiful time together?' he asked. 'I thought you wanted to be with me? Is that not what you desire?'

'You are not Korlandril,' Thirianna said again. She glanced over her shoulder and saw that the beach stretched away to the horizon in every direction. The thing pretending to be Korlandril grabbed her wrist again and held up the bracelet.

'Put it on,' he insisted. Thirianna splayed her fingers as Korlandril tried to force the band over her hand. He snarled and twisted her arm, forcing her to her knees. 'Put it on or I will get angry!'

The clouds had become very dark now and the sea was heaving, flecked with foam, the waves crashing noisily against jutting crystal shards that had thrust up from the sandy shore.

'Leave me alone!' shrieked Thirianna, squirming in the grasp of the imposter.

'We will be together for eternity, just as you desire,' said Korlandril. 'It is what you want above all other things.'

'It is not,' said Thirianna, falling still. 'I do not love you.'

'Everybody loves me,' said the apparition. 'Do not lie. Do not resist your own heart's desire.'

Thirianna kicked out at the creature's leg, ripping free her hand as it stumbled. The sand had become beads of black glass, shifting underfoot as Thirianna tried to get to her feet. The waves were black too, and the sky a menacing purple and red.

'You cannot leave me,' Korlandril shouted after her as Thirianna turned and ran.

She had taken only a few paces before she stopped, the apparition appearing in front of her.

'It is better that you choose to spend eternity with me,' it said. 'I can make your existence an unending pleasure. Love me as I love you and you will never know fear or anger or sadness again. Accept our love for what it is, binding and forever.'

The thing took a step closer, hand held out, but stopped and glanced up at the sky. Thirianna looked to the clouds as well and saw that they were parting. It looked like snow was falling, though the clouds were shredding above, turning to thin wisps of grey. The white shower fluttered closer and closer.

'No!' snarled Korlandril. 'Leave us in peace!'

As the flickering downfall of white came closer, Thirianna could see beyond that the world was melting away. The sky had becoming the whirling miasma of the webway, the sea likewise dissipating into tatters of colour.

THERE WAS NOT just one of the creatures, there were dozens. They were all possessed of half-male, half-female bodies, with a single breast each, and huge, glittering, entrancing eyes. Thirianna was surrounded by them, as the daemons stalked forwards on bird-like legs and taloned feet. They had long claws for hands, which snickered and snapped in a staccato rhythm as they closed in. The closest held a golden manacle and chain, and lunged for Thirianna, but she dodged aside to evade its clacking grasp.

Thirianna recognised them immediately and was terrified. They were lesser daemons, servants of She Who Thirsts, embodiments of the Great Enemy.

She tried to flee but was surrounded.

The daemonettes paused and looked around, themselves frightened in turn.

Trailing crystalline threads, the warp spiders descended upon the webway, tens of thousands of the tiny creatures. In a pale wave they swept over the daemons, miniscule mandibles biting deep, covering the creatures from clawed feet to crested scalps. The daemons fought back, slashing with their claws, raking great furrows in the mass of the white guardians.

More figures appeared from the gloom, shining white silhouettes bearing swords and spears. As blazes of pure light they struck into the daemons, shattering them, leaving blossoms of fading sparks as they cut and slashed at the immaterial creatures.

Thirianna felt the light folding around her, forming a cocoon of energy, gentle yet strong. The light infused her, seeping through her spirit, transforming her into pure energy. She felt the touch of another presence upon her thoughts, wordless yet reassuring.

She allowed the light to lift her and in moments she was away, flashing across the webway, leaving the battling apparitions far behind.

WITH A GASP, Thirianna opened her eyes. She swayed for a moment and then collapsed, her hand falling from the infinity circuit node.

She did not lose consciousness, but felt weak and dizzy, her vision swimming. It was not her body that ailed but her mind. Images from her experience flashed through her thoughts, disorientating her further. She struggled to compose herself and between the visions half-glimpsed a ring of other eldar around her, five in all.

She recognised Kelamith, his face contorted in a fierce scowl of concentration. His fingers twitched at his sides, while several runes spun around him, whirling about on eccentric orbits.

In a few moments the nausea passed and Thirianna was able to sit back against the curve of the wall, catching her breath. She shuddered at the recollection of what happened and her waystone burned bright upon her breast, glowing blue, hot to the touch.

She had been so foolish, so naive. What had she been thinking, to dare the webway alone, inexperienced and helpless? She started to sob, realising how close she had come to being trapped by She Who Thirsts. She had risked not just death, but an eternity of torment devoured by the creation of the eldar's own hedonistic past.

Still shuddering, she flinched as a hand touched her shoulder.

Looking up, she saw Kelamith. She expected a rebuke, but his face was kindly, his lips curved in the slightest of smiles. Taking his hand, Thirianna allowed herself to be helped to her feet.

'I am sorry,' she said, burying her face in the cloth of his robe, more tears flowing.

'It is I that am sorry, child,' said Kelamith, holding a hand to the back of her head. 'I should have been more watchful.'

Thirianna pulled back and looked at the farseer.

'I put all of us in danger,' she said. 'What if those... things had taken me, turned me to their cause?'

'They did not,' said Kelamith, patting her hand. 'That is a credit to you. You are stronger than you think; not every person can resist their wiles. Yet I apologise again, for I had seen that you would venture forth on your own. I did so, when I first started, and I thought it would be good for you to find your own way. I did not see how much peril awaited you, and I should have done.'

'You knew I would get lost?' said Thirianna. 'You allowed me to wander free, knowing what it might have led to?'

'Heed this warning,' said Kelamith, now with a stern expression. 'Of the many possible outcomes, only this one put you at risk. I judged it worthwhile to let you have your own time, thinking the chances of disaster were remote. Yet no matter how unlikely an outcome might be in regards to all of the others, while it remains possible it must be considered. Had I known for sure that this would happen, I would have intervened. As it is, I did not think you powerful enough to travel so far and become so embroiled in the eternal matrix.'

'The eternal matrix?' said Thirianna. She had not heard the phrase before.

'It is the realm that binds together the infinity circuits of all the craftworlds, part of the webway and part of something else,' explained Kelamith. 'It is as close to the unbound skein as any artifice of ours can be, made of the raw stuff of the ether. A novice such as yourself cannot usually travel far upon it.'

'And what will you do now?' said Thirianna, casting her gaze at the marble-like floor. 'I suppose I have proven myself very short-sighted. I will understand if you do not wish to be my teacher any more.'

'I think that more than ever I wish to be your teacher, child,' said Kelamith. 'You show great potential, not just of psychic power, but of curiosity, resolve and self-belief. These are vital attributes if you are to reach the full extent of a seer's abilities. I would be more worried if you had not explored on your own.'

Thirianna looked around and saw the other seers nodding in agreement.

'Return to your chambers. You have had an ordeal that would test the greatest of us,' said Kelamith. 'Think on what has happened to you, and with the next cycle come to me again and we will continue with your training.'

REUNION

The Twin Birds – Hawk and Falcon. All runes work in conjunction with each other, but there are several pairing and sibling runes that can only facilitate a true reading together. The most prominent of these are the Twin Birds, formed as one and divided only upon the skein. In many cases the two fates of different individuals may be deeply entwined, seeming as one; in such circumstance the Hawk and Falcon are able to discern points of digression, each following its own path to highlight possible divides and moments of reunion.

AFTER HER DRAMATIC first foray into the eternal matrix, Thirianna was content to roam the more orderly confines of Alaitoc's infinity circuit. Areas previously seen as staid and safe were now sanctuaries of stability for the seer, refuges she attended constantly to maintain her sense of self and a degree of mental balance.

She progressed well under the tutelage of Kelamith, using the infinity circuit to open up the vistas of the wider skein with greater control and focus. Her wanderings became more concentrated, though she lacked the true ability of free navigation and frequently required the guiding spirit of Kelamith to show her the way.

For some considerable time this continued and Thirianna honed her powers every cycle, growing again in confidence, the dark memories of her near-capture by the daemons receding.

After her latest session in the infinity circuit, Thirianna was not dismissed by Kelamith. Instead the farseer invited her to walk with him in the gardens outside her residence.

They talked about the lessons learnt and Thirianna's hopes for the coming cycles, but it was obvious that something else was on the farseer's mind. The pair of them stopped at the height of an arcing white bridge over a shallow ravine, the shadows of the dome's towers long across the hills and scattered woodlands.

'You have come a long way to mastering your psychic sense,' said the farseer, hands clasped behind his back. Thirianna leant on the rail and glanced down at the thin rivulet of water passing under the bridge.

'I feel as if I have only stepped into the shallows,'

said Thirianna. 'The sea of knowledge extends far further than we have travelled already.'

'That is true, and it is why we must now venture further from the shore,' said Kelamith. 'Until now, you have acted as your own anchor. As you experienced in your time upon the eternal matrix, there are limits to our power while confined by our bodily conduit. To see further, to wade further into the sea of knowledge, we must lay before us beacons to follow. In this way we can follow their direction far out into the future, but be assured of the direction home.'

The farseer brought forth a rune from his belt, no larger than the tip of his thumb. It was made of dark blue wraithbone, gleaming slightly with its own power. The rune spun lazily at the end of Kelamith's extended finger.

'The runes are our beacons, our stepping stones into the distance,' he continued. 'Until now you have used your mind and body to channel the power of the skein, and there are limits to what we can withstand. The runes provide new avenues of exploration. If you think of the barriers between reality and the future as a wall, the runes open new gates for us to pass through. Each has its own specific purpose, opening up new vistas beyond that wall and guiding our minds to their destinations. They also act as a valve, ensuring that the power we tap into does not overcome us, shielding our thoughts from She Who Thirsts.'

Thirianna shivered at the mention of the eldar's darkest foe and almost lost the meaning of the farseer's words. She pushed aside the rising memories of the webway to concentrate on what Kelamith had said.

'Each rune increases our power,' said Thirianna.

'In a way,' replied Kelamith. 'In themselves they contain no power, but they enable us to channel more psychic energy. It is a balance. To control a number of runes requires considerable mental dexterity and focus. At first, we begin with a single rune.'

'You think it is time for me to learn runecraft?' said Thirianna, excited by the prospect.

'Certainly it is, child,' said Kelamith. 'Each rune is a unique thing, bonded to its seer, an extension of their Form. When you come to me next cycle, I will take you to have your first rune fashioned.'

'Which shall it be?' Thirianna asked. There were several hundred that she knew of now, each with its own benefits and challenges, abilities and traps.

'We all begin with the same,' said Kelamith. 'The rune of Self. Our personal rune. It is our incarnation upon the skein and no runecraft is possible without it.'

They arranged to meet in the following cycle and Kelamith departed, leaving Thirianna to think on this next stage of her development. The possibilities intrigued her and the idea of taking this important step gave her a sense of achievement she had not felt since becoming a seer. The image of the rune of the seer and the rune of herself were as one in her mind, inseparable, one the symbol of the other. It was a sign of her progress that she was about to embody that image she held in her mind, and she returned to her chambers full of anticipation.

'Is this a trick?' Thirianna demanded, as Kelamith waved for her to enter the bonesinger's workshop.

'There is no trickery,' the farseer assured her.

'Yet you must know who practices his craft here,' said Thirianna.

'I do know,' said Kelamith, expression impassive. 'Yrlandriar is one of the foremost bonesingers of Alaitoc. He has fashioned many seer runes.'

'He is my father!' said Thirianna, knowing that Kelamith had to be aware of the fact.

'So you no longer profess to be the child of Wishseer Aurentian? A strange time to make such a confession,' said Kelamith, his eyes showing intrigue.

'Aurentian was more my father than Yrlandriar, after the death of my mother,' replied Thiriama. 'Yrlandriar is no father to me.'

'Yes, he is,' said Kelamith, unperturbed. 'You are very fortunate.'

'Fortunate?' Thirianna almost spat out the word. 'Yrlandriar is a selfish, cantankerous tyrant. I will have nothing to do with him.'

The farseer's patient expression did not change. He turned at the high archway and clasped his hands together. A glow of psychic energy lit up Kelamith's eyes and his voice took on the otherworldly cant Thirianna now associated with the farseer's forays onto the skein.

'Yrlandriar will fashion the rune of Thirianna,' he intoned slowly. 'With it, she will continue on the

Path of the Seer, learning her own fate and that of many others.'

'There are other bonesingers,' said Thirianna, unconvinced by this fatalistic declaration. 'I will have one of them fashion my rune.'

'That is not what will happen,' said Kelamith, his voice returning to normal, eyes dimming. 'Your objections are juvenile, not worthy of a seer of Alaitoc.'

Thirianna stood firm, unwilling to indulge in the farseer's manipulation.

'You think that I make this choice out of whim or spite?' asked Kelamith, a touch of anger now showing in his furrowed brow. 'Listen to me, child. As a seer you will see many fates that you cannot change. If you cannot accept them, you will be driven mad, tormented by possibilities that never existed. If your father does not fashion your rune, your time with me is finished.'

'Perhaps another farseer will continue my instruction,' said Thirianna, crossing her arms defiantly. 'Surely there is at least one other that sees my potential.'

'That is pride,' snapped Kelamith, causing Thirianna to flinch. It was the first time the farseer had raised his voice to her, and she felt a momentary pang of guilt. 'No other will take you, I will ensure that.'

'You are not being fair!' said Thirianna. 'It has been many cycles since my father and I spoke last, and I do not wish him to be a part of my life.'

'If that is the case, you have a difficult choice to

make,' said Kelamith, calm again. 'You can continue to shun your father and find another Path, or you can become a seer and reconcile yourself to his existence.'

Thirianna wrinkled her lips in distaste, prompting Kelamith to turn away and start back down the passageway towards the grav-disc that had brought them to the Dome of Artificers.

'Wait!' Thirianna called after him. She clenched her fists in annoyance, but kept her frustration from her voice. 'I will speak with Yrlandriar, but only to ask for a rune.'

Kelamith stopped and turned back, waving a hand towards the doorway.

'That is all you have to do, child,' he said.

Thirianna took a deep breath and headed through the archway, steeling herself for the impending confrontation.

THE CHAMBER BEYOND was large and semicircular, opening out onto an even wider expanse that ran across a large part of the width of Alaitoc. The room was bare, in surprising contrast to Thirianna's expectations. A few pedestals displayed small works of art; an open cabinet held various works-in-progress; a central table was home to an assortment of cups, dishes and plates holding the remnants of several meals.

All of this Thirianna took in at a glance; her attention was snatched away by the scene beyond. In the massive nave-like chamber there hung what appeared to be the spine and ribcage of some vast primordial animal. As Thirianna approached the open side of the room she recognised what she was seeing – the central structure of a starship.

Gleaming lights shone from the ivory-coloured wraithbone, illuminating every part of the ship-to-be. It was the first time she had seen such a vessel under construction and it took her breath away. All thoughts of Thirianna's many disputes with her father were forgotten, swept away by the majesty of the creation before her. It was a large vessel, though by no means the largest, stretching for half of the hangar's length. The scale was only brought home to her when she saw the tiny figures on the gantries surrounding it.

Though she was not well versed in such things, it looked to Thirianna that the bulk of the work had been completed. The dorsal structure and splay of curving spars towards the prow put her in mind of a shark, front-heavy but delicately poised. The rib-like spurs shortened towards the stern before they abruptly widened into a three-finned tail. Looking up, she could see the massive round apertures where the solar sails would be fitted and in the unlit gloom above she caught the glitter of the panels ready to be lowered into place.

As much as Thirianna saw the starship, she could feel it as well. The wraithbone pulsed slowly with psychic power, barely registering against the background of the infinity circuit, but with its own distinct timbre. The skeletal structure nestled on a cradle of crystalline towers, connecting it to Alaitoc, feeding it the power of the craftworld.

Thirianna studied the details, recognising some

of the fluted work along the sides of the fuselage as settings for gun batteries. It was a warship, and the knowledge brought a hint of menace to the entire affair. She imagined the laser turrets and plasma accelerators that would be fitted, turning this graceful piece of art into a machine capable of dealing unimaginable destruction. The steady throb of psychic power now seemed edged with waiting potential, a beast slumbering, waiting for the command to unleash its fury.

The eldar working on the slender gantries and scaffolding were dressed in light tunics and tight-fitting bodysuits. They were implanting crystal nodes and gem-like energy studs into the wraithbone, coaxing the psychoplastic to accept the jewels with whispered words and intricate gestures.

'This is… unexpected.'

Thirianna turned at the sound of her father's voice. He walked from under the crystal cradle to her right, his open-fronted robe reaching to the floor, an intricate set of musical pipes under one arm. His expression was stern, eyebrows meeting in a frown beneath a high forehead. Yrlandriar's black and purple hair was bound up in an intricate knot fixed with several jewel-headed pins and his hands were encased in metallic gloves, delicately segmented and chased with golden rune designs.

'Kelamith sent you,' he said, walking past Thirianna into his workshop.

'I did not desire this meeting, but I have been left no choice,' said Thirianna. 'Kelamith is stubborn.'

'A trait with which you are all too familiar,' said

Yrlandriar. He gestured and a stool rose up from the blue fabric of the floor, next to the table. As the bonesinger sat down, placing his pipes in front of him, Thirianna noticed he did not offer her a seat.

'I see you have lost none of your hypocrisy,' she said. 'If you could but spare a few moments of your precious time I am sure you could compose a whole treatise on the merits of intractability.'

Yrlandriar eyed her coolly, legs and arms crossed.

'Your foolishness begets response,' he said. 'That you chose to ignore my advice is further proof of your selfishness.'

'Advice?' Thirianna made no attempt to hide her scorn. 'You wanted to control me, and nothing less. Just as you wanted to control my mother.'

'You have none of your mother's qualities,' the bonesinger said, a sneer creasing his face. 'It is only good fortune that you did not share her doom. And now you wish to play at being a seer? How long before you grow bored of that?'

'It was your manner that fanned the fire of Khaine within me and drove me to the shrines of the Aspect Warriors,' Thirianna snarled back. 'Perhaps it was the same for my mother.'

'How little you understand,' said Yrlandriar, looking away. 'It was a desire to protect you, her child, that called to Mythrairnin.'

'And you blame me for that,' said Thirianna. 'I was only a child when she died, but you held me responsible. You could never accept that she chose me over you.'

'Perhaps it was your behaviour, your spoilt

demands and incessant complaints that drove her into the embrace of Khaine.' Thirianna could see her father was quivering with emotion, though whether grief or anger she could not tell. He looked at her again, eyes slitted. 'And despite what happened to her, you had to follow in her steps. I lost a life-companion to Khaine's wars, and my daughter abandoned me for his bloody embrace too.'

Thirianna sighed and took a step towards the door.

'Did you not have something to ask of me?' Yrlandriar asked.

'No,' Thirianna replied. 'You have not changed at all. You belittle everything I have achieved and I see that you seek only to use this arrangement to further spite me. I do not care what Kelamith says, I will find another bonesinger to fashion a rune for me.'

'So I was right,' her father said. 'You speak of spite, and then discard your future simply because of your feelings for me. You have no dedication. When Kelamith first proposed this to me, I had hoped you had matured. I see that you have not. If you cannot ask a straightforward favour of me, what hope have you of walking the twisting paths of fate? You are far too capricious, Thirianna; you always have been. You are too young to be a seer, and I will not help you.'

Thirianna deadened her thoughts to her father's continuing insults as she headed for the door. She stopped at the threshold, unable to leave without retort.

'You are lonely and bitter, and seek to blame others for your own shortcomings,' Thirianna said quietly. 'Perhaps I should pity you, but I cannot.'

Before he could say anything further, Thirianna left, hot tears welling up in her eyes.

Kelamith was waiting for her, sat on the padded couch at the centre of the grav-disc. Thirianna sat opposite, and buried her face in her hands. Saying nothing, the farseer commanded the disc to rise up, tilting gently as it took them back to the Chambers of the Seers.

THREE MORE CYCLES passed before Kelamith contacted Thirianna, requesting that she join him in their usual chamber. She had spent the intervening period in brooding isolation, frustrated by her father's attitude, the old wounds of their parting reopened by the encounter.

Kelamith said nothing of his intent for her, and Thirianna feared to ask. The farseer had been adamant that Yrlandriar would be the one to make her rune, and it was with little hope that Kelamith had changed his mind that Thirianna travelled to the Chambers of the Seers. She fully expected to learn that his tutelage would cease, and Thirianna prepared herself for disappointment.

'To see the future is a powerful ability,' said Kelamith, after the two had exchanged their formal greetings. 'Yet it is a transient thing compared to the ability to learn from the past. It is in the understanding of past, present and future that true knowledge lies. The past informing the present, the future judged on events that have passed. Without seeing the past and the present, the future lacks context and becomes a meaningless barrage of possibilities.'

'One does not need to extend great psychic power to learn the mistakes of the past,' said Thirianna, unsure what Kelamith was trying to tell her. It did not seem relevant to her current predicament.

'It is not required, but it can certainly aid us,' replied the farseer. 'We each have our memories, preserved for eternity. We can consult records, to witness the decisions and conclusions of our predecessors. These are valuable sources of knowledge, but the infinity circuit provides us with another.'

Kelamith gestured for Thirianna to merge with the infinity circuit node. She did so, lowering her consciousness into the psychic web of the craftworld. The transition was smooth, without effort, no longer requiring the mantras she had learnt from Kelamith. In many ways, becoming one with the infinity circuit felt to Thirianna as if she returned to her natural state, that being clothed in mortal flesh was a temporary inconvenience that would one day be discarded.

Kelamith's thoughts overlapped with Thirianna's, mingling yet remaining distinct.

'Until now you have only looked forwards upon the skein,' he told Thirianna. 'You know that time is not a fixed point, but a seamlessly unrolling stream of cause and effect. Upon the skein, we can not only seek that which will happen, but also that which has already happened.'

Thirianna felt a tug at her spirit and she complied with it, shifting from the artificial state of the infinity circuit to the realm of pure thought that was the skein. The last time she had travelled here, during the battle with the orks, she had kept her gaze low, glimpsing only the futures immediate to her. This time she allowed her gaze to roam more widely, drinking in the complexity and beauty of the unfolding universe, seeing the haphazard mesh of fate being revealed.

'You do not yet have your rune,' said Kelamith. Thirianna noted a hint of admonishment in his thoughts. 'I will have to guide you back, to memories you have misplaced and events that you have never witnessed.'

To Thirianna it seemed as if the skein inverted itself. The unravelling threads were spiralling together, becoming one, a myriad probabilities becoming defined causes. The images she glimpsed resolved themselves in reverse as time flowed backwards. She struggled to keep up, so swiftly did Kelamith lead the way, but she half-saw herself again and again, in various situations that she knew well: becoming lost in the webway; meeting Kelamith for the first time; her argument with Korlandril; sitting composing poetry in her room; eating a meal with Aradryan and Korlandril in the shade of a golden-leafed tree.

Back they went, further and further, Thirianna's life flashing past, until they stopped during her youngest childhood. Thirianna was amazed, watching her infant self sitting in her mother's lap, trying to grab at her long braid of hair. Sadness filled Thirianna at the sight, even as the warmth of the scene filled her with a sense of love.

'I remember this time,' said Thirianna, trying to think clearly amongst the tumble of emotions that threatened to consume her. 'Mother is singing to me. The *Lay of Eldanesh*. She had a wonderful voice.'

'And as a child that was what you remembered, your mother's voice, imprinted forever in your thoughts,' said Kelamith. 'However, our memories alone do not define a moment.'

He brought the pair of them out of the vision, sliding sideways to an intertwining thread, like stepping from one gravrail platform to another. The scene returned, subtly different.

Thirianna felt shock as she realised she was experiencing the scene through the memories of her mother. She had her baby daughter on her lap, and was idly singing to her while she waited for Yrlandriar to return. He had been called away from Alaitoc, to effect repairs to a starship that had been attacked by humans. She was worried, afraid he might never return, afraid of what would become of her daughter to be raised without her father.

Yrlandriar entered and her mother's relief flooded through Thirianna. She saw his warm smile as he slung his bag from his shoulder to the floor. Infant Thirianna had fallen asleep and she never stirred as Yrlandriar knelt and placed a kiss upon her head.

Thirianna broke from the scene, pulling herself back to the abstract whorl of threads, seeing the three lives entwined in that moment, one of them her own. She was both appalled and fascinated by what she witnessed. Kelamith was right; the power of the skein went far beyond simply showing images of the future. It provided her with the means to witness herself from the perspective of others, to learn what they had intended, what they had thought and felt beyond her knowledge.

'Now do you see why it is Yrlandriar that must cast your rune?' said Kelamith.

'No,' replied Thirianna. 'You seek to prove that he loves me, by showing me a scene from before my mother died. He changed at that moment and his love turned to disgust. I do not doubt that he loved me as a child, but I fail to see how any of this is relevant to my current path.'

'You have not paid attention to what I have told you, child,' said Kelamith, showing his irritation. 'To understand the universe we must understand ourselves. Your past influences your future, and just as you must come to terms and accept the possible futures, you must also reconcile yourself with the truth of the past. That is the purpose of the Path of the Seer, to seek self-awareness.'

'I know all too well the effect my father's behaviour has had on me,' said Thirianna. 'I suffer no delusions on that account.'

'Examine the threads of your life, and note those which are most closely bound to yours,' said the farseer.

Thirianna did so and though other lives touched upon hers, coming and going, there were two constants: her mother and father. It was to be expected and Thirianna did not see how this changed things. She followed the interlocked threads and then halted, suddenly terrified. One of the threads stopped abruptly.

Her mother's death.

'I have no desire to see this,' said Thirianna.

'Your desire is irrelevant, child,' said Kelamith. 'Examine closely the future course.'

The seer did as she was told, seeing the unravelling of the threads representing her life and her father's becoming distant from each other, spiralling away towards their own dooms. Witnessed in this way, the divide became even starker than the memory of that growing distance.

'More than any other, this moment has shaped your fate, though through no act of your own,' said Kelamith. 'If you are to learn from it, you must experience it.'

'No!' said Thirianna, but her protest went unheeded. Thirianna felt Kelamith's spirit merge with hers, dragging her down into the moment of the event, becoming a singularity with the thread of her mother's fate.

TWIN SUNS OF blue fire blazed overhead, shining down upon a dismal plain. Hills covered with brown grass and stunted trees stretched to the horizon, broken by shallow pools of dank water. The landscape was broken by bizarre ruins, jutting up from the soil in rows that radiated out from an immense pyramid at their heart. Most were little more than hummocks of overgrown stone, any markings long faded. Here and there needle-like monoliths speared from the grass at haphazard angles, their sides etched with odd geometric designs that flickered with fitful bursts of energy.

The pyramid glowed, bathing in the light of the

two suns, reflecting them with a baleful sheen, its smooth surface marked out with large designs similar to those on the needles. Black lightning crackled about its golden peak and leapt to the tips of angular monoliths arranged about its base.

The army of Alaitoc approached swiftly, embarked upon Wave Serpent transports and Falcon grav-tanks. Their shimmering shadows flitted across the dull heathland as they closed in from three directions. The engines of jetbikes flared as they sped ahead to scout out the ruins.

Mythrairnin disembarked from the Wave Serpent with the other warriors from the Shrine of the Cleansing Dawn, her shuriken catapult at the ready as she leapt over the remnants of a low wall to take cover. With a whine of engines, the Wave Serpent moved away to take up a supporting position, its twin bright lances swivelling left and right as the gunner sought targets for the weapons.

In a constricting ring, the eldar moved in on their objective.

Ahead, the pyramid blazed with a pulse of power, a beam of disturbing pale green light erupting from its summit to pierce the greyish-yellow sky. An immense portal ground open, revealing a shimmering gate criss-crossed by forks of sickly green energy.

Warnings were passed on from the jetbike riders, but all who approached the pyramid could see the cause of their concern. Rank after rank of warriors marched from the portal, their bodies fashioned in the likeness of golden skeletons. Each carried a rifle set with a long crystal that crackled with the same unnatural energy as the gateway.

The heavy weapons of the grav-tanks opened fire, lances of laser energy converging on the emerging phalanx of artificial warriors. Gold-coloured bodies were shattered, robotic limbs sent whirling through the air.

The command came through to advance and Mythrairnin followed her exarch, Gallineir, as he vaulted over a toppled monolith, heading directly for the foe. Around the squad, other Aspect Warriors advanced, flashes of colour amongst the dismal surrounds.

The emerging necrontyr paid no heed to their casualties. Indeed, those warriors that had fallen still possessed a spark of life. Some crawled onwards, others paused to reassemble their broken bodies, the strange metal of their construction flowing and churning as legs and arms and heads were reattached.

Other infernal creations emerged from hidden gateways around the pyramid. Across the ruins, floating machines with skeletal torsos and heavy cannons emerged from the depths. Gleaming warriors with sleek bodies and halberds edged with glowing energy fields stalked through the remains of the necrontyr city. Clouds of beetle-like constructs each as large as an eldar helmet boiled up from the depths, the swarms hissing and spitting arcane energy.

Dark Reapers added their missiles to the fusillade of the vehicles, the trails of their shots cutting through the flickering mesh of laser fire. Squadrons of jetbikes jinked and swerved in unison as they duelled with the metal scarabs, their shuriken catapults unleashing volleys with each pass. The scarabs engulfed the machines and riders, overloading engines with their energy fields, detonating in blossoms of green fire to destroy the eldar.

A squad of Howling Banshees just ahead of Mythrairnin readied their weapons and leapt from cover to charge towards the closest necrontyr warriors. Like puppets controlled by a single hand, the necrons turned as one and levelled their weapons. Blinding green energy flared, rippling through the Aspect Warriors. Mythrairnin felt fear tugging at her as she saw a Howling Banshee struck by one of the beams. The energy pulsed through the unfortunate Aspect Warrior, stripping away her armour, then her flesh, then her bones, disintegrating her into nothing in a matter of moments.

With an angry shout, Mythrairnin aimed her shuriken catapult and fired at the necron warriors. Her hail of fire caught one of the artificial soldiers in the chest, slashing through metal in an explosion of sparks. The necron stumbled and fell on its face.

Mythrairnin turned her attention to another and fired again, but no sooner had she let loose another burst than the first warrior was pushing itself to its feet again, surrounded by a nimbus of unnatural light. Its glassy eyes flared menacingly as its ruined torso rearranged, the discs of the shurikens spat from its reforming metal flesh to fall to the ground.

Mythrairnin fired again, and again, and again, as did the rest of her squad. Under the barrage of fire, the necrontyr were knocked down time and again. With each volley, those foes who recovered grew fewer. Yet the necrontyr did not pause in their relentless advance.

Metallic creatures shrouded with cloaks and tatters of decaying flesh joined the attack, their wickedly long claws slicing through the Striking Scorpions fighting to Mythrairnin's left. The death of each eldar was greeted by an unsettling screech of triumph.

The eldar fell back, pulling away from the main necron advance under the cover of their tank fire. In rippling lines they retreated before the necrontyr and then attacked again, the army of Alaitoc constantly shifting, never allowing itself to be trapped in the ruins.

Mythrairnin did not know how many times she had fired or how many of the constructs she had destroyed. The battle became a delicate dance of attack and withdrawal, its tempo dictated by the ebb and flow of the necron assaults.

The ruins themselves became weapons. What had first seemed to be decorative, geometric structures revealed themselves to be weapon turrets. The pylons spat forth coruscating blazes of disintegrating energy, killing two or three eldar with every blast.

It was clear to Mythrairnin that they had come too late. The slumber of the necrontyr on this world had ended and their awakening could not be halted. Still the commands were to maintain the attack. She did not question her purpose, filled with the knowledge that the farseers had predicted this tomb world would at some time in the distant future despatch a harvesting fleet that might well fall upon Alaitoc's ships.

The risk to the craftworld would have been enough to stiffen Mythrairnin's resolve, but through the fog of battle-lust she could feel something else pushing her on. Dim memories of her daughter flickered through her mind as she fired incessantly into the necrons. If there was a chance, no matter how remote, that these evil creations might harm her child, she would give her life to prevent it.

One of the suns was setting and in the dimming light, the pyramid changed. Another section of gleaming metal slid away to reveal an immense hangar-like space. From the darkness emerged a terrifying apparition, glowing with green energy. It looked like a cross between a building and a warrior, a huge construct with a dozen heads and batteries of weapons set about a complex, ever-shifting geometric core.

The necrontyr war machine loomed over the battlefield, sheathed in a baleful glow that warded away the blasts of bright lances and scatter lasers. An orb at its centre spun faster and faster, crackling with energy that crawled along arcane circuitry to the blisters of the weapons turrets.

With a blinding flash, green lightning arced down upon the eldar army, shredding tanks and Aspect Warriors in a barrage of pyrotechnic destruction. Whole squads were vaporised in a heartbeat. Falcons exploded or were sheared into small pieces or crashed into the ruins of the city.

The order came to retreat.

Within moments, the Wave Serpent that was to carry the Dire Avengers slid into view just to one side of the squad, sheltering behind a crumbled archway. Mythrairnin and the four other survivors headed towards the transport, pausing only to unleash one more volley at the necron warriors closing in on them.

They were almost at the Wave Serpent when the shadow of the necron war engine fell across them. A moment later, the ancient stones around them detonated as lightning engulfed the Wave Serpent. The transport exploded, sending a shard of hull scything through the Dire Avengers.

Mythrairnin was flung back by the blossom of fire and hurled into the remains of a wall. She stumbled as she tried to stand and realised dully that her right leg had been cut off by the blast of debris.

She saw the necrons advancing and suppressed a cry of fear and pain. Khaine was with her, and with Khaine's strength she would not die without some retort. She fixed on the image of her daughter's face and activated her shuriken catapult, sending volley after volley into the necron warriors stalking closer.

A bolt of green energy hit her, and for the briefest of moments her entire body filled with pain, every molecule torn apart.

THIRIANNA CLAWED AND struggled to rip herself from the grip of the skein, but Kelamith would not permit her to leave. Trapped, Thirianna caught herself in a loop, experiencing the last moments of her mother's life, desperate to cling on to any connection to her, yet torn apart by the nature of her doom.

Kelamith intervened, prising Thirianna's spirit away from the thread of her mother, withdrawing from the intimate contact so that she could establish some semblance of rational thought and balance.

'Why?' demanded Thirianna, recoiling with horror from the memory of what her mother had experienced.

'It is not the pain of your mother that you must understand,' the farseer replied, his voice distant and dispassionate.

Before Thirianna could raise any objection, she felt herself drawn down into the material of the skein again, this time flowing along a faint after-thread left by her mother's death, to where it intersected with the line of her father's life.

THE GLOWSTONE LET out only the feeblest amount of light, barely touching the blackness of the room. Yrlandriar sat cross-legged in the middle of the chamber, hands on his knees, staring at the darkness.

How could he tell Thirianna what had happened? How could he explain to her why her mother would not be returning?

These questions nagged at him, more than the grief that was even now crushing his heart and running veins of chilling venom through his gut. In a moment of self-reflection, Yrlandriar realised that it was not the thought of answering these questions for his daughter that so vexed him; he could not answer them for himself.

He knew it was a fallacy to expect meaning from the random chance of fate, and still he struggled to find some sense in the death of his beloved Mythrairnin. He could find none. He could find no solace in a meaningful death because he could not comprehend how it was that she had first taken to the Path of the Warrior. The causality of her ending led back to that decision, and it was this that defied logic more than anything else that crowded Yrlandriar's thoughts.

She had known death was a possibility and yet against all reason, Mythrairnin had abandoned her child to his care to follow in the footsteps of the Bloody-Handed God. It was a decision that seemed perverse to the artisan, to seek destruction instead of the joys of her own creation.

He had not wept. It seemed a pointless exercise in vanity, a physiological response that would do nothing to fill the gulf that yawned wide in the core of his being. He was empty and cold, all sense of love and warmth ripped from him for no reason at all.

The child would need him.

It was too painful to contemplate. Yrlandriar was surprised by his own reaction, yet every thought of Thirianna mutated into memories of her mother. They were so alike in many ways the slightest thought of his daughter sent spasms of grief through Yrlandriar.

There was nothing he would be able to do to ease the hurt, and Thirianna's grief would compound his own. Yrlandriar's misery would reflect in his daughter and her woe would stir his own. She would be better free from such a taint, able to live her life untouched by the gnawing sadness that would now be his burden.

THIRIANNA WAS STILL absorbing this, trying to reconcile her own memories of the time with the thoughts of her father, when Kelamith moved them again. This time it was to a juncture of her life and Yrlandriar's, and from the first moment she recognised it: the time before she had left to become a Dire Avenger.

'YOU CANNOT TELL me what to do!' screeched Thirianna, snatching up her bag of belongings. 'You just don't understand.'

'No, I do not,' said Yrlandriar, his heart sinking as Thirianna took another step towards the door. He had failed, and now Thirianna would suffer the same fate as Mythrairnin. He tried to calm himself, but the mere thought of his daughter becoming an Aspect Warrior filled him with foreboding.

'Can you not see how selfish this is?' he said, spitting the accusation at his daughter. Her anger deepened and Yrlandriar realised he was not conveying what he meant properly. She simply would not listen to what he was saying. 'Why do you have to do this to me?'

'This is not about you, father,' said Thirianna. 'Why does everything have to be about you? And you accuse me of being selfish!'

'You are making a mistake,' he said. He had let Mythrairnin leave for the shrines without argument and was not going to do the same with Thirianna. 'You are being hasty and immature.'

'I am not being immature,' said Thirianna, her tone cold. 'As a child you would always tell me what to do. I will not accept that any more. You cannot control me; I am not your possession. You should support me, and understand that I have to do this. I have little left to remember mother, but perhaps I can know her a bit better if I follow upon the Path she trod.'

'That path leads to death and despair,' said Yrlandriar. The slightest hint of the thought that Thirianna would die as well sent a chill through every part of him. It would be too much to bear and he could not allow it, for the sake of both of them. 'I forbid this. As your father, I cannot allow you to do this.'

'Forbid?' Thirianna's voice rose to a piercing pitch. 'Forbid? I am not some lump of wraithbone to be moulded and shaped and teased by your command. That is your problem, father. You think that you can be the master of everything you touch. Well, you will not be my master. Turn your fingers to another purpose and leave me to live my life as I choose.'

Yrlandriar could think of nothing else to say that he had not said already, over and over. He had known that he and Thirianna were becoming estranged, and had expected her to leave even sooner. Yet to learn that she was to tread in the footsteps of Khaine was too much for him to accept.

Thirianna stopped at the door and gave him a

final backwards glance. Was that hesitation he saw? Did she wait for some last argument from him to dissuade her from this madness?

It did not matter. Clearly he had failed. He had failed Thirianna and he had failed the legacy of Mythrairnin. Both of them were lost to him and perhaps they were the better for it.

'Just leave,' he said, turning away, finding no consolation in his decision.

AFTER RETURNING TO her body, Thirianna excused herself from Kelamith and left the Chambers of the Seers. She did not return to her own rooms, but instead took the gravrail across Alaitoc, back to the Tower of Ascendant Flames where she had been raised.

The tower was close to the hub of Alaitoc, the highest on the craftworld, a massive edifice of walkways and bridges and balconies and windows. She sat on a bench hidden away in the depths of the park surrounding the tower, beside a pool filled with blue-scaled skyfins and purple dawnsails. In the bushes nearby, a green-furred leathervole rustled through the fallen leaves, its ridged proboscis nuzzling through the mulch.

Thirianna allowed herself to relax, concentrating on the small details of the scene. Yet for all that she tried to separate herself from what Kelamith had shown her, the experience continued to tickle away in the depths of her mind. She had deliberately closed off the memories from the skein, unwilling to relive them until she had settled herself. It had been a cruel tactic of Kelamith, one that was now blatantly manipulative, and part of her railed against the farseer's transparent bullying.

Though she refused to recall in detail what she had witnessed, she could not avoid the imprint they had left upon her consciousness. Thoughts of her father were still overwhelmingly associated with frustration, but the edge was not so keen, her anger not quite so sharp.

Thirianna could not quite believe the cold-hearted behaviour of Kelamith in subjecting her to such distress, but she realised that whatever his intentions she was left to deal with the consequences.

Carefully, like someone opening a door a crack to peer into the room beyond, Thirianna peeled back the layer of ignorance shielding her recent memories. She veered away from those of her mother, instantly feeling a stab of pain as soon as she approached them. It was her father that concerned Kelamith, and now her, and so it was to that train of experience that she now paid attention.

Reviewing what she knew of Yrlandriar, she was no closer to forgiving him for his selfish ways. It had been wrong of him to shut Thirianna out from his feelings after the death of her mother, no matter how he justified it to himself.

Yet despite that, Thirianna had now seen herself through his eyes, and that was something she could not simply ignore. While his behaviour had been poor and his reasoning unsound, Yrlandriar's decision to withdraw into himself had not been helped by Thirianna's increasingly demanding nature. The more she had pushed for his attention, the further he had withdrawn from it, fleeing his daughter as if she were the spectre of her dead mother.

As hard as it was to accept, Thirianna came to the conclusion that she had acted selfishly as well. She had made no attempt to bridge the dark gulf between them and had simply expected her father to cross the divide and come to her.

Thirianna was upset and scared by how little empathy existed between her and Yrlandriar. How could father and daughter grow apart so swiftly? In retrospect, it occurred to her that it was what they had both desired, even if only subconsciously. Without Mythrairnin to bind them together, each of them considered themselves and the other best left to be on their own.

If Kelamith had expected some great change of Thirianna's outlook, some revelatory thawing of her feelings towards her father, he was going to be disappointed. The farseer's callous stunt in the infinity circuit did not deserve such a reward and Thirianna was appalled that Kelamith had thought it plausible. Despite everything, she still considered her father a stranger, and she owed him nothing.

Rousing herself from her reverie, Thirianna looked up at the Tower of Ascendant Flames, silhouetted against the dim glow of the dying star. She had been born up amongst the cloud-wreathed heights of the tower, but her life had not started until she had left. She could not defend her father in any way. He had not tried to do his best; he had made little attempt to give her the love and affection she needed.

With that thought came a realisation. It was not her father's love she desired, not his apologies nor his forgiveness. All she required of him was a rune, fashioned from wraithbone.

He was a stranger and she was attaching too many other emotions to the relationship. It did not matter whether they were father and daughter, whether they agreed on her choices in life. He was a bonesinger and she was a seer. She required a rune, and he would make it for her.

THE FOLLOWING CYCLE, Thirianna returned to her father's workshop. Yrlandriar was working on the starship frame, but she waited patiently for him to return, examining the pieces on display. Many were unfinished, their purpose, whether functional or artistic, not clear. Others were little more than three-dimensional sketches, rough shapes and angles that held some semblance of the form they would become but nothing more. There seemed to be quite a few of these which she had not seen before, which led Thirianna to wonder if perhaps Yrlandriar was trying in his own way to come to terms with their fresh meeting and not yet succeeding to find the means.

Her father announced himself as he returned, and Thirianna put back the object she had been looking at with a pang of guilt. Remembering how mortified she would have felt had someone been examining her poems, she suddenly wondered if she was intruding into Yrlandriar's privacy.

The bonesinger did not seem surprised at her presence.

'So you have come back, Thirianna,' he said, sitting beside the table again.

'I wish you to fashion a rune for me, father,' she replied, using her most formal tone.

'And why would I do that for you?' said Yrlandriar. 'What you ask for is not some bauble. What assurances will I have that my efforts will not be wasted? That half a pass from now you will not have tired of being a seer and moved on to your next flight of fancy?'

Thirianna refused to rise to the taunt, and held her temper in check.

'None of us know for how long we might tread a Path, and it is not for you to judge anyone but yourself,' said Thirianna. 'I am committed to learning the secrets of the seer. Such is my commitment, I am willing to offer you an apology so that we might understand one another better.'

Yrlandriar raised an eyebrow in surprise.

'An apology?' He seemed genuinely pleased. 'What is it that you regret so much that it is worth apologising to me?'

'I am sorry that we do not like each other better, and do not know each other better,' Thirianna said. She bit back the criticisms that surfaced in her thoughts and paused, taking a breath before she continued. 'I am sorry that I did not realise that as much as I needed your comfort and attention following the death of my mother, you equally deserved the time and solitude to deal with your own loss.'

Yrlandriar swallowed hard, his expression softening. He glanced away, towards the looming bulk of the starship, and his next words were softly spoken.

'I am sorry also, Thirianna,' said the bonesinger. 'Sorry that I cannot mend the past as I might repair a broken spar or heal a splintered node.'

'I need your help now, father,' said Thirianna, the words coming with difficulty. 'Will you fashion a rune for me, so that I might learn to be a seer?'

Still looking away, Yrlandriar touched a finger to the side of the table. A shallow drawer slid out, and from this the bonesinger brought out a small object, as slender as one of his fingers. Finally he turned his gaze to Thirianna and his face was stern.

'It is not yet finished, but I was going to bring it to you when it was complete,' he said. 'Your coming here stirred up many painful memories for me, but I cannot blame you for that. More than anything else I have created, this has caused me much hardship. It is your rune, wrought in wraithbone, conjured forth by my hand and my will. Perhaps you will care for it better than I cared for you.'

'Thank you,' said Thirianna, bowing her head. 'It means much to me that you have done this.'

'Though it was not my intention, I raised a daughter who was strong of will and knows what she desires,' said Yrlandriar, placing the unfinished rune on the table top. 'I wish I could take some pride from that, but it leaves me hollow.'

'Pride is fleeting,' said Thirianna. She felt uncomfortable with the silence that followed and Yrlandriar was faring no better, fidgeting with the fittings of his gloves. 'I hope you will deliver it in person when it is finished.'

'I hope it guides you to a fulfilling future,' said Yrlandriar.

'It is folly to chase after fulfilment,' said Thirianna. 'If you taught me anything, it is to accept what fate brings us, good or ill. To deny that is to forever post-pone contentment.'

Yrlandriar nodded thoughtfully, his gaze straying back to the starship.

'I will not keep you from your other work,' said Thirianna.

Her father said nothing in reply, so she turned and left, resolving to find Kelamith as soon as possible.

POWER

The Siren Mirror – Eldanesh's Shield. As the ward of the Sire of the Eldar turned back the blows of his foes, so the Siren Mirror acts to reconstitute the energies of an enemy. One of several runes whose use is specific to battle, Eldanesh's Shield works by channelling the power of the skein harnessed by the enemy, so that it might be wielded in the favour of the seer.

THE RUNE OF Thirianna floated a little more than an arm's reach in front of her, utterly still. She drew the image of the rune into her thoughts as Kelamith had shown her, creating a bond between the mental and the physical. The rune glowed slightly with the psychic power and Thirianna could feel more energy flowing into her mind.

She sat in the middle of the main chamber of her apartments, performing the exercises passed on by the farseer. At first she attained control of the rune, mastering it to her purpose. When balance was met, she took the power of the rune into herself.

Now that she had completed the first two stages, she could choose how to wield the psychic energy that was now hers to possess. Thirianna chose an external focus, using the rune to extend her influence on the physical world. She concentrated her thoughts, narrowing them to a single point at the centre of the rune.

The rune acted as an amplifier, adding power from the skein to Thirianna's innate psychic energy. With this, the seer reached out across the room, picking up several objects from the tables and shelves: a brush, a necklace, her discarded bag and a small bust of Asuryan. Thirianna's eyes flickered from one to the other as she moved them around the chamber, delicately placing each one in a new position.

She repeated the exercise, moving the objects back to their original places, but this time with her eyes closed, using only the psychic aura of the rune to guide her thoughts. With gentle psychic pushes, she nudged each object back into place.

Opening her eyes, Thirianna noted with some satisfaction that she had restored the room perfectly. She turned her attention to a wide dish set on the floor in front of her, a small square of cloth laid inside the metallic bowl. Thirianna set her mind to the task of examining the cloth scrap at the smallest level, passing into its weave, down to the individual molecules of the material. She set the atoms dancing, agitating them with the power of her thought, exciting the air molecules around the cloth.

After a few moments, the scrap burst into flames, burning with a pale blue colour. It quickly turned to ash, settling into the bottom of the dish, gently stirred by the breeze drifting in through the open window.

They were small things she did, but it was not safe to practise the greater powers that were being unveiled to her, at least not in the confines of her apartment. There were rooms in the Chambers of the Seers, rune-shielded and psychically warded, where she had unleashed some of the more extreme abilities she was now learning to control.

The rune had another purpose and it was to this that Thirianna now turned her attention.

With the image of her symbol still fixed foremost in her thoughts, Thirianna made the transition to the skein. No longer did she need the infinity circuit to make the journey; her thoughts were able to flow between the realms of the real and unreal with the smallest effort.

It was a liberating experience for Thirianna to know how far she had progressed. As Kelamith had told her, the runecraft increased her powers exponentially. As she floated in the aether of the skein, Thirianna marvelled at how much she could do with just a single rune, and was eager to increase her powers further. The most experienced farseers, like Kelamith, could control a dozen or more runes at a time. Thirianna could only speculate at the possibilities that would open up to her, though such a thing was still a distant dream.

Being one and the same with the rune, Thirianna was able to instantly find her own life thread in the insane tangle of the skein. She fixed herself upon the current moment, her rune appearing as a marker in her thoughts.

Kelamith had warned her not to roam too far ahead of the present, not until she was strong enough to cope with the multiplicity of fates that would unfold. After her wayward adventure in the webway, Thirianna heeded her tutor's warning and restricted herself to peeking just a few cycles ahead.

She was amazed by the number of overlapping threads, the volume of lives upon which every life touched, whether directly or indirectly. Decisions she made echoed up through the possible futures, creating branch after branch of potential fates. In turn, her life thread twisted and turned, shaped by events and the actions of others, sometimes becoming hazy during periods of great uncertainty, other times becoming taut and thick when she was in full control of her destiny.

One thread in particular bonded itself to hers very shortly, the next cycle in fact. She investigated, and found that it belonged to Korlandril. Everything became uncertain as she looked closer, the act of her observation obscuring the potentialities that were being revealed.

Leaving her rune as a beacon to bring her back, Thirianna moved away from her own life and followed Korlandril's. It was steeped in darkness and bloodshed, tainted by Khaine's touch as Korlandril followed the Path of the Warrior.

Something strange happened next and Thirianna could not quite work out what it foreshadowed. One of Korlandril's possible futures merged with that of another. The two existences did not just entwine or knot together, they became a single thread. Looking more closely, pushing back visions of bloodshed and battle that tried to encroach on her thoughts, Thirianna examined the composite thread and saw that it was not just Korlandril's life that was meshed within its fibres. There were others, coming from across the skein at different times, each becoming a small part of the whole.

The merged life of Korlandril and the others stretched on without turning or breaking, slashing through the future like a bloodied blade. With some shock, Thirianna realised what the skein was showing her. Korlandril's spirit was being subsumed into a greater presence, that of an exarch of the Bloody-Handed God.

Korlandril risked becoming trapped on the Path of the Warrior.

Thirianna located her rune and returned to it, before she effortlessly slipped out of the skein and back into her body.

She wondered what to do. She had not nearly enough skill or experience to delve further into Korlandril's possible paths and what she had seen was only one of several possible outcomes. As when she had foreseen his injury during the battle against the orks, there was no means by which she could accurately predict what would happen in the long term should Korlandril take one course over another.

The perils of causality, a lecture oft-repeated by Kelamith, came to Thirianna. It was a simple premise: by acting upon an observation one might bring about the foreseen, undesired event. Sometimes a seer's actions would influence the passage of fate, so that the observer became the cause. It was just one of many pitfalls waiting for the unwary voyager into the future, one that every seer had to confront if they were to fulfil their potential. The very essence of the seer was to guide Alaitoc and its people past the dangers and conflicts of the future; yet it was a delicate balancing act judging when to intervene and when to allow fate to take its own course.

In short, as Thirianna had once summarised it to Kelamith, the lesson was not to interfere unless you were sure of the outcome.

Thirianna was far from sure of the outcome if she chose to act on what she had seen. Could she prevent Korlandril's entrapment, or would she somehow, or had she already, precipitated it? Not only that, if she was to find herself in the position that she could avert Korlandril's journey to becoming an exarch, was it right that she should do so? Until she was more accomplished, she could not venture far enough across the skein to see the possible implications of Korlandril's futures.

Like so many of the questions posed by Kelamith, it was an impossible conundrum, one that was far beyond Thirianna's rudimentary scrying skills and ethical reasoning.

There was only one conclusion she could come to, though it pained her to admit, just as it had pained her to allow Korlandril to be injured. She was in no position to judge what was right and wrong and would simply have to allow what was to come to pass to do so. Though it might turn out to be a personal tragedy for Korlandril, and for Thirianna, Korlandril's possible entrapment could have implications far beyond their lives, and to change it might be to endanger the lives of others.

THIRIANNA WAITED BENEATH a snowpetal in the Garden of Heavenly Delights, reading a treatise on the Rune of the Golden Sail passed to her by Kelamith. She had seen herself meeting Korlandril here and despite her decision not to interfere with the course of events as she had foreseen, Thirianna had decided to allow the meeting to take place.

She felt Korlandril approaching, his warrior spirit cutting across the skein like a bubble drifting across a pool of blood. She turned and feigned surprise as he reached the shade of the tree.

Korlandril was dressed in a pleated robe of dark green, the same colour as the Striking Scorpion armour he wore in battle. He walked with quiet assurance, his eyes scanning the parklands constantly, seemingly poised for action. Thirianna could sense the spirit of Khaine hiding under the surface, a coiled serpent waiting for the opportunity to strike.

Pushing back a rising distaste, Thirianna remembered that they were friends and she embraced Korlandril, trying not to shudder at the warrior's cold touch. Taken aback, he hesitated before wrapping his arms around her.

'I heard that you had been injured,' Thirianna said, stepping back to regard Korlandril, assuring herself that he had recovered. It was better that she did not reveal her foreknowledge of his grim injury.

'I am healed,' he replied with a smile. 'Physically, at least.'

Korlandril gestured to the bench and the two of them sat side-by-side. Thirianna was about to ask him how he was feeling, but stopped herself. It was a foolish question, and one that would invite her to say something she might regret.

'What is wrong?' Korlandril asked.

Despite her earlier confidence, seeing her friend's concern weakened Thirianna's resolve. She could not simply let him become trapped as a warrior. She decided that even if she did not act directly, a timely reminder of the perils associated with being an Aspect Warrior would not go amiss.

'I was going to visit you, as there is something you should know.' It was a lie, but Thirianna believed it would be better for Korlandril not to know that she had intended to allow him to travel to his doom without her intervention. 'I would rather we spoke about other matters first, but you have caught me unawares. There is no pleasant way to say this. I have read your runes. They are confused, but many of your futures do not bode well.'

Korlandril spoke with assurance, dismissing her concerns with a frown. 'There is nothing to fear. I have suffered some tribulations of late, but they will not defeat me.'

'It is that which worries me,' Thirianna said. She reached out and laid her palm briefly on his cheek, but he flinched at the touch. 'I sense confrontation in you. You see every encounter as a battle to be won. The Path of the Warrior is taking its toll upon you.'

'It was one slip of concentration, nothing more,' said Korlandril, standing up. He stepped away from Thirianna. 'I stumbled but the journey goes on.'

'I have no idea what you are talking about,' said Thirianna. Korlandril's confidence had become defensiveness, his remarks an overreaction. 'Has something else happened?'

'It is nothing important, not of concern to the likes of you.'

'The likes of me?' Thirianna was upset more than angry. How swiftly Korlandril had forgotten the past they shared. 'No concern of a friend?'

Korlandril looked guilty, eyes downcast, unable to meet her gaze.

'I almost struck a genuine blow during a ritual settlement.'

Thirianna knew what a dishonour that would be. It also confirmed her suspicions. If Korlandril could not maintain control of his murderous impulses in the shrine, it was a sign of the growing grip Khaine had on his spirit.

'Oh, Korlandril...' she said.

'What?' he said. Anger flashed across his face, his

brow knotted, teeth briefly bared. 'You speak to me like a child. It happened. I will learn from it.'

'Will you?' There was no contrition in Korlandril, as if he sought confrontation. Thirianna remembered Korlandril's comment of 'the likes of you' from earlier and wanted to assure him that she understood better than he realised. 'Do not forget that I have been a Dire Avenger. Though that time lives in the mists of my past, it is not so old that I forget it entirely. Until recently I trod the Path of the Warlock. As a warrior-seer, I revisited many of my battle-memories, drawing on them for resolve and strength. I recall the lure of the Warrior's Way; the surety of purpose it brings and the comfort of righteousness.'

'There is no fault to be found with having the strength of one's convictions.' Korlandril's fists were balled and his shoulders hunched with aggression. It frightened Thirianna to see him this way, and the surety of what she had seen made her more determined to help him back from the brink of a lifetime of hatred and bloodshed.

'It is a drug, that sense of power and superiority,' she warned. 'The war-mask allows you to control your rage and guilt in battle, it is not meant to extinguish all feeling outside of war. Even now I sense that you are angry with me.'

'What if I am? You sit there and talk of things you do not understand. It does not matter whether you have trodden the Path of the Warrior, you and I are not the same. That much you made clear to me before I joined the Deadly Shadow. Perhaps *you* felt tempted by the power. I have a stronger will.'

Thirianna could not stop herself from laughing at the ridiculousness of the accusation. She had successfully passed from warrior to poet; he was the one that was becoming trapped.

'Nothing has changed with you,' Thirianna replied, angry as much with herself as her friend, for allowing herself to get involved. 'You have learnt nothing! I offer comfort and you take criticism. Perhaps you are right. Perhaps it is not the Path of the Warrior that makes you this arrogant; you have always been so self-involved.'

'Self-involved?' Korlandril's voice rose with disbelief. He stepped back and visibly took a breath, trying to calm himself. When he spoke next, his voice was scornful. 'You it was that fluttered in the light of my attention, promising much but ultimately willing to give nothing. If I am selfish it is because you have taken from me that which I would have happily given myself to.'

'I was wrong, you are not selfish,' said Thirianna.

She wondered how the two of them had ever been friends. Her patience was wearing thin with Korlandril's sense of self-importance. Had he always been this pompous?

'You are self-deluding! Rationalisation and justification are all that you can offer in your defence. Take a long look at yourself, Korlandril, and then tell me that this is my fault.'

Korlandril stalked back and forth for a moment, like a caged animal seeking escape. For a heartbeat, Thirianna feared the Aspect Warrior would become violent. It was clear that his war-mask was thinning, the rage of his battle-spirit mingling with his personality away from the shrine and war.

'You are jealous!' Korlandril rasped. 'Once I was infatuated with you, and now you cannot bear the thought that I might live my life outside of your shadow. Elissanadrin, perhaps? You believe that I have developed feelings for another, and suddenly you do not feel you are unique in my affections.'

'I had no idea that you had moved your ambitions to another,' replied Thirianna. She had no idea who Elissanadrin was, but if she was fool enough to consort with Korlandril, Thirianna felt sorry for her. 'I am glad. I would rather you sought the company of someone else, as you are no longer welcome in mine.'

'This was a mistake,' he said. 'You are not worth the grief you bring, nor the time you consume.'

A grim realisation dawned on Thirianna. Her fear of involving herself with Korlandril had been correct. Their confrontation was just another blow upon the slender barricade that kept Korlandril's anger in check. She began to sob, burying her face in her hands, knowing that she had probably moved him closer to entrapment, against her every intention.

She recovered a little and looked up, finding that Korlandril had departed without any farewell or parting word. It was with bleak thoughts that Thirianna left the park. Her unsubtle interference, despite knowing that it might prove ill, had possibly doomed her friend. Far from helping Korlandril, her clumsy attempts at a warning might well have brought about the very fate she had wanted to avoid.

Thirianna wondered, for the first time since she had escaped the webway, whether she was suited to the life of the seer. She had wanted answers, to know the consequences of her actions and their effect on others. In reality, the more she learnt, the further she delved into the secrets of the skein, the less certain she was of anything.

THE FLAMES THAT licked along the edges of the witch-blade were a pleasing violet hue. Thirianna's rune glowed with the same colour as it slowly orbited the hilt of the weapon, its aura dimming and brightening in tune with the ebb and flow of the psychic flames. The purple haze gleamed from Thirianna's rune armour and was reflected from the golden sigils inscribed into the walls of the hexagonal chamber.

Thirianna wore no helm – and had not drawn up her war-mask – and her eyes glittered with psychic power as she concentrated on the witchblade. When first she had taken it up, it had been an extension of her body. Now it was becoming an extension of her mind. With a thought, she reduced the flames to a dull gleam; with another they burst into full life.

Thirianna stepped and chopped, leaving a violet trail of light where the blade passed. She cut and thrust, side-stepped, parried and thrust again, the tip of the sword leaving a glowing imprint in the air. She had not noticed it before, but the burning trail of the witchblade left rune-impressions on the air, writing death and destruction in its wake.

Spinning to a new posture, Thirianna levelled the witchblade at chest height and unleashed the power of the psychic fire. The violet flames roared across the room, splashing against the rune-covered walls. Thirianna's rune spun madly, turning over lengthwise as she poured more psychic energy into the blast, adjusting the aim of the witchblade with small wrist movements.

Imagining an unexpected attack, she brought the weapon up to the guard position, as her mind wreathed the flames into a disc of fire to ward away the blow. She whirled, her robe flapping at her legs, bringing the witchblade to the attack in a new direction, setting loose three pulses of flame that exploded against the psychic shield of the wall in purple blossoms.

A chime sounded, alerting her to an approaching visitor. As she drew back her power, the swiftest delve into the infinity circuit revealed the arrival to be Kelamith. It was unexpected. She had not seen the farseer for more than a dozen cycles and it seemed that he had been content to allow her to practise with blade and rune without supervision.

Stowing the weapon in its sheath, Thirianna powered down the protective runes and opened the archway to allow Kelamith to enter. The farseer was dressed in his full regalia, his crystal-lensed helmet tucked under one arm.

'Battle approaches,' he said. 'Come with me to the council of seers. The autarchs will be needing our guidance.'

Thirianna nodded, and with a twitch of her finger sent her rune into a pouch at her belt. She opened her sword hand and the witchblade reluctantly floated back to its place on the wall. She followed the farseer through the Chambers of the Seers, heading towards the central hall where the council gathered. She had seen it before, a high-ceilinged dome of dark blue, pierced with diamond-like gems that glittered as the starry sky. Benches lined the walls, and to one of these Kelamith led Thirianna. He directed her to sit as other seers filed into the chamber, the farseers gathering on the central dais while the warlocks and lesser seers took their places on the marble benches.

It was quite a crowd, all thirteen of Alaitoc's far-seers present and nearly four times that number of other psykers. Thirianna exchanged thoughts of greeting with those around her and received the same in reply, some formal, others genuinely warm and welcoming. All was done without lips moving, telepathic contacts that took moments to convey what would take a lengthy conversation to say. A few remarked that this was Thirianna's first council and she responded with nervousness and excitement.

The autarchs then entered, emerging from the gra-vrail station beside the hall, coming from the Aspect shrines where they held their own gatherings.

The autarchs, three of them, were dressed in ornate armour. Thirianna could sense the antiquity of their wargear, generations of death steeped in the plates and mesh. Arhathain wore dark blue armour chased with gold detail, a white cloak hanging from his shoulders, a long spear in his right hand; Neurthuil's armour was also blue, though of a clear sky and decorated with silver, the metallic wings of her flightpack folded close, a three-barrelled lasblaster hanging from its strap over her shoulder; Akolthiar's armour was red and orange, his face hidden behind the grille of a Banshee mask, a long-muzzled fusion pistol at his waist, a red-bladed axe in hand.

All three had trodden the Path of the Warrior many times and all three had proven strong enough to resist the lure of Khaine. Though Thirianna had no desire to become a warrior again, she was filled with admiration and respect for the three commanders, inspired by their discipline and purpose.

It was Arhathain, chief amongst the autarchs, who spoke first.

'We have received warning from this council that a threat emerges.' His voice was quiet and assured, deep and full of authority. 'The word has been passed to the exarchs and the Aspect shrines ready for battle. We seek guidance from the council.'

'The council is ready to guide,' Alaiteir replied formally, the farseer gesturing to one of his companions.

'The skein ripples with conflict,' said Laimmain, her fingers moving as three runes emerged from her belt and took up station in front of her. 'Worse, the taint of the Great Enemy falls upon the thread of Alaitoc.'

An aura of consternation filled the hall and Thirianna's heart beat faster while recent memories threatened to surface. She pushed back the rebellious recollections and focussed on the farseers.

'An artefact has been unearthed, brought out

of hiding by the reckless inquisitiveness of the humans,' continued Kelamith. 'It is a small thing but possessed of a great power to corrupt.'

'For the moment it is dormant,' said Laimmain, picking up the explanation again. 'Yet the humans' curiosity and greed will cause them to delve into its properties and their spirits will be ensnared, their dreams given form by this subtle and deadly creation.'

'This wicked artefact will work its malice, eating at their minds, perverting their ambitions,' said Alaiteir. 'They will become enamoured of this thing, slaves to the will of She Who Thirsts.'

'Their depravity will be hidden at first, yet they are rulers of a world, important agents of the Emperor, and their corruption will go unnoticed but reach far,' said Kelamith. 'In just a short time, a passing of three of their generations, they will secretly revere the Great Enemy. In madness and desire, they will call upon She Who Thirsts to deliver them power so that they might escape the rule of the Emperor and thus seal their pact with darkness.'

'Such a thing would be ill enough,' said Anuraina. She summoned an image into being with a wave of her hand. It showed an arc of the galaxy, a swirl of stars that Thirianna recognised as being only a few light years from Alaitoc. 'In their ignorance, the humans will fail, but their inexpert ritual shall weaken the boundaries between the realm of the mortal and the immortal.'

The projected image swirled and changed. Thirianna recognised it as a vision from the skein, similar to the ever-fluctuating, slightly amorphous view from her own journeys into the possibility of futures. The vision centred on a particular star and then closed with the fifth planet in orbit. The sky around the orb seethed with daemonic energy, as the warp breached into the material universe, bringing the power of Chaos into the physical realm.

'The contagion from this daemonic invasion will spread to neighbouring star systems,' said Kelamith, as the image continued to evolve, presenting a view of debasement and destruction across seven more worlds. 'These forces will be harnessed by those who wish us harm. Guided by the Great Enemy, the forces of Chaos will strike at Alaitoc.'

The next vision was even more horrifying. It showed the vessels of the craftworld overrun by daemons of She Who Thirsts, breaking open the crystal vaults of the ships' infinity circuits, supping at the eldar spirits held within. Gasps and disgusted whispers rippled through the auditorium. Thirianna looked away, sickened by what she saw.

'All of this can be averted with a strike now,' said Alaiteir. The vision presented by Anuraina dissipated and was replaced by a shadowed view of a human citadel. 'The object that will cause so much strife is being brought here. It is poorly defended, a journey of no more than a few days from Alaitoc.'

'And what is the objective?' asked Arhathain. 'The item must be recovered or destroyed, that much is clear. What of its corrupting effect?'

'All in the citadel may have been touched by its presence,' said Kelamith. 'Even if we recover the artefact, who can say what its lingering taint might damage in the future?'

'All in the citadel must be slain,' said Alaiteir.

'Are you sure that is necessary?' asked Akolthiar.

'You seem concerned to protect the humans,' said Kelamith. 'We speak of only a few hundred lives, nothing more.'

'It is not the expenditure of the humans that I question,' replied the autarch. 'The more to be slain, the greater the risk to eldar lives. Not only will it require more warriors to risk themselves in battle, such a strike may provoke a response from the humans.'

'We have delved into this,' said Kelamith. 'There is no consequence to Alaitoc if we strike swiftly and surely. The humans will remain unaware of our part in the attack, and those that suspect will be left no proof of our involvement. Alaitoc will not be blamed.'

'If that is so, then I agree,' said Akolthiar.

'We have consent,' said Arhathain. 'We will begin preparations for a battleship to convey the warhost to this world. Opposition will be minimal. The Aspect temples will be sufficient to deal with the matter.'

'We shall continue to scry the battle-fate of your warriors,' said Laimmain. 'Several of us will accompany you to the world to ensure that nothing goes amiss.'

'And the artefact?' said Arhathain.

'We have already despatched a message to the white seers,' said Kelamith. 'They will meet us at the human world and stand ready to take possession of the artefact. The Great Enemy's wiles are many; be sure that your warriors are fully prepared.'

'The Aspect Warriors will not be turned by this object,' said Arhathain. He looked at the assembled seers. 'Be sure that none of your number are beguiled by its presence either.'

The farseers looked displeased at the suggestion, but bowed their heads in deference to the autarchs, formally passing on the burden of the battle to the military leaders.

When the autarchs had departed, a discussion ensued between the seers. It was decided that Kelamith and Laimmain would accompany the force, along with Thirianna, Aladricas and Naomennin.

'To practise one's skills in the peace and safety of the craftworld is one matter,' Kelamith said to Thirianna as they walked back to her apartment. 'It is another to employ them in the anarchy of war and unleash them upon living creatures. This will be a valuable if somewhat difficult experience for you.'

Thirianna said nothing, something in her memories stirring inside, haunting her. Kelamith detected her reticence.

'This is not some scheme of mine to have you confront your unkind past,' said the farseer. 'We will need your skills if we are to avert this threat to our people. Whatever issues you may have with the slaying of potential innocents, set them aside now. To see the peril and not act would not only doom Alaitoc, it would be an insult to those who have long striven to harness this power for our protection.'

'I understand,' said Thirianna, though she felt

uneasy about the coming battle.

'We do not leave for another two cycles,' said Kelamith. 'Use that time to confront whatever doubts are nagging. In battle, you will not be given the luxury of hesitation or laxity.'

'I will be prepared,' Thirianna assured him, though she was loath to reveal to herself the malign memory she had taken great pains to lock away in the deepest parts of her mind. 'When you call, I will be ready.'

THIRIANNA WAITED IN the dark antechamber in the Shrine of One Hundred Bloody Tears, sensing the exarch in the room behind her calling the Dire Avengers to battle. She knew that she would have to reach into her memory and bring out the experience she had shut away. It was concealed firmly behind her war-mask, and Kelamith had hinted that the coming battle might bring it forth without Thirianna's volition. Better now, she had decided, to confront this potential nightmare in the sanctuary of the shrine, than risk it taking her unawares at a critical moment.

She began the mantra that brought forth her war-mask. She paused as it was settling into place, keeping a hold of her normal self to avoid being consumed with bloodlust. The witchblade in her hands thrummed with life, woken by her dark thoughts.

Placing the blade to one side, disassociating herself from its war-hunger, Thirianna sat cross-legged in the middle of the chamber and closed her eyes. She pushed through the red film of the war-mask and opened herself to the memories that lay beyond.

Dozens of recollections flooded through her, each a vista of death, a vignette of bloodshed. She shuddered, caught between the horror of the atrocities she committed and the ecstatic feeling that had flowed through her when she had perpetrated them.

Yet there was nothing there that caused her greater concern than before. She had seen these things when she had prepared for the battle with the orks. There was another memory, so vile to her she had cast it down into the abyss of her thoughts, where even her warrior-self would not have to contemplate it.

She baulked for a moment, afraid to venture further. Her skin felt slick with the blood of those she had slain, her ears rang with their wounded cries and death rattles, her heart pounded with the sensation of their fleeing life.

Thirianna withdrew a little way, allowing the warrior-memories to recede, leaving her in peace again. She slowed her heart and breathing, instilling calm. If she were to unleash this dark memory she would have to do it swiftly, diving past the other recollections into its lair.

Hardening her heart as much as she could, filled with trepidation, Thirianna thrust herself into the past, sweeping past the battles into the dark maelstrom of her innermost secret thoughts.

IT WAS SOME kind of eating area. A long table flanked by high-backed seats stretched the length of the room, set with plates and candlesticks as if ready for a meal. Thirianna heard a whimpering noise and leapt onto the table. She ran along its length, picking her way between the dishes and candlesticks without thought.

At the far end of the room was another seating area, with overstuffed chairs and a round table. In the corner cowered a female human. With her were three children, one male, two female. Their faces were red and wet, their eyes glistening.

The taint of Chaos permeates this place, said Kelamith. *All must be purged.*

The humans made whimpering, animal noises as Thirianna brought up her shuriken catapult.

The eldest female, the mother, shrieked something, covering the children with herself. Thirianna ignored her wails and opened fire, shredding the woman's body.

The children screamed, their tear-streaked faces spattered with the blood of their mother. The largest of them, the boy, leapt to his feet and charged Thirianna. She reacted without thought, stepping aside from his clumsily swinging fists. She swung the shuriken catapult, bringing it down on the back of the boy's neck, easily snapping the young human's spine. He flopped to the lacquered floor without a further sound.

The two girls squirmed, trying to free themselves from the dead weight of their mother, eyes wide with horror as their brother's corpse twitched in front of them.

Thirianna looked at the youngest. She was barely old enough to walk, yet the look in her eyes seemed weighed with a lifetime of sorrow. The Aspect

Warrior fired again, ripping out the child's throat with a short salvo. The last struggled to her feet and turned to run. It was futile and she went down in a mess of blood and ragged dress, her blonde locks covering her face as she tumbled onto a rug.

Thirianna looked at the sprawling bodies, the swirl of their blood and the splay of their dead limbs. They had been so fragile, so easy to slay.

She laughed.

FALLING TO ONE side, Thirianna let out a wild howl of despair. Her own laughter echoed around the chamber, haunting and deliberate, full of contempt for life. The seer clasped her head in her hands, filled with guilt and shame, her body convulsing as she remembered every fleck of blood on the faces of the dead children. She saw the edges of the mother's ribs, bloody and scratched from the shurikens, poking out from beneath her laced bodice. She could smell the blood, hear the crying.

Every part of her wanted to flee. Thirianna resisted the urge to hurl the memory back into the blackness, a tiny part of her strong enough to face the full fury of her own violence. Over and over she watched the family dying, yet it never dimmed, and the memory of her exultation at the act wrenched at her spirit each time.

Panting, Thirianna forced herself to her feet. She had to accept this; she had to acknowledge that part of her capable of committing such an act. They were only humans, she told herself, but her justification felt hollow. They were not innocent, she reasoned, they were tainted by Chaos, but she knew that it was a delusion.

I am a murderer, she thought.

Another part of her mind railed against the accusation. Her war-mask flowed, bringing out her warrior spirit. She had been a Dire Avenger, incarnation of a purifying flame. She had slain hundreds, guilt or innocence were irrelevant.

It was not the act itself that so appalled Thirianna, it was the joy it had brought.

It sickened her, that laugh, the utter disregard for life that she had shown. It rang again in her ears, chilling, devoid of compassion. The slaughter may have been justified or not, it may have been a necessary precaution or cold-blooded murder. What Thirianna could not deny was the satisfaction it had brought. It had not been an act of instinct in the heat of battle, a life-or-death decision to slay or be slain. It had been cold-hearted, reasoned, and was all the more enjoyable for it.

The heinous act had thrilled her so much because she had known full well what it was she was doing. It was the simple matter of doing the unthinkable, without blame or shame, which had been exhilarating. It was a true moment of Khaine's bloody work, unhampered by logic or morality.

Another thought burst through Thirianna's internal recriminations. Even in her moment of high-handed triumph, she had known she was bewitched with the bloodshed. After the battle she had quit the Shrine of One Hundred Bloody Tears, turning her back on the Bloody-Handed God, forever expunged of her desire for war.

The act, callous as it was, had freed her from Khaine's grip.

Focussing on this, Thirianna recovered some of her equilibrium. As the visceral nature of the memory subsided, she was able to hold on to that simple fact: at her darkest moment she had triumphed. She had stood upon the brink of accepting Khaine's embrace, of becoming enamoured of death and blood-letting, but it had not trapped her.

It was the nature of the Path that a life be composed of many such moments, where one trod the line between safety and utter obsession. Thirianna had passed the test, and she had moved on. It was only from shirking her duty to those she had slain, by trying to forget them, that she had poisoned herself.

The memory was quickly losing its power to unbalance her. The more she examined it, the more Thirianna consoled herself to the grievous act. Confronting what she had done, she could feel the guilt and shame she had not felt at the time. In accepting the punishment, the raw feeling that sang along her nerves, she could atone for her bloody ways.

Reaching out a hand, Thirianna called to her witchblade. It leapt to her grasp, singing its own deadly song. She Who Thirsts threatened again, through the humans once more. Thirianna would have to kill again, not only to save her own life, but to save the lives of future Alaitocii. Human lives would be saved too, though they would never comprehend the benefit for themselves. The thought did not make what she had to do easy, but it made it a fraction more palatable.

Thirianna heard the dull chanting of the Dire Avengers in the adjoining chamber. Their ritual was coming to its climax, as each would be daubing the rune of the shrine on their foreheads and taking up their war-masks.

She crossed the room and lifted her helm from its hook. She too was ready.

THE ELDAR BATTLEPLAN was a thing of complex beauty. Like so many human worlds, the eyes of the defenders were ever turned outwards, seeking threats that would approach openly. Not only had they allowed the machinations of Chaos to enter unhindered into their lives, the humans were incapable of defending themselves against any foe more advanced. Their orbital stations and crude surveying satellites scanned the void for disturbances in the warp, expecting enemy ships to enter their system in the outermost reaches, far from the gravitational pull of their sun.

The eldar suffered from no such restriction. The webway passed close by to the human world and though it was not without some effort, it was a straightforward task to extend a temporary tunnel into the system. The battleship *Fainoriain* and two destroyers had exited the webway inside the ring of detection devices, and hidden by holofields and other screening devices, the eldar had devised their method of attack.

The Chaos artefact had been taken to the citadel

seen in the visions of the farseers. Swiftly monitoring the humans' unencrypted communications revealed that this fortress was a retreat for members of a mercantile cadre that effectively ruled the world under the auspices of the Emperor's agencies. It was protected by physical walls and gun turrets, but had no defence against the eldar.

In layout the fortress was an octagon, protected by walls of hewn stone, within which a courtyard of dull grey slabs contained several buildings. At each angle of the walls was located a defence battery, multi-barrelled cannons pointing to the skies beside small guardhouses. The main citadel was located not quite at the centre, a slightly smaller tower in its shadow. Several one-storey buildings surrounded these two structures, storehouses with wide doors and no windows. Flags hung limply from poles along the walls, and spotlights glared out into the night beyond.

Such defiance was in vain against the eldar.

The first wave of Aspect Warriors emerged from the webway within these defences and swiftly secured the walls and outer courtyard, cutting down all resistance with shuriken catapults and missile launchers. As the anti-air batteries were overrun, Swooping Hawks descended from the night skies to bolster the attack, dropping onto the worn battlements with plasma detonations and strobing lasblasters.

Thirianna noted in passing that Korlandril was amongst those fighting, the Striking Scorpions of the Deadly Shadow tasked with taking one of the warehouse-like outer buildings. He seemed to have recovered from his injury and his thread across the skein was strong.

Glad that her former friend would not suffer a repeat of the trauma of his last battle, Thirianna followed Kelamith down an alley between two of the warehouses. While Dire Avengers, Dark Reapers, Howling Banshees and Fire Dragons made the initial assault, the seers and a bodyguard of more warriors had left the webway in the vicinity of the command tower close to the northern wall.

Two squads of Warp Spiders heralded the second phase of the attack. Using their warp jump generators, the Aspect Warriors teleported directly into the main guard room within the tower, silently slaying the occupants in a matter of moments.

Thirianna and Kelamith led the squad of Dire Avengers from Thirianna's old shrine, the One Hundred Bloody Tears, accompanied by Arhathain. Poised between reality and the skein, Thirianna quickly led the others to a large portal of iron. She had foreseen the door opening as the occupants of the tower emerged to respond to the attack on the wall.

Sure enough, a few moments later, the sound of grinding gears and swinging levers could be heard. The gates opened inwards to reveal several dozen human soldiers wearing drab grey fatigues. Their uniforms were more like labourers' clothes, heavy overalls stitched with many pockets worn over white shirts. Their helmets were of grey-painted metal, steeply sloped with narrow cheekguards, and their squad leaders wore gorgets of silver and vambraces of the same.

The humans raised their lasguns slowly, eyes widening with shock and fear. The Dire Avengers opened fire, gunning down many, while Thirianna, Kelamith and Arhathain charged into the doorway.

Thirianna cut the legs from the first soldier as a blue las-blast deflected from her rune armour. She ducked under the butt of a rifle and chopped off the hands holding the weapon. A step to the left brought her behind the screaming man and a swift cut to the neck ended his suffering. Forewarned by the skein, Thirianna brought up her witchblade to deflect another las-bolt, before unleashing a fury of flames through a doorway to her right, incinerating another handful of humans.

Thirianna briefly felt the spirit of Kelamith as he flashed through the minds of the defenders, searching for information, stealing their dying thoughts. It felt a little like ransacking their graves, prising open their last hopes and fears for glimmers of useful intelligence.

'We seek the darkness below,' said the farseer. Thirianna glimpsed a vision of a room filled with crude communications devices. 'Their voice must be silenced.'

Arhathain led the next attack, the shuriken weapon mounted in his gauntlet spewing a hail of discs as he leapt down a flight of stairs towards the underground levels. The glow from his spear mingled with the light from Thirianna's blade and Kelamith's staff, bathing the stairway in a multicoloured swirl.

The Dire Avengers followed after their autarch, the two psykers bringing up the rear. More soldiers emerged from a row of rooms holding narrow bunks; unarmed, they were swiftly despatched.

At the end of the corridor, the room to the communications centre started to swing shut. Thirianna felt a huge build-up of pressure in the back of her mind, as Kelamith extended his will. The door was thrown open by the power of his thought, hurling back the two men who had been closing it.

Dial-filled consoles exploded as the Dire Avengers opened fire. Thirianna went through the door beside Arhathain, blocking a bayonet aimed at her gut. She slashed the tip of her witchblade through the human's throat, sending him reeling into another soldier. Jumping high over both men, Thirianna drove her blade into the back of another, before spinning on her heel to deliver the killing blow to the man who had been tripped.

Arhathain's spear blazed as he swept it through the bank of speakers and levers, sending molten metal splashing up the dark stone walls. An ear-splitting whine erupted from a damaged grille, a moment before Kelamith's staff silenced it, the farseer driving the ornate head into the bowels of the spark-spitting machine.

'It is done,' said Kelamith. The whine of shuriken catapults filled the passageway outside as the Dire Avengers responded to a fresh attack.

'The cordon is formed,' reported Arhathain. 'All squads are in position to move on the central building.'

'Wait!' snapped Kelamith.

A heartbeat later, Thirianna also felt something

changing. The skein was shifting, mutating and bending as new futures unfolded. A malign presence was spilling out across the threads of fate, bending them to its purpose.

'She Who Thirsts,' muttered the farseer.

Thirianna recognised the taint, awash with memories of being hunted in the webway. Now there was no attempt to beguile, no subtle twisting of desire. The daemons of the Great Enemy swamped the skein with their presence, responding to the threat to their artefact.

'We do not have time to wage two battles,' said Arhathain, also sensing something of the gathering daemonic threat. 'We have a limited time before we are detected and the humans respond in force.'

'Continue for the main tower,' said Kelamith. Thirianna felt him binding for a moment with the mind of Laimmain as the two farseers devised a plan to defend against the daemons. 'We shall protect your spirits as you protect our bodies. Thirianna, come with me.'

The two of them headed up through the communications tower, as Arhathain and the Dire Avengers left to join the main attack. Thirianna flowed between reality and unreality, the material and immaterial overlapping in her thoughts. As she negotiated a turn in the stairs, she felt the first pull of the artefact.

Tenebrous tendrils plucked at Thirianna's mental defences, seeking a means to penetrate her mind. Her rune glowed white-hot, fending off the attack, redirecting the psychic power pushing at the barriers erected around her mind.

Though she suffered no physical damage, the psychic attack left her dizzied. She could smell a sweet perfume, alluring, intoxicating. Her skin tingled within her armour, while a melodic harmony disorientated her, tempting her deeper into the skein.

She resisted the alluring deception, hardened to it by previous experience. Enraged, the daemons hurled themselves at the minds of the eldar, clawing and screeching, trying to overcome with brute force that which they had failed to circumvent by seduction.

Thirianna lashed back with her mind, sending a pulse of fire across the skein. Kelamith did likewise, and she felt the flames from the other seers scorching along the threads of the future, purging the daemonic presence.

Reaching the uppermost storey of the communications building, Kelamith withdrew from the skein for a moment, leaving Thirianna to fend for herself. Keeping only the smallest fraction of her essence in her body, she ventured further across the skein, following the path blazed by Laimmain, picking off stray motes of Chaos energy left in the wake of the farseer's offensive.

Immaterial hands plucked at Thirianna's thoughts, trying to prise open her passions, seeking weakness in her resolve. She felt the heartache of her discord with Korlandril and Aradryan and quickly responded with thoughts of her partial reconciliation with her father.

The daemons recited the words of her poems,

calling them out in trite snippets, twisting the meanings of the verses, making them sound pathetic and hollow. Thirianna refused to be goaded into a response. Instead, she followed the psychic echoes of the voices, tracking down the daemons and bringing the fire of purity to bear upon them. White flames licked across the skein, silencing the evil chatter.

There came a lull in the onslaught, the daemons retreating from the wrath of the eldar seers. Thirianna returned her consciousness to her body, noting that the entire psychic battle had taken less than a dozen heartbeats.

'Our foe is not yet defeated,' warned Kelamith, gesturing towards the door. 'We must join the attack on the central tower.'

The seers left the communications building and headed towards the central compound. Fires could be seen burning at several of the windows in the upper levels. There were eldar dead at the main gate, Howling Banshees riddled with bullets. Thirianna stepped over the corpses without a second glance, her war-mask inuring her to the horror of the scene.

As she followed Kelamith up a winding staircase, she was aware again of powerful energy flowing across the skein. The daemons came again, focussing their malice upon the psykers, drawn to their bright spirits.

Drawing power through her rune, Thirianna divided her attention between the real and unreal. With the daemons flooding the skein with their corrupting energy, it was impossible to draw on the power of her foresight, so it was with some caution that she stepped off a landing into one of the chambers of the citadel. She scanned the room quickly, while on the skein the daemons manifested themselves, appearing in a variety of hideous forms. The daemonettes she had encountered before could be seen, claw-hands slashing, jewelled eyes bewitching. With them came six-limbed monstrosities with lashing tongues. Thirianna focussed her powers, meeting the daemonic incarnations with an apparition of her own, flaming sword in hand.

Blade met claw in the ethereal world, as Thirianna leapt behind the toppled remains of a bookcase, lasbolts searing along the stained wood. She pulled out her shuriken pistol and fired back, felling one of the soldiers taking cover in a doorway opposite.

A claw snapped at Thirianna's face, deflected at the last moment by the hilt of her witchblade. She darted under another slashing claw and brought the sword up into the creature's chest, turning it to ash.

Kelamith entered the room, a ball of light erupting from the tip of his staff, hurling the humans back from the doorway. On the skein, a handful of daemons disintegrated into bodiless screams at the touch of his mind.

'Others are coming, stall their advance,' said the farseer, waving a hand towards another, smaller doorway at the far end of the ruined library.

Thirianna dashed down the long carpet, sword in hand, arriving at the door a moment before a human stumbled through, a pistol in one hand, chainsword in the other. Thirianna blocked the chainsword with her witchblade and fired her pistol into the man's gut, sending him backwards through the door.

In the skein, the daemons were acting strangely. They circled the bright sparks of the eldar psykers, constantly moving, feinting but not attacking. Thirianna could sense other energies at work, the power of the warp leaking through to the material world, the unreal becoming real through the machinations of the daemons.

Beyond the door was a small set of stairs leading down, no doubt used by servants so that they would not disturb their masters as they moved about the citadel. There were sounds of a struggle coming from below and Thirianna hurried down the steps.

The daemons were pouring their power through the nascent breach into the material universe, seeking anything to anchor upon. The dull, lifeless minds of the humans were hard to detect, but utterly unprotected. Urged on by a thought from Laimmain, the seers tried to intervene, placing themselves between the daemons and the humans, hurling bolts of fire to drive back the creatures of the Great Enemy.

The room below was some kind of storage area, the walls lined with shelves, barrels and crates stacked neatly to one side. A human female crouched behind one of the boxes, her head in her hands, mouth open in a silent scream. Thirianna stepped forwards, witchblade raised.

The woman's flesh pulsed, rippling with unearthly power as something slid into the body, pushing its way into the material world through her weak mind. Spines erupted from her back and shoulders and her hair fell out in clumps, leaving a distorted scalp coloured a dark pink. Fangs erupted bloodily from her gums and her fingernails turned to white claws.

With a screech, the daemon-thing leapt at Thirianna, slashing at the eye lenses of her helm. Sparks erupted from the seer's rune armour, throwing the daemonic creature back, the woman-daemonette smashing into the shelves to send shards of pottery crashing to the hard floor. Thirianna did not hesitate, lunging at the possessed human with witchblade outstretched. The sword passed into the daemon's gut, violet fire springing from the wound.

A psychic backlash ripped along the witchblade, taking Thirianna by surprise. She stumbled back, losing her grip on the weapon as she tumbled over piled sacks. The daemon-thing was not destroyed. A forked tongue rasped in and out of its fanged mouth as it stalked forwards, its dagger-like claws outstretched.

Thirianna formed a fist, enveloping her hand with psychic power. She sprang to her feet and punched the creature in the chest, driving her hand forwards with every ounce of physical and mental strength. The blow tore the daemon in half, a ring of purple fire exploding outwards, hurling body parts into the cluttered stores.

Here and there, the daemons were making other breakthroughs from the skein. Try as they might, the eldar could not shield every human mind. Thirianna could feel the artefact weighing heavily on the psychic plane, bending everything around it, forming an immaterial gravity well that drew everything towards it. Its presence was erratic though, coming in ebbs and flows, its power constrained by the will of the seers. It flared, sending out a corona of energy, shadowy tentacles seeking a mind to latch on to, to bring it to full awakening.

Thirianna heard the creak of a door behind her opening. Her witchblade flew into her hand as she spun around, ready to strike.

The blade stopped a hair's breadth from the boy's throat.

Thirianna trembled, looking into the wide, brown eyes of the youth. He was dressed in drab grey clothes, his jerkin buttoned tight, short trousers flapping around his knees. She noticed he was barefoot.

The boy said something to her in the garbled tongue of the humans, his face a mask of fear. He started backing away towards the door, eyes roving around the room, taking in the gore splashed everywhere.

'Slay him!'

Kelamith's command was a shout in the heart of Thirianna's mind. She almost acted on impulse, but stayed her hand again, refusing to strike the killing blow.

She could not do it. The council had decided that all had to die, but Thirianna could not bring herself to slay the boy out of hand. She was not the cold-blooded slayer of Khaine any more. Her witchblade twitched, eager for blood, but she held it back. Even with her war-mask in place, she could not spill the blood of the boy. He was no threat.

In the moment of her hesitation, Thirianna's guard in the skein wavered. A daemonic entity slipped past her straying thoughts, sliding into the youth. She watched in horror as his skin paled and his eyes darkened.

Flickering between the skein and reality, Thirianna could see the daemon within the boy's form, yet still she could not deliver the deadly blow. On the skein, she seized hold of the daemon and tried to drag it from the youth's body.

The child snatched up a broken piece of wood and smashed it across Thirianna's chest. Her rune armour absorbed the blow, flashing with light.

She struggled with the daemon, its psychic claws and teeth slashing and biting at her mind as it fought to keep the boy; she delved her thoughts into the raw stuff of the daemon, sickened by its touch but determined not to let go.

She warded away the swinging plank with her witchblade, guiding the blow harmlessly past her shoulder. The boy snarled and spat curses at her in his own tongue before jabbing the broken end towards her face. Thirianna ducked aside, slapping the plank from the possessed boy's grasp with the flat of her witchblade.

Now the daemon changed, melding itself around Thirianna, trying to draw her into the remnants of the boy's mind. His memories flashed across her consciousness: so few and all of them of a lifetime of drudgery and servitude.

'The boy is dead. There is nothing left to save.'

Kelamith's voice was calm, the words like cooling water on a fevered brow, calming Thirianna's ire. She realised her fear was giving strength to the daemon.

The harder she struggled to free the boy from its grip, the stronger it became.

Distracted, Thirianna reacted slowly to the youth's next attack. He snatched up a clay jug and hurled it into the side of her helm. The material held and she was unharmed, but the impact made her ears ring.

The witchblade called to her, resonating with Thirianna's war-mask. She was a killer, and the boy's life or death would not change that. The stain of blood was on her spirit forever. What was one more short existence in the torrent of blood she had unleashed in her life?

The daemon swelled with power, fuelling itself from Thirianna's doubt.

The boy's body rippled and bulged, hunching over as a tail tipped with a barbed sting erupted from the base of his spine. The sting jabbed towards Thirianna, almost catching her unawares. She ducked beneath the attack and stepped back out of range.

The boy smiled at her, the expression one of sublime innocence.

The daemon had gone too far and it flinched as it realised its mistake.

Thirianna levelled her witchblade at the boy. Purple flames sprang from the sword, engulfing the possessed child from head to foot. On the skein, Thirianna ripped free from the daemon, tearing it apart from within, shredding it with her naked rage.

The thing screamed, such a piercing, plaintive wail that Thirianna almost broke off her attack. She steeled herself and poured out more of her rage, turning the creature's physical body to a smouldering cinder even as she scattered its power, banishing it across the breadth of the skein.

As the charred remains collapsed into ash, Thirianna fell to her knees, moaning with despair. Her blade grew dark and her rune clinked to the ground as she retreated inside a hard shell thrown up around her thoughts.

KELAMITH CAME TO her quickly, on the skein and in person. He peeled away the protective layers encircling her mind while he helped her to her feet.

'Come and see that which has caused us so much grief,' he said.

Thirianna locked away the encounter with the daemon alongside her previous child-slaying, bringing her war-mask into full focus, shutting off the rampaging guilt that wracked her whole mind.

She was calm again.

The threat of the daemons had been dissipated but still Thirianna could feel the brooding presence of the artefact. It became a more diffused energy, spreading across the skein, looking for escape. The minds of the eldar were like a field of stars, and in turn each flickered with pale blue and delicate green shades as the Great Enemy sought to tempt them.

'TOUCH NOTHING,' WARNED Kelamith, his words echoing across the skein to the minds of the other eldar. 'Free your minds of desire and temptation.'

As the two seers headed up another staircase, Thirianna caught sporadic sounds of fighting. On the skein she could see the last few humans holding out in the room at the pinnacle of the tower.

The artefact made a last grab for attention, pouring its filthy power into the humans. Thirianna felt a moment of triumph from the object and saw a vision of a human leaping towards the box that held its power in check.

Something else flickered across the skein. They were there for a moment and then gone: Warp Spider Aspect Warriors, forewarned by Kelamith. The thread of the human's life ended abruptly.

A new aura of light filtered across the immaterial realm as Kelamith and Thirianna were joined by Arhathain on the top landing. Kelamith gestured for Thirianna to wait as the farseer and autarch entered the chamber together.

Thirianna turned at a sudden presence behind her. A group of grim-faced seers made their way up the stairs, all clad in plain white, heads shorn of all hair. Between them floated an ovoid container, dark red in colour and patterned with silver runes. Thirianna stepped out of their way, disturbed that they had no presence on the skein. As they passed, her spirit stone glowed white for a moment, touched by their energy.

When the white seers had entered, Thirianna moved to the door, just in time to see that not all of the humans were dead. The artefact gave a last pulse of power, imbuing life into the near-lifeless with a flailing tendril of energy. A human soldier surged from the wreckage of the room's furniture, one arm hanging limply by his side, a long wound in his thigh spraying blood as he sprinted across the room towards the artefact.

Arhathain reacted quickest, his spear singing across the hall to catch the human in the chest, hurling him bodily through the air. A blink later, several shuriken volleys and laser blasts passed through the air where the man had been. Arhathain beckoned to the spear and it twisted, ripped itself free of the dead human and flew back to his grasp. Unperturbed, the autarch approached the box and lowered to one knee beside it, studying the artefact closely.

Whispering protective mantras, the white seers closed around him, their robes obscuring all sight, their sibilant incantations growing in volume. The skein bent around them also, becoming a protective bubble that reflected back the thoughts of Thirianna as she tried to peer inside.

When they parted a moment later, silence descended. The box was gone but the wraithbone casket gleamed with a darker light, an aura of oily energy seeping from it. The casket weighed heavily on the skein, even the warding powers of the white seers unable to stop it from affecting the paths of fate around it. There was much blood and death surrounding the artefact, but Thirianna knew not to pry too closely, and averted her thoughts.

The white seers departed with their tainted cargo.

'Humans gather in force to destroy us outside the walls,' Arhathain announced, standing up. 'The garrison are all slain. Return to the webway and we will be away. Take our dead; we cannot leave them in this forsaken place.'

* * *

'WHO ARE THEY?' Thirianna asked, as she and Kelamith followed the white seers back to the transport pod that had brought them through the webway.

'A bridge, between the craftworlds and the Black Library,' replied the farseer. 'They are steeped in the knowledge of Chaos, and are immune to its charms and wiles.'

'They do not look like Harlequins to me,' said Thirianna, remembering the garish troupe of warrior-performers she had seen once as a child.

'Though the Harlequins know the location of the Black Library, they are not its only guardians,' explained Kelamith. 'They are far too capricious to be entrusted with such a thing, no matter how devoted they profess to be about the destruction of the Great Enemy. Wiser, sounder minds than those of the Laughing God's followers will study this thing and learn its secrets before it is destroyed.'

Thirianna thought how sheltered her life had been on Alaitoc. She had thought she had known everything about her people, both those of the craftworld and those beyond, but she was learning quickly that the remnants of the great civilisation they had once been were far more diverse and secretive than even she had known.

'That is true,' said Kelamith, detecting her thoughts. 'There are many things of eldar and alien origin that we have forgotten.'

'That is not a comforting thought,' said Thirianna.

'It was not intended as such,' replied Kelamith. 'Though you faltered today, you will grow the stronger for it. Though you can perfect the arts you

have already learnt, honing your runecraft and powers, you face another choice, child. It is not an easy
decision, and while many decisions may influence
the course of your fate, this one will without question decide your doom.'

Part Three

Farseer

SKEIN

The Hooded Shadow – Cloak of Morai-heg. The balance of fate can be both robust and delicate. Some dooms cannot be avoided, while others hang by a slender thread for their duration. Of the latter, there are some fates so highly attuned to influence that the simplest observation, the knowledge of their possibility, can render them inert. In order to look upon such visions, the seer must go forth in the guise of Morai-heg herself, protected from repercussion by the Hooded Shadow, lest their awareness of what they witness brings it to pass or quenches its potential.

THIRIANNA HELD HER rune just above her fingertip as she contemplated her future. It was to this point that she had been moving since leaving the Path of the Poet, an instance in her life that would have a profound effect on her existence, both of what came next and what she had already experienced.

She sat on the low couch below a window overlooking the parklands. The dome had moved to the dusk-like period of the cycle, an artificial twilight of deep reds and purples casting long shadows from the trees and rocks. The croaking of nocturnal amphibians could be heard in the distance, while moonsparrows and rasp owls disturbed the peace with their roosting cries and haunting calls. Swarms of tiny bats, each no larger than a fingernail, fluttered from their nests in the boles of the kaidonim trees, appearing as a drifting haze that floated just above the grassy hills.

All of the calm of the scene was lost on Thirianna as she studied the slowly revolving sigil of wraithbone. She admired the craft her father had put into its making. At first glance it appeared quite plain, a simple shape of two bars and three curves, encompassing the syllables of her name. On closer inspection, the surface was rippled with whorls and lines, almost invisible to the naked eye, like the print of a fingertip. Stranger still, the wraithbone was not static. The pattern shifted slowly; so slowly it could not be seen, but it definitely changed from one cycle to the next in subtle ways.

The design could be taken as a map, perhaps, charting the possible futures being played out by Thirianna's life. It might be a record of her past life, constantly updating as she moved across the skein of fate. For all Thirianna knew, it might well be a simple conceit of her father, an embellishment of purely decorative value.

Whatever the mutable pattern was, it could not offer Thirianna any guidance on the matter at hand. There was no pressure to decide her course; she continued to practise her scrying and her psychic abilities, and in a sense that was a choice in itself, a choice of non-commitment. Yet Thirianna knew her continued studies were not a resolution, but simply a means to allow her time to think.

It was tempting to use the rune to delve the future path, to see the consequences of one act or another on Thirianna's life to come. It was for that very reason she had chosen the Path of the Seer, after all.

Kelamith had warned against such a thing. Reading one's own rune was commonplace amongst seers. Thirianna had done it several times, but always the ending had been blurred, lacking true meaning or context. When she had fought in battle against the humans, it had been her rune guiding her step and her blows, but only from one moment to the next.

In this matter the rune could not help.

Thirianna had to decide whether the Path of the Seer would be just one stage of her life, as had the Path of the Poet and the Path of the Warrior and the other paths she had trodden before; the alternative was to dedicate herself to the ever-deeper study of the skein and to ultimately become one with the infinity circuit. There was no alternative. If she wished to be a farseer then she would be treading upon a road that led to two fates: accidental or violent death, or the near-life of the Dome of Crystal Seers. To truly understand the skein, to glean its most vital and hidden secrets, was to share in its power, to become part of it, eventually leaving behind Form and Being and becoming Mind alone.

The rune could not help because the situation presented Thirianna with a paradox. If she were to hold back and stay a simple warlock, she could not see far enough ahead to understand the future implications. If she wanted to know where her fate would take her if she became a farseer, the extension of her powers would continue to grow exponentially, taking her to places in the skein she could not yet comprehend, and thus would not understand yet.

Against Kelamith's advice and the logic of the problem, Thirianna had tried to locate her future self on the skein, as the farseer must have known she would. It had been a frustrating experience, full of circles and loops that became ever more complex and self-referential the further ahead she scryed. The divergences in her life became so maddeningly complicated and obscure that she had abandoned her forays into her future in order to preserve her sanity. She had stood on the brink of becoming wrapped up in her own convoluted destiny, never to escape, and at the last moment had heeded Kelamith's warning.

As many important decisions come to be, it was a straightforward question of whether she desired a varied life, or an existence dedicated to a single goal. Without any foresight, reduced to second-guessing fate, Thirianna could apply logic and feeling, but nothing more, and it was these two qualities that she had come to distrust and had led her to becoming a seer.

She looked again at the rune, wondering if there was some kind of message or secret intention of the spiralling design worked into its surface. There was only one person who could answer that question, and Thirianna found herself wondering what other advice Yrlandriar might give her.

She had not seen her father since he had presented her with the rune, passing by her apartment on a brief visit. The two of them had exchanged formal pleasantries but both had grown quickly uncomfortable with the notion of discussing deeper matters.

Part of Thirianna was loath to seek help from Yrlandriar. She had done well enough without his opinion before and it was likely to disagree with her own desire. Yet the avoidance of confrontation was morally cowardly; Thirianna's instinct was to continue on the Path and it was appropriate that she sought out challenges to that intuition to test her resolve. Yrlandriar was likely to provide such a thing, even if his opinion only served to bolster her dedication out of opposition to her father's wishes.

She reached into the infinity circuit, seeking the signature of Yrlandriar. He was working on the starship again and their consciousnesses touched only briefly long enough to agree a meeting later in the cycle.

Thirianna took off her seer robes and placed her rune inside a cloth-lined drawer in the wall beside her bedding. She pulled on a skin-tight suit of ochre, threaded with veins of gold, and a pair of high boots of dark blue. She styled her hair, strapped on a broad white belt, and drew on a long coat that matched the colour of her boots. She activated the mirrorplate and examined the results. She looked nothing like a seer, as had been her intent. If she was to make this decision clearly, she had to divest herself of the accoutrements of the seer, to discover if she was comfortable merely being Thirianna.

It was liberating at first, as she walked out of the apartments and joined the growing group of eldar at the gravrail platform at the edge of the park. Other than passing acknowledgement, no one else paid her any heed. Garbed as a seer she had been treated with more dignity and respect, but also a little suspicion.

The bullet-like carriage of the gravrail arrived and Thirianna boarded, joining a crowd of eldar heading rimwards for the night shows and darkened domes of dockwards Alaitoc. The carriage swiftly accelerated, turning the scattered lights of the towers and park to a blur, before the gravrail passed into a tunnel between domes and all became a soft white light.

Thirianna felt strangely alone. She was tempted to delve into the infinity circuit, but decided against it. Instead she sat watching the other occupants of the carriage as they travelled in pairs and threes and small groups, chattering happily or taking part in deep discussions with their peers.

At a glance it was impossible to say which path each of them was currently treading. There were a few subtle signs in clothing, jewellery, hairstyle and manner, but Thirianna felt half-blinded by having to resort to such techniques. As a seer she could glimpse the thread of everyone in the carriage and know instantly who they were, and what they did.

She tried to turn it into a game, to see if her old skills of observation had withered under the glare of her growing psychic ability. It was something to pass the time on the long journey.

Some of the others left and more came on board as the carriage moved from dome to dome, bringing in revellers from the Arcade of Distant Gravitas, dropping off severely dressed aesthetes in the Dome of the Kites. With each new influx, Thirianna studied them afresh, watching the changing relationships and unfolding destinies being played out in the flesh as she denied herself the vision of them on the skein.

Would they stay friends, she wondered? Who would grow closer and who would be drawn apart by the nature of the paths they followed? Would they be happy or sad? Which of them would lead lives of fulfilment or frustration?

It was an intriguing experience, to speculate on such matters. It reinforced the opinion of Kelamith, that rarely could the lives of individuals be turned to one fate or another. Only the great swathe of destiny could be altered, the life of Alaitoc steered on the correct path. It was a trap to think that every ill could be avoided and every boon enjoyed for each person. The gain of one was often the loss of many, and the gain of many made at the expense of a few.

As the carriage neared its destination at the docks, Thirianna was left with only a handful of others.

The cultured landscapes outside were swathed with darkness except for the scattered glow of lanterns on the rivers of the Dome of Eternal Winters and the gleam from the windows of spire-like habitats.

She was in no hurry and when the gravrail arrived in the dock area, she found a small vendor offering a variety of hot confectionery. Thirianna was amused to see that they were cooked over an actual open flame, giving them a rustic flavour she had not tasted before. Nibbling on the soft lumps of sweetness, she wandered to her father's workshop.

As she entered, she immediately heard voices raised in song.

She hurried to the hangar where the starship was being crafted, having never seen a chorus of bonesingers working together. She located them arranged around the prow of the ship, accompanied by several dozen lesser artisans lining the gantries and walkways surrounding the ship's skeleton.

The huge space was filled with rising and falling harmonies, resonating from the ribbed walls, rebounding from the vaulted ceiling. The sounds of pipes merged with the voices of the eldar, adding an undercurrent of a different rhythm and pitch. Every harmonic was precise, guided by the bonesingers to a particularly frequency, moulded to the pitch and tone desired.

The air was alive with psychic energy. The starship skeleton resonated with the power and the walls hummed with it. It was too tempting not to witness this extraordinary feat from the skein, so Thirianna slipped part of her mind sideways into the infinity circuit to observe the act of creation both physically and psychically.

The infinity circuit thrummed with the energy being channelled. The structure of wraithbone blended with the psychic circuitry of the craftworld, attached at several key nodes. Drawing on this power, the bonesingers were weaving a pattern of resonant psychic energies, overlapping matrices of power that when combined formed solid matter: fabled wraithbone.

Two curving spurs were being added to the front of the ship. Thirianna's guess was that the area would later house some form of sensory array, such was its position. With her eyes and ears, she had some vague idea of the wraithbone forming out of the air, growing from the existing skeleton, its creation setting up vibrations that cut across the psychic choir.

With her mind, she could appreciate the true beauty of the act. The nascent wraithbone existed as a potentiality within the skein, taking on infinite forms. As the bonesingers led the other artificers, the skein pulsed and flowed with their desires, their imagining of the ship's design acting as the guide of fate. Conforming to this shaped destiny, the wraithbone solidified from its amorphous state into a physical material, fulfilling the self-destiny of its existence.

Fuelled by the infinity circuit, the wraithbone was a distillation of the skein, an amalgam of hope and despair, opportunity and disappointment, love and hate, life and death. The songs of the artisans encompassed joy and woe, the realisation of dreams and the dashing of ambitions.

The wraithbone was glowing with its own chill light, its future shape appearing as a fluttering image on the edge of vision, molecule by molecule emerging from its potential to fulfil its destiny.

Thirianna's waystone, attuned to the psychic voice of Alaitoc, throbbed with the beat of the song of creation. It sang through her body and mind, filling her with vigour and hope. Her mind was ablaze with possibilities as she glimpsed the voyages of the starship-to-be, the trials and tribulations and triumphs of its crews splaying out from the wraithbone core at its heart, a thousand and more new fates unveiled in the act of its creation.

Slowly the chorus quietened. One by one the artisans finished their songs, until only the pipes and voices of the bonesingers were left, echoing faintly through the great hall. Each sang and played in isolation now, honing the last parts of the structure, discordance rising from the harmony. Sadness gripped Thirianna. Potential was becoming reality. Infinite possibilities were resigning themselves to a singular fate.

The last notes hung in the air for a time, shimmering along the whole skeletal structure. And then they were gone, leaving a perfect moment of silence.

Thirianna realised she was crying.

It was as if she had lived and breathed with the ship. In the last moments of the song she had been taken to distant stars and far-flung worlds. And at the very end, she had seen the destruction of this mighty vessel, its conflagration in battle. Even in its birth had been sown the seeds of its death, the fate of all things, from eldar to starship, flower to star.

As she recovered, it was hard for Thirianna to match the beauty of what she had experienced with her knowledge of Yrlandriar who had orchestrated it. The starship was as much part of him as it was anything else, something more than just the fruit of his labours. His imprint was within every part of it, meshed with the presence of the others who had joined in its making, a physical extension of his own thread of destiny.

For a moment Thirianna felt jealousy. It was such creations, such children born of wraithbone, which had occupied her father when he should have attended to the needs of his actual child.

She tried to suppress the feeling as she saw her father approaching, not wishing to engage with him in a negative frame of mind. She tried to mask the envy she felt, but could not help but wonder if the satisfaction of being involved in such a creation had outweighed Yrlandriar's feelings on becoming a father.

'I fear I am under-dressed,' said Yrlandriar as he stopped in front of Thirianna, his eyes quickly taking in her extravagant outfit. He wore his rune-embroidered robes and carried his pipes under one arm, hair tied back by a bland but neat band of silver.

'I felt like a change,' said Thirianna, taken off-guard by the comment.

She followed Yrlandriar into the workshop, and

sat down as a low seat emerged from the wall at a gesture from the bonesinger. He placed his pipes on the table and sat next to her, somewhat stiff and formal.

'I have a question,' said Thirianna, unsure how to phrase it.

'A question for me?' replied Yrlandriar, blinking with surprise. He regained his composure quickly. 'Ask your question.'

'The designs on the surface of the rune you wrought for me, do they have a meaning? Was it a pattern of your creation?'

Yrlandriar relaxed, comfortable with the nature of her inquiry. He stood up, opened a cabinet in the wall and took out a small crystal bottle and two goblets. He passed a cup to Thirianna and filled it with amber liquid from the decanter, before serving himself and placing the bottle back in its place. Thirianna noticed his actions were crisp and premeditated, a mark of physical as well as mental discipline.

'The design that you see is not an invention of mine,' said the bonesinger, shaking his head. 'The wraithbone is psychoreactive, as you know. It is responding to you, forming itself from your thoughts and feelings, binding itself to your spirit. What you see is a reflection of yourself, as realised by the wraithbone.'

'And will it ever stop changing?' Thirianna asked. She took a sip of the drink. It was honeywater, sweet and aromatic.

'Only if you stop changing,' replied Yrlandriar. He

sat down and looked at Thirianna but said nothing more. His finger tapped on the rim of his goblet, though whether from contemplation or impatience Thirianna could not tell.

'I sense that you have more than one question to ask of me,' he said eventually. 'Your first could have been easily answered via a more distant communication, yet you come to visit me.'

'I stand upon the crux of a choice,' said Thirianna, choosing her words carefully. She did not wish to betray her own feelings on the matter lest it influence her father's opinion. 'My runecraft has progressed well. I must choose whether I will devote myself to further study of its lore, or remain a warlock for the time being.'

'You are too young to become a farseer,' Yrlandriar replied promptly. He took a mouthful of honeywater and Thirianna realised that he was not going to offer any further explanation.

'Age is not an issue,' she said.

'Of course it is,' said Yrlandriar. 'You have more than half of your life ahead; it would be obscene to walk a single Path for all of that time.'

Thirianna was about to argue her case but stopped herself. What her father had said was true and it was not something she had properly comprehended. However, it irked her that he seemed so dismissive of the idea.

'If it is what I wish to be, what my destiny should be, that is of no concern,' she said.

'It should be a concern,' said Yrlandriar. 'There are a great many things you might yet accomplish even if you do not attach yourself to this single path.'

'You are a bonesinger and shall remain so until you die,' Thirianna pointed out.

'That is different,' said Yrlandriar.

'How is that so different?' asked Thirianna. 'What accomplishments of yours outshine the creations you now render? Is not your final path also your finest?'

Yrlandriar looked to speak, but then took another drink. He glanced around the workshop, the slight hint of a frown creasing his brow.

'Yes, that is true,' he said when he returned his gaze to his daughter. 'You will have a great deal of experience by the time you are my age. For many passes I have been a bonesinger and yet I still cannot reach the heights achieved by some of my predecessors.'

Thirianna was not sure if that was an endorsement or just a passing comment. Yrlandriar's expression was doubtful, but his words seemed to lend weight to Thirianna's choice by instinct.

'I did not learn to create starships from the air in a single cycle,' Yrlandriar continued, his expression lightening. 'Perhaps you are right. With many passes of study and experience you might become one of the greatest farseers of Alaitoc. That would be the reward for the sacrifice you would make.'

'Sacrifice?' Thirianna was not sure what she would be giving up. It seemed to her that now she had tasted the potential of seerdom, it would be hard to live without it.

'To experience a life not bound to the skein,' said Yrlandriar. 'Would you ever fall in love, in the knowledge of all the potential disasters that might befall the relationship? Would you have a child, risking seeing its death a thousand times over every time you travel the skein? The life of a bonesinger can be lonely, I assure you. There is little in the physical world that can match the harmony of spirit that comes from the act of pure creation. Yet it is nothing to the loneliness of the farseer. At a whim you can choose to see the death of everyone you have ever cared about and yet you must often choose to let it happen, for fear it will bring doom to others to interfere.'

Remembering her last encounter with Korlandril, Thirianna had known a little of that dilemma. She had hoped that by increasing her experience and power she would bring more surety to her decisions, but recent exploits trying to divine her own future had betrayed that belief as a myth. The further one could venture, the wider the uncertainties involved.

'I see that perhaps I have opened your eyes to something you had not considered before,' said Yrlandriar. He turned slightly towards her, goblet clasped in his lap. 'You alone will make this decision and you alone will bear the consequences of it. You ask what I think you should do? I can tell you that I would never exchange my time with your mother or the raising of you for a few extra passes studying the way of the artificer. There is a level I will never be able to attain, but it is a small price to pay in compensation for the legacy I have left in other ways.'

'I see,' said Thirianna. Her father's honest words

had sown doubt in her mind. She was back to the conundrum of the rune. How could she decide when she could not know what she would be giving up? She might not be a farseer and yet spend her life alone, leaving it without a legacy, her existence nothing more than something that happened and then was gone.

'Nothing is certain,' said Yrlandriar, reading something of Thirianna's dilemma in her pensive expression. 'You choose between two unknowns, and in this you are not less and no greater than any of us.'

'And if I choose to become a farseer, against your wishes?' Thirianna was not sure why she wanted to bait her father in this way, but it was a habit hard to break.

'My wishes are irrelevant,' said Yrlandriar, much to Thirianna's surprise. He smiled slightly at her reaction. 'We both know you will ignore them, and I cannot force my views upon you, that much is clear. So it is that I choose not to have any. Whatever you choose, I will try to remember that I am your father and I will give you whatever support I can. That is the best I can offer you.'

Thirianna could not quite believe what her father had said, and she ran his words through her mind again, trying to detect some hint of sarcasm. There was none.

'To be counted amongst the greatest of Alaitoc is not something to be dismissed lightly,' said Thirianna. She had read treatises and works from philosophers, poets and seers who had all left their lasting mark on the craftworld. To have her name listed amongst their like was tempting indeed.

'You think that fame is reward enough to forgo the life you might enjoy?' asked Yrlandriar. 'Is that a good reason to give up on everything else that might be?'

'It is *a* reason,' said Thirianna, laughing at herself. 'Only history will judge if it is good enough.'

'You are committed to this,' said Yrlandriar. 'I see it in your eyes. You see a future unfolding before you, shaped to your desire. It is not with joy that I realise this, but it is plain that you have cast your stone into the pool and now it remains to see how far the ripples will stretch.'

'I have,' said Thirianna. 'Too few of us pass our lives with true meaning and I will not be counted amongst those who came and went and were forgotten. I cannot change the past that exists between us, but I am happy that we have reached an understanding.'

'Enjoy it while it lasts,' said Yrlandriar, his expression stern. 'In time, the past and the present will be of no importance to you. I will be just another thread in the great tapestry of your destiny.'

THE FLUX THAT had beset Thirianna's thread on the skein settled with her decision. She spent some time exploring the possible fates, though she heeded Kelamith's advice not to stray too far into the future at this early stage.

Her life took on a regular pattern of study, exploration and tuition. Progress was steady but slow, the unwinding possibilities of the skein gradually revealing their secrets as Kelamith guided Thirianna along the pathways of fate.

Twenty cycles after making her decision, Thirianna was met mid-cycle by Kelamith, who took her to their favoured place in the parklands, overlooking the tumbled rocks on the hillside.

Kelamith had a box with him, no larger than his hand, fashioned from the wood of a liannin tree. A simple pattern was carved in the lid, showing a knotted design representative of the skein, winding about the rune of Morai-heg, the goddess of fate.

Thirianna took the proffered box uncertainly, surprised by the gift from her mentor.

'It does not come from me,' he said with a delicate shake of the head. 'Open it and things will become clearer.'

Intrigued, Thirianna lifted off the lid of the box and placed it beside her. Within, nestled in the velvet lining, sat two more runes. One was the Scorpion, the other was the Wanderer. Confused, Thirianna looked to Kelamith for an explanation.

'They come from Yrlandriar,' he said.

'Yes, I understand that,' replied Thirianna. 'I appreciate the gesture and the effort. What I do not understand is why he chose these two runes. Did he speak with you about the choice?'

'No,' said Kelamith. He leaned a little closer and spoke softly. 'Your father had paid greater attention to your affairs than perhaps you realise. Remember why it was that you first came to Alaiteir.'

'I was distraught, worried about my...' Realisation

dawned. 'The Scorpion represents Korlandril; the Wanderer is Aradryan.'

With a nod, Kelamith stood up.

'It is a fine gift, and I am happy to deliver it on Yrlandriar's behalf,' said the farseer. 'What have you learned about the Scorpion and the Wanderer?'

'The Scorpion is a rune of concealment,' said Thirianna, remembering the first descriptions from the texts she had read. 'It is used to find those fates that would otherwise be hidden to the observer. The Wanderer, well, that one is easy. It allows the seer to travel to distant threads, unconnected to others.'

'A very useful combination, and one that is within your power to wield wisely,' said Kelamith. 'I shall leave you to investigate your gift in your own time. Call on me if you need further guidance.'

Kelamith left her sitting at the top of the hillside. With a thought, Thirianna lifted the two runes from the box. Her own rune joined them from her belt and the three wove orbits around each other, interchanging positions as Thirianna concentrated on them, the circles and ellipses they described in the air pleasing to her eye.

The park was not the place to begin this new exploration of the skein. Thirianna allowed the runes to settle in the box. Kelamith was already out of sight, so she made her way to the Chambers of the Seers on her own, excited by the new possibilities presenting themselves.

As she arrived, she remembered to send a message across the infinity circuit, expressing her sincere thanks to her father for the gift. It was, she told him, the best thing he had ever done for her.

THIRIANNA WAS BAFFLED by her next forays onto the skein. She had thought that with the power of three runes to draw upon, the maddening anarchy of diverging futures would be made clearer. If anything, the skein had become even more complex to navigate.

She asked Kelamith about this, having become lost several times trying to locate occasions when her thread and that of Korlandril and Aradryan would overlap again. It was an exercise in curiosity more than anything else; thoughts of her friends came infrequently and it was with dispassionate interest that she viewed their unfolding lives.

'It is the nature of the skein that the greater we become, the more of it we see,' explained Kelamith.

The two of them shared a simple lunch in Kelamith's rooms at the heart of the Chambers of the Seers. His apartment consisted of two areas: one for sleep and one for study. Little space was given over to anything except the basic essentials for eating, drinking and sleeping. The rest of the apartment was filled with copies of treatises, complex fate charts notated by Kelamith himself, rune boxes and storage crystals.

The apartment was quite cluttered, unlike the cold, streamlined mind that Thirianna detected when she was on the skein with her mentor.

'But that does not make sense,' said Thirianna. 'The greatest seers can make distant, accurate prophecies.

How is that possible if the skein becomes ever more complicated?'

'You are using the power of the runes to expand your horizon,' said Kelamith. He picked at the scraps of food left in the dish set between them. 'You must learn to use their particular qualities to focus your vision on what you wish to see. The true art of the seer is to combine the power of many runes to hone in on a specific instance. Do not use them to look at the whole of the skein, but employ their channelled power to add layers of meaning to a narrow point of reference.'

'I think I understand,' said Thirianna. 'How should I proceed? What instance should I examine?'

'It does not matter,' said Kelamith. 'There is no means to know the import and probability of a divergence or convergence until one examines it.'

Thirianna was not satisfied by this answer, and Kelamith picked up on this.

'Do not be too hasty to know everything,' he said. 'Start with something simple, something small. Pick something that you know well.'

'I have tried that,' said Thirianna. 'I looked for Korlandril's thread, but I could not locate it. It is as if he has disappeared from the skein, and even the Scorpion cannot find it.'

'You are looking in the wrong place, then,' said Kelamith. 'If you are looking for an unknown, you must first begin with a known. I have shown you how to wind back the skein and look to the past. Use this to locate Korlandril's thread and then follow it forwards. Really, you should know this. It is a fundamental procedure.'

'You are right,' said Thirianna, pricked by the farseer's disappointment. 'I am sorry. I have been over-reaching myself, forgetting the process you taught to me. I will apply myself with more attention to detail.'

'It is not wrong to strive to see everything,' Kelamith said. 'It is the lure that brings us all to the skein. Do not fall into the trap of seeing everything whilst observing nothing. Small gates will often be the start of long roads.'

Thirianna was not quite sure what this last enigmatic statement meant, but she was eager to visit the skein again, fortified by Kelamith's advice. She asked leave of her mentor and returned to the Chambers of the Seers.

Remembering to apply herself to the basics, Thirianna forced herself to go through the entire ritual, even using one of the infinity circuit nodes to slip into the skein. She spoke the mantras in full, visualising and focussing on every syllable, concentrating on the meanings behind the words.

The skein appeared as it had done previously, a baffling labyrinth of emerging potentials. Thirianna ignored the temptation to go exploring and instead used her rune to latch onto her own thread. She wound it back, tugging the past to the present, until she found her last encounter with Korlandril.

Now that she had located his thread, Thirianna allowed time to wind forwards again. As she had done so before, she came across a tightly wound interlacing of threads, into which Korlandril's disappeared but did not emerge.

It was now that Thirianna channelled some of her energy through the Scorpion, allowing herself to pass into the tight knot of destinies, making her presence fine enough to pass through the grain of the tangle.

With some sadness, she realised what had come to pass. As she had feared, Korlandril had become too enamoured of his war-mask and was now trapped on the Path of Khaine. He was now an exarch, one spirit amongst many, his essence bound within a suit of ancient armour, rapidly losing its individuality as it was subsumed into the greater consciousness of the being known as Morlaniath.

So much for Korlandril, she thought. She felt a stab of momentary guilt at the thought that perhaps she had precipitated his fall into Khaine's clutches, but it quickly passed. Regret was misplaced on the skein. Here more than anywhere else it was plain to see the missed opportunities and squandered moments that passed by every living thing with each breath. The past, with its simple straight lines, fixed in place, could not be changed.

Thirianna corrected herself, remembering one of the early lessons taught to her by Kelamith. It *was* possible to change the past, through the power of the warp. Time in the realm of Chaos did not flow forwards and backwards. It churned and looped, and a seer with enough skill could, with great effort and a large amount of risk, move sideways from one flow to the next, and thus if gifted with a little luck, move his or her consciousness back in time.

There was grave danger to the seer; channelling so much power in the heart of Chaos itself was an invitation for daemonic attack even with the protection of the runes. This was not the greatest peril though. The past was meant to be set and it was impossible to foretell the consequences of any change made. Only the greatest catastrophes could be averted in this way, yet such action led to futures that were impervious to prophecy.

As Kelamith had concluded, it was far better to change the present than influence the past.

Thirianna switched her attention to Aradryan, having seen nothing of her friend since the battle at Hirith-Hreslain. She withdrew her focus from the Scorpion and channelled her power through the Wanderer, flinging her gaze wide to locate Aradryan's tangle of threads.

It took some time to find him. For a period he had been lost altogether and it was impossible to discern the reason. Thirianna noted this for a future conversation with Kelamith and concentrated on the slender threads she could find. Each was a tenuous causal link, made vague by Aradryan's unfettered desires. He was being ruled by emotion and whim, straying far from the Path, and thus cause and consequence changed quickly as his moods and feelings swung widely from one extreme to another.

Aradryan's growing capriciousness was clear to see as a series of threads that rapidly spiralled into a festering mess of contradictory lines of fate. Thirianna picked the closest, glimpsing her friend fighting aboard a starship of human design. She could not precisely locate the event in time and space, but it was not that distant; he was close to Alaitoc and the battle she saw would take place soon.

From this nodal point, Thirianna busied herself exploring the possible outcomes. In some futures, Aradryan died during the battle, shot or cut down by huge warriors garbed in the armour of Space Marines from the so-called Imperium of Mankind. Thirianna was amused by the conceit of the humans to claim the galaxy as their dominion, especially since such a claim was made in the name of a piece of rotting flesh sustained only by sacrificing their own kind. An Alaitocii philosopher, Nurithinel the Outspoken, had once claimed that the humans' worship of their corpse-Emperor was no worse than the interment of eldar spirits within the infinity circuit and had been hounded from the craftworld for the distasteful comparison.

Putting aside this diversion, Thirianna continued her exploration. In other futures, Aradryan survived, returning to his ship in triumph. In either case, he had risen to a position of some prominence in quite a short space of time, but backtracking along his lifethread did not reveal how this had come to pass. It must have been something that happened during the period in which his fateline disappeared from the skein.

Following the threads forwards again, Thirianna cast her vision further ahead. Here there was a dizzying multiplicity of outcomes: Aradryan dying in a variety of unpleasant manners; Aradryan travelling the webway to the dark city of Commorragh; Aradryan returning to Alaitoc with wanderlust spent; Aradryan being taken in by the Harlequins; Aradryan captured by humans and experimented on by their crude scientists.

Thirianna stopped, suddenly noticing a small detail that had flashed past in one of the first visions. She tried to find it again, but already the lines of fate were blurring together and splitting afresh as her friend's actions spawned new fates for him.

Thirianna withdrew from the skein, concerned with what she had seen. Detaching herself from the infinity circuit, she closed her eyes and concentrated, bringing back the image that had flickered past.

She saw Aradryan, garbed outlandishly, a pistol in one hand and a gleaming power sword in the other. He was fighting a human clothed in a garish uniform, with golden epaulettes and a peaked cap. It was not this that worried Thirianna; she had seen Aradryan fighting many different foes from orks to hrud to humans to other eldar. What had nagged her as it flashed past was where Aradryan was fighting.

She examined the vision again, bringing it to a stop at a certain point where she could draw back and see more clearly what was going on. She shuddered at what she saw.

Aradryan fought alongside other eldar, armoured in the colours of Alaitoc. Around him were many bodies, of human and eldar, and approaching was a squad of Imperial Space Marines liveried in red and white. What appeared to be the smouldering remains of a Phantom Titan, one of Alaitoc's greatest weapons, formed the backdrop.

Past this vignette, Thirianna saw something that horrified her as it confirmed her first suspicion. It was the glint of muzzle flare on crystal, and in that speck of light she could see what the las-blast was reflecting from. It was a crystal seer. In fact, she recognised him immediately, having spent some time in the Dome of Crystal Seers learning about her predecessors from Kelamith. The robe-clad statuesque seer was Anthirloi, who stood at one end of the Sighing Bridge.

At some time in the future, there was the possibility that humans would invade Alaitoc.

Thirianna opened her eyes, hands trembling, her heart thundering in her chest at the thought. It was not chance that had drawn Aradryan to that moment, it was entwined with his destiny, an emergent possibility brought about by his actions. Thirianna had not seen how or why Aradryan was tied up with the humans, or how it was that they had come to Alaitoc, but her instinct had been right to notice it.

She calmed herself, remembering that she had seen only potential, not certainty. Many had been the warnings made by Kelamith and the other seers not to take everything she witnessed as coming to pass. The vague nature of the vision, the uncertainty with which she had come across it and the fact that she had not been able to locate it again all pointed to an extremely rare happenstance. The chance course of events required to bring it about were astronomically slim, verging on the impossible.

Overcoming her first reaction, Thirianna returned to her chambers to think a little more on what she had seen. She revisited the vision several times in her memory, convincing herself that Alaitoc was the scene of the fighting. It was unmistakeable.

Yet if the violence she had seen would come about, the whole craftworld was embroiled in the battle. Such an event would be a massive weight upon the skein, entwining the fates of every eldar on the craftworld and every human they fought against. Other seers must have surely seen the possibility of such a cataclysmic event before.

Thirianna poured herself some sunbloom nectar and sat by the window. It was arrogance of the highest order to think she had unwittingly stumbled upon such a momentous occasion when the most experienced farseers of Alaitoc had no inkling of its existence. It was more than arrogance, it was vain fantasy.

She laughed at herself for being so concerned. In this she had really proven herself a novice. Kelamith had seen the doom of Alaitoc many times, and Thirianna was sure she would see it again too in the future. It was folly to react to such an unlikely possibility.

To occupy herself with other thoughts, Thirianna studied for the next few cycles, avoiding the skein except to strengthen her links to her new runes. Yet try as she did to forget what she had seen, it continued to haunt her. She dreamt about that moment, that silent scene of death and destruction, her mind giving voice to the fierce war cries, hearing the crackle of the flames and the snap of the humans' weapons. She smelt the blood and felt the fear, and woke in a terrible state of panic.

Frustrated with this turn, Thirianna sought out Kelamith. They met in the Chambers of the Seers and Thirianna explained what she had seen and how it had affected her.

'It is natural,' Kelamith assured her. 'No matter how rational and logical we may try to be about such things, we cannot fight against the visceral nature of such a vision. To be unaffected would be strange. The contemplation of our own death is serious enough. To witness the potential downfall of Alaitoc is of a much higher magnitude.'

'And it grows less with time?' asked Thirianna. 'It will diminish?'

'The sensation becomes less extreme and of shorter duration with each experience,' Kelamith told her. He looked away. 'It never wholly disappears.'

'Such a remote possibility is not worthy of consideration, is it?' asked Thirianna.

'It is not,' replied her mentor. 'To dwell on such possibilities is to invite a creeping doubt, one that will gnaw away at your ability to travel the skein with freedom. If you let such a thing hook its barbs into your thoughts, it will constantly drag at you, leading you back to the improbable and the destructive.'

'Yet what I saw could happen,' said Thirianna, remembering the vividness of her dreams. 'Is not the most distant possibility worthy of investigation?

This was not some minor battle I saw; it was a war for survival. If there is even the remotest chance that such a thing will come to pass, should we not bring it to the council's attention?'

'As a theoretical possibility, it is not without merits for discussion,' said Kelamith. He stood up and smoothed a crease in his robe. 'As a spur for further action, it is inconsequential. You are welcome to raise the matter at the next gathering of the council in four cycles' time.'

Thirianna thanked Kelamith for his time and consideration. When he left, she realised she had much to do if she was to present what she had seen to the farseers and autarchs. Even if the catastrophe she had seen was of almost no import, it would be a good opportunity for her to present her first real vision to the council members.

THE FARSEERS AND autarchs came together in the Hall of Communing, an open, column-lined dome at the edge of Alaitoc. Only a force wall shielded the inhabitants from the depths of space, so that the council was surrounded by a field of stars with only the ground beneath.

Thirianna waited patiently while other matters were attended to. The council discussed several visions reported by the senior farseers and the autarchs requested guidance on military endeavours and excursions they were planning. Thirianna listened with interest to everything said, noting the lyrical, narrative form adopted by the farseers when they explained their visions. There was a style to the language that conveyed the sense of what they had seen, taking those who had not witnessed the visions as close as possible to the experience.

Thirianna hastily reconsidered her own submission for the council's deliberations, couching her report in more fanciful terms while the members discussed messages that had arrived from Ulthwé warning of a renewed attack against the Imperium of the humans, launched by renegades dwelling in the warp storm that had engulfed the heart of the ancient eldar empire. It was decided that a small force would be despatched to aid Ulthwé should the need arise, but the farseers saw no need to investigate more fully; Ulthwé was home to Eldrad Ulthran, agreed by all to be the most powerful farseer alive, and there was little Alaitoc could add to his greatest divinations.

The council proceeded for most of the cycle, until the open invitation was accorded to the members to bring up minor matters for discussion. Thirianna caught Kelamith's eye, who introduced her to the council as his pupil and then motioned for her to begin her address.

'I have seen the death of Alaitoc,' Thirianna began, wanting to capture the attention of everybody present. 'In flame and smoke, by plasma and missile, our world is ravaged by the unending hatred of the humans.'

She paused and looked around. Some of the seers watched her with polite, vacant expressions. A few were holding conversations with those around them. Many seemed bored or amused by what she said. It was not the reaction she had hoped for and she considered her next words carefully.

'The Space Marines will come, the fell warriors of the Emperor, and they will bring with them the doom of many,' she continued. 'I have seen Alaitoc's domes torn asunder, our halls ravaged by war, our people slain in their thousands.'

Her claim was not technically true – she had been unable to locate the thread again despite many attempts in the last few cycles – but the spirit of what had been locked into her memory was the important point.

'A time will come when we must stand strong against this threat, for all that we hold dear, our very existence, will hang in the balance,' Thirianna told them, eyeing the assembled council members. She tried not to look to Kelamith for assurance, but glanced in his direction nonetheless. Her mentor looked no more interested than any of the others. She forged on, skipping the rest of the introduction, hoping that it was her delivery that fell on deaf ears and not her message. 'Cataclysm will come, brought upon us by the actions of one of our own. I have seen this fate, spawned by the recklessness of one that I know. In hi–'

'When?' asked Arhathain, cutting through Thirianna's tale. 'Please be more specific.'

'I...' Thirianna's nerve broke as she looked at the autarch, who sat with one eyebrow raised in questioning, lips pursed with irritation. 'I am not sure, autarch. The thread is indistinct, the timing uncertain.'

'Very well,' said the autarch. His expression softened, yet his look of benign pity stung Thirianna more than his annoyance. 'Such is the nature of the skein. Perhaps you could tell us what this acquaintance of yours will do to precipitate this unheralded attack on Alaitoc?'

Thirianna looked down at her feet, feeling guilty for wasting everybody's time with her nonsense.

'I am not sure, autarch. He is an outcast, his future wild and free, difficult to follow.'

'That is to be expected also,' said the autarch, not unkindly. 'You are Thirianna, yes? I know that this must be quite frightening for you, so please do not feel you are being judged. Your inexperience should not be held against you. Is there another here who can better explain what form this threat will take, or the nature of the event that must be averted to prevent it?'

The assembled eldar looked at each other and Thirianna desperately wanted one of them to indicate that he or she had also seen something of what Thirianna had encountered. None did so, and a quiet murmuring spread through the council, adding to her embarrassment.

'Thank you, Thirianna,' said Arhathain. 'If you do discover any more information on this matter, be sure to bring it to the attention of Kelamith.'

Thirianna's shame could not delve any deeper into her heart. Instead it turned to anger, her frustration with herself becoming frustration at the council.

'Please let me finish,' said Thirianna. 'This is important. I saw Alaitoc under attack. I was not mistaken.

If what I saw comes to pass, we shall all be slain and the craftworld destroyed.'

Thirianna heard quiet laughter and looked around the council, furious with the disrespect they were showing her.

'At least we should investigate further,' said Thirianna. 'The remotest possibility that Alaitoc might be attacked is surely something we should take seriously?'

'An attack that none of us has foreseen except you?' This came from Anatharan Alaitin, the eldest of the farseers. 'While we spend our time chasing this dream of yours, who can say what other issues we might miss? I am sorry, Thirianna, but you will have to present us with a better case than you have. Spend some more time on it and if there is more to be learnt you will learn it.'

'I need your help to do so,' said Thirianna. She held out an imploring hand to those around her. 'I have not long trodden this Path. I have but three runes to control. There are those here that can steer a dozen times that number. Will one of you follow me and help me locate this disastrous fate?'

She looked now at Kelamith, but Thirianna's mentor gently shook his head. None of the others offered her any comfort. Thirianna turned her attention back to Arhathain, hoping that he might indulge her, even if only out of pity.

'A life lost, a starship destroyed, an Exodite world attacked, a threat to another craftworld, all of these things I could dismiss,' she said. 'Yet I saw none of those things. However faint the possibility, no matter how tenuous the thread I found, it is there. And if it is there, it may come to pass. This is our home of which I speak: Alaitoc. Judge this wrongly and we all suffer.'

'The council has heard your petition, yet we have found no cause on which to act,' said Arhathain. His narrowing eyes betrayed his irritation at Thirianna's continued insistence.

'My apologies for wasting the council's time,' said Thirianna, sitting down. Inside she raged at her casual dismissal by the great of Alaitoc. Had one of them seen what she had seen, she had no doubt that further action would be called. Their doubt was personal, and all the more hurtful for that. It was Thirianna they did not trust and it did not matter what she said, they could not submit to the idea that she had glimpsed something that they had all missed.

FOR SEVERAL CYCLES after the council, Thirianna avoided the Chambers of the Seers, ashamed at the reaction she would receive. She stayed in her rooms, brooding on the indignity of what had happened. The more she considered the events of the council, the greater her conviction became that something had to be done about the vision.

Spurred on by the desire to redeem herself, Thirianna tried to rise to the challenge posed to her by Arhathain. If she could locate something on the skein that vindicated what she had seen, it would give her a reason to broach the subject again with Kelamith and the others.

Knowing what she did might be dangerous, Thirianna delved into the skein again, determined to find some other evidence of the possible fate she had witnessed. Ignoring the warnings made against spending too much time away from her physical self, Thirianna spent most of each cycle skimming across the skein, using the Wanderer to guide her to random shreds of future, hoping that she might come across the previous thread she had found.

It was hopeless. It had been a rare chance that had brought the vision to her in the first instance, and it would require hundreds of cycles of searching at random to find it again. At the end of the second cycle of hunting, Thirianna tried a different approach. She reasoned that if what she saw would come to pass, at some point in the future it would affect her. If she followed enough of the threads of her own destiny, one of them would lead her to the catastrophe she had seen.

For a whole cycle Thirianna searched, pausing only briefly to eat and drink, but still she could not find the elusive thread she sought. She blazed across the paths of her future selves looking for the slightest glimmer of recognition. Yet the further ahead she looked, the more unlikely it became that she would find what she was looking for. The event she had witnessed would happen sometime in the current pass, that much she was certain. She restricted her search, ignoring the more distant echoes of times to come, hoping to come across some evidence of the turmoil that would surely engulf her should the humans attack Alaitoc.

She found nothing.

Thirianna verged on abandoning the search. It seemed most likely that whatever Aradryan might have done had passed by and that a different course had been set. The glimmer of possibility had not come to fruition and Alaitoc was safe.

This conclusion did not sit well with Thirianna as she once again resumed her quest. As she looked for a link between herself and the momentous event, using the Scorpion to delve deeper into her near-future to divide and tease out all of the half-chances and near-misses, she stumbled upon an unexpected scene.

The threads she followed barely touched on hers, yet there was a causal link somehow. The essence of Morlaniath, the exarch Korlandril had become, was also involved, entwined momentarily with the fate of Arhathain. Following the course of these events, Thirianna saw Arhathain bringing the council together again, instructing the senior seers to direct some of their effort into investigating Thirianna's claim.

Thirianna left the skein, amazed at what she saw. Somehow it was possible that she could convince Arhathain to take her seriously; that was all she wanted. She knew it was likely a fool's errand to seek out the fate of Aradryan and expect a revelation, but it rankled that the council had given her no credence at all.

Thirianna slept for a short while, her dreams still mired in the death of Alaitoc, and rose again as soon as she had regained a little of her strength. The long journeys into the future had taken their toll on her mind and body, even after only a few cycles, but she gathered what stamina she could and set out again, following the trail left to her by the Scorpion. After a while, she located the moment of Morlaniath and Arhathain coming together.

She focussed all of her thoughts on that event, prying open the skein to witness what might come to pass.

THE EXCHANGE TOOK place in the Chamber of Autarchs, empty save for Morlaniath and Arhathain. At first Thirianna could not hear what passed between them, but as she focussed her mind, blocking out the peripheral information, concentrating on the two speakers alone, she caught scatters of their conversation.

'Perhaps you seek war, for that is your nature,' says Arhathain.

'I cannot make a war, if that is my desire, it is the council's choice,' replies Morlaniath.

'Every day our seers uncover a thousand dooms to Alaitoc,' says Arhathain. Thirianna senses disinterest in him. He has heard the arguments before. 'We cannot act on every vision; we cannot go to war on every doubt. Thirianna herself cannot provide us with clarity. We might just as well act on a superstitious trickle of foreboding down the back of the neck.'

'She lacks the proper skill, the means to give you proof, hold that not against her,' counters the exarch. Thirianna wondered why it is that he takes up her cause. 'Give her the help she needs, to prove her right or wrong, she will keep her silence. This doubt will hold her back, it will consume her thoughts, until you release her. You have walked many Paths, seen a great many things, lived a great many lives. That life you owe to me, I remember it now, so many cycles past. I was your guardian, the protection you sought, a true companion. I remember the debt, the oath you swore to me, it is now time to pay.'

A DISTANT TIME flickers across the thread, distracting Thirianna for a moment. She sees a young Arhathain, fighting as a Swooping Hawk on the world of Nerashamensin. A human twisted by the worship of the Chaos Gods emerges from the shadow of a broken doorway, a crude gun in her hands. She aims at Arhathain. The Chaos-worshipper falls, a chainsword cutting her head from her body as the Striking Scorpion Elidhnerial strikes from the dark interior of the building.

Several lifetimes pass. Elidhnerial becomes an exarch, joining Morlaniath. Morlaniath is awakened by the anger of Korlandril and the two become as one.

Thirianna marvels at the convoluted nature of history and destiny. The original Morlaniath, Elidhnerial, Arhathain, Korlandril and Thirianna bound together by distant ties that none of them is aware of.

ARHATHAIN FROWNS AND turns away, pacing to the far side of the rostrum at the centre of the hall.

'The one I made that promise to died ten passes and more ago,' he says softly, looking up at the circular opening at the top of the dome. A distant swathe of stars is strewn across the blackness of space. 'I did not swear that oath to you. It is not Elidhnerial that asks me to repay that debt, it is Korlandril.'

'I am Morlaniath, Elidhnerial too, and also Korlandril. The debt is owed to me, to all the parts of me, united in spirit. Who save me remembers, can repeat the words used, heard them spoken by you?'

THIRIANNA REMEMBERS THE words too. She can repeat them. She saw the debt of thanks sworn by Arhathain. The debt Elidhnerial-Korlandril-Morlaniath now wishes repaid.

'IF I DO not do this?' asks the autarch.

'Your honour is forfeit, and others shall know it, I will make sure of that.'

The autarch turns and directs an intense stare at Morlaniath. Thirianna senses his loathing for the exarch.

'You will not call on me again in this way?' says Arhathain.

'Your debt will be repaid, to Elidhnerial, and we shall speak no more.'

Arhathain nods reluctantly and stalks up the shallow steps of the chamber.

THIRIANNA BROKE FROM the vision with her head pounding, her breath coming in shallow gasps. It was the first time she had witnessed the future in such specific detail and her mind throbbed with the energy she had used to render it.

Arhathain's change of heart now made sense, but it left Thirianna with another question: why had the exarch Morlaniath intervened on her behalf?

Thirianna did not have the strength at that moment to delve back into the skein to discover the truth. She would have to apply some reasoning to the matter herself. She lay on her bedding and closed her eyes, pushing away the numbness that was welling up inside her thoughts, trying to focus on the problem.

The only connection she shared with Morlaniath was Korlandril, who had become part of the exarch's fractured personality. It was possible that some remnant of the relationship between Thirianna and Korlandril was inside the lingering spirit of her former friend. She wondered if she could appeal to that transient fragment of the exarch, to entreat him to act on her behalf.

Yet that provided another problem. If she was to reveal how she knew the exarch had influence over Arhathain, it would invite suspicion from Morlaniath. Though it was accepted that the seers had to scan the fates of every individual, Thirianna had intruded upon a very private matter, one that would cause the exarch to take offence.

She would have to approach the matter in a different way, without giving away the fact she knew about Morlaniath and Arhathain's history. If she could somehow sow the seed of the idea in the mind of the exarch, there was a chance he would act as she had seen, and thus Arhathain's command to the council to help her would be realised.

Thirianna smiled. The disastrous last meeting with Korlandril had shattered her confidence in her ability to intervene in the way a seer should. This latest encounter renewed her confidence. This was exactly why she had become a seer, to act and not react. By her hand she could set in motion a course of events that would be to her benefit.

The thought of such a thing thrilled Thirianna. For her whole life she had been prey to the whims of fate, unseeing of the future, unable to do anything but respond to protect herself. Now she would prove that she had moved beyond that.

She would truly be a farseer.

ON THE LONG journey to the Aspect shrines, Thirianna's determination started to falter. Caught up with ideas of how she would prove her worth to Kelamith and redeem herself in the eyes of the council, she had commissioned a skyrunner to take her across Alaitoc. Her enthusiasm had ebbed as she considered how she was going to confront the exarch Morlaniath.

Her nervousness increased as she approached the forbidding portal that concealed the Shrine of the Hidden Death. She had allowed herself to forget a cardinal rule of farseeing: not all futures come to pass. It was only a possibility that Morlaniath would heed her, and then only a possibility that he would intervene for her, and on top of that there was no assurance that the help of other seers would aid her in detecting even a glimmer of what she had seen before.

In the heat of the moment she had failed to consider the alternatives. Enthused with sudden optimism, she had not investigated the other out- comes of the encounter. Morlaniath might refuse to see her. She might be humiliated, turned away by the exarch. Worse still, Arhathain might learn of her manipulation and her reputation would be forever tainted by the act.

This thought expanded, as Thirianna realised that her movements on the skein had been open to see. The use of the Scorpion made it less likely she would be discovered, but if Kelamith or any of the other farseers investigated thoroughly they would eas- ily follow the trail she had left. Even success might damage her standing.

The gate to the shrine was inconspicuous in itself, a small emerald-coloured doorway within a narrow archway. Thirianna stopped in front of the gateway, unsure how to attract the attention of Morlaniath. When she went to the Shrine of One Hundred Bloody Tears, she was admitted without effort; the gate before her was solidly closed.

There was still time to pull back from the thread she was about to spin. She could turn around and return to the skyrunner, allowing events to follow their natural course. She had not committed herself to any act that would change anything.

The door sighed open behind her. Thirianna turned quickly, surprised by this. A tall figure clad in ornate armour stood in the open gateway, face hidden behind the expressionless mask of his helm. Thirianna felt the rune of the Scorpion in a pouch at her belt jostle in recognition, tugging at her thoughts.

Foolishly, she had expected to see Korlandril. Instead she was confronted by a Striking Scorpion exarch, full of brooding menace. Death surrounded the warrior like a cloak, its touch cold to Thirianna's psychic sense. She retreated from the presence, suddenly afraid.

'Is that you, Korlandril?' she asked.

'I am not Korlandril, though he is part of me, I am Morlaniath.'

It was as Thirianna had feared. Korlandril had been absorbed by the meta-spirit of the exarch. Morlaniath did not seem to recognise her. Beyond the exarch stretched low dunes of red sand, the haze of heat obscuring the distant dome wall. Here and there scrubby patches of candlewood broke the undulating wilderness, the scent of their small but pungent blossoms wafting from the open gate. A blood-red orb hung low on the artificial horizon, bathing the scene in a dim, ruddy light.

'Why do you disturb us, coming here unbidden, breaking the gold stillness?' asked Morlaniath.

There was anger in his voice and Thirianna backed away, every doubt she had crowding into her thoughts. She shook her head, wishing she had not come here.

'This was a mistake,' she told the exarch. 'I should not have come. You cannot help me.'

Morlaniath stayed silent for a moment. Thirianna

could detect turmoil in his spirit, but was too frightened to examine it any closer. She kept her mind firmly detached from the skein, not wishing to experience the horror of the exarch in anything but his physical form.

The exarch's disturbed spirit settled again. 'Now that you have come here, seeking guidance and truth, speak your mind with freedom,' said Morlaniath. 'If I can assist you, if you have hard questions, perhaps I can answer.'

Thirianna approached and stared past Morlaniath, taking in the wide vista of the desert. Her gaze turned to the exarch.

'Is there somewhere else we can speak?' she said

'The shrine would not be fit, farseers enter with risk, and I am loath to leave,' the exarch declared.

Thirianna agreed. She had no desire to set foot in the Striking Scorpion shrine. It was a hard enough task to attend the Shrine of One Hundred Bloody Tears; to enter an unfamiliar Aspect shrine would test her nerves to their limit.

'Can we perhaps walk awhile?' she suggested. 'I do not feel comfortable discussing matters on your doorstep.'

Morlaniath turned away without a further word. After a moment the door did not close and Thirianna assumed she was to follow the exarch. She stepped into the dome, booted feet sinking into the soft sand. Morlaniath strode ahead, poised and graceful, while Thirianna struggled to keep up with his long strides. Squinting against the artificial sunset, she saw that they headed towards a shallow oasis gently fed by irrigation webs beneath the sands. Clusters of red-leaved bushes hid the water's edge, bright white stars of blossom poking from the foliage.

It was a place of surprising peace, an oasis in more than just the physical sense. Morlaniath crouched at the water's edge for a moment. At the back of her thoughts Thirianna could feel the skein undulating as the exarch's many memories of this place came together.

'This is… pleasant,' said Thirianna. She looked for somewhere to sit and on finding no seat or rock, lowered herself onto the warm sands.

Morlaniath looked at her, eyes concealed behind the red lenses of his helm. It was an unsettling sensation and Thirianna gathered her robe about herself and tossed her hair over one shoulder as a distraction from that dead gaze.

'It is the birth in death, the hope in hopelessness, life amongst the barren,' said Morlaniath.

Thirianna gathered her thoughts. She counted the present situation a success, uncomfortable as it was. The harder part was perhaps to come. She had to put across her thoughts in such a way that the exarch would wish to help her. She did not look at him when she spoke. She gazed thoughtfully into the waters. Insects skimmed the surface, sustained by its tension.

'I have foreseen troubling times for Alaitoc, perhaps something worse,' she said.

'You are now a farseer. Such things will be your life, why do you come to me?' said Morlaniath. His voice was flat, giving away nothing of his mood.

'I am told that I am in error,' explained Thirianna. 'The farseers, the council of Alaitoc, do not think my scrying will come to pass. They say I am inexperienced, seeing dangers that do not exist.'

'Likely they are correct, your powers are still weak, this path is new to you,' said Morlaniath. Though the exarch's words were disheartening, Thirianna drew some strength from the indication that Morlaniath knew who she was. It was possible some part of Korlandril still existed inside. 'I do not see my role; I am the exarch here, not one of the council.'

'You don't believe me?' said Thirianna.

'You offer me no proof, and there is none to give, belief alone is dust,' replied Morlaniath.

This was proving even harder than Thirianna had envisaged. She needed a strategy, an approach that might appeal to the vestiges of Korlandril harboured inside the group-mind of the exarch. To give herself time to think, Thirianna stood and walked to the pool's edge. She dipped her booted toe into the waters, sending a ripple across the surface. It was a subconscious act, but it created a reaction in the exarch. His thoughts were disturbed, just as the water was disturbed. Thirianna thought of the skein; of the ripples caused by action that spread across space and time.

Korlandril was in there somewhere; perhaps she could bring him to the fore with something familiar to both of them.

'I followed the fate of Aradryan,' she said. She could not judge his thoughts, his face hidden from view, but she could sense another bubble of activity within Morlaniath's spirit as he searched his memories. She pressed on, hoping that Korlandril still recognised the name. 'Our three destinies are interwoven. More than we have seen already. Yours is not ended, but will soon; his is distant and confused. Mine… mine is to be here, to tell you these things to set in motion future events.'

This last was not entirely true, but Thirianna considered herself an agent of destiny now.

'What is it you have seen, what visions bring such woe, what do they mean for us?'

A single personality was asserting itself; Thirianna could sense it in the skein, one thread growing thicker than the others. Her eyes confirmed as much; one of the spirit stones in the exarch's armour glowed brighter while the others dimmed. It had to be Korlandril, becoming more focussed, drawn out by familiarity. That he had asked the question bolstered Thirianna's confidence again. The exarch wanted to know what she had seen.

'Aradryan dwells in darkness, but there is also light for him,' she said, affecting the tone of language used in the council. If it was right for the autarchs it might work on the exarch. 'But his darkness is not confined to him. It spreads into our lives, and it engulfs Alaitoc. I do not know the details; my runecasting is very crude at the moment. I feel he has done something gravely wrong and endangered all of us.'

'Your warnings are too vague, they contain no substance, we have no course of action,' replied Morlaniath. He turned his head away, his attention straying back towards the shrine hidden somewhere in the dunes.

Thirianna gave voice to her disappointment, finding no more support here than in the council.

'That is what the council says. "How can we prepare against something so amorphous?" they asked. I told them that more experienced seers should follow the thread of Aradryan. They refused, claiming it was an irrelevance. Aradryan is gone from Alaitoc, they told me, and he is no longer their concern.'

The exarch did not reply to this immediately. Thirianna felt a tremor of contact buzzing through her mind. She risked a glance into the skein and saw Korlandril's thread touching upon hers. Korlandril's, not Morlaniath's. He was remembering her. Hopefully the memories were good ones. His next words dashed that hope.

'Continue your studies, delve further into this, to seek your own answers,' said the exarch.

'I fear there is no time,' said Thirianna. She had to force Morlaniath to confront the issue now. 'This is imminent. I lack the strength and the training to see far ahead.'

'Others have not seen it, your fresh cataclysm, who are stronger than you,' remarked the exarch. Korlandril's spirit was weakening again, moving away from Thirianna. 'I must concur with them, who have trodden the Path, who see further than you.'

'It is such a small thing, whatever it is that Aradryan does,' Thirianna said quickly, making a last effort to establish a connection with the afterthought of Korlandril. She reminded herself that she had seen

Morlaniath convince Arhathain to help her. It was possible, if she could find the right approach. She stooped and took a pinch of sand, rubbing her fingers to spill it to the ground until she held a single grain. She flicked it into the waters of the pool. 'Such a tiny ripple, we can barely see it, but a ripple nonetheless. The anarchy of history tells us that momentous events can start from the most humble, the most mundane of beginnings.'

'I have no aid for you, no council influence, and I agree with them,' said Morlaniath. 'Go back to your studies, forget this distraction, I will not assist you.'

The words were harsh, the essence of Korlandril fading away. Disappointment welled up from within Thirianna. She had failed to accomplish even this simple task.

'I feared the worst, and you have proven me true,' she said, trying hard to hold back the tears that threatened to spill down her cheeks. 'Korlandril is not dead, but he has gone.'

'Which you once predicted, that both of us would change, for better or for worse,' said Morlaniath. Thirianna wondered if the exarch was throwing that sentiment back at her out of spite or merely making an observation. 'I am Morlaniath, you are Thirianna, Korlandril is no more. Seek contentment from this, do not chase the shadows, only darkness awaits.'

'Do you not remember what we once shared?' she said, out of desperation.

'I remember it well, we shared nothing at all, I have nothing for you.'

Thirianna straightened and wiped a gloved finger

across her cheek, a tear soaking into the soft fabric.

'You are right,' she said. 'I will leave and think of you no more.'

She bunched up her robe and strode up the encircling dune, heading towards the main portal. She felt the presence of Morlaniath behind her for some of the way, shadowing her progress, and then he stopped, leaving her to depart.

She felt a trickle of psychic energy and the portal ahead opened. In that instant, the exarch's mind was open, and out of desperate instinct, Thirianna made contact for a moment, propelling her sadness and shame into the mind of the exarch.

The link broke and she passed out of the dome, at a loss as to what she would do next.

IT WAS LATE in the following cycle when Thirianna received a summons from Kelamith to attend him in the Chambers of the Seers. It was most definitely a summons and not an invitation, and Thirianna's thoughts were quivering with trepidation as she made her way to see her mentor.

She found him alone, standing in front of the Orb of Elmarianin, a great sphere of ruby-red crystal almost as tall as the farseer, which glimmered with psychic energy, motes of power moving slowly through its depths. The farseer's face was reflected ruddily in hundreds of its facets, each appearing slightly different.

Kelamith turned at her approach, expression stern.

'It is a curious thing,' said Kelamith, gesturing to the orb. 'Created by Elmarianin before I was born, this device allows the seer council to combine their powers of divination. Its use takes a toll on the infinity circuit and those who employ it.'

'Yes, I have read about the Orb of Elmarianin,' said Thirianna. She was confused, unable to see the point being made by the other farseer.

'Speaking of curious things, I have just returned from a gathering of the senior seers,' continued Kelamith, eyes fixed on Thirianna. 'We we're called together by Autarch Arhathain. He has reconsidered your contribution to the council and feels it merits more attention.'

Thirianna felt a surge of satisfaction, though she tried hard to conceal it. Then worry took its place.

'I am honoured,' she said. She kept her expression neutral, wary of betraying any sense of guilt. 'Did the autarch explain his change of mind? Did my arguments perhaps persuade him to judge again what I have seen?'

'He was reluctant to expand on that point,' said Kelamith, still staring intently at Thirianna. She sensed curiosity rather than suspicion and relaxed a little. 'It is almost without precedent, for the council to return to such a decision. Arhathain was most eloquent in his persuasion, insistent even. We have acquiesced to the autarch's wishes, and will search for this doom you witnessed.'

'I am pleased,' said Thirianna, knowing that it would be strange for her to pretend indifference at such a turn of events. 'I also hope that I am mistaken, and that more experienced minds brought to the matter will allay any fears the autarch may have.'

'Indeed,' said Kelamith.

He turned back to the orb, laying a gloved hand upon its surface. When he spoke his tone seemed casual, but his words struck a chill through Thirianna.

'It is a grave offence to mislead the council,' said Kelamith. 'The skein is not a plaything. It is a powerful force, one that we must always approach with due gravitas and dignity. To use its power for selfish means, to pursue self-aggrandisement, is to invite anarchy.'

Thirianna said nothing, though her heart beat faster. She calmed herself quickly, rationalising that if Kelamith and the others believed she had acted wrongly in some way, they would not have agreed to Arhathain's request for further investigation. Kelamith was baiting her, she decided, trying to get her to reveal her secret.

'Do you know the punishment for such a transgression?' said the senior farseer. Thirianna could see him watching her in the reflections of the orb. She shook her head. 'It is a cruel thing, one that we each despise, yet it is one of our oldest laws. One who misuses the skein in a grievous manner is banished from the council of seers.'

'That seems justified,' replied Thirianna, unsure what was so heinous about such a punishment.

'The offender is barred from all rune-casting, and to ensure compliance the perpetrator is taken to the Halls of Isha,' continued Kelamith. His voice was quiet, filled with sadness. 'He or she is subjected to a procedure that removes the parts of the brain that bolster our psychic strength. The criminal is cut off from the skein, unable to interact with the infinity circuit.'

That sounded a lot worse to Thirianna, though she still did not understand why Kelamith seemed to loathe it so much. His following words brought home the full extent of the injunction, as he turned and looked at Thirianna directly.

'It is a far harsher punishment than death,' he said. 'It is the ultimate banishment, Thirianna. Forget for the moment the power to traverse the skein and witness the future. Think on those things that you take for granted, small acts you perform every day. Your chambers respond to your thoughts, warming and cooling, lightening and darkening as you desire. You would only be able to communicate through the spoken word, unable to access the infinity circuit.'

He took a step closer, eyes boring into Thirianna.

'Even more than that, you do not see what you would lose by such a punishment. We each touch upon one another in subtle ways. We read each other not just physically but with our thoughts. We have bonds between us stronger than family and friendship. Every Alaitocii is bound together through the infinity circuit, and every craftworld tied to a single fate through the eternal matrix. To be cast from that is to be something other than eldar. Loneliness and despair, cut off from that most instinctive of contact, will haunt the criminal. They will watch and hear life around them, but they will not feel it.'

It was truly a greater punishment than Thirianna had appreciated. To lose one's sight, one's hearing, one's sense of touch or smell would be unfortunate enough. To have part of one's spirit taken away, to be rendered mundane, to lose a huge part of the essence of being eldar, would be crippling.

'That is severe indeed,' she said, keeping her tone even. 'With such an injunction as a threat, I cannot imagine anyone wishing to transgress such a law. I cannot imagine it has ever been put into practice.'

'Then your studies are incomplete,' said Kelamith. He waved a hand to the orb. 'Elmarianin suffered such a fate. His genius in creating this device was marred by his motives for doing so. He did not like the idea of the council holding power over him and so he sought to place himself above the other seers. He was the most powerful seer Alaitoc has known, and could wield the orb by himself. He used its power to interfere in the lives of the council, placing them in his debt, creating weakness and division.'

'How was he stopped?' Thirianna asked. She was horrified by the tale and wondered why she had not heard it before.

'One of the seers, Aranduirius, was brave, and spoke to the others of Elmarianin's manipulation of her,' said Kelamith. 'Each put aside their pride and confessed Elmarianin's control, spurred by Aranduirius's example. Together, as a council, they confronted him and subjected him to the law.'

Kelamith came closer, seeming to grow in height as he approached, until he was standing less than an arm's length away; his presence invaded the space around Thirianna but she could not step back. The witchlight gleamed in the farseer's eyes and when he spoke, it was with the distant tone Thirianna recognised as his voice of prophecy.

'Thirianna is taken to the Halls of Isha, where she undergoes the Ritual of Cleaving,' intoned the farseer. This was not idle threat; this was a vision, one of Thirianna's possible futures. She backed away, frightened by the pale blue orbs that stared at her. Kelamith followed, taking a step closer, keeping within touching distance. 'She is shamed, cast out of the council. Her mind is broken, her ambition crushed. In atonement she seeks the Path of Service. Still she does not find peace. Her empathy has been taken, her telepathy stolen. She wanders Alaitoc, a ghost-like creature subjected to scorn and pity in equal measure. Alone, cast out, terrified by the long half-existence that stretches before her, Thirianna takes the star-walk, casting herself into the void from the Bridge of Tranquillity.'

The horrifying gleam of Kelamith's eyes seemed to envelop Thirianna as he projected the vision. She drifted for a moment in the freezing vacuum, as empty as the void that consumed her.

Thirianna shrieked and fell back, landing heavily. When she looked up, Kelamith was standing over her, the witchlight gone, one hand extended to help her up.

'That future will not come to pass,' said the farseer, pulling Thirianna to her feet. He shook his head with disappointment. 'You think I am so vile as to heap such a punishment upon a misguided act?'

'I don't know,' said Thirianna. She trembled, the

memory of her freezing death still grasping her heart with its cold touch.

'What you did was vain, and foolish, but no more than some of the other things you have done since coming to me,' said Kelamith. He laid a hand on Thirianna's shoulder and squeezed gently. 'I must believe that you acted out of genuine concern for Alaitoc, and your persistence does you credit. So too the manner of your manipulation. Now you have witnessed properly the power the skein grants to us, and I trust that you will not abuse it again.'

'Does the council know of this?' Thirianna asked, wondering if Kelamith's forgiveness might prove irrelevant.

'They do not,' said the farseer. 'They are quick to put down Arhathain's change of heart to a whim of interest. You must recover yourself; other members of the council will be arriving soon.'

'They are coming here?' Thirianna glanced at the glowing orb.

'It will be the quickest way to put this matter to rest. If there is some echo of Alaitoc's doom to be found, we will find it.'

THE SKEIN WAS alight with the prying minds of the eldar. They stood in a circle around the Orb of Elmarianin, each surrounded by a small constellation of orbiting runes. The air glowed with the ruddy power of the orb and the witchlight of the seers, casting marbled reflections of red and blue across the chamber. The facets of the massive gem reflected the assembled seers, picturing them from every perspective, alone and together. The bright points of light shifted in its depths, converging and splitting, forming arcs of light that mirrored the patterns being woven by the seers' runes.

The gleam of the orb grew stronger as each psyker moved his or her mind into its crystalline form, refracting their spirits through the prism of its construction, their foresight multiplying and diverging.

Thirianna channelled herself through her rune, letting consciousness slip into the orb, feeling its cold edges breaking apart her thoughts, disassembling her mind. Ignoring the strange sensation, she did her best to guide her fellow seers to the location of the event she had seen.

She cast the Wanderer, attaching it to her own rune, so that it would bring her to the thread of Aradryan. She felt the minds of the council nearby, watching her, judging her. She tried to put aside their scrutiny. It did not matter if they faulted her technique as clumsy or her divination as naive; all that mattered was finding the glimmer of Alaitoc's death.

Aradryan's life unfolded rapidly as Thirianna surged across the skein, following the winding trail of his fate. She felt a little guilty, exposing her friend's being to the observation of so many, but she knew no other course to take.

Some of the seers were already branching off, intrigued by spiralling possibilities hinted at by the outcast's actions. Having agreed to Arhathain's wishes, they put their full effort into resolving the problem. Thirianna would have felt pleased by this dedication had not a few of them remarked beforehand that they were keen to get this nonsense dealt with quickly so that they could return to their normal studies.

Aradryan's immediate future settled quickly, the disparate strands melting away as possibilities were ended. His fate was narrowing to a point, a single strand from which he could not escape.

The farseers crowded close, eager to see this pivotal moment.

A pulse shook the skein. To the eye of Thirianna's mind, it took on a blood-red hue and a deep rumble echoed across its length and breadth. Crimson blood flowed along every strand, dripping from life to life, while fire sprang into being, burning vast swathes of the skein.

A single rune blazed above all others. Like a beacon of white fire, the symbol of Khaine the Bloody-Handed obliterated the skein, devouring all life.

The war god's heartbeat reverberated again, and was answered by another thunderous tremor. In the heart of the craftworld, nestled in the wraithbone core of Alaitoc, the Avatar of Kaela Mensha Khaine started to awake.

War. Terrible, all-destroying war.

In the light of the baleful rune, the seers scurried and panicked, racing across the skein, searching desperately for the catalyst of such devastation. They fragmented into splinters of thought through the power of the orb, hunting along several strands at once, covering swathes of history.

As the light of Khaine faded, as the flames died

and the blood dried, the skein was rewritten, revealing its secrets.

The thread of Aradryan coiled about Alaitoc like a serpent constricting around its prey. His fate, his life, surrounded the craftworld, squeezing it from existence.

The seers delved through the knot, confronted by images of burning towers and falling spires. Human tanks rumbled along the Boulevard of Languid Praise, while Imperial Space Marines blasted at the doors to the Dome of Eternal Peace.

Death, fire, war. All of Alaitoc was crushed beneath it, the craftworld's future disintegrating under the weight of attack.

This was no distant possibility. The threads of fate were growing rigid, hardening into certainty, coalescing into a single unavoidable destiny.

The seers conversed quickly amongst themselves, recovering from the shock of the sudden change in fortunes. They needed to know what had happened, what Aradryan had done to create such a doom and why they had not been able to witness it earlier.

Thirianna already knew, or guessed she knew. She had seen it before and the memory of it had lodged like a shard in her mind.

She called to the other seers as she raced back through the outcast's life. As she expected, the possibility had become reality. She peeled open the skein to reveal Aradryan's piratical attack on a flotilla of Imperial ships.

The humans sought revenge for their fallen.

It was an extreme response. The attack on the

Imperial convoy did not seem to merit such an overwhelming attack. Yet the consequences were clear to see, the path from the cause to the effect as straight as possible, one linked directly to the other.

Several of the seers departed, Kelamith amongst them, to bring this dire news to the autarchs, so the council of war could be gathered and plans set in motion. Those that remained, Thirianna included, began to search for a solution that would avert the disaster.

They examined the future potential of Aradryan, but no alternatives were revealed. The seers turned their attention to the humans, picking up the straggling strands of their lives. Military commanders, a planetary governor, the Chapter Master of the Sons of Orar Space Marines; all were examined and all could not be diverted from their course. Something had been set in motion, larger than any individual. There could be no timely assassination to curb the growing threat. No pre-emptive strike would stall the Imperial behemoth gathering its might.

Thoughts then turned to moving Alaitoc, though the craftworld was only part of the way through its star-fuelled regeneration and to leave now would be a major hindrance to her future health. The seers explored the possibilities regardless, but found that escape from the attack was impossible. Whether they remained or moved, the humans somehow were able to find Alaitoc and launch their attack.

They were too late. They would have to stand their ground and fight.

One-by-one the remaining seers departed, leaving

Thirianna alone amongst the frayed threads of Alaitoc's future. Her heart was heavy with grief, no thought of vindication entering her mind.

Kelamith intruded upon her woe.

There is still hope. The attack cannot be forestalled, but the war is not lost. The future beyond is filled with immense uncertainty. We will fight the humans and we will be victorious. Dark days will beset us, but we will endure and we will recover. This is not the first time Alaitoc has faced immediate peril and through our endeavours it will not be the last.

The farseer was gone again and Thirianna was alone.

She moved her consciousness to the present, to a moment experienced with Aradryan. He was asleep in his cabin aboard his ship, intoxicated with a cocktail of exotic spirits and narcotics. Thirianna felt weak, her force dissipated by the effect of the Orb of Elmarianin. She gathered up what was left of her psychic strength and concentrated it into a single thought: a warning.

She touched upon Aradryan's drug-fevered mind, connecting him for an instant to the coil of his life strangling Alaitoc. The craftworld was in grave danger and would need every Alaitocii, outcast or not, to help defend her. Aradryan had to return, to restore the balance he had selfishly disrupted.

Thirianna lurched out of the skein, utterly drained. Pain thrummed through her synapses and her body ached, tested to the limit by the amplifying effect of the orb. She decided to return to her chambers. Other, loftier minds could concern themselves with what would happen. When she had recovered she would play her part in the events to come.

War was fast approaching and she would need all of her strength.

WAR

The Bloody Hand – Khaine. There is one rune that a seer loathes to employ, for it is a terrible rune; all too often it is the doom of the seer. Yet there is no other rune that can replicate its power, for in war and bloodshed are many fates decided. In matters of battle, the rune of Khaine must guide the eye of the seer, to bring about the demise of the enemy and ensure the Bloody Hand does not fall upon the friend. A terrible rune, used to trace the fate of Alaitoc's Avatar. It is a treacherous rune, possessed of its own fierce pride, and will try to steer the seer only to fates that end in tragedy.

THE AVATAR WAS awakening.

Thirianna could feel its bloody call in her bones.

The touch of the Avatar stretched to every part of Alaitoc, its wakening dreams of bloodshed permeating the infinity circuit, rousing the ire of all on the craftworld.

As a former Aspect Warrior, Thirianna was more susceptible to the sensation than those who had never walked the Path of the Warrior. Her war-mask, held in dormancy, quivered inside her mind, seeking to rise up in response to Khaine's call to arms. It was ever-present, gnawing at her thoughts when the council of war was convened between the autarchs and the seers. She could sense its effect in the warlocks and felt its power swirling from the military leaders.

The task was straightforward. The seers would divine the nature of the human attack, trying to foresee the direction and nature of the assault. With this information the autarchs would devise a suitable battle plan. In turn, the seers could travel the skein to explore the possibilities opened up by the courses of action chosen.

Straightforward, but far from simple. So many strands of fate had to be examined it was impossible to foresee every eventuality. Promising threads petered out into inconsequence, while mundane events proved to have profound implications. The life or death of a particular individual could hold the balance between victory and defeat; whether that was an autarch or a guardian, a Space Marine captain or a lowly human soldier. Whether a squad held its ground for a moment longer, or fell back a moment sooner, created new vistas to contemplate.

The greater part of the burden of prophecy fell on the shoulders of the most experienced farseers. They could utilise their runes of Khaine to travel the bloodiest pathways, weighing up life and death with incredible accuracy.

For the warlocks, and lesser seers such as Thirianna, their task was to provide an overview of the unfolding events. They lingered on the periphery of the skein while the most powerful minds delved deep, watching the great play of events as the senior seers used their many runes to twist and bind, separate and cut the threads of destiny.

Thirianna had been presented with the rune of Alaitoc by Kelamith. It was a powerful symbol, binding her fate to that of the craftworld. As the seer who had first witnessed the potential doom, it was her responsibility to stay focussed on that moment.

Over and over she saw the craftworld destroyed or overrun.

If the fleet engaged the attackers early, the enemy smashed past and landed without interference; if the starships protecting the craftworld held off their attacks the enemy were too numerous to hold back while they bombarded Alaitoc from space.

If the eldar held the landing points, they were drawn into bloody, attritional fighting. Victory came at too high a price, the population of Alaitoc so diminished that it never recovered. If the humans were allowed to gain too much of a foothold, large portions of Alaitoc were destroyed, never to be rebuilt.

It was an agonising experience for Thirianna, who

sat at the heart of the destruction like the silver scales of Morai-heg, weighing one outcome over another.

The autarchs asked constant questions, demanding details of the forces the humans would bring to bear, the types of weapons they carried, the tactics they would employ. No detail was considered insignificant. The war host of Alaitoc was deadly but finely tuned. Each squad of Aspect Warriors, each tank and transport, each Titan and starship had a role to fill in the great tapestry that was being woven. If part of the thread was too weak, the whole picture came apart.

Arhathain, veteran commander and hero to Alaitoc, suggested a swift counter-attack, taking the battle to the humans before they had approached Alaitoc. The seers complied, investigating the outcomes of such a strike.

Too few warriors, came the response. The Imperial fleet being sent against Alaitoc would absorb any damage inflicted and the surviving Aspect Warriors would not have the strength to hold against the humans left behind.

Seeing that invasion was inevitable, the autarchs considered their alternatives. Did they fight for every piece of the craftworld or sacrifice areas for strategic gain? Here the prophecies were more encouraging. As sufficient as the Imperial ships were to break through the orbital defence, the skein showed that they could not hold onto large amounts of territory. An occupation of Alaitoc would be impossible, the threat of a long, drawn-out war remote.

This pleased the autarchs, and they pried further

into the potential strategies they might employ. The war host was a fluid, moving thing, able to strike and withdraw, constantly attacking whilst using speed and misdirection as its defence. If it was possible to avoid fighting the humans head-on, the eldar would gradually sap the strength of the invaders.

Thirianna was overwhelmed by the vision that followed. Large swathes of Alaitoc lay in ruins. Domes were shattered and the passageways choked with the dead. The delicate ecological balance of Alaitoc was destroyed, deserts encroaching on forest domes, swamps swallowing terraces and vineyards, wildernesses engulfing parks and gardens. The infinity circuit faltered, sporadic and weak.

Yet the Alaitocii survived; enough to renew and rebuild. Their homes were devastated, many loved ones lost, but the people of Alaitoc endured. In time the craftworld would recover, and though most of a generation would be lost, Alaitoc would rise from the ashes of invasion like the phoenix of Asuryan, its power diminished but not gone.

The exhausting work continued, honing the strategy over the coming cycles. The seers came and went as their stamina dictated, adding their power to the effort when they could, resting and recovering when they were spent. Thirianna was sent back to her apartments several times by Kelamith, to sleep amongst dreams of flank attacks and diversions, air assaults and orbital battles.

Slowly the plan came together, like the orchestration of a great composer. The autarchs pored over the visions of the seers, homing in on areas of vagueness, mustering the resources of the craftworld to meet the threats that emerged with each prophesied scenario.

The resultant consensus was in part a military strategy and in part an ethos to be adhered to. War brought too much flux to the skein for every outcome to be known, and despite every effort of Thirianna and the rest of the seer council, there was no surety of any particular event coming to pass. The plan consisted of layer after layer of contingency, of response to gains and losses as fluid as the war host itself. Every margin of victory or defeat was analysed, and plans constructed to deal with the consequences.

After so much effort, the best the autarchs hoped for was a chance for victory. They could be no more prepared than they were, yet chance, or perhaps fate, would still play a major part in the battles to come. Victory was not guaranteed, indeed was far from certain, and depended upon a great many things coming to pass as the eldar desired.

In that time, Thirianna learned a lot about humans and their way of war. Through the visions granted by the skein, she saw the paradox in their nature. In one regard they were blunt and predictable. They lacked any kind of subtlety, preferring their brute strength over sophistication. They could be trusted to tackle any obstacle the eldar placed before them head-on, and in this was found their greatest weakness. They could be lured and directed, forced into battles that favoured the eldar. Their xenophobia, their creed of self-punishment and sacrifice could prove their undoing, bringing them into battles that they could not hope to win yet ones they would fight out of blind devotion and hope.

Yet for all their barbaric ways, the humans were also fickle. In each of them nestled the seed for great heroism and great cowardice. Compared to the lives of the eldar, the humans lived for a brief moment, and their threads were little more than remnants scattered across the skein, the vast majority passing their lives without meaning or impact on the wider universe.

A few of them were different, but were not necessarily marked out by status or rank. A lone sergeant might rally a line rather than flee; a medic might brave a storm of fire to rescue an officer who goes on to lead a new attack; a gunner mans his weapon when others have retreated to hold back an Alaitocii counter-attack.

Not only did moments of positive qualities make the picture unclear. Unexpected cowardice, ill discipline, poor communications on the part of the humans could unsettle the plans laid by the eldar. Just as the Alaitoc war host had to be precise and focussed in its movements and attacks, the responses of the enemy had to concur with the desires of the eldar.

It was with hope rather than confidence that Thirianna left the final meeting of the council. She had played her part in preparing Alaitoc for war; now was the time for her to ready herself so that she might influence the battle by her own hand.

* * *

THROUGHOUT THE SCRYING and the planning, the pull of Khaine had strengthened. The Avatar's coming was fast approaching and Thirianna could feel the white heat of its awakening burning through the infinity circuit.

The exarchs were assembling, ready to present the Young King to the Avatar of Khaine. The infinity circuit trembled with the impending events, flashing images of war through the mind of Thirianna. She saw not just the battles to come, but conflicts past, across the galaxy. In her dreams she was a hundred different warriors striding across a hundred different battlefields. She brought death to the foes of Alaitoc as the war god incarnate led the battle host of the craftworld.

As the ceremony reached its climax, the skein fell still, pregnant with potent possibility. Thirianna felt the moment of sacrifice as the Young King was offered up. The rune of the Young King disappeared from the skein and the rune of Khaine took its place, dimly glowing, casting its presence across every future.

The Avatar's spirit roused itself from dormancy with a psychic roar that caused all on the craftworld to pause, shaken by a wave of anger and a momentary thirst for blood.

Thirianna had been asleep, dreaming of skies alight with green fire and dark towers toppled by the might of Alaitoc. She sat bolt upright in her bedding, heart pounding, breath coming in shallow gasps. Her war-mask surged up from the interior of her mind, blanketing all other thoughts. The seer relived her own battles, each passing in an instant, a dazzling, dizzying montage of slaying. Countless were the enemies that had fallen by her hand.

The moment passed.

Sitting in the darkness of her room, Thirianna felt relaxed and alert. The tension of the last cycles had drained away, replaced with energy and purpose, invigorated by the coming of the Avatar.

The enemy approached and Thirianna was ready to fight.

THE SEERS HAD the best view of the opening stages of the war; better even than the captains and their crews aboard the starships gathering on the outer edges of the star system. The farseers came together in the Chamber of the Dawning World, a dark circular hall whose floor was inlaid with concentric circles of runes cast from precious metals that glowed with the power of the infinity circuit.

Each farseer had been ascribed a region of the skein to watch. Thirianna watched the unfolding fates of more than a dozen starships, from frigates to battleships, as they took station hidden in the gravity well of one of the outer planets.

The arrival of the humans was imminent and plain to see. Their ships bulled their way through the skein, casting long shadows on the warp that even the most inexperienced seer could detect. They were accompanied by a whispered moaning, their warp engines leaving torment and misery in their wake. Their rough passage formed eddies of power that made their direction and speed easy to calculate. Daemons and other predators trailed after them, drawn by the aura of life that leaked from within the crude warp shields protecting the human vessels.

The runes of the farseers danced around each other, combining together to form a picture of the star system as accurate to the seers' eyes as if they were gods looking down upon the dying star and its orbiting planets.

Yet this picture was not of the present but the future. It told a tale of what might be rather than what was. In the elaborate dance of fate, squadrons of attack craft whirled about each other while human strike cruisers and eldar destroyers duelled with laser and shell and torpedo.

The humans arrived, their warp engines splitting apart the aether, sending a shockwave ripping across the skein, momentarily blinding Thirianna and the others.

The first flotilla disengaged from the warp exactly where the council had predicted. The humans' backwards technology forced them to spread their fleet during entry, while crude scanners peered into the star system gathering data.

The outlying ships of Alaitoc were already moving, engines charged from their solar sails, drifting undetected from the cover of asteroid fields and gas clouds. The humans were still half-blind as their ships scoured the star system with laser and microwaves, and in their moment of weakness, the eldar struck the first blow.

Launching salvoes of torpedoes, the Alaitocii

announced their presence. Waves of frigates made attack runs on the lead human ships, their laser batteries rippling along the energy shields encasing the armoured vessels.

Thirianna was impressed for a moment. The human ships were protected by warp-based technologies, their fields dissipating the energy of the fusillade into the alternate realm. With each barrage stopped came the scream of the warp, every failing shield a tiny pinprick break through the thin barrier between reality and the immaterial. She had not believed them capable of such technology, though it was still simplistic compared to the eldar mastery of the warp.

The humans struck back as best they could, launching flights of bombers and waves of torpedoes. Their clumsy cannons hurled plasma and huge explosive shells, but their tracking systems were unable to cope with the holofields hiding the eldar vessels. The frigates skipped away from the counter-attack, a few suffering minor damage from the sheer weight of fire furiously hurled out by the human guns.

The runes moved, growing brighter or darker as fortunes favoured one ship or another. Khaine's rune howled madly as a human ship exploded, consumed by its own reactor. At least half a dozen of the other vessels were severely damaged, their threads bleeding on the skein as they limped away from the eldar attack.

The main force of the invaders now appeared, arriving in small groups scattered around the edges of the star system. This also the seers had foretold, but the fleet of Alaitoc was not numerous enough to cover every approach. The farseers had located the flagships and the vessels with fates that would favour the humans and the autarchs had concentrated the efforts of the fleet towards them, determined to snuff out their potential before it could be realised.

The eldar attacks were fast and damaging, but could not be sustained against the immense fire-power of the arriving ships. The autarchs had heeded the warning against a prolonged battle, and duly the fleet responded, melting away into the void before they suffered badly from the humans' retaliation.

The first phase was complete. There was no future in which the humans had been prevented from entering the system, but damage had been done. More importantly, doubt had been sown in the minds of the enemy commanders. Thirianna could see their threads wavering, splitting rapidly as they considered their course of action. A myriad scenarios filtered across the skein: the humans gathering into a single fleet and driving straight for Alaitoc; the enemy vessels dispersing, attempting to make their own way towards the craftworld before gathering for the attack; lighter vessels sent rapidly ahead to scout the way while the lumbering battle cruisers and bat-tleships followed behind.

To confound the planning of the humans, eldar vessels continued to make hit-and-run attacks, directed towards lone and vulnerable vessels by the autarchs, who in turn were guided by the constant commentary from the seers.

'The *Finrairni Ano* and *Lasthetin* are the stalkers of

the void, moving along the bloody crescent,' intoned Thirianna, her words spoken without thought as she concentrated on the visions filling her mind, channelling what she saw into a stream of description. 'A human light cruiser delays, suffering engine trouble in the shadow of the ninth world. The fiery blooms upon the arc of the stars wither the enemy, and in shadow we pass into light.'

A chorus of voices filled the chamber, the words and the images behind them directed through the infinity circuit to the waiting autarchs who passed on the messages to the admirals and captains of the fleet.

The ships themselves were part of the skein, their wraithbone hearts merged with the eternal matrix, forged from the infinity circuit of Alaitoc. No light or radio wave could travel as quickly as thought on the skein and every movement and action of the humans was almost instantaneously known to those aboard the craftworld.

The artful interplay of rune and fate was a graceful veneer atop the violence unleashed. Thirianna could feel every death brought about, played out in flickers of desperate struggle across the skein. Bodies froze in the void and burned in the fires of expelling gases. Mothers and fathers, sons and daughters perished, consumed by plasma and laser. Pain and fear flowed, feeding the rune of Khaine. Dread stalked the strands of fate, sapping the strength of the living, turning heroes to cowards. Blood was spilled, its taste lingering in Thirianna's mouth. Every thread that ended was a life lost, human or eldar.

The skein was awash with destruction, yet Thirianna drew on her war-mask to endure. She distanced herself from the struggle, seeing only sundered destinies and paths of hope. She did not let her anger come to the fore, instead she viewed the unfolding war with dispassionate eyes. To feel was to invite doubt and there could be no room for that.

The humans floundered for some time and Thirianna sensed discord flowing through their fate. Internal division, debate, was splitting asunder their threads. All the while the eldar continued to shadow the humans' ships, waiting for any opportunity to pounce, seizing on any moment of unwariness.

THE SECOND PHASE of the attack was a drawn-out affair. The invading fleet broke into three waves, much like an ancient column of advance with a vanguard, main force and rearguard. Picket ships were despatched by the human commanders to keep watch for the Alaitocii attacks, while several squadrons of the fastest starships broke ahead to secure the orbital area between the fourth and fifth planets.

Several times the enemy tried to lay traps, leaving vessels seemingly isolated and ripe for attack whilst in reality help remained near at hand. The skein revealed the blatant trickery behind these ploys and the eldar ignored the bait, instead launching raids against other parts of the enemy fleet.

For cycle after cycle the humans encroached on the space around Alaitoc. Having split their fleet, the enemy commanders ensured that no part was left too far away from the others, nor too close, and so their advance proceeded at the pace of their slow battleships and sluggish transports.

It was impossible to watch the skein for so long without pause, and the seers divided their labours so that some rested while the others watched for any new threat or opportunity. Like a choreographed performance in the Dome of a Thousand Shadows, the farseers passed on what they had seen to each other, their runes touching and parting, forming new patterns with each turning cycle, the collective far stronger than its individual parts.

The humans were direct but not hasty, and the skein was filled with images of the inevitable clash. As the seers had witnessed, there would be no stopping the humans from launching a direct attack.

Yet the delays of the humans provided some hope for the Alaitocii. The longer the invading fleet took to arrive, the more raids and passing attacks the craftworld's fleet could make.

The vanguard flotilla did its best to sweep away the waiting eldar ambushes, but their ships were too few and too slow to catch the elusive eldar vessels. Forewarned of any sudden changes in direction and speed of the enemy ships, the line of eldar vessels protecting the craftworld was able to quickly adjust, vanishing before retribution found them, stealing away to new hiding places.

As time passed, the Alaitocii were helped in other ways. More ships arrived through the webway, bringing back warriors and rangers who had been away from the craftworld. One particular arrival caused quite a stir on the skein.

On board were three of the greatest warriors of the eldar, the Phoenix Lords. They were the founders of the Aspect shrines, whose names were legend. Three founders of the Aspect shrines: The Cry of the Wind, Baharroth; The Harvester of Souls, Maugan Ra; The Shadow Hunter, Karandras.

Three Phoenix Lords, almost without precedent, had come to Alaitoc for a single purpose: war.

Thirianna marvelled at the threads of these remarkable beings. Their lives stretched back to the time of the Fall, where their fates had blossomed into life under the leadership of the First Exarch, Asurmen, yet their origins were hidden by the great shadow of She Who Thirsts. Their threads also stretched forwards into the impossibly distant future, to the final battle known as the Rhana Dandra, the Last Battle against Chaos.

Yet the threads were not a single thread, each was bound to dozens of other lives across their span. Other strands joined those of the Phoenix Lords, winding close about them before becoming part of the whole. Thirianna had seen something similar in the lives of the exarchs, their essence made up of a composite of eldar spirits. Examining them more closely, Thirianna saw that the initial appearance was deceptive. The lives were absorbed by the Phoenix Lords but the original thread continued on, bolstered by each new knot along its length.

As she was about to turn her attention elsewhere, Thirianna noticed something familiar about the thread that represented Karandras, the Shadow

Hunter, Phoenix Lord of the Striking Scorpions. There would come a miniscule break in the near-future, but the splitting of fate, the ending of a life, was swiftly healed by the binding of another strand: Korlandril's. Thirianna was not sure what this presaged, but she did not have the time to investigate further.

Another rune threw itself to the fore, demanding attention from every seer.

The Wanderer rose high above the skein. Aradryan, unwitting instigator of this unfolding catastrophe, had returned to Alaitoc.

'You will not see him.' Kelamith's statement was definite, though it was an assertion rather than a prophecy. 'Your fate and his are too tightly bound for you to cause any more disruption.'

'How can you deny me?' argued Thirianna. 'Aradryan is my friend, I should speak with him. Am I not owed this small courtesy for my part in warning you of the peril that has beset us?'

'Your part in this remains unclear,' said Kelamith. 'The decision of the council is final. You will not see the renegade.'

'He is outcast, not renegade, there is a difference,' said Thirianna.

'That too will be for the council to decide,' said Kelamith. 'Aradryan's actions have brought untold disaster upon Alaitoc, whether he knew the danger or not. You have seen the skein, the uncertainty that surrounds your friend. He is a highly disruptive force and we do not yet know to what consequence his coming here will lead.'

'He brings reinforcements,' said Thirianna. 'Surely that will count in his favour. You see as well as I do the rune of the Laughing God. Harlequins accompany him, plus many outcasts of Alaitoc that wish to defend their home.'

'And that will be placed on the balance of judgement by the council,' said Kelamith. He made a short, chopping motion with his hand, a sign of irritation and an indication that the conversation was finished. 'Return to your duties and concentrate on your work.'

Thirianna held her tongue, knowing that to argue longer would achieve nothing and risk further admonishment from Kelamith. She glared at the farseer's back as he left the chamber, indignant at the council's decision to subject Aradryan to their judgement.

She made her way to the Chamber of the Orb, where the defence of Alaitoc had been moved. The divinations were becoming more intricate, as the human fleet massed again, barely three cycles' travel from Alaitoc. The humans appeared to have stalled, and were busily reorganising their ships; flurries of transports and communications were exchanged as they devised the final plan for their attack.

Half a dozen seers were immersed with the Orb of Elmarianin, keeping watch on the movements of the humans. Every ship had been brought back for the close defence of Alaitoc; the humans were gathered en masse and provided no easy target for attack. Perhaps, wondered Thirianna, they were hoping the eldar would foolishly try to confront them in a massed battle. Such a move would never happen. For the Alaitocii to surrender their advantages of speed and manoeuvrability would be a move of utter folly.

As the cycle passed into the night phase, Thirianna examined the humans with her companions, whilst allowing herself the occasional moment to look at the fate of Aradryan. The council's decision was in the balance, whether Aradryan was declared renegade and told to depart or if he would be welcomed back to the craftworld. His own temperament further complicated matters and several of his futures showed Aradryan leaving in anger or contempt at the council's behaviour, abandoning Alaitoc to its fate.

The humans had settled upon their course, the threads of fate coalescing once more, becoming a bright path that led directly to the rune of Alaitoc at the centre of Thirianna's thoughts. Out in the darkness of space, plasma engines were flaring into miniature suns, powering the Imperial vessels along that path.

TRAILS OF FIRE criss-crossed the starry sky as missiles and torpedoes streaked across the firmament. The blinding flash of laser weapons flitted through the darkness, while blossoms of brief flame erupted in the void. Squadrons of graceful destroyers tacked effortlessly to bring their weapons to bear while battleships slid gently through the maelstrom, their batteries unleashing salvoes of destruction, open bays spewing wave after wave of darting fighter craft and wide-winged bombers.

On the skein, the threads of fate looped and coiled, colliding with each other as ships exchanged volleys of fire and torpedoes streaked through space. Within every strand were dozens of others: the lives of the eldar crews. Within the threads of the human fleet, the mass of fates entwined together was enormous, an impossible tangle of humanity in which it was impossible to tell who would live and who would die. Death was indiscriminate, laying low admiral and crewman alike, favouring none.

The seers had narrowed down the possible landing sites of the attack to three locations. The autarchs had arranged their forces accordingly, ready to respond as the course of destiny became clearer. Squads of Guardians and Aspect Warriors waited in their transports, spread across Alaitoc.

The infinity circuit was afire with the tension, the minds of all aboard the craftworld concentrated upon this single effort. Thirianna could feel expectation and fear from the many; anger and anticipation from the Avatar and the Aspect Warriors.

Breaking the cordon of eldar ships, an Imperial frigate approached the voidward rim of Alaitoc, heading towards the Dome of Crystal Seers. Thirianna could see the slab-sided, brutal vessel through the thousand eyes of Alaitoc's sensor batteries, encrusted with cornices and buttresses, its prow a giant golden ram shaped like an eagle's beak. Flashes rippled from bow to stern as it opened fire with deck after deck of guns, the flares cut through by the searing beams of laser turrets arranged along a crenulated dorsal deck.

Anger rippled through the craftworld and Alaitoc responded. Like a wounded beast, the craftworld lashed out at its attacker, sending a storm of lightning and laser leaping from defence turrets and anti-ship guns. The human frigate was enveloped by fire, shields scourged by the ire of Alaitoc. Under the torrential fusillade its hull quickly broke, sending plumes of burning air into the vacuum. The furious fire continued until the ship's plasma reactor was breached, turning it into a brief-lived miniature sun.

The breakthrough of the frigate was only the first foreseen by the seers. Thirianna saw more Imperial vessels smashing their way into range of Alaitoc. She spoke quickly, sending messages directly to the ships' commanders placed under her guidance, redirecting them so that they would be able to blunt the reckless human attacks.

The eldar ships glimmered with holofields, appearing as shimmering ghosts to open fire before disappearing against the star-filled backdrop. Human void shields sputtered with blue and purple flares as they unleashed bursts of energy to shunt the attacks of the eldar into warp space.

Despite the efforts of Thirianna and her companions, the relentless ferocity of the humans would not be turned aside. The skein was awash with their hatred, their loathing of the eldar a unifying force that drew together disparate fates, focussing them upon a single goal: the destruction of Alaitoc.

The humans drew inexorably closer, their coming

heralded by fresh waves of torpedoes and the glare of attack craft. Burning hulks drifted in their wake, both human and eldar, debris gently spiralling away from shattered wrecks. The humans seemed bent on their course, coming straight for Alaitoc like armoured comets, punching through the craft-world's fleet, heedless of the damage inflicted upon them.

There were too many converging destinies to keep track of them all and too late Thirianna saw a cruiser bursting past the burning remnants of one of the destroyers under her watch. She sent a warning to the captain but even his swift vessel did not have time to escape. Hundreds of explosions filled the void around the fleeing eldar ship, making a mockery of its holofields. Distraction and misdirection were no defence against the scattered bombardment unleashed by the human cruiser.

Broken in half, solar sail shredded, the eldar destroyer slowly disintegrated. Thirianna found painfully few threads of those aboard, the lives of a handful of crew who had reached the escape shuttles in time.

The cruiser ploughed on, intent on bringing its weapons to bear against Alaitoc. Thirianna reached into the infinity circuit, connecting with the minds of the gunners and urging them to concentrate their fire on the looming Imperial ship.

There were too many threats though, and her call was lost amidst the clamour of other farseers sending their own warnings.

Thirianna latched on to the thread of the human

cruiser, flying ahead along its path to locate its destruction. She found nothing to give her hope, as she watched the long lines of armoured doors opening again to reveal bristling gun batteries.

At the last moment the weapons of Alaitoc heeded her call for attention. Laser fire converged on the cruiser and its shields rippled, dissipating the blasts with actinic flares. Its bow erupted with blossoms of orange and moments later the streak of torpedoes hurtled towards Alaitoc, breaking into hundreds of smaller missiles as they crashed into the craftworld.

Thirianna felt the impact in her spirit as well as in the trembling beneath her feet. It was as if her own body was pierced, and she recoiled from the infinity circuit as more salvoes from the cruiser's gun decks slammed into Alaitoc, crashing against the energy shields that protected the domes.

Forcing herself to endure the pain, Thirianna strove to unwind the coiling thread of fate that surrounded the cruiser. Transports were arriving in its wake. They could not be stopped. The barrage from the cruiser continued for some time and then fell silent, the flare of laser and shell replaced by the small pinpricks of assault craft engines.

Thirianna glanced ahead along the skein and saw human soldiers disgorged from the ramps of their drop-ships. She knew where the first boarding parties would land.

'Autarch Arhathain, the humans will come first to the Tower of Ascending Dreams.' She sent the message and turned her attention back to the skein, seeing the interplay of fates crystallising as the defenders of Alaitoc responded to the news.

'Come with me.' Kelamith broke Thirianna from her contemplation. She withdrew from the skein and found the farseer standing next to her, staff and sword in hand. He wore his jewel-lensed helmet, his voice carried to her across the skein.

Her own witchblade thrummed into life at her belt, detecting imminent battle. Around her, the other farseers and warlocks were also readying for physical conflict, leaving those with no war-masks to continue to monitor the skein.

'We have done what we can from here,' said Kelamith. 'We set foot upon a new path. Now we must take a more direct role.'

BY THE TIME Thirianna had reached the arterial passageway adjoining the Chambers of the Seers, a Wave Serpent transport was already waiting for her, summoned by Kelamith. Two more of the sleek machines glided into view as the ramp in the back of the first opened to allow Thirianna to board.

Inside were ten guardians, clad in armour made up of yellow polymer mesh overlaid with plates of deep blue. Ten helmeted heads turned towards Thirianna as she embarked and ten shuriken catapults were raised in deferential salute.

Kelamith's thoughts touched upon Thirianna's mind.

The Passing Spectacle. Stop the humans from reaching the Plaza of Shattered Memories.

She acknowledged the instruction and passed it on to the pilot of the Wave Serpent. The transport rose into the air as the ramp silently closed. Thirianna's last glimpse outside was of the two other Wave Serpents falling into formation behind.

As they sped along a cross-world highway, Thirianna slipped into the skein, focussing her mind on the spiralling pathway known as the Passing Spectacle. It acted as a bridge across a gorge-like split between two of the craftworld's domes, leading from the docks at the Tower of Ascending Dreams to the Plaza of Shattered Memories.

She foresaw human soldiers advancing quickly to the base of the pathway, three squads of them led by an officer in a heavy coat. They carried simple lasguns and their fear resonated along the thread of their fate; they had strayed too far from the other landing parties, misdirected by Alaitoc itself, and would be easy prey.

Thirianna followed this train of thought and glimpsed the humans being cut down in a crossfire of shurikens. She reached across the skein to the minds of Nathuriel and Unarian, the leaders of the two other guardian squads placed under her command.

'Depart at the Crescent of the Dawn and approach the Passing Spectacle from starwards. We will draw the enemy onto the bridge, allowing you to strike from behind.'

'Understood, Farseer Thirianna,' the two squad leaders replied.

The use of her honorific sent a brief thrill through Thirianna, but it was soon surpassed by a wave of anxiety. She looked again at the skein, going further into the future to locate the consequences of her plan.

All was well. The advance party of humans would be destroyed and the bottom of the Passing Spectacle secured. Several possibilities spawned from the act, all of them leading to fresh attacks against Thirianna and her warriors. She saw herself meeting another human officer blade-to-blade in one of the scenarios, her witchblade matched against his chainsword. The farseer emerged victorious, though several of the guardians would lose their lives defending the passageway.

There was another possible fate emerging. It was extremely vague, the hint of a possibility. Something was obscuring the skein, a presence she could not quite discern. With a thought, she tugged the Scorpion from her belt pouch and set her mind to the task of deciphering the riddle.

There was a figure cloaked in uncertainty, bound within the skein in a way Thirianna had not seen before. It troubled her that this person's actions were hidden. He was definitely human, his short, brutal fate tying a knot around the graceful arc of Thirianna's own thread. She could not see how the division came to pass, it was mired in circumstances beyond prediction, but on one path her life ended and on the other she killed the human.

A word from the Wave Serpent pilot informed her that they would soon be arriving at their destination. Thirianna took the last few moments to scour the skein for wider information.

The humans had forced a landing, several hundred

of their soldiers breaking through the dock defences to create a safe zone for more drop-ships and shuttles to land. They were trying to unload their heavier weapons from the transports, but were being subjected to withering fire by several guardian squads supported by heavy weapons on anti-grav platforms.

The grander scheme was unfurling as the autarchs had dictated. It was usual for the Aspect Warriors to bear the brunt of the fighting, with the militia of the guardians acting as a reserve to counter-attack against enemy breakthroughs. However, the divining of the seer council had foreseen problems with this approach; some greater force of the humans was also held in reserve and once committed would sweep away all resistance. The source of this strength was unclear, but the autarchs had decided that the guardians would bear the brunt of the early fighting, preserving the fighters of the Aspect shrines to confront this later threat.

The Wave Serpent slid to a halt, the ramp opening with a hiss of escaping pressurised air. Stepping out onto the pale grey of the Passing Spectacle, Thirianna realised that Alaitoc had drained the area of air, leaving only a thin atmosphere for the humans to breathe. With the aid of their helmets, the eldar had more than sufficient air to sustain them, another factor in their favour.

Thirianna and her squad took up position opposite an archway not far from where the Passing Spectacle blended with the lower levels of the dock. The humans would be entering soon and she warned her guardians to be ready while she checked to make sure the other two squads were in position to strike.

The hallway in which they waited had a low, oval cross-section, flattened underfoot by a pathway of marble. Columns lined each side of the passageway, providing cover for Thirianna and her warriors.

'They are coming,' announced Thirianna, sensing a tremble on the skein caused by the approach of the humans.

The first soldier through the door seemed utterly unaware of his peril. Thirianna allowed a few more to enter before giving the order to open fire. Shurikens hissed down the passageway, slashing through the soldiers' grey uniforms, leaving arcs of blood spattered on the floor and walls.

Thirianna warned her guardians to take cover a few moments before a sporadic blast of ruby-hued las-fire flared from the archway as the following soldiers opened fire. The guardian nearest the door staggered out from behind a column, clutching the side of his helm. The name Temerill flashed through Thirianna's mind a moment before another las-bolt caught the guardian in the chest, burning through the breastplate of this armour, sending him reeling to the floor.

His thread had ended.

Thirianna drew her shuriken pistol and fired back, her salvo joining with the fire of the others to cut down the three humans who were crouched in the archway. Sensing the moment for action, Thirianna stepped out into the corridor and ran forwards, her witchblade flaring into life. She threw herself into the cover of a las-scarred column a heartbeat before another volley erupted from the outer hallway.

Thirianna glimpsed into her immediate future, judging whether to attack or stay in the sanctuary of her hiding place. She saw herself being struck by several las-bolts, but none penetrated the psychic field of her rune armour.

Witchblade levelled towards the arch, Thirianna stepped out from behind the pillar and focussed her mind. She filtered her psychic power through the anger of her war-mask, sending it coursing along the length of her weapon. Violet flames spewed along the passageway, roaring through the archway to engulf the soldiers beyond.

Thirianna felt four more lives flicker into nothingness.

'Fall back towards the ramp,' she told the others, noting the arrival of the human officer. He would lead the attack, the humans storming along the passageway with knives and bayonets. Thirianna saw that such a move would be most unwelcome at this moment in time and signalled again for the guardians to retreat a few dozen paces to the archway behind them.

As the humans launched their fresh assault, Thirianna sent the call for the other two squads to make their move. The humans barrelled forwards into the fire of her guardians, ignoring the several men that were cut down by the welcome of the eldar's shuriken catapults. The slow, clumsy humans wore ill-fitting suits of drab grey and black camouflage, stitched with skull and eagle insignias on their arms and chests, their helmets fitted with silvered visors that hid the upper part of their brutish faces.

Like the guardians had done before, they took up positions behind the protection of the columns, lasguns propped against the burnt and chipped masonry. Thirianna saw the darker uniform of the officer striding through the gateway, his deep voice echoing along the passage as he bellowed at his troops and waved them forwards again.

Half of the humans let loose a volley of las-fire while the other half ran on, their breathing laboured, bayonets glinting in the light of the screaming las-bolts.

At the same moment, Unarian's warriors emerged from the far archway, weapons at the ready. Their burst of fire struck the enemy soldiers from behind, shurikens tearing through cloth uniforms and flesh.

Thirianna signalled for her squad to attack, and led the charge back into the corpse-choked corridor, her rune armour flaring with las-blasts. She singled out the human officer amongst the panicking soldiers, picking loose his thread from the tangle of the others. With a flick of her wrist, she sent a whining bolt of psychic energy into the ungainly crowd of humans. It struck the officer in the back of the head as he was turning to look at Unarian's warriors. Hair and skin charred instantly and with a high-pitched scream the officer toppled forwards, his pistol clattering across the floor as it fell from his grasp.

The men he had been leading lived for only a few moments longer. A few managed to snap off ragged shots, killing two of Unarian's guardians, before they too were ripped to shreds by the coordinated shuriken volleys.

Thirianna checked the skein. Not a single human thread was left; all were dead.

More were approaching quickly, though not so fast that they would arrive before Thirianna had readied a fresh welcome for them. The passageway was too narrow for all three squads to defend, so she dispersed them through the surrounding rooms.

She looked down at the bodies of the dead humans, shocked and yet pleased by how easy it had been to outwit them. She cautioned herself against over-confidence. A momentary glance at the skein showed that her shadowy confrontation was becoming more likely. A circle of burning iron surrounded her rune, slowly constricting around her.

This was just the first skirmish in a battle and the first battle in a war that she had seen would last for several cycles. There was still a lot of fighting and killing to be done.

THE INFINITY CIRCUIT was alive with reports of the humans' activities. The farseers passed on what they saw on the skein, their communications appearing to Thirianna alongside glimpsed images of the visions, while the autarchs issued their responses.

Alaitoc itself reacted to the presence of the invaders, reconfiguring walkways and passages, closing off domes and opening up new pathways for the eldar to encircle their foes. Air was expelled from some areas while others were flooded with noxious gases, suffocating the humans in their hundreds.

Darkness enveloped other portions of the craft-world, allowing Striking Scorpions to attack from the shadows, slaying their foes unseen. The docks were subjected to barrages of flickering light to blind the humans, leaving them vulnerable to assault by Warp Spiders and Shining Spears. Sound was also used, to deafen the unprotected ears of the attackers, while their crude radio-based communications were easily blocked or subverted by the energies of the craftworld. The spirits of the infinity circuit were channelled to launch a massive psychic attack, driving the humans mad with visions of death and terror.

Thirianna and her guardians had seen off two more assaults against the Passing Spectacle, though both had been lacklustre in their execution. A swift foray through the skein confirmed Thirianna's suspicion that these attacks were intended merely to keep her small force in place while the humans gathered numbers for a serious push forwards.

She highlighted this turn of events to the autarchs, who set in motion several more guardian squads and two squadrons of war walkers to come to Thirianna's aid. A breakthrough by the humans starward of Thirianna's position meant the reinforcements would not arrive until the next clash had begun.

'We must hold the bridge for as long as possible,' she told her warriors, who now numbered only twelve. If they tried to hold their ground in the teeth of the enemy attack, they would be surrounded and wiped out. 'Be ready to withdraw to the Passing Spectacle at my signal.'

It took some time for the humans to organise themselves for the renewed offensive. During the long pause, Thirianna studied the skein in more detail, trying to figure out the most likely routes of advance they would use. Her attention was drawn to the mysterious figure that was now appearing prominently through her own thread. Using the power of the Scorpion, Thirianna dug into the nature of this individual, and found herself touching upon another mind on the skein.

She recoiled in shock, her mind awash with images from the human psyker. His thoughts were anarchic, lacking the focus of an eldar seer, but the tendrils of his power stretched into many threads, drawing on a large reserve of energy. His mind was protected by a burning shield, which both warded away the prowling daemons but also acted as a beacon to them. If Thirianna's mind was a swift skiff skimming across the waves of the warp, eluding detection, the human was a loud and angry gunboat that bullied its way through the tides of energy.

The human psyker was not far away. Now that Thirianna had identified him, she could sense his location instinctively. Along with several armoured walkers, he had joined a force of nearly fifty humans preparing for the next assault. His presence was highly disruptive; the soldiers alongside the psyker were suspicious of his powers.

They were right to be worried. The psyker tapped into the warp without the benefit of runes, channelling the raw energy of Chaos. Though his mind was wrapped up in protective hymnals and armoured with bluntly fashioned talismans, if they failed he had no other defences against possession or psychic feedback.

The rattle of a large-calibre automatic weapon heralded the next assault. On awkward legs, a human war engine three times as tall as Thirianna stalked through the gloom, a multi-barrelled gun beneath its cockpit spewing fire. Fist-sized projectiles tore through the walls of the passageway and surrounding rooms.

Darting out of cover, the guardians opened fire, but their shurikens inflicted little damage on the walker's armoured hull. Another followed, its rapid-firing laser strobing red beams down the passageway, scorching marks across the pillars and walls.

Behind the walkers advanced several squads of infantry, the psyker amongst them. He was easy to pick out, dressed in a long coat of purple and gold, with a high red-lined collar. His head was shaved bald and Thirianna could see the scars and bulges of implants inserted beneath his scalp. A wispy beard trailed from a narrow chin and his eyes were like beads of green glass. The psyker awkwardly held some form of laser pistol in one hand and a wand of curious design in the other. The rod was tipped with a crystal shaped like a skull and the glimmer of psychic energy surrounded it.

Two of the walkers and a third of the soldiers had come through the archway when Thirianna sent the signal to Alaitoc to close the doorway. The walls shifted, the petal-like plates of the door swishing into place in an instant; an unfortunate human was caught halfway through and was sheared in two by the closing portal.

At the same time, the light crystals blinked out, plunging the passageway into utter darkness. The guardians opened fire, able to see through the heat-sensing lenses of their helmets; Thirianna's helm had the same but her psychic eye highlighted the enemy even more clearly.

She leapt out of cover and ducked beneath a random cannonade of shells from the lead walker. Guided by her prescience she dodged to the right as the fire of her companions whickered through the darkness, cutting down a handful of humans. Three more steps took the farseer up to the first walking machine. Fire leaping from its edges, she swept her witchblade towards the gun of the walker, slicing its barrel clean through.

She jumped back as the pilot tried to fire again. The cannon exploded as its shells jammed in the breech, sending flame and debris up through the floor of the cockpit to mangle and incinerate the pilot. The walker sagged to the left, crashing into a column in a shower of dust and sparks.

A bright light filled the passageway, gleaming from the wand of the psyker. Thirianna was caught in the open, facing the full force of the incoming volley of las-fire. She somersaulted behind the wreckage of the walker as red beams filled the corridor, her rune armour flaring with energy as several bolts found her.

'Avert your gaze,' she told her warriors as she sent another signal to the infinity circuit. If it was light the humans desired, it was light they would have.

Alaitoc flooded energy into the passageway, the walls themselves shining with psychic power, harsh white light blazing into the eyes of the incoming humans. Thirianna vaulted over the downed walker, eyes closed, guided by her psychic sense. Fire streamed from her witchblade, engulfing the next walker, lapping around the edges of the cockpit, licking along hanging pipes and cables.

Fuel lines burst, spewing fire over the walls and ceiling as the machine erupted into a column of flame.

Thirianna continued her course, charging into the closest knot of humans. They were recovering from their blindness, but not quickly enough to see the farseer sprinting into their midst. Her witchblade flashed left and then right, decapitating two of the soldiers.

As she parried a lunging bayonet, Thirianna directed her guardians to the left. They opened fire at her urging, scything down more humans while she ducked under a heavily gloved fist and drove her witchblade through the gut of another man.

Lightning poured down the passageway from the psyker's outstretched hand, leaping through three of the guardians, cracking open armour, scorching flesh and snapping bones. Thirianna felt the pulse of energy along the skein as the psyker drew in another surge of power. She acted without thought, snaring the psyker's thread with her own, cutting off the supply of psychic energy.

The psyker choked and stumbled back with a

howl of pain as Thirianna kicked aside one of his bodyguard. Blue energy enveloped Thirianna as the psyker flung out his wand, power coursing along the skein, engulfing the strand of Thirianna's life.

Her rune armour burned with white light for several heartbeats, absorbing the brunt of the attack. It was not enough to shield her from all damage though as the psychic blast throbbed through her thoughts, burning her mind from the inside.

Snarling away the pain, Thirianna unleashed the fury of her witchblade, purple flames setting fire to the psyker's long coat. He flailed wildly, bolts of power erupting from his eyes as he stumbled backwards, his own attack swarming around him, consuming him from within.

Thirianna had no time to follow up the attack. The butt of a rifle struck her in the back. She rolled with the blow, rune armour clattering on the hard floor, and spun on her heel as she came back to her feet. The tip of her witchblade found the human's chest, punching through breastbone into his heart.

The psyker's thread had come to a ragged end.

Aware of a pounding at the closed archway, Thirianna dipped into the future. The third walker was ramming itself against the door and cracks appeared where the artificial petals joined.

'Pull back to the Passing Spectacle,' she ordered, sending another sheet of violet flame into the humans, driving them back towards the archway.

The guardians retreated, sending more shurikens down the corridor as they melted back towards the bridge.

Thirianna reached a psychic hand into the skein and snatched up the threads of the humans, crushing them together in an immaterial fist. The men around her stumbled into each other and groaned with pain, giving her the opening she needed to break free. Without a backwards glance, she dashed back down the corridor, reaching the safety of the next doorway just as the humans recovered and sent a barrage of red bolts after her.

Including the farseer, there were eight of them left, against at least twice that number of humans. A shuddering crash announced the collapse of the far portal and Thirianna corrected herself: at least four times that number of enemies.

The span of the Passing Spectacle was not without cover. Though it had no rail as it spiralled up over the interdome gulf, it was lined with high pedestals on which were set busts of renowned Alaitocii from the craftworld's long history.

Beneath the bridge stretched the expanse of the chasm, an expanse of gigantic interlocking crystals that formed the bedrock of the craftworld, their depth lost amidst a layer of glittering mist.

The humans advanced cautiously, allowing their remaining walker to take the lead. Thirianna and her squad kept just out of sight, pulling back each time the machine's laser tracked towards them.

They had completed three of the five loops of the spiral when Thirianna ordered them to hold their ground. The reinforcements were approaching rapidly, but the humans would reach the top of the Passing Spectacle before they arrived if they continued to advance at their current pace.

Settling into what cover they could find, the guardians opened fire, sending a storm of shurikens towards the walker. Sparks flew from its armour, but it was not slowed. The marble-like surface of the bridge was scuffed and scratched by the walker's iron feet as it plodded forwards.

Its lascannon spat out a beam of red. A plinth shattered, sending shards of Neruenthia the Foreshadowed spraying into the guardian behind. The eldar's bloodied remains toppled over the edge of the bridge and disappeared into the depths.

Thirianna searched the skein for the fate of the walker's pilot, seeking some means to bring about his death. She located it, a bright, burning strand, as the walker opened fire again, obliterating another of her guardians. She cast about along the neighbouring threads and drew two together.

As the walker's lascannon swivelled towards its next target, a sleek shadow emerged from the fog of the chasm. Its holofields shimmering blue and yellow, the Wave Serpent rose above the Passing Spectacle. The holofields dimmed for a moment as its turret turned towards the walker. Twin trails rushed from its missile launchers and a few heartbeats later, the human war engine was wracked by two detonations, sending its mangled remains careening off the edge of the span.

More transports rushed from the depths, their turrets raking the advancing humans with shuriken cannon fire and stabs of blue plasma from their starcannons. Moving in from the base of the bridge, a trio of war walkers stopped the humans' retreat with a barrage of high-explosive missiles and scatter laser fire.

Rivulets of blood coursed down the Passing Spectacle, dripping over the edge into the misty chasm below. A few of the humans had survived, crawling into the cover of shattered plinths, their threads waning, their lives leaking away.

Thirianna did not pause to enjoy the moment of victory; the skein was alive with movement as more and more humans deployed onto the craftworld. Several hundred were pressing towards her position, far more than could be held.

Another force was heading towards a neighbouring bridge to rimwards, and they would cross into the next dome soon. Searching for some way to delay them while she redeployed her growing force, she found a stray squad of Striking Scorpions not too far away.

Her mind touched upon that of the exarch and she recognised Morlaniath. His thoughts were immersed in shadows and death as his squad raced across Alaitoc aboard their Wave Serpent. Thirianna pushed through the chilling aura and sent him an image of the unfolding battle, allowing him to see the disposition of the squads and vehicles in the vicinity. She bound together several fates, addressing several dozen eldar with her thoughts.

'The enemy make progress along the Well of Disparate Fates. Walk the red path with them, drive them back to their landing craft.'

The runes were set in motion as the Alaitocii

responded to her request. None were close enough to aid her at the Passing Spectacle and a swift survey of the unfolding future revealed that the bridge would not be held against the next attack, even if every eldar with her laid down their lives in its defence.

It was time to draw back to the next line. While she and others held where they could, a concerted counter-attack was being made to reclaim the landing grounds seized by the invaders.

Guided by Thirianna, her small force withdrew to the dome gates at the top of the spiralling bridge. The first humans were already at the base, streaming past the bodies of their dead compatriots, urged on by a bellowing officer whose mind was like an iron cage, impervious to Thirianna's scans.

She waited until the humans were halfway up the bridge before interfacing with the infinity circuit. She arrowed through the conduits of the Passing Spectacle, becoming one with the craftworld, closing off conduits and crystal pathways. With a last thought, she speared back along the bridge, detonating its wraithbone heart as she passed.

The Passing Spectacle erupted into shards from the base, falling in jagged lumps, pitching the advancing humans into the mists below, their screams swallowed by the swirling fog. Thirianna felt a spark of sorrow at the act but it did not last long; if Alaitoc was to be kept safe, much of it would have to be sacrificed for the ultimate victory.

With the humans' axis of advance cut off, Thirianna moved her troops back from the fighting, joining up with several Aspect Warriors squads, a pair of Falcon tanks and several guardians crewing anti-grav support weapons. They moved as one along the Boulevard of Undimmed Glories, preparing for the next phase of the battle.

Something bright and powerful burned across the skein, spearing into the heart of Alaitoc's rune. Thirianna recognised it immediately and felt a shiver of apprehension. The hidden strength the seers had witnessed, the play of their deadly reserves, was unfolding. A red-and-white fist closed on the craftworld, smashing through hundreds of strands of fate.

Thirianna sped across the infinity circuit to the counter-attack against the landing site, seeing dozens of eldar lives shorn short by the reserves being committed. She saw giants, garbed in thick, powered armour. Their livery was a vivid red, their shoulder pads and insignia painted in stark white. Thirianna looked into their spirits and saw warriors hardened by lives of battle, their minds honed to sharp points, their existence directed towards the singular purpose of war.

She snatched what information she could, hearing devotional speeches directed to the spectre of their founder, and glimpsed a world where humans teemed like insects in gigantic cities that pierced polluted skies. She was overwhelmed by shadows of childhood memories of bitter fighting in dark, twisted tunnels, desperate struggles with sharpened metal splinters and home-made guns. They were killers raised from birth, their instinct for slaying honed since infancy in a world where the ruthless lived and the meek did not.

Yet all this was banded about by a willpower of steel, contained by the training of their masters and their dedication to their cause, forged into a cold fury, a righteous anger now directed at the eldar of Alaitoc. They were natural killers, who took joy in slaying, given the greatest armour and weapons the humans possessed, instilled with fervour for destruction like a war-mask that was never removed.

They were not human at all. An Aspect Warrior embraced the touch of Khaine and became a heartless killer, but he or she remained eldar in spirit, able to set aside their destructive impulses when not at war. These warriors had left behind concepts of mercy and desire for peace, and sought only conflict and bloodshed. They were more than human in many ways, yet to Thirianna's mind they were also less than the basest creatures, as crude as orks in their warlike desires, an affront to the galaxy, serving no part other than as harbingers of slaughter. That the self-declared Emperor of Mankind had desired them to be this way betrayed his barbaric nature.

Thirianna shuddered with fear at what she saw, momentarily gripped by panic.

The Sons of Orar, lauded and feared Space Marines of the Emperor, were about to commence their attack.

DESTINY

Alaitoc – Sword of Eldanesh. One of the first runes, Alaitoc signifies the cutting of ties, the sundering of past from present and present from future. For the seers of the craftworld that bears its name, Alaitoc is the hub about which all other runes are cast, determining the fate of the craftworld and its people. It is also a protective rune, which in dire circumstances can be used to cut through the skein, ensuring sanctuary from daemonic intrusion.

THE BATTLE FOR Alaitoc continued to rage. The attack of the Space Marines had bolstered the flagging invasion of the humans, sending the craftworld's defenders reeling back towards the central domes.

Seizing control of several arterial routes, the attackers were advancing at speed, the charge led by the red-and-white-armoured warriors of the Sons of Orar. In their wake followed columns of infantry, tanks and artillery, ready to bring the full weight of the humans' strength to bear against the Alaitocii.

As had been agreed by the council before the invasion, parts of Alaitoc were surrendered without a fight. Force domes and energy shields were removed, exposing the advancing army to the ravages of open space. The great arches along the Way of Unerring Moonlight were sealed. The bridges across the Valley of Benign Modesty were cast down.

The humans were subjected to constant harassment from the swiftest eldar troops. Swooping Hawk Aspect Warriors flitted above the advancing lines, showering down las-fire and plasma grenades. Shining Spears darted from side tunnels, cutting swathes with shuriken fire and laser lance before dashing to safety. Warp Spiders teleported into the heart of the enemy, unleashing the monofilament webs of their deathspinners before withdrawing.

The eldar gave ground and counter-attacked with precise purpose. The enemy could not be halted, but they could be stalled and redirected. Every effort was made to divide the human forces, allowing isolated companies to be picked off by superior attacks. Tanks were led down dead-ends, forced to withdraw and advance again, only to find their new routes blocked to them.

The Space Marines were the toughest proposition. Individually and together they were a match for the

Aspect Warriors. The only means to combat them was to bring them out into the open, where the Titans and other large war engines of Alaitoc could be brought to bear against the superhuman adversaries.

Thirianna received a message from Kelamith as she mustered several batteries of heavy weapons to meet an armoured thrust along the Starlit Causeway. Her fellow farseer requested that she met him in the Well of Silent Affection, a hall located close to the Chambers of the Seers at the core of Alaitoc.

She had known this time would come, but the thought still sent a shiver of trepidation through the farseer. There was only one reason to visit the Well of Silent Affection: to awaken the dead of Alaitoc.

THE HALL WAS well named, its strange acoustics absorbing every sound, muffling Thirianna's footfalls as she crossed the pale blue floor to join Kelamith. The walls were covered with a labyrinth of crystal cables, the infinity circuit laid bare. The energy conduits pulsed and flashed with light.

Kelamith had beside him a wraithbone chest, its lid open. Inside were several dozen waystones, each settled within its own niche within the interior. His expression was hidden behind his ghosthelm, but his voice betrayed his sombre mood.

'It is our duty to rouse the spirits of those passed, that they might fight for the future of generations to come,' said the farseer.

He plucked the first waystone from its nest and held it in its hand. It fitted snugly in his palm, a pale blue ovoid with a pearlescent sheen. Kelamith walked to the infinity circuit conduits, which were gathered in a spiral around a small aperture. He placed the waystone into the waiting hole.

Removing his glove, Kelamith took a sharp-edged rune from his belt: the symbol of Death. With this, he nicked the tip of his finger, allowing a single droplet of blood to emerge. The rune floated up from his fingers and hovered around the waystone as the farseer touched his finger to its cold surface.

The infinity circuit was set alight by the ceremony, psychic energy blazing through the pathways as Kelamith's blood seeped into the waystone.

A bright flash zoomed along the conduits, a spark of white fire, drawn by the farseer's tiny sacrifice. The speeding bolt followed the conduits around the waystone, circling swiftly before disappearing. A moment later the waystone gleamed with inner power, highlighting the farseer's helm and armour with a blue glow.

Kelamith plucked the spirit stone from its place. With measured stride, he crossed the hall to the other side. A wave of the hand drew back the veil of the thin walls, revealing a long line of alcoves. Within each stood a wraithbone form, each taller than an eldar. Their smooth, slender limbs were shaded in blue and yellow, the colours of Alaitoc. Domed heads like helms shone blackly in the light of the infinity circuit.

In their hands the immobile constructs held wraithcannons; Thirianna could feel the dormant warp cores of the weapons imprinting upon her thoughts.

As Kelamith approached the first artificial body,

the helm-like head opened up, revealing a niche within for the spirit stone. The farseer placed the spirit stone in its receptacle and stepped back. The head closed down as psychic energy flared through the wraithbone, glowing from jewelled nodes fashioned within the artificial body and limbs. The black head paled, becoming white with inner light.

The wraithguard turned its head towards Kelamith and then moved its immortal gaze to Thirianna. She could sense its confusion, plucked from the eternal energy of the infinity circuit and placed in a new body. On the skein, a faint thread of fate glimmered into being, a life born anew, however fleetingly.

There is coldness. The ghosts walk amongst us.

The wraithguard's thoughts were confused, scattered. Thirianna felt Kelamith reaching out with his mind, linking his thread to that of the wraithguard, infusing it with his own purpose.

The construct raised its weapon and took a step towards the farseers.

Alaitoc in peril. War. I am ready.

At a signal from Kelamith, Thirianna accompanied him back to the box of waystones. She took one of the stones from the box and followed the same ritual as Kelamith. As her blood touched the waystone, she felt a flicker of connection between herself and the infinity circuit.

It was unlike any experience she had encountered before. She became a part of the infinity circuit in a way that was far deeper than her previous contact. She saw not the flow of psychic energy, but the spirits of the dead that generated it. No longer were its pulses and phases an abstract phenomenon; they were the spirits held within the circuit moving about the craftworld bringing their dormant consciousness to where it was needed.

She latched on to one of the passing spirits, feeling its distant, detached essence. It perceived her only vaguely but was lured by the connection, following the trail she had left on the infinity circuit.

She pulled back from the dead spirit a moment before it passed into the waystone, fearing that part of her would become trapped within it. Unformed questions nagged at Thirianna's thoughts as she took the spirit stone to the next waiting wraithguard.

Placing the stone within the core of the construct, Thirianna felt a name impressed upon her memories: Naetheriol. She had been a poet, a Dark Reaper, a pilot and a mother. A life full of experiences flashed through Thirianna as Naetheriol's spirit merged with the wraithbone of her new body.

Waking. Darkness.

Thirianna guided Naetheriol from her alcove, allowing her to glimpse the world through the seer's eyes, parting the misty veil of death that fogged the spirit's perceptions. Leaving a gleaming star of clarity in the dead eldar's thoughts, Thirianna turned back to the chest, ready to repeat the procedure.

When they were done, Thirianna and Kelamith had roused thirty wraithguard. It was not a large number, but they were formidable fighters. Their wraithcannons would be a match for the Space Marines' armour and their wraithbone bodies could withstand incredible amounts of damage.

Yet they would not be the deadliest weapons to be let free from the Well of Silent Affection.

Moving to the far end of the hall, Kelamith uncovered the bodies of the wraithlords. Though similar in design to the wraithguard, these constructs towered above the two seers, their long limbs carved with miniscule runes. Bright lances and missile launchers were fixed to mounts on their shoulders, scatter lasers and long power swords were gripped in massive fists.

Only the strongest spirits could power such constructs and Kelamith produced the rune of Khaine from his pouch as he returned to the waystones. Thirianna attached herself to his thoughts as the farseer delved into the infinity circuit searching for suitable candidates.

His psyche came upon the shrines of the Aspect Warriors. Every living exarch was already fighting, but there were several suits standing dormant in forgotten shrines. Kelamith opened up the wards that kept these war-like spirits away from the mass of the infinity circuit and Alaitoc shuddered with their rush of anger.

Vengeful, full of hatred, focussed on death and destruction, the spirits of the dead warriors screamed through the infinity circuit, seeking release. It was a simple matter to guide them along the conduits to the waiting wraithlords.

The first Thirianna recognised, albeit from a strange perspective. He was Kenainath, a Striking Scorpion exarch, the former mentor of Korlandril. His body had only recently succumbed to the weight of time and his spirit was almost fully formed; it had suffered little of the dissipation of essence that beset the wraithguard.

The exarch flowed into the wraithbone body that was chosen for him and raised twin fists that crackled with energy. A shuriken cannon on his shoulder moved in its mount as Kenainath spread out into the systems of his new-found body.

I serve Khaine again, sooner than expected; I shall bring ruin.

Three more wraithlords were given life, each fuelled by the spirit taken from a dormant exarch. Kelamith and Thirianna were joined by several other seers and each took five of the wraithguard to act as their warriors. They were sluggish to respond at first and Thirianna extended her thoughts into the wraithbone shells of the constructs, guiding them after her with her will.

The wraithlords, possessed of greater clarity, departed for council with the autarchs, leaving Thirianna with Kelamith.

'I see that your fate and that of Korlandril are as yet still closely entwined,' remarked Kelamith as he walked beside Thirianna, the ten wraithguard following with long strides behind them.

'Korlandril is no more, and Morlaniath who he has become has but a short fate remaining,' replied Thirianna.

'Yet it is fitting that you should share one last encounter, to complete the circle that was started,' said Kelamith.

'As you request,' said Thirianna.

The two of them parted company, boarding separate cloudskiffs with their immortal charges. Thirianna allowed the wraithguard to slumber while she searched the skein for Morlaniath. She found him in the Dome of Midnight Forests and directed the skiff pilot to take her there.

ONLY THE RUDDY glow of dying Mirianathir lit the sky of the dome. Beneath the ruddy shadows of the lianderin, the Alaitocii gathered. Grav-tanks prowled along the pathways while scores of Wave Serpents shuttled back and forth delivering squads to their positions. Here the eldar would make their next stand, able to rake fire across the wide clearings from the cover of the scattered woods. Every valley would become a killing field, every brook and meadow a graveyard for the invaders.

Disembarking from the skiff, Thirianna urged the wraithguard into motion. They followed her along a silvery pathway that cut through the lianderin trees as she followed the thread of fate towards Morlaniath. A Wave Serpent caught up with them as they crossed a bridge over a narrow stream, dropping off three warlocks: Methrain, Nenamin and Toladrissa. They accompanied Thirianna as she led the wraithguard into the trees again, heading for the centre of the dome.

She found the exarch and other Striking Scorpions in a clearing looking down on a long valley that stretched to the edge of the Dome of Midnight Forests. Morlaniath's squad was made up of the survivors of the Hidden Death, Deadly Shadow and Fall of Deadly Rain shrines. They had suffered badly in the Space Marine attack and Thirianna could sense apprehension amongst the Aspect Warriors, mixed with anger and a strong desire for vengeance.

Had it not been for her witch sight, Thirianna would have not known the Aspect Warriors were nearby, concealed in the shadows of the forest. The clearing was dominated by a Cobra tank, a massive war engine mounting a distortion cannon in its low turret. As with the wraithcannons of her bodyguard, Thirianna could sense the warp core powering the weapon, though the rent it made in the skein was far larger. A pair of Vyper jetbikes circled through the trees around the clearing, keeping watch for approaching foes.

Thirianna allowed her mind to touch upon the strand of Morlaniath, attracting the exarch's attention. She raised her witchblade in a salute to the ancient warrior.

'Our fates share the same path again for a while,' she said.

Is this coincidence, or a machination, brought about by your hand? The exarch's thoughts came as a chorus of voices, tainted with bitterness, an after-echo of Korlandril's past.

'I am not senior enough to influence the judgement of the autarchs,' replied Thirianna. 'Some have fates closely entwined; others have strands that never touch. We are the former. Do you not remember where you are?'

Thirianna had recognised the place immediately, and with a deft thought looped back the thread of

Korlandril's life, briefly laying it alongside that of the exarch. She felt a flash of recognition as the exarch's eyes fell upon a tall statue at the edge of the clearing, of an eldar warrior kneeling before the goddess Isha, catching her tears in a goblet.

'I PRESENT *The Gifts of Loving Isha*,' he announced with a smile.

There were a few gasps of enjoyment and a spontaneous ripple of applause from all present. Korlandril turned to look at his creation and allowed himself to admire his work fully for the first time since its completion.

THIRIANNA SMILED AT the memory shared, having never experienced Korlandril's pleasure at that moment. It was odd to her that such happiness would turn to such sadness swiftly after. With what she knew now, it was clear that Korlandril's psyche had been far from stable, his artistic temperament masking a deeper flaw.

I remember clearly, when disharmony reigned, when my spirit was split. This was my new birthplace, the path leading from here, which brought me full circle. It is no more than that, a place in a past life, of no special accord.

Korlandril had been consumed by this being, but his memory still lived on. She wanted to give that ghost of the friend she had known some comfort in the last moments of its existence. She had some time to search the skein, using the Wanderer to pull together disparate fates conjoined with the statue Korlandril had created.

She found what she had been hoping to see.

'Many new paths spring from this place,' said Thirianna. 'Some for good, others that lead to darker places. Your work began those paths, even if you did not intend it. We are all linked in the great web of destiny, the merest trembling on a silken thread sending tremors through the lives of countless others. Just a few cycles ago a child sat and stared at your creation and dreamed of Isha. He will be a poet and a warrior, a technician and a gardener. But it is as a sculptor that he will achieve great fame, and in turn will inspire others to create more works of beauty down the generations.'

I need no legacy, I am an undying, eternal warrior.

For most that would be true, but for Morlaniath, for the spirits that made him, that would not be so. Thirianna had seen his fate, to momentarily become one with Karandras the Phoenix Lord, imbuing his lifeless form with fresh energy and then dissipated upon the winds of the skein.

'No creature is eternal: not gods, not eldar, not humans or orks. Look above you and see a star dying. Even the universe is not immortal, though her life passes so slowly.'

What will become of me, have you divined my fate, looked upon my future?

The question unsettled Thirianna, both because of the answer and because the exarch was of the mind to ask such a thing. Clearly he detected something of the doom that was fast approaching, sensing his place on the skein though not appreciating it fully. It was better that he did not try to second-guess what would come to pass, but was focussed on the battle to come.

She fell back on a trick that Kelamith had often employed when avoiding questions Thirianna had asked: enigmatic obfuscation. To seem wise and yet say nothing was an art she had been slowly studying since becoming a seer.

'We all have many fates, but only one comes to pass. It is not for me to meddle in the destiny of individuals, nor to look into our own futures. Trust that you shall die as you lived, and that it is not the True Death that awaits you, not for an age at least. Your passing will bring peace.'

I suffer many deaths, I remember each well, never is it peaceful.

Thirianna was bombarded by a succession of images as the exarch experienced his past deaths again. She broke off her contact with Morlaniath, sensing the skein swirling, new fates unveiled as the humans launched their next attack.

THE DOME OF Midnight Forests was rocked by a massive explosion. A plume of smoke billowed across the forests as the humans breached the dome to rimwards. Screeching and twittering, flocks of birds exploded from the canopy, flitting across the dark sky in their terror.

The crack of Space Marine bolters and the zip of lasers echoed in the distance.

The enemy are upon us! The infinity circuit carried the thoughts of Arhathain, bringing the autarch's words to every eldar on the craftworld. *The next battle begins. Do not sell your lives cheaply, nor forget the artistry with which we fight. They day has not yet come when the light of Alaitoc will be dimmed.*

THIRIANNA WATCHED THE slowly unfolding battle from afar, though the slaughter felt all too close as it shivered across the skein. The Space Marines spearheaded the next advance, punching through the thin line of eldar who had been set to defend the breach.

Support weapons and Falcon grav-tanks poured their fire into the advancing warriors of the Emperor, but they would not be stopped. The Space Marines overran the hills on which the batteries had been positioned, unleashing hails of explosive bolts from their weapons, driving off the grav-tanks with missile launchers and lascannons, chopping down the survivors of the crews with chainswords and knives.

The Imperial forces crept up the valley, their position given away by a trail of fire and explosions. Thirianna divided her attention three ways: keeping the wraithguard alert and ready to act; monitoring her own thread of fate seeking danger; following the thoughts of the seers and exarchs as the battle progressed.

Like a stain, the humans spread across the skein, their filthy lives polluting the bright eldar threads they touched. Blood flowed in their wake, of both sides, and Khaine was their constant companion.

Vampire bombers rained down sonic detonators and Swooping Hawks showered the advancing humans with plasma. The skein rippled with the warp jump generators of the Warp Spiders and shuddered from the carnage being unleashed.

The eldar forces moved under the direction of the autarchs, falling back, regrouping, attacking again. The beauty of their battle plan was laid out on the skein, a graceful, curving picture of ever-shifting momentum, drawn and re-drawn with each passing moment.

The humans, in contrast, were a blunt spear, cast towards the heart of Alaitoc without thought. They drove all before them, leaving the skein a tangled, rank mess. The Space Marines were the bright tip of the spear, death to all they touched, so that soon the eldar melted away before them, unwilling to lose more warriors in a vain attempt to halt the Sons of Orar.

Thirianna barely noticed as a squadron of war walkers passed by and headed down into the valley, so intent was she upon the diverging strands of destiny. Nothing had become clearer about Alaitoc's fate since the invasion had begun; the craftworld's future was mired in darkness and uncertainty.

Neither side weighed more heavily on the scales of fate and the future remained finely balanced, easily tipped one way or the other by a small act of heroism or cowardice, luck or ill fortune.

The humans continued their bloody advance, now unleashing the power of artillery guns dragged onto the slopes of the valley. The large cannons pounded the upper reaches of the valley, thinking they targeted the defenders of the craftworld. Nothing was further from the truth.

Forewarned of this development, the Alaitocii had pulled back out of the valley, leaving the artillery to hammer empty groves and destroy the cover that would have later protected the human advance. Thirianna was saddened by the smashed trees, each of which was immeasurably older than the creatures that destroyed them. The Dome of Midnight Forests was one of the most ancient parts of Alaitoc, created before the Fall to be the lungs of the original trade ship that would later become the vast craftworld.

She felt her anger duplicated across the skein. Runes of Isha wept as the bombardment continued and the rune of Khaine burned fiercely, brought to renewed life by the ire of the eldar. Thirianna assuaged her anguish with glimpses of the future, taking comfort in the scenes of dying humans she saw there, punished for the affront of their attack.

In the wake of the artillery barrage, the humans pushed on quickly, seeking to seize the head of the valley with a thrust of tanks and armoured personnel carriers. They brought with them a smog of exhaust fumes, their clattering, roaring engines echoing up the valley.

The Alaitocii responded, moving swiftly back into the positions they had abandoned. Falcon grav-tanks brought destruction on white beams of bright lance fire. Vyper jetbikes sped through the flames and smoke, missile launchers spitting trails of explosions.

As squads of grey-clad soldiers evacuated the burning wrecks of their transports, war walkers and jetbikes attacked, shuriken cannons and starcannons ripping through the survivors, painting the rucked mud red with the blood of the invaders. Warp Spiders materialised to engulf floundering human soldiers in webs of deadly monofilament that sliced through flesh and bone, dissecting the screaming soldiers within clouds of constricting mesh. These were joined by a battery of doomweavers that sent even larger swathes of the lethal fibres across the valley, engulfing whole companies.

As before, the humans looked to the Space Marines to fight back hardest. Thirianna was disconcerted by the seeming foresight of the humans. Whenever the eldar unleashed a backlash against the enemy, it always seemed to fall upon the regular soldiers and not the elite warriors.

Now they came on in their red-and-white tanks and transports, racing past the burning hulks of the other vehicles, their weapons spitting death at the eldar war engines. Vypers were brought down in hails of heavy bolter fire and Falcons turned to burning cinders by the shafts of lascannon beams.

The valley was lit up by plasma and laser as both sides exchanged furious volleys, each testing the resolve of the other. The Space Marines headed into the teeth of the storm unleashed by the Alaitocii, utterly heedless of the danger.

The farseers sensed trouble, Thirianna amongst them. She delved into the future and saw what would happen if the eldar tried to halt the attack with brute force: piles of dead Alaitocii and the dome in ruins.

The warnings sounded across the infinity circuit

and the Alaitocii gave way, surrendering the slopes to the advancing Space Marines rather than suffer unsustainable casualties.

Into this newly-won ground the rest of the human army advanced again, shielded by the tanks and power armoured warriors from the Sons of Orar. Starshells were sent into the dark sky to illuminate the carnage and in the flickering white light of falling phosphor Thirianna could see hundreds, thousands of humans marching up the valley.

She spied an opportunity. The Space Marines were holding their ground in the open, allowing their less-armoured companions to seek the shelter of shattered tree trunks and deep craters. She let her mind touch upon the thoughts of the Cobra tank destroyer that lay waiting in the clearing, sending them a vision of the vulnerable Space Marines.

Spurred by Thirianna's instruction, the Cobra lifted effortlessly from the flattened grass, arcs of energy coruscating along its distortion cannon, throwing dancing shadows across the clearing. The skein bucked and twisted as the warp core opened, drawing in energy directly from the immaterial realm.

Images of the Chaos realms fluttered through Thirianna's thoughts; impossible vistas and baying calls filling her mind.

The lead Space Marine tanks were almost three-quarters of the way along the valley. Lascannon blasts stabbed from them into the darkness, setting fire to trees, gouging furrows in the ground as the enemy sought the elusive eldar.

With a thrum that set the ground shaking, the Cobra opened fire. The air itself screamed as the distortion cannon tore at its fabric, a rent appearing in the air above the closest Space Marine vehicle. Thirianna's head throbbed with the pressure of the energies unleashed, the skein itself shrieked as it was wrenched into the material universe.

The gap opened by the blast widened into a whirling hole framed with purple and green lightning, its depths a swirl of colours and reeling stars. Thirianna's spirit stone was hot upon her breast as she felt the pull of the warp, the lingering power of She Who Thirsts tugging at the edges of her essence. To open the realm of the Chaos Gods was always risky, inviting terrible consequence, but the effect more than outweighed the dangers at this time.

A Space Marine tank lurching down the left slope was dragged to a stop by the implosive energies of the warphole, its tracks grinding vainly through the soil, smoke belching from its exhausts as the driver gunned the engine in an effort to maintain traction. With a drawn-out creak, the vehicle lifted from the ground, tipping backwards, stretching and contorting as the breach into warp space opened wider. Rivets sprang free and disappeared into the ravening hole, followed quickly by the tangled remains of the gun sponsons. An armoured figure was drawn out of the top hatch and spun crazily into the maw of the warp a moment before the tank slammed upwards and was sucked into the spiralling vortex.

Thirianna could feel the remnants of the tank and its crew lingering on the skein. They were not dead, not all of them. Their souls cried out in torment, subjected to the raw, ravaging energies of the warp, their minds exploding with the power of the immaterium flooding through their psyches.

She felt satisfaction at their deaths and stayed for a moment, relishing the after-echoes of doom that faded from the tattered ends of their threads.

With a crack like thunder the vortex closed, sending out a shockwave that sent a nearby Space Marine transport slamming into a tree with a shower of leaves.

The clearing fell still again as the Cobra's cannon recharged. Undaunted, the humans continued their advance, almost reckless in their haste to close. The humans had learnt from their earlier mistakes and the artillery opened fire again. Thirianna traced the shells across the skein, fearing that they would land close by. Instead they were directed to the outer slopes of the valley, where the eldar had been taking shelter from the advance.

Dozens of strands were cut short in the thunderous detonations. Fire spread along the valley, leaping from tree to tree, a pall of smoke blotting out the light of the descending starshells.

The Space Marines had pushed forwards again and one of their largest tanks had come within range of the clearing. Lascannon blasts seared through the darkness, shrieking off the Cobra's curved hull. The super-heavy tank lifted again as more power surged along the length of its main gun. Again came the scream of tortured reality and the concussive blast of the warp vortex forming. More than a dozen armoured figures and a pair of troop transports were sucked into the energy maelstrom, their forms thinning and twisting before they disappeared from sight while raw psychic energy forked to the ground from the breach's undulating rim.

Wrecks and bodies littered the valley floor, but the Space Marines had gained the higher ground to either side and from their vantage point their tanks poured chattering fire into the treeline. Within this cordon, batteries of self-propelled guns lumbered into position, bringing them into range of the dome's heart. A least twenty tanks grumbled towards Thirianna's position, painted in the same grey as the soldiers' fatigues. Four brightly coloured Space Marine transports charged ahead of the advance and would be at the edge of the clearing shortly.

Thirianna recognised the scale of the threat immediately, but as soon as she moved to the skein for a solution she found that help had already been despatched.

Hidden in the darkness by its holofields, a Phantom Titan carefully made its way through the trees. Thirianna soon heard the snap of branches under the towering war machine's tread and could feel the psychic power of the spirit stones bound within its wraithbone frame.

She allowed her mind to flow within the Titan's structure and for a short while shared in the vision of its crew.

FROM ABOVE THE treetops the triplet crew looked down the valley, the dome canopy of their cockpit alive with runes highlighting the positions of friends and foes, the whispers of the spirits roaming through the wraithbone Titan constantly buzzing in their ears.

They guided the tread of their machine to avoid the Striking Scorpions hidden at the base of a statue, and stepped between them and the Cobra. They dimmed the power to the holofields and redirected it to the weapons as bright red symbols flashed across the view.

The shoulder-mounted missile launchers opened fire with a flurry of blazing trails that engulfed the lead tanks of the enemy. Hulls were split open by the armour-piercing warheads and engine blocks shattered by their detonations.

Acting in concert, the three eldar turned the Titan and swung its tremor cannon into position. They locked on to their target and plotted the most destructive arc of fire. Agreeing in unison, they unleashed the power of the tremor cannon's generator.

Protected within the head of the Titan, the crew were shielded from the throbbing violence of the sonic weapon. They watched with some satisfaction as the weapon traced an invisible path through the enemy vehicles. The air danced with agitated molecules, the weapon starting to tremble in its mounting as it unleashed a counter-harmonic, sending out a ground-shattering beam of sonic energy.

Where the line touched, the ground erupted, a huge gout of earth and rock rupturing into a widening crack that zigzagged along the hillside. Tanks shook themselves apart as the beam crossed over them;

Space Marines were flattened inside their armour; unarmoured soldiers were torn limb from limb by the sonic energy coursing through their bodies.

The spirits of the Titan gave warnings that the weapon was overloading and the crew shut down the supply of power. While the tremor cannon recharged they launched another barrage of missiles into the infantry fleeing from the carnage they had wrought. Several tanks were still heading closer and so the crew turned their attention to the pulsar.

Lances of pure energy split the darkness of the Dome of Midnight Forests, each pulse of light smashing into an enemy tank, splitting it apart with one hit. Ammunition set off secondary explosions inside the turret of one, while the engine of another detonated in a huge ball of fire and gas, a cloud of jagged debris scything down the humans nearby.

THIRIANNA WITHDREW FROM the Titan as the Cobra fired again and the valley descended into an anarchy of swirling vortexes, wailing sonic explosions and the steady strobe of the pulsar. Shells screamed in return, flashing past the wavering image of the Titan to crash into the trees beyond the clearing.

The farseer sensed the runes changing, moving away from the valley to another attack to starwards. She felt the request from another farseer for aid and passed this on to the two massive war engines. Together they departed, ready to lend their firepower to where it would do the most harm to the enemy.

Thirianna could feel the tension in the clearing

was increasing; Morlaniath and his warriors were eager for battle, hungry to avenge their fallen. She sensed the exarch's growing excitement at the thought of imminent close-quarters combat.

'Arhathain is mustering forces for a counter-attack along this axis,' she told him, watching the developing manoeuvres through the lens of the skein. 'We wait for the reinforcements and then we will advance.'

Make ready your wargear, more warriors arrive, we shall be fighting soon, she heard the exarch tell his squad.

The battle continued, the greater part of its ferocity moving to other parts of the dome. In the valley, the Imperial troops secured their positions, digging crude entrenchments and piling up lines of earthworks. They seemed to be preparing for a counter-attack and she passed on this information to Arhathain, who was in the process of mounting just such an assault.

It seemed a rash move until Thirianna cast her gaze wider. She had been focussed primarily on the valley, and with only some thought to the wider dome. Now she looked across Alaitoc and saw that the humans were making advances elsewhere, four lines of fate converging on the centre of Alaitoc. They seemed to be heading directly for the Dome of Crystal Seers and the Chambers of the Seers, somehow knowing that the nerve centre of the craftworld lay in and around those places.

Not for the first time, Thirianna sensed a guiding hand directing the movements of the humans.

There was someone else on the skein, someone not of Alaitoc.

Before she could investigate further, she was interrupted by an inquiring thought from Morlaniath, who wanted to know how the wider conflict progressed. She thought it was irrelevant at the moment, but she was not a lone commander and it was part of her role to pass on such information to the exarchs.

She decided to speak to the exarch in person, suddenly cautious of the enemy presence she had detected on the skein. She crossed the clearing quickly, leaving her wraithguard to protect the approach from the valley.

'We have abandoned the Dome of Lasting Vigilance, and the humans control more than a quarter of the access ways to Alaitoc's central region,' she told Morlaniath. She delivered the report without much enthusiasm, distracted by more personal concerns. 'We still hold the domes around the infinity circuit core. It is Arhathain's wish that we drive these humans from this dome so that we can mount an attack on the flank of their other forces, severing them from their landing zone in the docks.'

'The enemy prepare, waiting is a peril, how soon do we attack?' said Morlaniath.

Thirianna moved across the skein, touching on the minds of the other seers, anxious not to transmit her thoughts too far lest they be intercepted by malicious listening minds.

'The counter-attack is almost ready,' she said eventually. 'The humans' rough defences will be no obstacle. They think only of left and right, forwards and backwards. They still forget that we do not have to crawl along the groun–'

Fire burned across the skein. Fire and shadow, blood and death.

The farseer stopped and turned her gaze beyond Morlaniath and saw flickering light in the woods casting long shadows amongst the trees.

The Avatar was approaching.

Its presence joined the minds of the hundreds of eldar converging through the trees at the head of the valley, linking them together in one bloody purpose. Thirianna could feel hundreds of guardians and Aspect Warriors advancing through the woods around her, all mustered around the burning incarnation of Khaine. Far above, Swooping Hawks circled in the thermals of the burning tanks while dagger-winged Vampire bombers cruised back and forth awaiting the order to strike.

A coldness seeped into Thirianna's heart and she looked across the clearing to find the Shadow Hunter, Karandras, in the darkness of the trees. There was a flicker of connection between his spirit and that of the Striking Scorpion exarch, a moment of contact and recognition.

She glanced at Morlaniath, knowing what was to come. She said nothing, leaving Korlandril's fate to run to its swift conclusion.

WITH THE WRAITHGUARD behind them, Thirianna and the warlocks joined the force advancing with the Avatar. The presence of Khaine's incarnation drove the eldar forwards, filled with dreams of retribution, united in their cause to cleanse Alaitoc of the human presence that stained the craftworld.

'My attention is required elsewhere, trust the Avatar to lead.' Kelamith's presence was distant, moving to one of the other warzones. With a moment of misgiving, Thirianna realised that she was the last farseer left in the Dome of Midnight Forests. Her unease passed, burned away by the proximity of the Avatar.

She studied the skein, noting the patterns of advance that would be followed by the attacking eldar. Aerial and support weapon bombardment would herald the attack, while the ground forces slipped around the ends of the defensive lines and took the human army from the flanks.

They encountered the outlying forces quickly: squadrons of walkers and squads of Space Marines. Battle raged amongst the thinning trees as the Avatar led the attack down into the valley.

Thirianna found herself on the left flank, accompanied by Dire Avengers and Dark Reapers. Several squads of Space Marines waited ahead, their heavy weapons already firing on the advancing Alaitocii.

She despatched the Dark Reapers to a bluff overlooking the enemy positions and forged ahead with the Aspect Warriors and her wraithguard. Explosive bolts erupted from the Space Marines' positions behind rocks and splintered trees.

Drawing on the power of the skein, Thirianna swathed the fates of those around her with a maelstrom of energy, misdirecting the enemy fire, distracting the aim of the Space Marines so that they fired at shadows.

Not all of the Space Marines' fire went astray. Bolt rounds cracked from the bodies of the wraithguard. A ball of plasma flew up the ridge towards the Dark Reapers, sending charred bodies flying into the air.

Into this torrent of fire advanced the eldar, cloaked from view by Thirianna's psychic manipulations. Several of the Dire Avengers fell to the storm of bolts and missiles raging along the slope and a wraith-guard collapsed in a heap as another plasma bolt caught it full in the chest; fewer casualties than they would have suffered without the farseer's protection.

Thirianna had done enough and the wraithguard were now within range. She poured consciousness into their half-dead minds, allowing them to see as she saw.

The wraithguard lifted their weapons and fired.

The warp rippled open through a cluster of mul-ticoloured stars, ripping apart the armour of the Space Marines, tearing their spirits from their bod-ies. Thirianna winced at the psychic howling that swept across the skein but urged the wraithguard on, firing their weapons again and again.

The return fire from the Space Marines was lessen-ing.

The Dark Reapers now added their missiles to the attack, blossoms of fire springing into life along the Space Marines' defences. The Dire Avengers sprinted forwards under the cover of this attack, their shuriken catapults slinging a hail of monomolecular-edged discs into the armoured giants confronting them.

Seeking the best angle of attack, Thirianna roamed across the skein as she advanced behind the wraithguard. Around her, the warlocks hurled bolts of fire and threw crackling spheres of psychic energy.

On the skein, Thirianna felt the touch of something alien in her thoughts. She ducked away but returned swiftly, seeking its source. Following the threads, she saw a second force of Space Marines readying to attack, a reserve that would throw back the eldar advance and drive them from the dome.

Every attack and counter-attack was being met by the Space Marines. Thirianna searched fervently for their seer, amazed that a human could be so gifted. She corrected herself; her foe was not human. She searched along the strands of the Space Marines' lives and located what she was looking for.

The Space Marine psyker was well hidden, shielded by centuries of discipline and dedication. His mind was almost as strong as an eldar's, yet it had been honed into a sharp weapon, capable of slicing through fate with a thought.

Yet for all his power, the Space Marine could not match Thirianna for prescience. He had not yet recognised the unfolding fates of the eldar attack; the Space Marines were not yet ready to respond.

If Thirianna could slay this psyker swiftly, his warning would not come, and the eldar attack would succeed.

She summoned her warriors to her and pressed on, searching the skein for a sign of her elusive foe. He could not wholly contain the power leaking from his mind and she found him with a squad of

Space Marines a little further along the ridge, directing the actions of his followers.

Thirianna looked for other forces she could bring to bear, but they were all committed to the attack with the Avatar. Even if the Space Marine counterattack was forestalled, Thirianna could see how closely-run the battle would be. She could not afford to withdraw any more forces to help her.

'Follow me,' she told the eldar around her, instilling purpose into the minds of the wraithguard.

Emerging from a shallow ravine, Thirianna found her foe: an armoured transport that looked more like a mobile bunker than a vehicle. Beside the huge tank stood a cluster of warriors in red-and-white armour, one amongst them marked out by his blue livery. As soon as Thirianna laid eyes on him, she knew what she faced. Librarians they were called by the Space Marines, and this one was ranked highly amongst them.

She drew on the Scorpion to slide close to his thoughts, slipping prompts and subtle images into his mind, seeking to direct his attention elsewhere. She was met with a wall of willpower that seemed forged of iron, rebounding her attempts at manipulation. Thirianna tried again and fared no better, unable to penetrate the solid shield of faith and devotion that protected the Space Marine.

She would have to end this physically.

The farseer and her warriors slipped along the slope as quickly as they could. The wraithguard were not so fleet of foot as the living eldar and Thirianna was forced to leave them behind, despatching

Toladrissa to look over them.

The Dire Avengers and seers moved quickly down the valley, heading towards the bright searchlights of the Space Marine command vehicle. Thirianna could feel the Librarian's thoughts searching for her, alerted by her ill-considered attempt to infiltrate his thoughts. She drew a veil around her spirit, concealing herself behind the power of the Scorpion.

Time was running short. The Avatar and the main force were approaching the moment of commitment. Thirianna tried to warn the other seers, seeking aid from Kelamith, but they were occupied with their own problems and she realised she faced this task alone. If she failed, the Alaitocii counter-attack would fail. If that happened the Dome of Midnight Forests would fall to the enemy, allowing them to breach the infinity core that lay in the adjoining dome.

That could not be allowed to happen. For the final stage of Alaitoc's defence, the humans had to be kept in the ring of domes surrounding the core, allowed this close but no further.

The eldar leapt over the rocks and scrub, closing in on the jutting cliff where the Space Marines were stationed. The Dire Avengers opened fire as soon as the first enemy came into view.

The Space Marine fell, his thick armour scored by hundreds of shurikens, weaker joints and eye lenses shredded and shattered by the fusillade of discs. Almost immediately the other Space Marines returned fire, fiery bolts screaming back into the attacking eldar, three Dire Avengers smashed from their feet by bloody impacts.

Methrain and Nenamin cast their singing spears into the Space Marines, the triangular heads of the weapons gleaming with psychic energy. Both struck their targets, cutting through armour and fused ribcages to pierce vital organs. Thirianna let fly a ripple of lightning from her sword as she sprinted forwards, shattering the armour of another Space Marine.

The Librarian turned swiftly, instantly alert to the threat but, thanks to Thirianna, not psychically forewarned. Like the others he was clad in powered armour, of a deep blue, only his shoulder pads sharing the heraldry of his companions. His armour was scuffed and scored from fierce fighting and Thirianna sensed a wave of malicious intent. The Son of Orar held up a staff topped by an ornately carved rendition of a ram's head. The skein buckled as he summoned power, drawing in an immense swell of energy. Thirianna leapt to her right as a blast of pure white light erupted towards her, obliterating two of the Dire Avengers following behind the farseer.

Thirianna dodged back and forth as boltgun rounds split the air around her, runic wards blazing into life as some struck home. In moments she had closed the gap and was swinging her sword at the Space Marine's helmeted head. The Librarian met her witchblade with the haft of his staff, smashing Thirianna to one side with his raw strength.

With his other hand he drew a shimmering sword, psychic energy playing along the crystalline seams threaded through the blade.

The Librarian swung at Thirianna's head as he tried to reach into her thoughts and shred her mind. She deflected the first with her witchblade and the second with a deft turn of thought, sending the psychic blast back to where it came from.

The staff blazed again, hurling Thirianna from her feet as serpentine psychic energy crawled across her rune armour. She recovered swiftly, jumping to her feet to avoid a second blast. Fire raged from her sword, catching the Librarian in the shoulder, scorching paint and leaving a blackened sworl across the grey material beneath.

She saw his head was surrounded by a tracery of cables and wires and could feel the psychic power flowing along these conduits. She fired her shuriken pistol into the Space Marine's chest and he turned a shoulder towards her to catch the flying projectiles on his armoured pad.

The pistol shots had been a feint. The Space Marine was out of position as Thirianna spun past him, jumping up to lance the tip of her witchblade into the gap between helm and the power plant of the Space Marine's backpack. Cables exploded with raw psychic power as the edge of Thirianna's weapon swept through the psychic wiring.

The Librarian lashed out with his staff, catching Thirianna in the back, sending her face-first into the dirt.

She did not need to see her foe to strike.

She snatched up the Librarian's thread of fate, now blazing and hot without the defences of his psychic hood. She sent a surge of power racing along its length, pouring all of her hatred and rage into the blast.

Rolling to her feet, Thirianna turned in time to see the Space Marine reeling back, his eyes burning through their lenses, staff and sword falling from his spasming hands. Thirianna could feel the iron shields of his mind closing down and knew she had only another moment to finish this.

She leapt, bringing down the witchblade with all of her force, infusing the weapon with the last of her mental strength, turning it into a diamond-hard blade that split the Librarian's head from scalp to jaw.

Thirianna landed as the Space Marine's body crashed to the ground, brains and blood spilling from the fatal wound.

Desperately Thirianna returned to the skein to see if the Space Marines had been pulled back to reserve, ready to thwart the eldar assault.

Relief flooded through her as she saw the Avatar striding into the heart of the humans' defences, cutting down everything in its path. The Aspect Warriors tore into the Imperial army while aircraft raked them from above. The humans fled the assault, the Space Marines falling back to the edge of the dome, far from the infinity core.

Alaitoc's rune wavered, balanced between salvation and death once more.

The hawks circle. The time to strike is nigh.

Thirianna knew the meaning of the words sent to her by Kelamith. She reached to her belt to cast another rune: the Wanderer. Exhausted, she had enough strength left to spare for a moment of worry. For her whole life she had striven for control. She had laboured hard to manage her own affairs and choose her own direction. Her stomach sank at the thought of what she had to do, but there was no option, it had been agreed by the council.

The skein rippled as she poured what little remained of her willpower into the Wanderer, sending the signal for the final phase of the battle to begin. The infinity circuit blazed with the single rune and the skein became a maelstrom of energy, swirling all about the sigil.

The fate of Alaitoc was cast and Thirianna had left it in the hands of the selfish, capricious Aradryan.

It was now up to the outcast to bring peace to Alaitoc.

Discover the fate of Alaitoc in book three of the Path of the Eldar series, *Path of the Outcast*.

ABOUT THE AUTHOR

Gav Thorpe has been rampaging across the worlds of Warhammer and Warhammer 40,000 for many years as both an author and games developer. He hails from the den of scurvy outlaws called Nottingham and makes regular sorties to unleash bloodshed and mayhem. He shares his hideout with Dennis, a mechanical hamster sworn to enslave mankind. Dennis is currently trying to develop an iPhone app that will hypnotise his victims.

Gav's previous novels include fan-favourite *Angels of Darkness* and the epic *Malekith*, first instalment in the Sundering trilogy, amongst many others.
You can find his website at:
mechanicalhamster.wordpress.com

Also by Gav Thorpe

◀ TIME OF LEGENDS ▶
THE SUNDERING

BOOK 1: MALEKITH

UK: 978-1-84416-673-2
US: 978-1-84416-610-7
Digital: 978-0-85787-057-5

BOOK 2: SHADOW KING

UK: 978-1-84416-816-3
US: 978-1-84416-817-0
Digital: 978-0-85787-058-2

BOOK 3: CALEDOR

UK: 978-1-84970-050-4
US: 978-1-84970-051-1
Digital: 978-0-85787-152-7

Prince Malekith is one of the mightiest heroes
of the elves. His deeds are legend, his admirers
are legion. But Malekith's bitterness and secret
ambition will lead his people into a devastating
civil war that will end in the destruction of
his lands and the breaking of the bonds of
fellowship between the elves. It is a war that
will echo down the ages.It is the Sundering.

**AVAILABLE IN PAPERBACK and EBOOK FORMATS FROM
WWW.BLACKLIBRARY.COM**

An extract from Caledor
by Gav Thorpe

DURING THE DARKEST years of Ulthuan, the two greatest elves to have lived were at the forefront of the war
against the daemons of Chaos. The first Phoenix King,
Aenarion the Defender, was aided by Caledor Dragontamer, and the two lords of Ulthuan held the daemon
hordes at bay for more than a century.

Caledor it was that saw the attacks of the daemons
would never cease while the wild winds of magic blew
across the world. The Dragontamer studied long and
hard the mystical secrets of Chaos, gaining an insight
into the immaterial realm beyond any other mortal.
Seeing that the magic flowing into the world from the
Realm of Chaos in the north sustained the daemons,
Caledor set about preparing a mighty spell that would
create a vortex of energy on Ulthuan to siphon away
the winds of magic. Many were the arguments he had
with Aenarion over this course of action; Aenarion
feared rightly that the weapons and armour of the elven
lords were forged by the same magic that sustained the

daemons and without it the isle he ruled would be defenceless.

The two never came to agreement on the matter, and when Aenarion's wife, the Everqueen, was slain, he ignored Caledor's counsel and sought out the Sword of Khaine to strike down the daemon hosts. The Phoenix King became a dark, vengeful warrior, and founded the kingdom of Nagarythe in the north of Ulthuan, and ruled from the citadel of Anlec. The Dragontamer quit his alliance with Aenarion and his own kingdom, named after Caledor, turned its efforts to the creation of the magical vortex.

Though once friends, the two great elves never again wholly trusted each other, but at the moment of greatest peril, Caledor and Aenarion both played their part in the defeat of the daemons. Caledor began his ultimate spell upon an isle in the waters of Ulthuan's Inner Sea. Seeing what the Dragontamer intended, the daemons threw their armies at Caledor and his mages. Aenarion came to Caledor's aid and held back the legions of Chaos to give the mages time to complete their incantations.

Both were to sacrifice themselves. Though victorious, Aenarion and his dragon, Indraugnir, were grievously wounded in the battle. True to the oaths he had made, Aenarion flew north to the Blighted Isle to return the Sword of Khaine to its black altar; neither king nor dragon were seen again. Caledor and his followers became trapped within the eye of the vortex, frozen in time by the spell, doomed to an endless existence as conduits for the magical energy.

Thus the lands of Caledor and Aenarion were left without their rulers; Caledor in the mountains of the south, Nagarythe in the bleak north. The distrust that existed between the two kingdoms did not end with the deaths of their founders, but grew greater. The successors of the elven lords would not surrender power to each other and each claimed credit for the victory over the daemons.

When Aenarion's son, Malekith, desired to inherit his father's position as Phoenix King, the princes of Caledor resisted. They reminded the elves of the other realms that Malekith had been raised in a place of darkness and despair, and that the Dragontamer had prophesied that the descendants of Aenarion would be forever tainted by the curse of Bloody-Handed Khaine.

The First Council of princes chose Bel Shanaar of Tiranoc to be Phoenix King, thus ensuring neither Caledor nor Nagarythe would hold the greatest power in Ulthuan. Malekith accepted this decision with dignity and the Caledorians likewise endorsed the choice of Bel Shanaar.

Under the reign of this new Phoenix King the elves rebuilt their cities and explored the world. Colonies were founded across the oceans, and the influence of the elven kingdoms spread far and wide. Always wary of each other's status and power, Nagarythe and Caledor continued their rivalry for centuries and though peace existed between the two kingdoms, their distrust of each other deepened, the princes of each accusing the other of being jealous, arrogant and self-serving.

So it was with some annoyance, and a little trepidation, that Prince Imrik of Caledor heard the news that Naggarothi banners had been seen approaching his camp. The general of Caledor's armies in Elthin Arvan, the lands east of the Great Ocean, Imrik was grandson to the Dragontamer, younger brother of the kingdom's ruling prince, Caledrian.

The arrival of the Naggarothi was untimely. Imrik and his warriors had spent twelve days pursuing a horde of savage orcs and goblins through the wild lands in the south of Elthin Arvan, and that day would bring their foes to battle.

'The Naggarothi seek to steal our glory,' Imrik said to his companions, his youngest brother Dorien and cousin Thyrinor.

The three sat in Imrik's pavilion, already in their armour of golden plates and silver scale. The herald who had brought the news of the Naggarothi arrival waited nervously for his general's command.

'They believe they can take a victory here and claim these lands for themselves,' said Dorien. 'Send them away with a warning that they trespass on Caledorian soil.'

Thyrinor shifted uncomfortably in his seat and raised a hand to Dorien to ask for his peace.

'It would not be wise to provoke them,' said Thyrinor. He turned to the messenger. 'How many do you say they are?'

'Twelve thousand, my prince,' replied the herald. 'Of which four thousand are knights. We counted them as they forded the Laithenn River.'

'They'll be here well before noon,' said Imrik. 'They marched all night.'

'We should ready our army and attack the orcs before the Naggarothi get here,' said Dorien, standing up. 'They cannot claim credit for a battle that was finished before they arrived.'

'Not yet,' said Imrik. 'I will not be forced into hasty battle.' 'So what would you have us do?' said Dorien. 'Share the glory with those cold-blooded killers?'

'We'll prove ourselves greater,' said Imrik. He signalled

for the herald to approach. 'Ride out to the Naggarothi and tell their prince to come to me.'

The messenger bowed and departed swiftly, leaving the three lords of Caledor in silence. Imrik waited patiently, arms crossed, while Dorien paced to and fro. Thyrinor moved to a table and poured himself wine mixed with water, which he sipped with an agitated expression. After some time, he turned on Dorien with a frown.

'Sit down, cousin, please,' Thyrinor said sharply. He swallowed a mouthful of wine. 'You prowl like a Chracian lion in a pen.'

'I don't like it,' said Dorien. 'How did the Naggarothi learn of our pursuit, and how did they catch us so swiftly? And if my pacing vexes you so much, feel free to step outside, cousin. Or would that be too far away from the wine ewers for you?'

'Stop bickering.' Imrik's quiet instruction stilled the pair. 'Dorien, sit down. Thyrinor, drink no more. Our army readies for battle while you squabble like children. Wait.'

Dorien acquiesced and sat down, sweeping his long scarlet cloak over one arm of his chair. Thyrinor emptied his goblet and placed it on the table before returning to his seat.

'How can you be so calm, cousin?' said Thyrinor. 'Do you expect the Naggarothi to be our allies?'

'No,' said Imrik, unmoving.

'You give them opportunity to snub us,' Thyrinor said. He threw up his hands. 'Why attempt an embassy you know will not succeed, cousin?''Because they would not,' said Imrik. 'We behave with dignity.'

'As if the Naggarothi care about our dignity,' Dorien said with a snort of derision. 'They will see it as weakness.'

'Do you see it as weakness, brother?' asked Imrik. His eyes fixed Dorien with an intent stare.

'No,' Dorien replied, a little hesitant. 'I know we are not weak.'

'That is all that matters,' said Imrik. 'I care not for the opinions of the Naggarothi.'

Again the elves fell quiet. Outside, the clamour and bustle of the mustering army could be heard. Captains called out for their companies to assemble and piercing clarions signalled the call to battle.

Imrik passed the time in contemplation of the battle to come. The Naggarothi were an unwelcome distraction. He had not become Caledor's most lauded general by allowing himself to be distracted. The prince knew his companions thought him brusque, cold-hearted even; he considered them boisterous and hot-headed. The prince was content with his life. The chance to prove himself in battle, to show his worth as an heir of the Dragontamer, was enough. Even the small exchanges with his brother and cousin left him agitated, and glad to be far from the court of Caledrian. Here in the colonies an elf could make a name for himself with honest endeavour, away from the personalities and politics of Ulthuan.

It had been such constant wrangling that had driven him to Elthin Arvan. Though descended from the line of Caledor, Imrik had little aptitude or desire for magical ability and so had dedicated himself to mastery of the sword and the lance, and the command of armies. He shared his people's distrust of the Naggarothi, but also held them in some grudging respect; their accomplishments in war were unmatched by any other kingdom, including his own.

In particular, he admired their ruler, Prince Malekith.

Imrik would never say as much to another elf, but the achievements of Malekith were an example to be followed. Such admiration was shadowed by irritation too; had Imrik not shared his lifetime with Malekith he would have been renowned as the greatest general of Ulthuan. As it was, he was famed in Caledor and amongst a few of the colonial cities that knew of his exploits, but his victories and conquests were otherwise drowned out by the accolades heaped upon the prince of Nagarythe.

Imrik curled his lip in a silent snarl, annoyed that despite his efforts, he had allowed the Naggarothi to interrupt his pre-battle preparations. Dorien and Thyrinor looked at their commander, alerted to his annoyance.

'Call the army to order,' Imrik said, standing up.

He lifted his sword from where it leaned against the side of his chair, and buckled its golden sheath to his belt; his ornate helm he tucked under his arm. The hem of his cloak brushing the intricately embroidered rugs on the floor, Imrik led the other two elves from the tent.

The air was damp and the sky overcast, a thin mist obscuring the heathlands on which the elves had made camp. The pennants atop the pavilions hung limply in the still air, wet from rainfall in the night. The small town of gaily coloured tents was alive with activity as retainers bustled to attend to the needs of the captains and knights. Spear companies marched briskly to the mustering south-east of the encampment, their silver armour and dark green shields dappled with water droplets.

Imrik turned to the west and strode along a temporary causeway laid across the grass and heather. Gilded harnesses studded with rubies and emeralds jingled as a squadron of knights rode across the pathway ahead, dipping their lances in salute as they passed in front of their general, white steeds stepping briskly. Imrik raised his hand in acknowledgement.

Passing between an open-sided armoury and a store tent, the three princes reached the dragon field. Three of the mighty beasts lazed on the stretch of rocky grassland, expelling clouds of vapour from their nostrils. Two were the colour of embers, with deep red scales and orange underbellies; the third had an upper body of dark blue like twilight, its legs and lower parts the colour of slate. All three raised massive heads on their long necks at Imrik's call.

'Time for battle!' shouted the general.

The dragons heaved themselves up with growls and snorts, yellow eyes blinking slowly. The largest, one of the red-scaled pair, stretched out its wings and yawned wide, fumes smoking from its gullet.

'So soon?' the monster said, its voice a deep rumble.

'Are you tired, Maedrethnir?' said Thyrinor. 'Perhaps you wish you were slumbering beneath the mountains of Caledor with your kin?'

'Impudent elf,' said the dragon. 'Some of us must remain awake to keep you out of trouble.'

'Perhaps you would prefer to walk?' suggested Thyrinor's mount, the blue dragon called Anaegnir. She flapped her wings twice, buffeting the elves.

Young elves in the livery of Imrik's household emerged from the camp, bearing the ornate saddle-thrones and weapons of the dragon princes. When the harnesses were fitted – an involved operation that required much cooperation from the dragons – the three princes pulled themselves up by ropes to the backs of their mounts. They buckled belts across their waists, leaving their armoured legs to hang free across the necks of the beasts. Each was handed a lance by his retainer; weapons forged of silvery ithilmar, three times as long as an elf is tall, garlanded with green and red pennants. The princes took up high shields and hung them from their saddles.

When the retainers had retreated a safe distance, Imrik leaned forwards along Maedrethnir's neck and rubbed a hand along his scales.

'South-east, to the army,' said the general.

Maedrethnir launched into the air, the grass flattened beneath the thunderous flapping of his wings. The other two dragons followed swiftly, and all three princes circled higher and higher above the camp.

The altitude granted Imrik an impressive view of his army assembling. Two thousand knights drew up in squadrons a hundred strong, their banners and pennants rippling as they trotted across the wild heath. To their left, the spear companies formed; blocks of five hundred warriors, nine in all, ranked ten deep behind their standards. Twenty wagons formed a column behind the spearmen, each drawn by four horses and bearing two bolt throwers and their crews. Archers, some three thousand more elves, waited in companies beside the spearmen.In green and red and silver, the elven host stretched across the dark moorlands. Turning his gaze to the south-east, Imrik could make out the distant curve of a river, rushing down from the high mountains jutting above the horizon. From above it was easy to see the route taken by the orcs; a swathe of trampled grass and bushes that meandered towards the river. The smoke of hundreds of fires obscured the wide waters much farther to the south where the greenskins had made their camp.

As Maedrethnir tilted a wing and dipped towards the army, Imrik heard a distant shout. Looking over his shoulder, he saw Dorien waving his lance to attract attention. When he saw that Imrik was watching, he pointed the lance tip to the west. Imrik told Maedrethnir to turn to the right so he could see what had attracted Dorien's attention.

A column of black and purple wound alongside a narrow stream: the Naggarothi. Their armour glittered with gold, their knights in the vanguard setting a swift pace while the infantry followed as quickly as possible. Imrik spied something else, a shape above the army of Nagarythe.

'What is that flying above the Naggarothi?' he asked.

Maedrethnir turned his head to look, gliding effortlessly in a slow arc towards the other elven host.

'A griffon and rider,' said the dragon, with some distaste. 'Shall we teach them not to intrude upon our skies?'

'Take me to them,' said Imrik.

Beating his wings, Maedrethnir soared higher and turned towards the Naggarothi. Looking back, Imrik saw Dorien and Thyrinor following. With his lance, the general signalled for the other two princes to join the army. Thyrinor took the instruction immediately and turned away; Dorien did so only reluctantly.

As they flew towards the Naggarothi, Maedrethnir dipped his long head towards the ground.

'A rider,' he said. Imrik looked and saw a lone elf on a white steed, galloping back towards the Caledorian camp.

'Take us down to him,' said Imrik. 'Let's hear the Naggarothi reply.'

The rider reined in his steed as the dragon and prince

descended steeply. The horse stamped skittishly as Mae-drethnir landed a short distance away, the messenger's steed letting out a whinny of unease. The herald patted the beast on the shoulder and urged his mount closer, so that he could be heard without shouting.

'General, the Naggarothi prince declined your invitation,' said the messenger.

'Does this prince have a name?' Imrik asked.

'He is Maldiar, my prince,' replied the herald. 'A lord of Athel Toralien.'

'Never heard of him,' said Imrik. 'Must be one of the upstarts Malekith made prince before he disappeared into the northern wastelands.'

'Indeed, my prince,' said the other elf. 'He bade me to tell you that the Naggarothi do not accept demands from Caledorians. I am sorry, my prince, but Maldiar also instructed me to tell you to abandon your attack on the orcs and claims he alone has right of conquest in these lands.'

'We shall see,' said Imrik. 'Return to the army and tell my captains to be ready to advance.'

'As you command, my prince.' The herald turned his horse away; it leapt gratefully into a gallop to race away from Imrik and his monstrous steed.

'Let us meet Maldiar,' Imrik told Maedrethnir.

A rumble shook the dragon's chest, which might have been a laugh, and he powered into the sky. Dragon and rider headed towards the Naggarothi, skimming over the heath just above the height of the few scattered trees that broke the rough hillscape.

The griffon rider – Maldiar, Imrik assumed – had noted the approach of the Caledorian prince and directed his own winged mount head-on towards Imrik. As the other prince came closer, Imrik could make out more of Maldiar and his beast. The prince wore silver and gold armour inlaid with rubies; the eagle-like head of his griffon was feathered with blue, black and red, and its hindquarters were striped white and black, its claws the colour of blood.

The griffon let out a high-pitched shriek as the two princes closed in each other. Maedrethnir shook with a deep growl in reply, smoke leaking from his nostrils.

'Force them down,' said Imrik.

Maedrethnir surged higher, climbing above the griffon, and then stooped with wings furled, heading straight for the Naggarothi prince. Neck straight, jaw open, the dragon looked like he would crash into the griffon and rider. At the last moment, he opened his wings and stopped in mid-air, sending a rush of wind over Maldiar. The griffon swayed and dipped in the draught, tumbling a short distance before righting itself. Maldiar's shouted curses drifted up to Imrik but the Caledorian ignored them and pointed to the ground.

With Maedrethnir hovering just above and behind, Maldiar descended, guiding his griffon to land upon an outcrop of rock rising up through the sea of gorse and grass. Imrik and his dragon spiralled around them three times before landing within lance-reach. The griffon was a large beast, three times the size of a horse, but it was dwarfed by Maedrethnir, who loomed over creature and rider with wings outspread, blocking the morning sun.

'How dare you!' rasped Maldiar. 'This is an insult! By what right do you interfere with my rightful progress?'

'I am Imrik of Caledor. You have no rights here. These will be my lands.'